Books by Christine Trent

A Royal Likeness

The Queen's Dollmaker

A Royal Likeness

CHRISTINE TRENT

KENSINGTON BOOKS
www.kensingtonbooks.com

KENSINGTON BOOKS are published by

Kensington Publishing Corp.
119 West 40th Street
New York, NY 10018

All Kensington titles, imprints, and distributed lines are available at special quantity discounts for bulk purchases for sales promotion, premiums, fund-raising, educational, or institutional use.

Special book excerpts or customized printings can also be created to fit specific needs. For details, write or phone the office of the Kensington Special Sales Manager: Kensington Publishing Corp., 119 West 40th Street, New York, NY 10018. Attn. Special Sales Department. Phone: 1-800-221-2647.

ISBN-13: 978-0-7582-3858-0
ISBN-10: 0-7582-3858-4

First Kensington Trade Paperback Printing: January 2011
10 9 8 7 6 5 4 3 2 1

Printed in the United States of America

For Jon,
who was, is, and always will be
the love of my life

PROLOGUE

Paris, October 1802. "For what reason do you wish to leave France?" Fouché looked at her with the hooded eyes she remembered painfully well.

"My business partner, M. Philipsthal, wishes for me to join his Phantasmagoria show in London." Marie kept her voice steady and tried not to break her gaze from his, fearing he would see it as a sign of weakness and deny her a passport.

"When do you plan to return?"

"When my purse is full." She inwardly chastised herself for her sharp tongue, but calmly kept her hands clasped loosely before her as the minister of police continued his review of her application across his desk.

"And at what point will you be overflowing with riches? Have you set a date for this, or shall I simply indicate your return date as 'when Madame Tussaud achieves victory'?"

"No, monsieur, I believe I will be gone about a year. With your kind permission, of course."

"Of course. What does it mean here that you intend on taking 'thirty character figures' out of France? Are you moving your entire salon? You said you were just joining Philipsthal's show temporarily."

Marie drew in her breath as she tried to think how to best answer. Her future depended on her next words to this man she both feared and detested, but it was not the first time she had encountered him. How had a forty-one-year-old wife and mother of two young boys ended up in the company of the frightening and pitiless Fouché, *again?*

She resisted the urge to rub her eyes.

Born Anne Marie Grosholtz, Marie had grown up in the household of Philippe Curtius, a Swiss physician for whom her mother was a housekeeper. He was skilled in wax modeling, which he used to illustrate anatomy. His work was admired by the Prince de

Conti, who became his patron and encouraged him to move to Paris and set up a wax figure cabinet. His first exhibition was held in 1770 and Marie quickly became a studious and talented apprentice.

In addition to learning wax modeling, she also trained in political savvy. She watched as Curtius hosted elegant salons for French aristocrats such as the prince. These stylish members of society were invited to the exhibition's location in the fashionable Palais Royal. Over wine and fine music, they could stroll about looking at his life-sized wax figures of their friends and other notable famous people. It soon became a fashion to hire Dr. Curtius to have a personal replica of onesself made.

But when the political winds began shifting and revolution became the maxim, Curtius speedily altered his exhibition. The watchman at the front door was no longer a prim man dressed in white livery, but was instead replaced by a lout dressed sansculotte style. Gone were the elegant, fussy, bewigged aristocrats talking about fashion and love affairs. Curtius invited the more disreputable figures of society to his salon—now more politically termed a wax cabinet—such as Robespierre, Marat, Danton, and the loathsome man before her now, Joseph Fouché.

Curtius ensured that wine flowed liberally and that he displayed only wax figures that would not be offensive to the revolutionaries. Any figure remotely aristocratic was rolled up in protective sheets and stored out of sight. Marie took note that although Curtius was heartily welcoming of his new clients, he made sure that he never expressed any opinion whatsoever about their activities. For this reason he managed to avoid any irrational indictments on their part, while remaining completely informed on the ever-changing political climate in Paris. His show flourished.

Despite her adoption of Curtius's methods, Marie was not so fortunate in avoiding calamity during the 1794–5 year of terror. While Curtius was away on a trip to the Rhineland in July 1794, Marie was denounced by a dancer at a nearby theatre, who was supplementing his income by serving as the local executioner's assistant.

Despite his knowledge of her innocence, Fouché did nothing to help her and she remained in prison for about a week awaiting execution, until a friend of Curtius's heard about her plight and intervened on her behalf.

After that, she retreated back to the shadows of the exhibition, which she had inherited upon Curtius's death in late 1794 and had worked tirelessly on ever since. Even a late marriage at age thirty-four to a civil engineer named François Tussaud and subsequent children had not slowed down her pace nor her ambition for success with the exhibition, still called Curtius's Cabinet of Wonders.

But the show was not without its financial difficulties after years of national strife and the death of its original owner. When Paul de Philipsthal, an old family friend and fellow showman, returned from a booking of his Phantasmagoria show in London, he raved about the English audiences, who were fresh and eager for entertainments. Taking Marie aside, he suggested that she slip over with a collection of Curtius's wax figures to add a new dimension to his own show. They would form a partnership, and with his experience of the London theatre and her talent for wax sculpting, their show could not fail to draw enthusiastic spectators.

So here she was now, seeking a passport from Joseph Fouché, who had somehow managed to separate himself from the devastation of the Terror and become Napoleon's minister of police. She focused back to answering his question.

"Exporting my wax portraits will give the English an opportunity to see the cultural and artistic preeminence of the French. They will either come to admire us, or fear our natural superiority."

Fouché hesitated. "But we want to keep talent in France, and *you* have talent."

"Most of the figures I will take were made by M. Curtius. *He* had talent, as well you know."

"Mmm, yes, he was a good fellow. Served an excellent burgundy. I remember you skulking about in the corners while we talked of world events." Still he vacillated. What effect would the effigies of revolutionaries who had died on the guillotine have abroad? Would it intensify hatred between the two countries? *Would he be blamed for the escalation of bad feelings while Napoleon worked toward the subjugation of the English?*

Unlike most of his contemporaries, Fouché had managed to assert himself into the highest levels of both the revolutionary government and then that of Napoleon Bonaparte. This he did with an acutely developed sense of pragmatism and a considerable streak of cruelty that he employed without hesitation in order to maintain his political power. His years of switching allegiances and staying ahead of his opponents had given him the capacity for simply being able to *smell* when something in the air was not quite right, much as a dog uses this sense to avoid poisoned meat.

The supplicant before him must have understood his indecision, for she suggested to him with just a hint of artificial helpfulness, "As you know, I have modeled both the first consul and his wife, and they will be part of the exhibition in London."

And that was what was so irritating, wasn't it? This petite but energetic woman before him was in favor with Napoleon and Josephine, having modeled them both to their utter delight. Did he dare do anything that might offend them now, despite what repercussions it might have upon him later?

The moments ticked away as he struggled with a verdict. He could not quite assess what Madame Tussaud's real motivations might be, but neither could he feel that she would do any harm.

With a resigned sigh, he picked up a pen, dipped it into his silver inkwell, and signed his name to her documents, giving her permission to travel to England for an indefinite period. He hoped he would not regret it.

Even as she witnessed the crates filled with wax figures being loaded onto the ship, Marie could hardly believe her good fortune. She looked one more time at Fouché's signature on her papers before folding them up and tucking them into the pouch she had sewn into her dress for traveling. Her four-year-old son, Joseph, danced excitedly by her side, ecstatic over the thought of his first great adventure.

She had had little thought for the sea voyage until now, so busy was she with preparations. It had not been easy to pack up the fragile wax figures to be transported by caravan over bumpy roads and then carefully—she hoped—stored in the ship's hold for the brief journey across the Channel. Marie deliberately avoided tearful farewells with her husband and her mother, instead spending her last hours leaving them with dozens of little instructions for care of the Salon de Cire in her absence.

Her real emotions were focused on two-year-old Francis, who was too young to make such a journey with his mother. She clutched him tightly, and whispered in his ear that when she returned to France it would be with a full purse and dozens of playthings for him. Unaware of the import of the moment, her son chirped and giggled and gave her a sloppy kiss on the cheek.

With eyes full of tears threatening to spill forth, she was glad enough to turn away and board the carriage that would take her and Joseph to their ship.

The Channel was choppy and unkind, and most of the passengers were simply relieved to finally see the white cliffs of England. Marie, though, was ecstatic. She had done it. She had survived the Revolution, slipped past Fouché, avoided her husband's reproaches for leaving him, and was now determined to remake her wax salon into a breathtaking attraction like no other.

What matter that she now had to face a customs official who was sure to faint dead away after opening one of her vast packing cases to find a glass eye peering up inquisitively at him?

PART ONE

London

☙ 1 ☙

London, January 1803. "Ow! Nicholas, I need another bandage."

Marguerite's husband rushed into the workroom with a bundle of muslin strips.

"You've hurt yourself again? I'm going to send those new carving tools into the Thames. This is the third time this week a knife has slipped in your hands."

"I know. And look what happened." Marguerite held up her latest creation, a fashion doll commissioned by a local dressmaker who intended to show off a new ball-gown design on it for several of her select clients. But the doll's head would have to be redone, as there was now a deep gash across the left side of its face.

"Why don't you let Roger handle the carving?" Nicholas asked.

"I probably should, but I'm so frustrated with trying to perfect wax heads that I wanted to retreat back to the familiarity of working with wood. I'm good at that. At least, I used to be." She held up her left thumb, the muslin hastily wrapped around it now beginning to seep blood.

Nicholas put his arms around his young wife and lifted her up onto the large worktable, which was littered with scraps of fabric, bundles of straw, blocks of wood, and other materials of the trade.

"Sweetheart, you are the best dollmaker in London. Wax is still a new medium. I've no doubt you will eventually be the best wax dollmaker in all of Europe."

"I'll never be as good as Aunt Claudette."

"No, you'll never be your aunt Claudette." He wrapped his arms around his wife and kissed the tip of her nose. "Much to my great relief. I couldn't bear to be married to a woman of lesser talent than you."

"Mr. Ashby, you're very fortunate that I am of such a forgiving nature that I can overlook your insult to my beloved aunt and mentor. Otherwise, I might be forced to employ my shrewish tone of voice."

"Is that so? And what does a lady shrew look like in her natural state?" He scooped her off the worktable and cupped one hand around the back of her neck while using the other to pull her thick auburn hair out of the knot she employed to keep it out of her face while working. It slid down her back like the flow of warm brandy from a decanter.

"Now I remember the fair young maiden I fell in love with at Hevington a decade ago. She was covered in wood shavings even back then."

Bells jangled as someone entered the front door. Marguerite disengaged from her husband's embrace and went from the back workroom out to the front of the shop.

It was Agnes Smoot, returning from an errand.

"Letter just come for you, Mrs. Ashby."

Marguerite took the proffered folded square from the shop's seamstress with her unhurt hand. "Thank you, Agnes. Has Roger returned yet from making deliveries?"

"No, mum, not yet. D'you want to see him when he gets back?"

"No, I'm sure he doesn't want to hear of my epic battle with a carving knife." She held up her bandaged thumb.

"Again, mum?"

"Yes, again, unfortunately." Marguerite returned to the workroom where Nicholas was busy arranging some scraps of wood according to size, while whistling softly under his breath. She held up the sealed correspondence.

"Speaking of Aunt Claudette, I have a letter from her. Would you like to read it with me?"

Nicholas stopped what he was doing and lit a small lamp to better illuminate the letter. Claudette Greycliffe's writing tended to be faint and spidery, and it could take them an entire evening to decipher her longer missives.

January 15, 1803
Hevington, Kent

My dearest Marguerite,

I trust all is well with you and that you are capably managing the recent influx of orders for the Season.

Are the troubles with France affecting your ability to obtain supplies? I expect old Boney won't be letting any French brocades leave his shores.

Forgive my intrusion, dear. Sometimes I get lonely for the excitement of the shop. Send along a project for me, will you? I should love to wield a knife again. It feels like an eternity since I held a block of wood in my hand.

William and I send our love to both you and Nicholas. Will you be coming to visit soon? Little Bitty is dying to show you her new cat that she found hiding under some shrubbery. It's a mangy thing—one eye missing, an ear clipped, and its tail bent horribly out of shape—but Little Bitty carries the thing with her everywhere. I believe this new addition to the family makes the animal-to-child ratio at Hevington nearly two to one.

William says the family estate is being turned into a wildlife menagerie. I haven't the heart to tell him yet that I have my eye on one of those new bullmastiffs that are becoming popular. They are supposed to be very good guard dogs, but I suppose that like every other creature that migrates onto Hevington, he will become spoilt and lazy.

With my greatest affection,
Claudette

P.S. Why don't you come for a week or so next month? William wants to teach the children blindman's bluff, and you certainly don't want to miss that spectacle.

"Aunt Claudette sounds a little lonely, Nicholas."

"Lonely! How could she have time to be lonely? She manages a careful and virtuous household, contains three noisy and active children, and hosts numerous fashionable parties, yet the woman is still inexplicably graceful. No wonder Uncle William adores her."

"Why, you foolish man! Not ten minutes ago you were glad I wasn't Aunt Claudette."

Claudette Laurent, the daughter of a great French dollmaker, had been orphaned in France at the age of sixteen, but found ship's passage to England and worked as a domestic servant for several years under a harsh mistress before finally risking all to start her own doll shop. Marguerite's widowed mother, Béatrice du Georges, had become friends with Claudette aboard the ship bound for England and so, along with five-year-old Marguerite, the three had lived, worked, and survived together. Although her mother had been involved in the shop, it was the young Marguerite who had shown a talent for dollmaking. Claudette encouraged her interest and the two became close, with Marguerite referring to the older woman as "Aunt" Claudette.

William Greycliffe was a man of minor aristocratic connections who had pursued Claudette relentlessly despite her initial disdain of him. Even now Marguerite loved to hear stories of their courtship told for the thousandth time.

When Béatrice died suddenly, Claudette and William brought the teenaged Marguerite to live with them at their Kentish estate of Hevington and Claudette made Marguerite her de facto heir in the doll shop. As time passed, Claudette turned more and more of the responsibility for the shop over to Marguerite as she became involved in raising her three children and managing the estate with William.

Nicholas was one of a set of twin boys born to James and Maude Ashby, Claudette's and Béatrice's domestic employers upon their arrival in England. Nicholas's heart burned with youthful passion for Béatrice, who gently refused him. He avidly followed the women's progress after they left the Ashby home and even visited on occasion. Following Béatrice's death, Nicholas finally took note of Marguerite and promptly fell in love with her saucy temperament. For Marguerite, Nicholas filled the need for gentle sweetness that her mother's death had yanked away from her, and the two had been inseparable during the intervening ten years.

"Oh, Nicholas, let's go for Shrovetide as Aunt Claudette suggests. We haven't been to Hevington in months. We even missed the lighting of the Yule log this past year. Besides, Rebecca is probably old enough now for a baby house and we could take one to her as a gift." In the coziness of the warmly lit workshop, full of the smell of freshly shaved wood, she reached her arms around her husband's neck and pressed her lips to his.

He responded in his familiar way, sliding both arms around her waist and burying his face in her neck.

"Very well, Mrs. Ashby. We'll leave the shop in the care of Roger and Agnes, and plan for a long visit to Hevington. But before you begin packing trunks, I believe there is some more immediate business that requires your attention," he said, gently dropping kisses along her exposed neckline.

"Is that so, Mr. Ashby? Pray, what business could be of such consequence that it calls for my *immediate* attention?"

"It's a very private matter. Come home now, woman, so we can, er, discuss it before it loses the strength of its importance." He playfully smacked his wife's bottom and ushered her out of the shop, humming a happy but aimless tune.

February 21, 1803. The evening before their scheduled departure for Hevington, Marguerite and Nicholas returned to the closed doll shop so she could put together a small box of miniature furniture and other accoutrements for the baby house they had already packed to take to Claudette's daughter, Rebecca.

Miniature dolls' houses, called baby houses, were becoming increasingly popular in England. Claudette had once spoken wistfully about the houses her father carried in his doll shop back in France, which led to an expansion in her own shop's trade in these diminutive pieces. In addition to offering miniature replicas of tables, chairs, beds, carpets, paintings, and dishes, Marguerite had started designing tiny scale-sized families to inhabit them.

She rummaged patiently through a box of petite tissue-wrapped dolls, searching for one painted with Rebecca's cobalt eyes, eyes that defined her as her mother's child.

"Marguerite, the hackney will not wait all night for us. Isn't the house and its furnishings enough for one child?"

"I suppose so, but I know I painted a baby-house doll that resembles her. I want her to have it. Maybe in this drawer? No, not here. I should look on the fabric shelves. Nicholas, would you go back to the workroom and see if you can find any more boxes of baby-house dolls?"

While Nicholas retreated to the back of the shop, she continued her search, the sound of her husband's gentle whistling floating high over the tops of shelves loaded with every manner of elegantly dressed doll. Marguerite's stock ranged from the little baby-house dolls all the way up to the *grandes Pandores*, life-sized dolls built on metal frames, which Aunt Claudette had made popular among the aristocratic English. The *grandes Pandores* were Claudette's favorite dolls, but Marguerite preferred the nimble skill involved in the tiniest of her creations. Besides, the *grandes Pandores* required the wax heads that were so dratted difficult to create as flawless pieces.

A distant shouting from outside overtook the comforting sound of Nicholas's whistling. She paused from what she was doing to listen, but the noise abated and she returned to her task.

Nicholas returned to the display room at the front of the shop. "Sweetheart, there are no baby-house dolls in the workroom. I'll go up to the attic and see if Roger may have stored some up there."

"And I'll continue looking down here. I'm just certain that we have more of these dolls in the shop."

Nicholas Ashby's tall but lanky frame disappeared from view again. He had grown in height as he became an adult, but had never filled out in an obviously muscular sort of way. Still he had the strength of two men, and Marguerite loved watching him haul large planks of wood from delivery wagons into the shed behind the shop. Even Roger, as enormous and barrel-chested as he was, could not out-lift Nicholas Ashby.

But Nicholas's interest in the shop stopped with physical duties. He was content to let Marguerite deal with customers and manage the financial affairs of the shop, much as her mother had been happy to let Aunt Claudette do years ago.

So engrossed was she with her thoughts and her search that when the projectile came through the window on the other side of the shop she was at first confused as to whether the sound had come from outside or the attic. The growing clamor outside on the street settled her confusion.

"Nicholas? Nicholas! Come quickly!" Marguerite called up toward the attic entrance, but he did not answer. He must have gone into the far reaches of the attic, which spanned the forty-foot length of the shop. She stood up, brushing dust from the sturdy, brown woolen skirt she wore most days when working.

Ever brash as a child and no less so as a woman, Marguerite marched to the front door of the shop and flung it open. The hackney was gone, and she was stunned to see a group of about twenty men, mostly drunk and on the brink of irrationality. They carried torches and clubs and the occasional pitchfork, and were gabbing loudly about a hanging at Southwark.

Why were these drunkards marching on respectable Oxford Street, and why in heaven's name were they congregating outside her shop with obvious ill will?

"That's her, Mr. Emmett. She's the doll lady we told you about, Marguerite Ashby." Through the smoky haze of the torches Marguerite could not see individual faces well, but the voice was coming from the back of the assembly.

"Yes, I have that figured out, Reggie. Your assistance is appreciated." A man who could have been one of any number of different merchants stepped forward so that Marguerite could see him. He was as short as Nicholas was tall but built like a bull. He swept an exaggerated bow.

"Mr. Emmett at your service, mistress."

"Yes, I have that figured out, Mr. Emmett." Hoots of laughter were interspersed with calls for Mr. Emmett to "get to it."

"Well now, mistress, we've just heard some disturbing news. News that might have a serious impact on your little trade here."

"News? What news?"

Reggie's voice rang out again. "She's a liar, Mr. Emmett. She knows all about it!"

The other men grumbled their agreement.

Marguerite stared steadily at Mr. Emmett with her arms crossed in front of her. "Hurry up with what you have to say so I can be about my business. I'm a law-abiding woman running an honorable shop with her husband."

"Is that right?" Mr. Emmett stepped closer and his frame filled the doorway. Up close, Marguerite could see that his eyes were bloodshot from drink and hidden rage, and he stank of a laborer's sweat. She calculated whether or not to scream for Nicholas but was unsure whether he would hear her, and as of yet she was not sure what might infuriate these men further.

"So is your husband here right now, mistress?" Mr. Emmett's gaze was thoughtful.

"He is. Shall I get him for you?"

"She's still lying, Mr. Emmett! Ain't no one else here except probably some spies hiding out."

Mr. Emmett's darting eyes spoke his indecision over whom to believe.

"C'mon, Mr. Emmett, are we going to do what we came here for? We're almost out of ale and I've a powerful thirst."

Marguerite maintained her own gaze. "And what did you come here for?"

"We're here to put a stop to the French intrigues coming in through Ireland, and that would include Colonel Despard and his bunch, plus all the French rabble like *you*."

"What French rabble? I'm an Englishwoman. Who is Colonel Despard?" Marguerite was trying desperately to figure out what he was talking about.

"Not with a fancy name like Marguerite you're not. A good Englishwoman would be Margaret or Margery. Your name has you dead to rights a lady Frog."

Marguerite drew in a breath in an attempt to be patient. What was taking Nicholas so long in the attic? "My mother was French. I have lived in this country all my life and am married to an Englishman. What is this nonsense about French infiltration through Ireland?"

"Ever since the French peasants started their revolution, the Irish have been hoping for a chance to bring popery back to England. Stinking papists the French and Irish are. They've been looking for a way to bring down the right noble house of Hanover so they could bring in French rule and turn us all into foppin' Frogs. So they found a half-wit in Colonel Despard to do their work. He stole over here from Ireland slippery as an eel and planned to kill our good King George. But the Irish and French are no match for smart Englishmen and he was found out. So today we all went and watched him and his gang swing from the gallows and get their heads chopped off, and now we're going to help out the Crown by getting rid of the rest of the French influence in England, starting with *you*, Mrs. Marguerite Ashby. We know all about this shop's wicked dealings."

Mr. Emmett's speech seemed to momentarily exhaust him, but it reenergized his mob with shouts of "fire the store" and "kill the French whore."

"So you see, mistress, we have two choices here. Either you can leave peaceably while we can look for hidden messages and contraband, since we didn't 'spect to find you here anyway, or if you want to be bothersome we may have to take further measures. And we're not opposed to those further measures." He reached out a hand and roughly caressed her right breast.

Marguerite instinctively slapped his face. A grave mistake. Mr. Emmett's face was now mottled red to match his eyes over the insult, while his cronies both laughed and urged him on to despoiling her. He grabbed her arm and pulled her close.

"I've half a mind to teach you manners right here, mistress, even though you'll probably give me the pox."

"What the devil is going on here?" Nicholas came striding into the room with a small crate under his arm. He tossed it to one side to confront the group of men.

"Who are you and what do you want here?"

Mr. Emmett reflexively dropped Marguerite's arm to face his new adversary.

"We're doing work on behalf of His Majesty, ridding England of what you might call subversive French influences."

"I would call it no such thing. And if you're looking for local French residents to accost, what are you doing here?" Nicholas was cautiously approaching the intruder.

"Your little wife here was born a Frogette, wasn't she? We think she's probably helping ol' Boney infiltrate England. Wasn't she once arrested for sending good English coin over to France?"

"That was her aunt—"

"No difference. She probably taught your wife how to stuff them dolls, and we mean to inspect them to be sure she isn't sending money or messages to Bonaparte."

Nicholas remained calm, although Marguerite could see one small vein throbbing over his left eyebrow, the only sign that his normally benign temper was on the verge of eruption.

"My wife's aunt was falsely accused of these activities, evidenced by her subsequent marriage to Lord Greycliffe, an honorable man."

"Maybe that's so, maybe it's not, but we've walked a long way from the hangin' and we plan to do what we came to do."

"Sir, you and your followers will leave these premises with haste. I will not have my wife plagued and threatened."

"We'll leave when we've a mind to. After our mission is finished."

"You'll leave when *I've* a mind for you to do so. Which is now." Nicholas's voice was still calm, but his resolve was unmistakable.

The mood began to alter noticeably among the crowd outside. It was amusing when a defenseless little woman sassed back, but it was an entirely different thing when some coxcomb started making threats, now wasn't it? The men became restless, pacing like jackals back and forth, waiting for their leader to make the kill so they could each have a share.

Mr. Emmett moved imperceptibly forward, just enough that Marguerite stepped back reflexively, allowing him fully into the shop. He put a hand forward to move her out of his way and Nicholas reacted instinctively like a lion protecting his pride. But the jackals were waiting for such a move. He stepped forward to push Mr. Emmett away from Marguerite, eliciting a sharp yelp of surprised outrage from the man. It served as the attack signal for the rest of the pack.

Marguerite was roughly elbowed and jostled as several men lunged into the shop, their eyes full of expectant treachery. Nicholas took several steps backward, knowing he had become prey.

Marguerite felt, more than saw, the splintering crack that accompanied the connection of a broken wood beam against her husband's left arm, sending him sprawling to the floor and sliding across the dark oaken surface into a tiered display of fashion dolls.

The grouping of sixteen dolls had been created as a tribute to King George's family. On the top tier were the monarch and his wife, Queen Charlotte. On the next tier were his married children, and the bottom shelf displayed his remaining spinster daughters, who were probably destined to retain their single status.

As Nicholas careened into the display, the dolls crashed into a heap around him. He brought his hands up to protect his face from the descending silk-encased wooden projectiles, but not before the princess Augusta fell against his nose on her way to landing next to him, her head turned toward him as though to survey the damage she had done.

Mr. Emmett barked at the others and pointed. "That's just what a French spy would do, boys—hide her traitorous goods inside playthings made up to look like the good king's family. She'd think that right funny. Those dolls are where we start looking."

Nicholas's nose was askew and bleeding profusely, yet he valiantly brought himself up to one elbow.

"You will not destroy—"

Another mob member silenced him by kicking him in the stomach. Nicholas doubled over, groaning.

Please, Nicholas, Marguerite silently prayed. *Show them your secret might and strength.*

As though encouraged by his wife's silent entreaty, Nicholas rose to all fours, then shakily stood, his waistcoat stained with a mixture of blood and floor dust.

The jackals were stunned by his fortitude and stopped long enough to watch his progress from the floor to an upright position.

Between clenched teeth, he fearlessly addressed Mr. Emmett again.

"You . . . and your boys . . . have been warned for a final time. I want you . . . out of this place of business . . . now."

Marguerite crossed wordlessly over to his side and leaned against him. To the onlookers it appeared that she was showing unity with her husband, but in reality she was supporting him, with one arm around him and the other gently holding his injured arm.

Nicholas gratefully leaned against her. The interior of the doll shop was now at a taut standstill. The hungry mob, having all slipped inside the premises, still looked to Mr. Emmett for orders, ready to pounce when he gave the go-ahead. Mr. Emmett, though, seemed a bit unsure of himself.

His next words startled Marguerite. "Well, I s'pose we can leave well enough alone, can't we? No need to rough up a lone shop owner and his wife. After all, they've been warned about what happens to traitors in this country, right?" He drew a finger across his neck for emphasis.

Several of the men protested with moans and grumbles. Reggie spoke up the loudest. "T'isn't fair, Mr. Emmett. You agreed with us that they were foreigners dressed in English wool and needed some comeuppance. We should be breakin' up those dolls. Who knows what they might be hiding in 'em. Why are you turnin' your mind?"

"Because, you balmy idiot, it just don't seem right to rampage on a lady whose husband is standing right here. Maybe we'll come back some other time if we hear that she's making an agitation."

"Aw, Mr. Emmett, you're not afraid of her husband now, are you?" Reggie was whining now.

"I'm not afraid of anything. C'mon, pints of bitters for the lot of you at The Lamb and Flag. Let's go."

The men, now deprived of their quarry, were deflated, but Marguerite did not dare let out her breath yet. To her surprise, Nicholas held out a hand in friendship to Mr. Emmett, and he clasped it in return, softly mumbling an apology for the disturbance. She stayed at Nicholas's heels as he escorted the men out.

As the last of the men were leaving, Nicholas shut the door forcefully. An enraged howl burst forth from the other side followed by muffled arguing.

"I told you, Mr. Emmett! He did it on purpose. My foot, he slammed the door on my ankle. I won't have it—I won't have it. Look, it's already looking busted up."

"Reggie, let's go. You won't even feel your foot after you get a little more to drink and Sadie sits in your lap."

From inside the shop Marguerite and Nicholas could sense discontent stirring in the crowd over how Mr. Emmett was handling the insult to Reggie. Nicholas said quietly, "Let's go through the back and step into the shed until this rabble is gone."

"You didn't shut the door on his foot on purpose, did you, Nicholas?"

Nicholas put a finger to his lips, his face expressionless. "Let's go, before Reggie bursts something in his constricted little brain."

Marguerite took his uninjured arm and they turned away from the door. In an instant, their world was a cacophony of splintering wood, shouting, and the clomping of shoddily clad feet on the shop's floor. She was separated from Nicholas by the men stampeding in through the broken door and found herself crushed against the shop's counter, across from where the royal family display had been overturned.

Several men addressed their attentions to those dolls, as well as others on shelves lining the shop. The artfully draped satin fabrics that created platforms on each shelf for the dolls to live upon were whisked away and their residents went tumbling to the ground. Disappointed that this did not cause most of the dolls to break apart, men began picking up individual specimens and hurling them against walls in order to separate their heads and limbs from their torsos.

In the distance, Marguerite could hear a plaintive wailing, but realized it was coming from her when one of the men shook a dirty hand in her face and snarled, "Quiet, or I'll settle you down with this." He gestured lewdly, but was too excited to return to the fracas to pay her that much attention. He abruptly turned away from Marguerite to grab a miniaturized flower-seller from the hands of someone else, and began slamming it repeatedly on a display table, hoping for some secret treasure to come out of it.

All around Marguerite swirled a confusing pattern of fabrics, doll parts, and sweaty bodies, reeking from their wild activity. The scene was cloaked under a heavy layer of smoke settling into the room from the torches the men were brandishing over their work. She remained paralyzed against the counter, too terrified to move in any way that would bring attention back to her.

Mr. Emmett no longer had control of his troupe of troublemakers, and as such was joining into the melee as heartily as the rest of them. Marguerite watched helplessly as he picked up the box Nicholas had thrown to one side and dumped the tiny contents onto a table. He picked up a doll from the pile and began fingering its clothing.

"Hey, look at these! They aren't any longer than my finger. No one would suspect something this small of holding contraband, so I bet it does." He held up the blond-haired figure for the others to see before using a club against it on the table, as though trapping and killing a wild pig. In one swing the tiny doll was obliterated.

It was the doll Marguerite wanted to take to Rebecca.

She looked around the room, trying to find her husband through the acrid gray plumes and the ongoing tumult.

He was near the entry to the workroom at the back of the shop, standing but shaking. His nose looked like a large knot on his face and his usually neat attire was rumpled and bloody. She caught his eye and he gave her the briefest nod, indicating that she should follow him.

He's still determined to go to the shed.

But Marguerite was stopped before she could take even a first step forward to join her husband.

As their search revealed no secret treasure, money, or correspondence, the men's discontent took a vicious left turn once again toward Nicholas. A group of four of them angrily approached him.

"Why isn't there anything here?"

"What've you done with the contraband?"

"Mr. Emmett said this was a French hideout."

Marguerite could practically hear their jaws snapping at Nicholas. She began to edge her way quietly toward him, unsure how she was going to break through their collective bulk to join her husband, much less how they were going to escape through the back door of the shop.

But her husband was not yet finished with the rabble. He pulled up his tall frame and stood as straight as he could, saying in as loud and clear a voice as his injuries would allow, "I've already said repeatedly that we carry on no dishonest business here. You have plundered a respectable shop in a very fashionable neighborhood, and you can be certain that the papers will carry news of it right away."

While he spoke, Marguerite continued inching her way back to her husband, lifting her skirt lightly with both hands to ensure she did not stumble and draw attention to herself.

"The only thing that's going to be carried right away is *you*."

Drat that Reggie, she thought. *Was it just liquor that made him so cantankerous?*

"Sir"—Nicholas's breathing was becoming ragged through his nose—"I am telling you for the last time—"

"You're telling *us?* Why, you're nothing but a French doxy whore lover. We'll be doing the telling here."

Reggie had inserted himself as the leader of the pack, his thin chest puffed forward in self-importance. Mr. Emmett was now just another rabid dog. Reggie reveled in his new position.

"And what I'm telling you is that me and these boys are here to serve England by rooting out undesirables."

"You've nearly destroyed this shop and found nothing in the process. You found nothing because there is nothing to find. What more do you want?"

"Satisfaction is what we want. And we haven't had it yet."

Nicholas raised a hand in a peaceful gesture, but it was interpreted as aggression by Reggie, who sought the slightest provocation in order to escalate his power.

Whatever Nicholas said next was drowned out by Reggie's belligerent roar. In the span of seconds, Reggie had grabbed a pitchfork from another man's hands and thrust it up to Nicholas's face, still shouting. It was impossible for Marguerite to hear anything Nicholas was saying over Reggie's yelling and the rush of blood in her own ears, but her husband was standing his ground with the trespasser. She watched as Nicholas brought up both hands this time to shove the pitchfork away from him.

Reggie's fury was now beyond redemption.

Grabbing the pitchfork with both hands for leverage, he thrust it viciously into Nicholas's stomach. Marguerite felt a bitter nausea that overrode the heat, the smoke, and the noise as she witnessed at least three of the prongs entering his torso.

This is not real. This is not happening. This is madness. Wake up, I must wake up!

She shut her eyes for the briefest moment and reopened them. The scene remained the same, except that Nicholas had fallen to the ground on his side, the weapon still lodged in him. Reggie rolled Nicholas onto his back with one foot and used the same foot to steady himself against his victim as he pulled the pitchfork out of his body. He wiped the tines against his pants leg and casually handed it back to the pitchfork's owner.

The shop went completely silent except for the crackling of the torches.

"Blast, Reggie," said the man with the pitchfork. "Did you ever kill a man before?"

"No, this was my first. Wasn't that hard, really."

Marguerite swallowed the fear rising in her throat, which threatened to disgorge the contents of her stomach, a supper shared with Nicholas just an hour previously.

She tamped down the fear, and quickly replaced it with white-hot rage at the sight of her husband lying motionless on the floor. How dare they attack her husband, her innocent husband, and this defenseless shop, for no reason other than to vent against some imagined adversary. What insanity had befallen the kingdom that marauding bands of drunkards could willfully attack its loyal subjects?

Nicholas, I must get to Nicholas. He needs help. I have to find a doctor for him.

Without thinking, she picked up a Chinese vase from the counter, a gift from a grateful customer. With a force that can only come from that unhappy blend of grief and wrath, she hurled the vase over the men's heads at the only remaining unbroken window of the shop. Both window and vase exploded into countless delicate shards from the impact.

At least a dozen heads snapped up in one motion, all eyes on Marguerite.

"Damn you, get out! All of you. You're nothing but a bunch of mangy curs and you will get out this *instant.* I hope you rot in hell. No, wait, I don't want you to rot. I want you to feel pain without end. I hope Satan himself stabs all of you over and over every day for eternity. And that your nose is broken once a week, always, and that you forever taste your own blood from your wounds." As she screamed her curses at the men, she picked up and threw anything her hands blindly grabbed from the counter. Scissors, inkwells, and fashion-plate books all went plunging through the air seeking random targets.

Would no one on the street come to their aid?

But even Reggie was sufficiently subdued by Marguerite's wild madness. The men all eyed one another nervously, and as a single mind decided that between the proprietor's stabbing and his wife's raving, they had seen enough action for one inebriated evening. Without waiting for direction from either Reggie or Mr. Emmett, the men scurried for the door and freedom while Marguerite spent herself on heaving every last projectile she could find.

A new silence engulfed the shop as she realized they were gone and she was hurling epithets at the empty space. Breathing heavily from her effort, she grasped the edge of the counter.

Did I say all of those things? I must have been possessed. Oh dear God, Nicholas.

She ran to where Nicholas lay on the floor, his torso engulfed in blood. She dropped to her knees next to him and threw herself on his chest.

"Oh no, Nicholas, no, sweetheart, can you hear me, please say something, I love you so much, darling, please say something, are you breathing, Nicholas?"

She lay atop him utterly still for a moment, and was rewarded with the sound of raspy breathing. She sat up and looked at him.

"My love, are you awake? Can you hear me?"

His eyes fluttered open and focused on her with difficulty.

"Quite a . . . show . . . you were very brave, my love." He coughed, screwing up his eyes from the pain.

"I was just senseless for a moment. Nicholas, I'm going to find a doctor for you now, to come and tend to your wounds. You'll be fine in no time at all."

"You must continue to be brave . . . not going to be fine . . . love you, Marguerite . . . sorry we do not have a child to carry on . . . shop . . . you're my fiery little rebel." He tugged at a pin in her hair and released her tresses.

"Nicholas, stop. Stop it this instant. Your wounds can be mended. You just need a doctor's attention. I'll run out now—"

With a surge of his hidden strength she knew so intimately, he grabbed her arm. "Don't leave . . . won't do any good . . . stay with me. Stay here with me. Here." He tugged at her arm.

She yielded to his pull and lay at his right side, his good arm wrapped around her and her right arm over his oozing chest.

He turned enough to kiss her forehead. His lips were dry and coarse. He murmured "I love you" once more before falling into a labored sleep, his breaths sharp and uneven.

Much as she wanted to run out to seek a doctor or do something—anything—to help, she lay still next to her husband. His tight grip on her probably would not prevent her leaving anyway. As his breaths became shallower, she splayed her hand across his chest to ensure she could feel every motion of his upper body. Her hand became sticky with her husband's blood. She glanced downward and saw that her own clothing was as stained as his.

How can it be that last night I made love to my husband, and tonight I am lying next to his dying body?

His breaths were now not only shallow but irregular, and he emitted a faint rattle. Marguerite nearly stopped breathing herself, fearful of making any movement that would disturb her husband. The metallic odor of his profuse bleeding caused her forgotten nausea to make an inconvenient reappearance, but she swallowed hard and mentally forced it away.

And then with a great *whoosh* Nicholas's breaths stopped altogether and he released his firm grasp of her. Was he . . . ?

She labored up onto one elbow. Nicholas's eyes remained shut, but now he appeared to be resting peacefully. She pressed her hand—the blood on it now dry—gently against his chest.

Nothing.

Nothing at all.

A long and piercing wail escaped her chest and yet again she had to suppress an overwhelming desire to retch. She lay back down next to her husband, exhausted, but determined to stay with him until she was certain his soul had departed for good.

2

Hevington, April 1803. "Lady Greycliffe, would you like to wear your lavender silk or your gold-threaded ivory gown to supper with Lord and Lady Balding?" Claudette's maid asked from the doorway of the library.

Claudette Greycliffe looked up from where she was arranging flowers in a vase while her husband sat reading a book on the classification of clouds in his favorite chair, a copper-colored leather cover over an old Jacobean frame that had faded and cracked exactly along the lines of William's sitting position. It was the only piece of furniture in Hevington that looked as though it belonged in the charity box, but William refused to part with his comfortable reading spot. Upon their marriage eleven years ago, Claudette was given free rein to redecorate as she saw fit, as long as she did not touch what she thought of as the King James Monstrosity.

"I think the lavender one, Jolie. Be sure to see to the gloves I wear with it. I believe there was a seam coming undone last time I wore them."

"Of course, madame. My lord, I picked up the post in the front hall on my way here." She offered the latest edition of *The London Gazette* to William before departing.

He lay down the science volume and opened the four-page newspaper, scanning it for anything of note. He loved to summarize the day's events for his wife.

"Hmm, looks like the news just made it here that Cardinal de Rohan died back in February. He was living in Baden. It says he spent his last few years and the remainder of his wealth in providing for the poor clergy of his diocese who were obligated to leave France during the Revolution. Good penance for that man, considering what he did to bring down his queen with that damnable necklace affair."

William continued folding and scanning the pages. He sat up with a start and muttered an oath under his breath. "The Treaty of Amiens is collapsing. No surprise there. That pompous rooster Bonaparte won't rest until he's invaded England and made us all his obedient little hens. He needs to be taught proper manners."

"William, I don't mean to be flippant, but Bonaparte's war with us is the least of my concerns, at least as compared to Marguerite. I don't know how to reach her." Claudette continued assembling flowers from Hevington's gardens.

William put the paper down in his lap. "This has certainly been worse than when we lost Béatrice, hasn't it? Of course, then she had Nicholas to comfort her. Now . . ." He let his words trail off.

Claudette blew pollen off the sideboard that held the arrangement and surveyed her handiwork on the cluster of newly bloomed orchids she had just gathered.

"There's no comforting her now. When Marguerite thought she might be pregnant, I thought I saw a small flicker of happiness in her. But when that hope wasn't realized, she just sort of slipped out of reality."

Almost as if in response to hearing her name mentioned, Marguerite appeared in the doorway that Jolie had just vacated.

"Aunt Claudette, I'm going to the North Bridge."

Several small bridges spanned streams across the Hevington property. The North Bridge was the longest of these bridges and the farthest from the house. Since her arrival at Hevington two months ago, Marguerite had taken to spending hours walking back and forth over the bridge, talking to herself. Some of Hevington's servants began gossiping that the mistress's guest was a bit touched, but William sternly informed the household that such talk would not be tolerated. The gossip subsided, but Claudette still saw knowing looks passing between servants whenever Marguerite was around.

"Of course, dear. Enjoy yourself. You'll return for supper, won't you?"

"Mmmm, what? Oh, I'm not hungry. Please don't wait for me."

"You may not be hungry now, but you will be in several hours. You *must* take some nourishment."

"All right, then, I'll come back. Send someone for me, will you?" As Marguerite turned to go, Claudette saw that there was a hastily mended tear in the young woman's dress, a gown that should have joined William's chair in the charity box long ago. Her hair was sloppily pulled together in the back, and did not look as though it had been washed or brushed in weeks.

As the door clicked shut, Claudette told her husband, "There must be something we can do to lift her out of her melancholia. I just wish I knew what it was."

"If you can figure out something, all the resources of Hevington and the Greycliffe family will be at your disposal. As long as it doesn't include any trips to France." He snapped his paper back open but looked at her teasingly over the top edge of it.

"I don't think we need to worry about any future journeys to my homeland."

Claudette had nearly been guillotined in Paris during the Terror. Her salvation had come in the form of William Greycliffe, and the pair married soon after.

Since then, Claudette had maintained an idyllic existence with William and their three children, and had gradually turned over her shop's management to Marguerite.

But the idyll was forever gone now.

Deep, quiet, lovable Nicholas. Struck down so violently in front of Marguerite. William had hired a man to investigate who Mr. Emmett and Reggie were and locate them, but the ruffians had disappeared into the background of London and could not be found. Meanwhile, Claudette was coordinating a refurbishment of the shop, in hopes that it could be reopened in time for the next Season.

How were they all to bear losing Nicholas? More importantly, how were they going to keep Marguerite steady and rational?

There must be something they could do to lift the girl's spirits.

Marguerite was relieved to get away from Claudette and William. She trailed her fingers along the railing of the bridge as she walked over it for the hundredth time. She paused at the top of the arch and leaned over the side to look down. A young bullfrog leaped through the reeds along the jagged edge of the water and landed with a noisy plop in the water before extending his legs for a leisurely swim across.

I wish I could be as carefree as you, Mr. Hoppy.

The bridge was the only place she found solace. The house was distantly visible from it, yet she had a vista of several hundred acres of tidily plowed fields and gardens beyond Hevington's boundaries. People rarely ventured out this far and she could be completely alone with her thoughts.

The pain of Nicholas's death pierced her anew each time she came here to mull over her situation. She relished the anguish, since it transported her away from the peace and calm that was a natural part of life at Hevington. She resented the tranquility because it seemed to mock Nicholas's death. How could people and animals and flowers and trees continue in their daily routines of life and growth? Didn't they realize that her husband was *dead?* Gone. Never to tease her again. Never to remove the pins from her bundled-up mass of hair and run his fingers through it.

She leaned over farther. Her hair made a blurry reflection in the water. She had made a halfhearted attempt that morning to pin it back, but it was falling out of its combs and hung in limp hanks around her.

I don't care. Without you, Nicholas, I have no reason to primp and worry about fashion.

She knew Aunt Claudette was giving her concerned looks, and undoubtedly she and Uncle William were talking about her. They just did not understand that there was no meaning to her existence any more. In fact . . .

She pulled back from the edge and finished crossing the bridge, doubling back on the ground to approach the water's edge. She didn't think it was too deep here, not enough to drown on purpose, but if she accidentally hit her head on something perhaps she would fall unconscious and drown. Then maybe she wouldn't feel the fluid filling her lungs. Just an easy sleep, then reunion with Nicholas.

These kinds of thoughts were entering her mind with more regularity as of late. Aunt Claudette said that the passage of time would heal her sorrow, but she was wrong. Time just ravaged her senses even more.

Marguerite pushed through the reeds where the frog had jumped in and stood there, water covering her boots and soaking the lower third of her dress, which was a depressing shade of brown that resembled nothing more than stable muck. She stood still in the gently flowing stream, letting it chill her feet and legs. Abruptly she sat down in the water. Her dress floated up around her and the cool liquid surged up around her breasts. She placed her arms in the water and lifted her face to the sunshine, which was as warm as the water was chilly.

All I need to do now is lean all the way back and let nature do the rest. I'm sure it will be over in a matter of—

"Mistress Ashby! Mistress Ashby!" She heard a horse gallop up and stop at the base of the bridge. She sat back up and attempted to push the dress down under the water. It refused to stay under the surface, so instead she struggled to get up on the muddy floor of the stream. Finally getting herself erect and sloshing her way out of the water, she saw that it was one of Hevington's footmen who disturbed her reverie.

"Mistress Ashby, Lady Greycliffe sent me to find you. Said it was time for supper and that you should come back now to change for the meal. She said I should escort you back on Nell. If you're ready, that is." He dismounted to help her.

The footman was giving her the peculiar look that all of the servants gave her when they thought she wasn't paying attention. It wasn't that she didn't notice their distaste for her, it was that she didn't care. Too tired to care. Of course, right now she was looking even more disheveled than usual, which should serve as tantalizing kitchen gossip later. She could imagine him running to Cook to tell her that Mistress Ashby was trying to swim in a shallow stream. Together they'd probably light a candle to ward off any evil spirits she may have brought with her to Hevington. Sometimes servants still clung to the old ways.

"No, I'll walk back. Tell Lady Greycliffe she need not worry about me."

"As you wish, mistress." He turned his back to mount Nell again, but not before Marguerite caught him quickly giving himself the sign of the cross.

Marguerite trudged her way back, changed her clothing and shoes, and joined William and Claudette in the small dining room, her hair still damp and smelling brackish. An assortment of dishes covered the table and Claudette had dismissed the staff, preferring instead to serve privately, away from the servants' curious eyes.

"Where are Edward, Rebecca, and Little Bitty?" Marguerite tried to muster up more enthusiasm regarding their whereabouts than she actually felt.

"I had them eat in the kitchen then go back up to the nursery to play. I thought the three of us could enjoy a nice meal together without the clattering of the children about." Claudette served Marguerite and William from several silver salvers before sitting down herself at the intimate round table.

Marguerite knew instantly that they were about to have "a talk," since Claudette disliked to be away from her children any more than she had to be. If she had dismissed both children and servants, things could not bode well for Marguerite.

With her silver fork Marguerite picked out the contents of her oyster loaf without actually eating any of it. The crust was warm and crisp, and would probably be quite delicious if she had any desire to taste it.

"I had Cook make your favorite. You love oysters."

"Thank you, Aunt Claudette," she replied listlessly. From the corner of her eye she could see that look passing between Claudette and William again. That unpleasant combination of pity, trepidation, and confusion that she was used to seeing on everyone's faces. It was funny how much alike the two of them had become, not only in gestures but in looks. Both were blond and fair, although Claudette's hair tumbled in a mass of tight coils when not pinned up, whereas William's hair curled gently at the nape of his neck. Neither had a gray hair between them. But both had deeply colored eyes that darkened perceptibly when upset or angry, although Claudette's eyes were the more surprising to behold in their deep shade of cobalt.

Uncle William opened the discussion by clearing his throat loudly. Dear Uncle William. So protective of the women in his world, and willing to do anything for the one woman he loved. His rescue of Aunt Claudette from prison had been nothing short of miraculous.

Although the family knew the story well, Uncle William was reticent to tell of his brave escapade to others. Brave yet unpretentious, she thought. Just like Nicholas. Except Uncle William had had time to work out a plan for rescuing Aunt Claudette, whereas Nicholas was blindsided by a pitiless horde of bullies. How different it might have been if Nicholas had had more warning—

William's *harrumph* interrupted her again.

"Well, Marguerite, what do you think?"

"What? I'm sorry, Uncle William, I wasn't listening." She attempted her best smile, knowing it was just a thin pink line in the center of her pale face.

"Claudette and I were thinking that you might want to consider returning to the doll shop. Making dolls again might lift your spirits and take your mind off things."

What?

She looked from her uncle back to her aunt. Surely this was a jest, intended to startle her out of her doldrums.

"You're not serious, are you?"

Claudette took over the conversation. "Dear, we just want to help you. The workers are almost done repairing the windows and giving the entire interior a fresh coat of paint. Agnes and Roger cleared away the doll debris and are very anxious to return to work again. William is going to travel to London next week on other business, and perhaps you'd like to go with him to see how the shop fares. It's waiting for your talented hands to return to it."

"I'm content to stay here with you awhile longer."

"And we're delighted to have you." Claudette reached an arm across the table to squeeze her hand. Marguerite hated these displays of affection and concern, since they usually resulted in uncontrollable bouts of crying for her.

"But Marguerite, you need something besides your nightmares to occupy your mind, lest you lose your sensibilities."

"My sensibilities are fine. I just want to be left to myself. To think."

William joined forces with his wife. "To think of what? Nicholas? We all grieve him, my dear, but we must continue to live."

"And why is that?"

"Er, why is what?"

"Why is it that we must all continue to live? I see no purpose in it for myself. My husband is gone, no chance for a child to comfort me, and as far as the Kentish countryside is concerned, I am nothing but that unfortunate Greycliffe relation."

Much to Marguerite's relief, William and Claudette were silent after that, concentrating on their own plates of food. For several minutes there was no sound other than knives cutting against china. An audible intake of breath from Claudette was Marguerite's signal that the talk was not over. As Claudette poured refills of claret for all three of them from a crystal decanter, she said, "Marguerite, we're very concerned—"

"Yes, I know how concerned you both have been and I—"

"—about you and we feel it is now our duty to do something about it."

Marguerite bit off the remainder of her retort. It sounded like they were going to force her into something vile.

William continued for his wife. "If you do not wish to return to the doll shop, you simply *must* do something else. You can remain at Hevington the rest of your days if you wish, but, my dear, you *will* find something to occupy your time and help you with your grief."

"I won't do anything you say. Neither of you can possibly understand my wounds. They will never be healed. Ever. I've learned to live with them, and you should as well. If it bothers you for me to continue living here, I'll . . . I'll—do women retire to convents anymore?—I'll send myself away somewhere." Marguerite felt like a petulant child but could not help it. In an even more childish gesture, she threw her monogrammed linen napkin to the center of the table and fled the room for the safety of her bedchamber.

"Well," William commented. "I suppose that went a bit better than the last time we tried talking to her. Maybe there's hope for her after all."

A week later, a servant announced an unusual visitor.

"Lady Greycliffe, Mrs. Maude Ashby and her son are here to see you and Mistress Marguerite in the front parlor." The young maid bobbed a curtsy and disappeared.

Claudette and Marguerite were sitting together quietly in the library reading. Marguerite's eyes had passed sightlessly over the words in a copy of Rousseau's *Émile,* a book her aunt had given her as a gift, but she snapped to attention at the mention of her mother-in-law's name.

"Maude! What do you suppose she's doing here, Aunt Claudette?"

"I don't know. She saw me at the funeral, which I'm sure satisfied her annual requirement for letting me know how much she despises me. I suppose we won't know why she's returned until we see her. Join me?"

The two women walked arm in arm down the stairs to the front parlor. Claudette noted with approval that even though Marguerite was still looking a bit frayed around the edges, her gown today was neat and clean, and she did not smell rancid, which indicated a recent bath.

Together they entered the room where Maude and Nathaniel Ashby waited. Maude rose from the settee while Nathaniel remained standing by the fireplace, preening himself in the mirror above the mantel. Maude hissed at him and he turned around to Claudette and his sister-in-law.

"Why Miss Clau—I mean, Lady Greycliffe—it's always a delight to see you. And Marguerite, you're looking very well."

If possible, Nathaniel had grown more portly since they had last seen him at Nicholas's funeral. Nathaniel had been a greedy, grasping child, and his gluttony had extended into adulthood. He sought women, food, and diversion with equal abandon. What he did not typically do was seek social calls with female relatives who bored him.

Marguerite stared at her in-laws sullenly. Maude Ashby had been furious when Nicholas married her, hoping for a quality match for her son and not a coupling with an orphaned French waif, particularly not one whose mother had been a servant in her own household. Fortunately she had not married Maude's favorite son, Nathaniel, who was the biggest brute of all his classmates but could do no wrong in his mother's eyes.

Although Maude had resented the marriage from the outset, she grudgingly came to accept it and even at one point had assisted them with the decorating of their London townhome. But Maude's opinion of her daughter-in-law had reverted to that of family interloper once Nicholas died. She even intimated at the funeral that his death could have somehow been prevented by Marguerite.

So why was she here again? If there was anyone she despised more than Marguerite, it was Claudette. From the moment Claudette had arrived on her doorstep with Béatrice and young Marguerite with a letter of reference for domestic employment, Maude had been nothing but supercilious with them all. When Claudette left Maude's employ abruptly after being falsely accused of wrongdoing in the household, the famous Maude Ashby temper went into full operation, and the hatred the woman spewed covered households all over London.

However, time had been gracious to Maude Ashby's looks and figure. Now a woman in her fifth decade, she was still sleek and attractive, although with a tempered ferocity simmering visibly beneath the surface. *A bit like a panther,* Marguerite thought wryly. *I must stay out of reach of her claws.*

"Nathaniel and I have missed seeing you, Marguerite," Maude said while ignoring Claudette's presence completely.

Marguerite watched as Claudette pulled herself up to full height.

"Welcome to Hevington, Mrs. Ashby."

Her address forced Mrs. Ashby's attention in return. "Lady Greycliffe," she said through gritted teeth.

Even worse than Claudette's insulting departure from her employ was her audacity in marrying a man who had frequented the Ashbys' supper parties and was a rising aristocrat. Maude was angling to use her association with him to improve her own social standing, but his marriage to Claudette had destroyed her plans. The homage demanded by the Baroness Greycliffe's position tasted to her like sour milk lapped from a crystal dish.

"To what can we attribute the great honor you do our household today?" Claudette asked. Like Marguerite, she was impatient to end the interview, yet curious as to why they had made the journey all the way from London to see them.

"Nothing other than a deep concern for our dearest sister and daughter. We just wanted to see how you were getting on, Marguerite."

Clearly this was not going to end quickly.

Claudette rang for tea and cakes and invited the Ashbys to sit down. When they were comfortably seated and refreshments had been served, Maude started circling stealthily around her point.

"Marguerite, dearest, how has your health been?"

"My health? What do you mean?"

"Nothing in particular. You've just been through a great deal of distress. Have you had any illnesses as a result?"

Whatever was the woman about? Had the servants' gossip reached her ears all the way in London?

"Illnesses? No, I don't believe so." She looked at Claudette for guidance, but got a helpless shrug in return.

"You know Nathaniel has taken over more and more of his father's business what with Mr. Ashby's heart condition. And you're doing a fine job of it, aren't you, pet?" Mrs. Ashby adored Nathaniel above all else, other than her own reputation.

Nathaniel responded to his mother's praise with predictable pomposity. "Simple, really. The old man just doesn't have the head for figures that I do." He looked down at his fingernails in a useless attempt to appear modest.

"I see that congratulations are in order for you, Nathaniel." Marguerite couldn't understand where this strange conversation was going to end up.

"I do so wish he would get married to a respectable woman, though, and stop all of his naughtiness with common women. Son, you're such a handsome and clever man. I'm sure there is a young lady of quality who would be honored to be seen on your arm."

"When I'm ready, Mother. Right now I'm still enjoying myself." He was lately enjoying himself with Lydia, one of the housemaids his mother had brought in to expand her staff as a show of the Ashby family's promising rise in Society.

The Ashbys would never be accepted by Society, so why did the woman keep on with the charade? Well, it kept him well supplied in female companionship. He folded his hands on his emerging paunch in satisfaction.

"Enjoying yourself in the gaming hells, more like. You're a thirty-four-year-old man who should be considering his future, especially when he has a father who is not well. We need a future generation to carry on the family name."

"Father has plenty of years left in him. Let's not whack the old man off yet. Besides . . ." Nathaniel gave a nod toward Marguerite.

"Yes, of course." Maude turned away from her son to give Marguerite her full attention, smoothing back her tightly coiffed hair with an exquisitely manicured hand. Her claws were filed to points.

"As you know, my dear, you have always been so highly regarded by Mr. Ashby and me and it just *distresses* us so deeply to think of you wasting away out here in the country."

Why did Marguerite have the sense that Maude was crouching in the tall grass, waiting to pounce and nip her head off with one sharp bite?

"You've no need to worry, Mother Ashby. I like it here at Hevington. No one bothers me and I have free run of the estate."

"Well, I'm sure that cavorting about the horse pastures may seem like an amusing pastime, but I'm sure we all agree that it can be damaging to a delicate woman's health."

Marguerite felt her temper beginning to flare and pressed her lips together to maintain her outward composure before replying.

"I had no idea you were so concerned for my well-being, Mother Ashby. Especially considering your total disinterest in my affairs since Nicholas died. As I recall, your carriage could not pull away from the funeral quickly enough to get you back to London. Wasn't there some social event for which you were anxious to return? Did your merry party companions find it odd that you had only spent a single day grieving for your son?"

Marguerite paused only for a quick breath and to take a moment of pleasure in the look of pure astonishment on Maude's face. Nathaniel still sat there like a perched chicken with his hands folded over a stomach entirely too distended for a young man of his age. She was startled to see almost a look of—was that approval?—on Aunt Claudette's face.

"But now your concern for your daughter-in-law has you racing back to Kent to see of what service you can be, and to pretend that you are now anxious that the bloom may have fallen off the rose of my ruddy good health. Pray tell, what scheme is prowling around in your mind that compels you to take interest in my tragic affairs? Lest it be some wild thought that Nicholas might have some sort of bequest that I am withholding, let me assure you that everything we had together was destroyed in Aunt Claudette's shop. That shop was our entire life, and now it's all gone. I don't wish Nicholas gone, but I certainly do wish you gone, Mother Ashby."

Marguerite was shaking. She couldn't believe it. This was the longest dialogue about Nicholas she had had since his death without breaking into a disheveled heap of weeping. Claudette was slowly nodding her head in encouragement of her tangible fury.

Maude held up her hand in appeasement. "Why, Marguerite, you misunderstand me. We are absolutely concerned about you personally. Especially since you might be carrying Nicholas's offspring. Perhaps his son."

"But I'm not with child. I'm absolutely certain of it."

"Yes, so Lord Greycliffe told me in his return letter to my inquiry. But, child, it's still early and you might not be showing yet."

"My courses started again last month." She reddened at having to speak so indelicately in front of Nathaniel, but he seemed oblivious to the entire conversation now that it was not focused on him.

"Again, you might not be showing yet, and we have to be absolutely *certain* of the truthfulness of your statement, don't we? After all, any child of Nicholas's is really an Ashby, isn't it? And we would want to be sure he grows up in a loving and proper environment with his *true* family, not out here in some remote village where he'll never have an opportunity to meet young ladies of breeding."

Claudette cut into the conversation. "Mrs. Ashby, are you implying that Lord Greycliffe's name and connections would not suffice to give Marguerite's child a good launch when the time came?"

"But I am not—" Marguerite said.

Maude Ashby sniffed. "I said nothing of the sort. You're just simply so far away from the city out here, and the society pages don't mention you much, which tells me that you don't come to London often."

"Aunt Claudette, you're letting her—"

"Mrs. Ashby, you are treading perilously close to the end of my hospitality."

"Ah, but I see Marguerite protests that she is not expecting, although *you* do not. Perhaps I am correct in my suspicions. And as such, I am recommending that you return to London with us, Marguerite."

"*What?*" Marguerite and Claudette gasped in unison.

"We have a coach large enough to take you with us this very night, once you get yourself packed up. You'll have a comfortable room and can sit and read or embroider or wander the hallways to your heart's content until we know undeniably whether or not you are carrying a child. My grandchild. The Ashby name will live on through this child, since Nathaniel may not ever father a successor." She cut her eyes over to Nathaniel, who appeared to be enjoying the fracas among the women.

"If you prove to be without child, then I will send you back to Hevington straightaway. Trusting, of course, that you have not taken advantage of my dear Nathaniel's sensitive feelings by then. However, if you are expecting, you will remain at our home until such time as you bear the child, and then of course we would insist that you leave him with us, to be raised with his true family." Maude nodded, an indication that she was finished and that all parties were to accept her proclamation.

Even Claudette was speechless at the woman's audacity. But now Marguerite found her mettle, much as she had when she went on the offense against the mob in the shop. This felt as much an affront to her as that had.

"Mother Ashby, have you completely taken leave of your senses? I have told you repeatedly that I am absolutely, positively not with child. But if I were—and I am not!—it is beyond the pale that you would come here while I grieve my husband to suggest that I willingly go as your prisoner to be poked and prodded by doctors for the next month while you make a decision as to whether or not I'm going to produce a grandchild for you to manage and oppress.

"You've already extended past Aunt Claudette's good graces of hospitality, and you've just stepped beyond the bounds of my own goodwill. I recommend that you leave now before this gets any worse, if that's possible."

Maude was unsettlingly serene. "Yes, I can understand your unease now that I have pointed out the obvious. Nevertheless, it shall be as I say. Would you like to come with us now, or perhaps Nathaniel can return for you in a week to let you get your affairs in order?"

"Mother Ashby, I will *never* go back to London with you."

"But you will."

Drat the woman. She practically purred in self-satisfaction.

"Why in heaven's name would I do this?"

"Because it would just be so *unfortunate* for people to continue thinking that you're hiding out here waiting to bear someone else's bastard child. Tongues are wagging, my dear, and I have no reason to correct people's impression."

"But I've been in mourning with my relations. Everyone knows what happened to me—it was in all the London papers. The only way they could think I've done something illicit is if—oh!" Marguerite shuddered involuntarily. She felt a streak of pain start at the base of her neck and run up behind her right ear. She'd been experiencing blinding headaches since Nicholas's death.

"Is if what, dear?" Maude's eyes narrowed into contented slits.

"Is if . . . is if . . . *you* were spreading rumors about me."

"I? Spread rumors?" Maude rose, as did Marguerite and Claudette, which signaled to Nathaniel that the interview was over and he was to rise as well. He tugged on his waistcoat to ensure it covered his abdomen. As if completely oblivious to what had just happened, he extended a warm farewell.

"Good to see you, Lady Greycliffe. Next time we'll bring Father. He always enjoys a good cigar with Lord William. Marguerite, a pleasure. Indeed a pleasure."

Marguerite stepped back in revulsion from his attempt to place a brotherly kiss on her cheek. Undaunted, he moved in on an unsuspecting Claudette and planted a moist and loud smack on her right cheek before she had the sense to step away.

Maude gave her parting shot. "Remember, Marguerite, that I cannot hold on to your good reputation for you forever. You'll have to make a decision quickly. I'll send Nathaniel back in one week for you."

Maude Ashby held her head high and proud as she left Hevington, as a woman who had successfully completed her mission of havoc.

Marguerite sank down on the parlor's pale green settee that Maude had just occupied, and Claudette sat next to her. "Oh, Aunt Claudette, what a ridiculous situation I am in. What should I do?"

Claudette's mouth was a grim line. "We'll think of something. Maude Ashby is nothing if not utterly predictable in her self-serving conduct. Perhaps William can go to London and bring pressure to bear."

"No, I could not stand for him to have to rescue me like that. He'd have to drag the Greycliffe name through the slops in order to clean my own. You've both been too kind to me for me to allow that to happen. Perhaps I should leave the country. Surely I can find relatives of my mother's back in France who will take me in for a while."

"No! There will be no traveling to France! William forbids it," she added.

Marguerite took her beloved mentor's hand. "Aunt Claudette, all of that was long ago."

"The Terror may be over, but the strife with France goes on and on. William expects that we will declare war on that country any day. I'm not sure we have the strength to stand up to Napoleon. In any case, it would be foolish and dangerous to go there for respite while Maude Ashby's gossiping settles down."

"I suppose you're right. Nothing good ever comes from dealings with my mother-in-law."

"I disagree. I see color in your cheeks, the first I've seen in months. And anger has ignited your soul. I'd say Maude's visit was very good."

Claudette lifted Marguerite's hand to her lips. "Darling girl, I think you may recover yet. And I think this talk of France has given me an idea."

Surrey Street, London
April 18, 1803

My dearest Claudette,

What an age it has been since we last saw one another. I'm happy to know that you found out that I have brought my exhibition to London. I suppose I should have told you myself, but I've been so busy with making new wax figures, handling daily receipts, and caring for my boy Joseph that all else simply flies from my mind.

My condolences on your family's loss, both your ward's

husband and the destruction of the doll shop. These are indeed fanatical times again, although it doesn't seem as though they ever stopped, does it? I try to stay personally unnoticeable and let my wax figures promote themselves. I never again want to end up in a prison cell, whether in France or in England. But I guess that's not a guiding principle I have to recommend to you, is it?

With regard to your ward's predicament, I fully sympathize and send my warmest salutations to her. She is more than welcome to join me at the Lyceum Theatre. Her dollmaking skills will be well applied here to waxworking, and it would be a great relief to have more help than my five-year-old son. My partner, Philipsthal, is more concerned with publicity for his Phantasmagoria show than with helping me with my work.

Please send Marguerite as soon as possible. She should bring along any carving tools, paintbrushes, etc. that she has.

Fondly,

Marie Tussaud

"William, Marie is enthusiastic about the idea." Claudette brought the letter around to where he was sitting in his old King James Monstrosity with a copy of an American book on chess that had just arrived on a packet from Philadelphia. William had recently become fascinated with the game and was trying to teach it to Edward. This book promised to help the reader master the game quickly.

He lifted his head from the book for a quick kiss from his wife. "Splendid. How do you think Marguerite will react?"

"I'm not sure. But I've given instructions for a private supper in the small dining room just in case."

3

An unusually cool May drizzle accompanied the coach on the long trip from Hevington to London, but dissipated as they reached the city's outskirts. Marguerite tensed as the carriage jolted along London's old cobblestones, fearful that they would be driving past, or near, the doll shop, but Uncle William's driver seemed to know that he should avoid that neighborhood entirely. William and Claudette sat companionably quiet across from her.

She started breathing normally again as they entered Westminster and made their way to the Strand. This was not a part of the city Marguerite had ever visited during her entire life in London because of its shabby reputation. Once an area of palatial homes belonging to the great families such as Essex, Northumberland, and Somerset, it had experienced a period of gradual decay. Most of the residences had been demolished and then replaced by low taverns and brothels. Recently it was undergoing rebirth with the construction of circuses, theatres, and other houses of entertainment. The roads here were uncobbled and rutted, but the frenetic energy of building and growth roused excitement even in Marguerite's fractured heart.

At Claudette's urging, Marguerite had discarded her threadbare dresses to which she had become so attached in her misery, and allowed her aunt to send off to London for a set of serviceable work dresses, two aprons, a cloak, and one fancy gown, as well as some new undergarments. They would be delivered shortly to her new lodgings in the same building where Madame Tussaud was staying with her young son, Joseph.

Marguerite had been more receptive to the idea of joining Marie Tussaud's traveling wax exhibition than either William or Claudette had imagined she would be. The encounter with Maude Ashby had jolted her out of her melancholy and given her anger and fear to feed on. The anger and fear had given her a sense of purpose and the realization that if she did not do something about her own situation, others would. And it might have had unpleasant results far beyond lying back permanently in the cool stream waters of Hevington.

The opportunity to meet Aunt Claudette's old friend Marie Tussaud, of whom she had heard much, was compelling, as was the thought of doing something—anything—other than dollmaking.

Marie had been the art tutor to King Louis XVI's sister Elisabeth when Claudette first met her. Claudette's London doll shop had risen to enough prominence that she began receiving orders from Queen Marie Antoinette, herself an avid doll collector. In 1788, an invitation arrived for her to come to France to meet the queen and make plans for a special doll Marie Antoinette wished to commission. This doll was of her closest friend, the Princesse de Lamballe. During the visit Claudette met Marie Grosholtz, who had not yet married François Tussaud. The two became fast friends, as Marie found many similarities between waxworking and dollmaking. Through the years of the Revolution the two maintained contact, even though Claudette had made her home in England. Both were devoted to the French royal family, although after her own imprisonment Marie learned to conceal any preference for either revolutionaries or monarchs, instead keeping her head down and focused on managing the waxworks exhibition left to her by Philippe Curtius.

If anyone beyond Aunt Claudette would understand Marguerite's deep anxieties about death, it would be Madame Tussaud.

When Claudette had first presented the option to her, Marguerite was surprised at her own acquiescence. The dust-up with

Maude Ashby had invigorated her to the point that she no longer strolled the North Bridge contemplating how to do away with herself, but instead paced back and forth in silent conversation with Nicholas, pondering how to outwit her sly mother-in-law. The woman was sorely mistaken if she thought Marguerite was going to let Society be tempted into thinking Nicholas Ashby had been a cuckold. She was even more mistaken if she thought Marguerite was going to live in her clutches again, undoubtedly as little more than a mere servant. No, she had to devise a plan to stay out of the Ashby clutches. For all she knew, when Maude realized Marguerite was not pregnant she would then decide Marguerite should marry Nathaniel, who showed promise of becoming every bit as pompous as his mother.

And how could she avoid marriage with him if living under that woman's roof?

Furthermore, what dishonor would it do Nicholas's memory for her to go to their home under a cloud of suspicion, if she was pressured into an unwanted marriage with his twin?

She shivered with distaste.

"Is everything all right, Marguerite?" Claudette's bright blue eyes peered at her in concern. "Are you having regrets?"

"Not at all. I'm still just coming to terms with the past, I guess. Foolish notions. I'm fine, Aunt Claudette, I really am. And I promise to try very hard to move forward with my life."

"I know you'll do very well under Marie's tutelage. Just think, William. A renowned waxworker in the family. Why, she'll be famous!"

"More famous than you?" William's voice was full of amusement.

"Infinitely more famous. Waxworks have been fashionable in Paris for years and you know how you Englishmen are always years behind French styles. You'll now be up-to-date in your smart entertainments." Claudette gave William a sly look out of the corner of her eye.

"Is that right, Lady Greycliffe? I believe we'll have more discussion about *entertainment* after seeing Marguerite settled in."

They teased just like she and Nicholas once did. How much

she admired this couple, still in adoration of one another after nearly a dozen years of marriage, childbearing, and the daily routines of life. Marguerite felt a sudden and sharp pang of longing for her husband. The grief churned and twisted for several moments, then was gone. William and Claudette had not appeared to notice her pain. Heavens, was she finally recovering?

"Pay no mind to William, Marguerite. He gets more and more foolish the older he gets. Oh, we're almost there. Would you just look at that!"

The Lyceum Theatre, where Madame Tussaud had her wax exhibition, was located on Wellington Street, just off the Strand. As the carriage pulled to a stop in front of the building, Marguerite looked up in amazement. The theatre was built to resemble an ancient Greek temple. Six columns perched on black marble bases soared up into the air, supporting an overhang covering a large expanse of portico. Inside the great portico hung four enormous chandeliers, an outdoor extravagance. The building behind rose even higher than the entryway, gleaming from new sand-colored paint.

What must the interior be like? she wondered.

As if reading her mind Claudette said, "I hear that the inside is large enough to hold a circus. I certainly hope there isn't one in there now. I don't think the smell of animal droppings is quite fitting with Marie's elegant creations."

The three of them climbed out of the carriage and smoothed the wrinkles out of their clothes. William instructed the driver to return in an hour, then they went in to find Madame Tussaud's exhibition, still known as Curtius's Cabinet of Wonders, even though Curtius had been dead for nine years.

The interior was as glamorous as the entry suggested it might be. Crystal chandeliers dangled in resplendent brilliance from the lofty ceiling painted in various Greek allegories. The bright red carpet had a random pattern in it, done to look as though crystal baubles had dropped from the chandeliers and shattered on the floor. It was breathtaking.

After several inquiries of passersby, they learned that Tussaud's exhibition was located next to Philipsthal's Fantastic Phantasmagoria Show. They climbed a wide set of steps to another floor in a wing off the center of the building.

Here they discovered the entrance to Philipsthal's show. They were greeted by a large sign proclaiming:

PHILIPSTHAL'S FANTASTIC PHANTASMAGORIA SHOW
A GRAND CABINET OF OPTICAL AND MECHANICAL CURIOSITIES
AMAZING INVENTIONS! WONDERS FROM AROUND THE WORLD!
BE AMONG THE FIRST TO COMMUNICATE WITH SPIRITS
FROM THE BEYOND.
PAY A VISIT TO A SORCERER AT WORK.
FOR A LIMITED TIME ONLY!

And in very tiny type beneath all of this:

CABINET OF WONDERS IN GALLERY TO THE LEFT

"Communicating with spirits? Does Marie's partner claim to be a medium?" William asked Claudette.

"I don't know. She didn't mention much about him."

"Curious that his sign makes so little mention of her exhibit."

"Uncle William, let's go find Madame Tussaud." Marguerite was impatient to meet her new mentor and get a glimpse of what a wax exhibition looked like.

They parted the curtains covering the doorway located several steps to the left of the Phantasmagoria show. Marguerite gasped at what she saw.

Beyond the curtain lay a gallery nearly forty feet long, with no other patrons in sight. The sparkle-infused carpeting of the hallway continued the length of the gallery. At five-foot intervals were double-armed sconces high up on the pale blue damask walls. The walls met ceilings adorned with plaster friezes surrounding more crystal chandeliers.

Candles burned brightly in each sconce, their wax dripping onto glass catch plates fixed at the base of each sconce, throwing a comforting glow over the room's inhabitants. Beneath each sconce stood a gilded Greek column about three feet in height. Atop each column was a bust of some famous figure of English society. Each bust faced either right or left, and had a regal draping carved into its base and covering its shoulders. A placard on the wall under the sconce provided a visitor with the name of the historical figure and a brief biographical sketch. Some had been typeset, and some were written in a loose scrawl.

Interspersed randomly throughout the gallery were life-sized figures, bewigged and clothed as if real human beings. Marguerite was reminded of nothing more than the *grandes Pandores* of the doll shop.

In the center of the exhibition hall sat a raised platform. Atop the platform was a glass-encased sarcophagus. Were the contents of that real or wax? Marguerite wasn't sure she was ready to know.

At the end of the gallery lay a door to some unknown room. It sprang open and a petite woman in a plain dress and lace cap bustled out.

"Sorry, friends, I am working in my closet. Admission to the Cabinet of Wonders is—"

The woman stopped and took in who her visitors were. Then covering the distance still separating them, she burst into a torrent of French.

"Claudette! I didn't realize you were arriving this exact day. This must be your William. Very pleased, sir, very pleased. And this is Mrs. Ashby. Lovely girl. Happy you are here. There's much to learn."

Marguerite tried to keep up with the barrage of dialogue. Her mother had taught her French as a child, but she hadn't used it much since her mother died. After the execution of Marie Antoinette, doll orders from France had declined rapidly and eventually disappeared altogether while Claudette still ran the shop, so there had been little reason for Marguerite to practice it. She had just figured out that Marie Tussaud was welcoming her, mostly because the woman was grasping her hand and pumping it up and down, when the Cabinet's proprietress turned around and called back to the rear door.

"Joseph! Nini! Come, boy, I need you."

The door opened again and out came a young boy, walking with an intent and purpose of a much older young man.

"How may I be of service to you?" The child spoke in precise English and executed a very elegant bow before his guests.

"This is my boy, Joseph. I call him my Nini. He's a good boy. Only here nine months and knows English. Soon he will be a native, won't you, Nini?" Marie placed a hand on Joseph's head.

Joseph was dressed in a miniature uniform resembling that of a soldier. His heavily lashed, inquisitive eyes were the color of cocoa, and were obscured by his hair, which swept across his forehead in a determined march down into his dark pools of vision.

"Yes, Maman. Do you need me to take admission?" The boy switched back and forth from English to French easily.

"No, no, these are your *maman*'s friends. These are Lord and Lady Greycliffe. Lady Greycliffe was your *maman*'s friend in France. And this is Mrs. Ashby, Lady Greycliffe's former ward. She's to be our new apprentice. You like that, eh, Joseph?"

The boy frowned, unsure. "What will the new apprentice do?"

"She'll learn wax modeling. She'll help your *maman* with the exhibition."

"But that's what I do."

"Yes, son, but *maman* needs another adult to help, too."

"Oh." Joseph cut his eyes over to Marguerite. "As you wish, Maman."

Before a threatening cloud of silence could envelop them, Claudette changed the subject.

"Marie, my friend, you have quite a collection of marble busts here. Show them to us."

"Marble! No, not stone. Wax. All wax. Come, look." She led them to a column near the center of the gallery. "See?" She tapped the figure on the shoulder. "Voltaire in wax."

They crowded in to examine the French philosopher's figure. His wax portrait was of him near the end of his life.

"Madame Tussaud, did you sculpt him from life?" Marguerite asked.

"Yes, I do life mask of him before he died."

"Life mask?"

"Yes, I will teach you."

They wandered through the gallery looking at other wax portraits such as that of the American Benjamin Franklin, a favorite of both the French and the English. Marguerite and Claudette were impressed by the casting of the figures, which was much sharper and better defined than what they had been able to do with their wood molds, and they said so to Madame Tussaud.

"Yes, my process has improved. I will teach Mrs. Ashby everything. Now, do you wish to see my secret figures?"

She led them through the rear door of the gallery, which opened into a space that was a jumbled combination of storage, art studio, and exhibit space. It reminded Marguerite of the doll shop's workroom, except it was larger and contained piles of wax bricks.

"I don't let visitors back here because it will scare them, but I show you, Claudette."

She drew them to the rear of the space, where several large crates were stored. Lifting the hinged lid on one of the crates, she motioned for them to look inside. Nestled in the crate was a figure of a woman that lay on a reclining couch, her arm across her forehead in repose. Upon closer examination, they could see that the woman appeared to be breathing. Claudette uttered a spontaneous "Oh my!" and Marie laughed in her sharp, birdlike way.

"Do you like it? This is Madame du Barry, favorite of King Louis XV. She may have met her end at the blade like so many others—oh, sorry, my dear—but she lives on here in wax. My mentor, Curtius, made this about thirty years ago for his salon in Paris. I plan to put up a separate curtained area to display it. For a separate charge."

William, Claudette, and Marguerite nodded in agreement.

"I have more to display with her. Look over here." She led them to another crate, opened it and removed one cloth-covered object from several. It was a replica of the guillotined head of Louis XVI. She held it by a wood post inserted through the base of the neck. Made in wax, it had stringy hair sewn into its scalp, and red paint had been applied around the neckline to give the impression of blood. It was quite theatrical, but the resemblance to the late king was unmistakable.

"Marie!" Claudette shrieked.

"Hah! Too much for your dollmaker sensibilities."

"Too much for anyone's sensibilities! Please, put it away."

"Wait," Marguerite commanded. "I would like to see it."

Nodding her approval, Marie handed it over to her new apprentice.

Marguerite held the head at arm's length, scrutinizing it, then bringing it close to sniff it. She wrinkled her nose.

"It smells dreadful. Is that part of its realism?"

Marie looked confused, so Joseph jumped in to serve as translator for his mother. Marie laughed, or rather barked, in return. "No, it's just remnants of glues and paints and plaster sitting together for so long in a closed crate."

Marguerite looked at the face again. "These figures seem gruesome at first, but it seems as though people here in England would want to see what King Louis looked like. I've only seen drawings of the late king, but it seems to me that this is a very good likeness."

"It *is* a good likeness. It's from his death mask."

"What is a death mask?"

"I put a plaster mold on his face after his execution to ensure I get all the details."

"Do you mean . . . after he was . . . you went and . . ." Marguerite held the head back out at arm's length for Marie to put away.

"Yes, some of the best figures are made from the infamous. The infamous usually get that way by having bad ends. I try to be on hand for these bad ends. It became a habit after revolutionary mobs forced me into it."

"Are you saying that you attend executions?"

"If it is someone worthwhile, yes. Never just for shock. Always someone famous. Already we have Marie Antoinette, Marat, Robespierre, and the king, and a few notorious Englishmen. We must get the death mask while the subject is still fresh."

"We?" Marguerite's voice was barely above a squeak.

Joseph imitated Marguerite's high-pitched "we" while translating, and was rewarded with laughter all around. Emboldened, he provided his own response.

"Are you frightened, Mrs. Ashby? Mama does not let me go with her to make death masks, but I am not afraid at all. When Maman says I'm old enough, I'll be the one to go with her, and you can stay home and be afraid."

Marguerite realized that she had a formidable opponent in the form of her employer's son.

"I've no doubt of your bravery, and I am most happy to see you display your courage in the graveyards of London. I don't believe I'll be ready to visit another grave site again in my entire life."

After concluding the tour of the back room and the outer gallery, Marie Tussaud invited them to tea and cakes at her rented rooms, where Marguerite's things had already been sent. She closed the exhibition for the day, quietly tutting in French about the loss of income from closing early, and they all went to the Surrey Street lodgings in the Greycliffe carriage. On arrival, Marguerite watched as William had the driver fetch a wrapped package from their luggage before joining the women and Joseph in the entrance hall.

"My driver will take care of unloading your belongings into your rooms, Marguerite, although you'll have to unpack yourself."

"I don't mind at all, Uncle William. It will keep my mind occupied as I get adjusted to being in London again."

The landlady, Mrs. Slade, greeted them, curtsying hastily upon realizing by William's dress that an aristocrat stood before her. She showed them around the building, consisting of four apartments, two on the ground floor and two on the floor above, divided by a worn but sturdy staircase.

Marie and Joseph kept their lodgings on the ground floor to the left side of the staircase. Marguerite was shown to her new quarters, located on the upper floor on the other side of the house. Her bedchamber was simply furnished with a quilt-covered bed, a plain oak table and chair for correspondence, and a washstand. An embroidered sampler dated 1765, by someone named Lizzie, hung over the bed. A small room beyond held hooks for dresses, hats, and other belongings. It was a far cry from her luxurious surroundings at Hevington, and would even be considered greatly reduced circumstances from the townhome she shared with Nicholas, but it didn't matter. Marguerite had little care for her living quarters as compared to her interest in her new apprenticeship, and said so aloud upon seeing Claudette's distressed look.

A parlor located behind the staircase on the ground floor was shared by the residents. Its furniture bordered on the shabby side, but it had a serviceable spinet in one corner and a four-shelf bookcase weighed down with well-worn books, mostly on botany, theology, and literature. The books had belonged to her deceased husband, Mrs. Slade told them.

"And now would you like tea?" she asked.

They sat in the parlor while Mrs. Slade bustled off to get their refreshments. The relaxed surroundings soon had Claudette and Marie chattering quite happily in French about their shared experiences, while William and Marguerite took turns listening in and poring over the shelved books. Joseph's translation skills were not needed, so he amused himself by teasing a spider that had been perfectly content in her web atop a window sash.

The only break in their conversation came when Mrs. Slade returned with a tray of tea and cakes. They praised the landlady's rich caraway seed cake, and returned to their chat after Mrs. Slade's lengthy explanation of how the recipe had been handed down through her family.

After Mrs. Slade's departure, Claudette's and Marie's French became so rapid that not even William could follow.

"William, did you bring it in with you?" Claudette's voice broke back into English, disturbing the cadence of the discourse.

He straightened up from where he had been pulling out a rare French volume on chess. "What? Yes, I did."

He handed his wife the paper-wrapped parcel that he had set on a table just inside the room. She untied the string securing it.

"Marie, do you remember this?" Claudette held up a large doll with a sweet, narrow face, dressed in a once-elegant dress that was faded by wear and time.

"Ah, yes, the princesse. I am still missing her. I wasn't able to do her mask. Maybe I will do her figure from memory one day."

Marguerite recognized the doll as a replica of the Princesse de Lamballe, the close friend of Marie Antoinette and the subject of Aunt Claudette's most revered commission.

"I miss her as well, Marie," Claudette said. "Sometimes it's still too much to think about."

"No tears, no tears, my girl. Eh, what about another figure of you?"

"Of me?"

"Yes. I'd like to make a tableau of the Revolution. When the public is ready for it. I will put on display my death masks of the king, the queen, Marat . . . and you, as one who was dear to the queen yet avoided the guillotine."

Claudette declined. "I have enough unspeakable memories of that interlude without a permanent reminder of my horror set up as a public spectacle."

Marie Tussaud shrugged. "Well, maybe you change your mind one day. Do you still have the figure I give you for your wedding?"

Marie had shipped a large crate to William and Claudette upon their marriage. Inside they found a life-sized wax figure of Claudette carving a doll. Claudette kept it in a special room back at Hevington, along with the Princesse de Lamballe doll.

"Of course I still have it. The children love it."

With an exaggerated look at his pocket watch, William pointed out to his wife that it was time to be going. Marie embraced Claudette fervently before departing for her own quarters with Joseph. Marguerite walked with William and Claudette to the front door.

"Remember that you're always welcome back at Hevington. Anytime."

"I know, Uncle William. Thank you both for everything."

Claudette produced a tiny parcel from inside her reticule and offered it to Marguerite. Inside was a watch pin, the casing worked in intricate silver filigree.

"Aunt Claudette, this is beautiful."

"It's from William and me, so you can track the time until we see you again." Claudette fastened the brooch to the bodice of Marguerite's dress before clutching her niece tightly.

"We'll miss you. But I know this is the right thing for you. And, dear"—she released Marguerite enough to put a hand against her face and whispered so no one else could hear—"promise me you might consider finding another young man one day."

The sharp pain twisted through Marguerite again briefly.

"No, Aunt Claudette. I can't go through this pain again. It's too much. I barely survived the first time. I couldn't endure it a second time."

Claudette patted her face. "You may eventually change your mind. At least I hope you will, for your own sake."

Marguerite watched from the entryway as they returned to their carriage. All of her luggage was gone, placed in her room by the driver while they were having tea. She waved furiously as they departed, holding back sentimental tears at seeing her two favorite people left in the world rumble away from her down the dusty street.

She shut the door and rested her head against it. Like the door, her old world was completely closed to her now. Her stomach gave voice in no uncertain terms that she was a cluttered mix of trepidation, excitement, and guilt as to her feelings of anticipation over her new life.

"Nicholas," she whispered. "If you're watching, please be happy for my newfound fortune. I miss you, darling, but I have to do something for my sanity and to stay out of your mother's clutches."

With that, she straightened her back, turned toward the stairs, and walked deliberately up to her room to begin the task of unpacking.

☙ 4 ☙

It was Madame Tussaud's custom to walk the half mile each morning from her lodgings to the Lyceum Theatre to save on hackney fares. Much of this walk was past the recently completed Somerset House, an enormous complex of government offices on the site of an earlier Tudor palace. Tussaud did not alter her practice with Marguerite's arrival. During the walk each morning she would discuss what important things had to be done before the exhibit opened for the day, and on the return walk she verbally totaled the day's receipts and ran through an oral ledger book. Joseph, an extraordinarily mature boy, walked dutifully alongside his mother, on the opposite side from Marguerite.

On her first day as Tussaud's apprentice, Marguerite was given the first of many sets of instructions as they walked toward the theatre.

"We will help each other—this is good. I teach you waxworks, and you teach me better English. Nini is a good boy, but not patient enough with my language. Did I tell you he's only here nine months and already he speaks like an *indigène?*"

Marguerite smiled. "I believe you did."

"Yes, he's a good boy to his *maman*."

Based on Claudette's recollections, Marguerite knew Marie to be at least forty years old, but her face spoke of a much younger woman, despite all of the heavy cares she had already borne in her life. Her petite frame was quick and birdlike in its movements. She spoke sparingly, as if saving up her words for a winter freeze. Her broken English was interspersed at times with French, particularly when she was upset or angry.

Marguerite asked her new employer about her heritage while sweeping the gallery floors that first morning.

"Yes, I'm born in Salzburg and my mother worked for my uncle Curtius as housekeeper. When he goes to Paris for his patron, the Prince de Conti, he sends for us and we go to live with him. My uncle kept a very popular exhibit in the Palais Royal. Famous everywhere. He teaches me waxworks as I will teach you. Most of the collection here is made from his hands. Here is one I've done."

Marie led her to a figure near the rear of the gallery. Lifeless brown eyes stared at an unknown point in time. His thin face looked haggard and bulges protruded from under his eyes. Wispy stands of curled hair lay lank against his scalp. Instead of the street clothing given to most of the busts, this one was dressed in a uniform with some kind of military sash over one shoulder.

Marguerite studied him. "I don't know who this is."

"This was one of my first since I have been in England. You may know about this man. He was very bad. Tried to kill English king and seize the Tower of London. Came to a bad end a couple of months ago. I took a death mask before his friends buried him. Very popular here in the exhibit. I was lucky Admiral Nelson got sentence commuted to hanging and decapitation or head would be in no condition to—what's the matter?"

Marguerite blanched and felt the floor shifting beneath her. She reflexively grabbed the top of the bust's head for support then snatched her hand away as if touching molten rock. This must be Colonel Despard, the traitor that cursed mob complained about, and whose actions so deeply affected her own life. She looked down at the placard, which confirmed it. She took a deep breath.

"Nothing at all. I was just a little light-headed. I should have eaten breakfast."

"Yes, I tell you at home you need more food than that little bit of toast you ate. Waxworking is hard work."

"You're right, of course. I'll be much more careful."

Marguerite realized that this apprenticeship might prove to be much more demanding than dollmaking ever was.

During her first two weeks in the exhibition, Marguerite did little more than sweep, dust, and assist Marie with rearrangement of the figures. Her mentor seemed to have an inexhaustible combination of ways to arrange them to make the exhibit seem "different" without actually adding anything new. They rearranged the gallery every couple of days. Sometimes they were lined up as soldiers, as Marguerite had seen them on her first arrival at the exhibition. Sometimes they grouped busts by subject, such as decorated war heroes together in a cluster or perhaps well-known politicians in an arc facing one another, then they put full-length characters together as though they were at a garden party. On other days, Marie might decide to create a visual maze of the busts and figures, forcing visitors through a winding path of wax statues. Each morning Marie would decide whether to make any changes, and the three of them—little Joseph included—would work furiously to change the setting prior to opening the doors at ten o'clock each morning. After that, Marguerite would retreat to the workroom to arrange supplies and clean, coming out only when summoned by Marie for a menial task. Joseph remained at his mother's side, welcoming guests as Marie collected admission fees.

Each evening after the exhibit closed around eight o'clock, they typically stopped at a street vendor's cart for bread, hard slices of cheddar, and perhaps some smoked fish or sliced lamb, before walking the few blocks back to their lodging. Marguerite fell into a pleasantly tired, dreamless sleep each night, a welcome relief from the months of nightmares at Hevington. Even her headaches were subsiding.

One morning prior to opening time they were visited by a tall man with deeply recessed eyes and a shock of thick black hair. His looks were not handsome as much as they were arresting. Marguerite estimated that he was taller than even Uncle William, except that this man's presence was far more imposing, almost regally so. He looked quizzically at Marguerite and gave her a polite nod, but did not question her presence.

"Madame, I have come about your payment for—"

"Shush, do not speak so in front of others." Marie was visibly agitated. "We will go to the back. Mrs. Ashby, you please finish preparing Sir Francis." She motioned for the man to follow her to the workroom.

Marguerite returned to smoothing out imperfections on Marie's latest creation, that of Sir Francis Burdett, a member of Parliament who had visited France during the early years of the Revolution. His wife, Sophia, had encouraged him to visit Madame Tussaud to have his own model made, in honor of his successful efforts at prison reforms. Marie had negotiated for the figure to remain in the exhibit for a week before turning it over to him. Today was to be the first day of his display and it was vital that it look perfect before its final placement in the center of the gallery. While Marguerite used a dampened cloth to press out any lingering rough spots, Joseph used a footstool to reach up and drape a blue velvet cloak around the figure's shoulders for dramatic effect.

Although Joseph spoke to Marguerite as little as possible, the miniature adult had softened a bit and was at least willing to work alongside her. Since she had arrived, Marguerite had not yet been permitted to collect admissions, interact with customers, or work with wax beyond last-minute detailing. Yet little Joseph went wherever his mother did and had a larger role than the apprentice did thus far, so he treated Marguerite with a magnanimity that was amusing to see in a young boy.

In the early hours of the day the entire theatre was quiet, so when voices rose in the workroom, Marguerite could hear snippets of their conversation. Marie's voice took on a shrillness and in short order both were quarrelling in French.

"Fifty percent of receipts . . ."

"Bills are due . . ."

"The landlord plans to . . . fixtures . . ."

"Gas! The man is mad."

". . . have been successful here . . . successful elsewhere."

Joseph made a motion as though to join his mother in the workroom, but Marguerite put a cautionary finger to her lips and shook her head.

"Whatever goes on in there is between your *maman* and that gentleman. Who is he?"

"That's Mr. Philipsthal, Maman's partner."

"The man with the show next door? The Phantasmagoria?"

"Yes, Maman came to England so he could make her famous."

Interesting. There seemed to be a disagreement on the road to fame.

"Have you been to the Phantasmagoria show, Joseph?"

Joseph looked at her with incredulity. "Mrs. Ashby, I have responsibilities here. There is no time to visit his show." Really, it was difficult to keep from giggling when he became so expressive and adultlike.

"I understand perfectly. I should like to see it, though. After all, don't you wonder what an invisible girl looks like? Or sounds like, I suppose."

"Not at all, Mrs. Ashby. I'm too busy with Maman."

At that moment, Marie and Mr. Philipsthal came out from the back room. Marguerite kept her head bent over her work. As the tiny woman strode by, frizzed hair peeping out from underneath her cap, she spoke without stopping. "Marguerite, I must speak to Mr. Winsor. Today you learn to take admissions. Nini, you show her."

Joseph's face was one of dismay, but Marguerite had little thought for him. Mr. Winsor was the Lyceum's owner. What had happened that necessitated that immediate meeting? But Marie was gone before she could ask.

If Joseph was a mask of disappointment, Mr. Philipsthal's face was one of great hope. "Madame, I do not believe I have had the pleasure of meeting you, although I was most entranced by your beauty earlier." He swept an extremely elegant bow. His French accent spoke of culture and grace and manliness. "Now that my business is concluded, I hope we can be properly introduced."

"I am Marguerite Ashby, Madame Tussaud's new apprentice. I have been here only a short time."

"Marguerite." It rolled on his tongue like a fine wine. "Such a lovely name. Are you a French émigré, too?"

"My mother came to England when I was about five years old. I think of myself as purely English."

"Miss Ashby, have you been to see my Phantasmagoria show?"

"Mrs. Ashby. I am widowed, sir. No, my time here at the wax exhibit is greatly accounted for and I have little to spare for other activities."

"My condolences on your loss. Your attire suggests you are no longer mourning. Is that so?"

"Not formally, no."

"Then as Madame Tussaud's business partner I insist that you attend the show one evening, and that you permit me the great pleasure of treating you to supper afterwards. Would Friday next be convenient?"

"Oh, I'm not sure that I have time for leisurely pursuits."

"Nonsense. I'm certain Madame would be happy to see her charming new apprentice enjoy a few hours on her own. Besides, she is a great aficionado of my show. If you are to learn our business, it makes sense for you to see many aspects of it."

"But thus far I have not done much in the way of—"

"Mrs. Ashby, please do not mistake my intentions. I simply wish to be considerate and . . . neighborly. You need not fear me."

But it wasn't fear she felt. It was sheer terror at the thought of being courted by a man. Was his insistence that he had no designs on her a ruse? Or had she become irrational beyond all reasonable expectations?

Calm yourself. Not everyone has ghastly intentions toward you.

"I suppose that would be fine. Provided Madame Tussaud will not need me that evening."

"Excellent. I presume you are staying in the same lodgings with her? Very well, I'll be there promptly at seven o'clock to escort you back here."

"Thank you, sir."

Madame Tussaud had responded to Marguerite's query about taking time to go to the Phantasmagoria show with a snorted "Humph" and a muttered "waste of time it is" but did not try to prevent her from going.

Mr. Philipsthal was as good as his word, and arrived at Surrey Street promptly at seven o'clock. Marguerite was glad Aunt Claudette had convinced her to take one fancy gown. She had not had need to dress elegantly for so long that she found herself actually laughing when she fumbled with pinning a fringed shawl around her shoulders.

Nevertheless, she thought herself presentable when Mr. Philipsthal arrived, and his appreciative eye confirmed it. He, too, had taken care with his appearance, and sported a gleaming gold watch dangling from his waistband.

At the Lyceum Theatre many other carriages were arriving and dozens of well-dressed gentlemen and their laced and feathered ladies stood milling about the entrance. Torches posted near each of the exterior columns blazed, illuminating the street, and the chandeliers under the portico brightly reflected the anticipation of the patrons.

"I've not seen such elegantly dressed people here before. Are all of them here for your show?" Marguerite asked.

"Hopefully so. Mr. Winsor let part of the Lyceum to an orchestra, and they may be having a concert tonight. He's trying to promote the fact that he is slowly installing gas lighting throughout the building. It's the latest thing and very expensive—just what attracts the upper class."

Their hackney finally maneuvered into position in front of the theatre and Mr. Philipsthal offered Marguerite his arm as they walked into the building. At the entrance to his show stood a uniformed young man taking admissions. The ticket seller began to say, "Welcome to Philipsthal's Fantastic Phantasmagoria Show. Seats in the balcony cost—Mr. Philipsthal, sir, my apologies. I didn't realize it was you."

"It's all right, Jack. I'm just escorting Mrs. Ashby to her seat."

"Yes, sir."

Inside the darkened theatre Mr. Philipsthal led her to a circular staircase to one side. At the top of the staircase he guided her to a small, empty box of four seats. He took her gloved hand and bowed over it.

"Mrs. Ashby, I will take my leave of you now."

"Pardon me? I thought we were watching the show together."

"Alas, I must be on hand to manage certain aspects of the show. I will return promptly at the end to escort you to supper."

He departed with another small bow. In minutes his small theatre had filled, and a stage worker extinguished candelabra around the theatre. When he was finished, only two multistemmed candelabra on the stage remained lit. The room quieted, and Mr. Philipsthal appeared on stage from behind the hanging gold curtain.

In a low, ethereal voice, quite unlike his own, he intoned, "Gracious ladies and distinguished gentlemen, welcome to my Phantasmagoria show. I am Paul de Philipsthal, the proprietor of this show, and it is my greatest honor to have you here as the very first witnesses of several special oddities, never before seen in England or the Continent. Please prepare yourselves to be thrilled, amused, and yes, even shocked. Ladies, you may need your handkerchiefs to contain your screams. Husbands and fathers will need to keep a strict eye on their women in case they should faint dead away."

Philipsthal stepped back behind the curtain, while a collective murmur went through the crowd. Even Marguerite found herself sitting forward in her seat.

Appearing next on stage was a man dressed in a Cossack's uniform, with red baggy pants gathered below the knee, high-top leather boots, and a long red tunic cinched at the waist with a colorful printed sash. On his head perched a bucket-shaped hat adorned with a long white tassel that covered most of his face. He was rolled out on a small platform by a stage worker.

After positioning the Cossack in the center of the stage, the stage worker ran behind the curtain, and for several moments all was deathly still. Then from the orchestra pit in front of the stage began wafting pulsating notes of music Marguerite had never heard before. The Cossack began kicking up his legs and slapping his thighs in response to the tune. His repetitions became faster as the music increased its tempo, and just as the music reached an overwhelming crescendo, sending the man into a speed of movement impossible to sustain, the orchestra abruptly fell silent and the man ceased his dancing.

The audience clapped delightedly to show its appreciation for the man's performance, but he did not bow to accept the crowd's applause. Instead, he stood stock still. Mr. Philipsthal reappeared on the stage and turned the platform around to show the audience that the man was just a mechanical device. His clothing did not stretch completely around him, and his interior workings were quite visible from anywhere in the theatre.

But how did he start moving? Marguerite wondered. There was no one on stage to manipulate him. It was as if he had indeed danced on his own.

Mr. Philipsthal rolled the Cossack offstage to thunderous applause, and from the other side of the stage entered another worker pulling an enormous wooden cage on wheels. The cage was gloriously painted in reds, blues, and yellow, and swaths of deep blue cloth covered the top of it, draping gracefully down its sides.

Inside the cage was an enormous tiger.

Mr. Philipsthal made his entrance once again and stood next to the door of the cage, placing one hand on its lock. "My dear friends, tonight you are among the first to see Tippoo, a ferocious man-eating tiger, captured by the East India Company, but not before it mauled to death the son of the great General Munro."

A ripple of recognition dashed through the audience. They knew Sir Hector Munro was a general who had defeated his enemy, Tippoo Sahib, known as the Tiger of Mysore, in a fight of Indian and French forces against the British East India Company just a few years earlier. Munro's son was attacked by one of Sahib's tigers and died in agony twenty-four hours later.

"And now"—Philipsthal extended his other arm—"we welcome with us tonight Major Ellery, who was present at the mauling and has sought vengeance for the past four years."

A man in a military uniform entered from the opposite end of the stage and stood next to the cage, glaring at the tiger.

"When I release the lock to the cage, Major Ellery will come face-to-snout with his longtime enemy, Tippoo. Are you ready, dear friends?"

A woman seated somewhere near the front of the theatre—it was difficult for Marguerite to see in the dark and from her elevated position—shrieked, and a gentleman nearby picked her up and carried her up the aisle and out of the theatre. The remainder of the audience was hushed, holding its collective breath in anticipation.

Philipsthal quickly released the lock and ran around behind the cage. The cage was towering enough that even from Marguerite's lofty position she could not see where he went. The major took a step to the cage, putting his right foot up into it and was greeted with a roar of such magnitude that the very walls of the theatre shook. More screams sliced through the air and the fear of the spectators became palpable.

Major Ellery recoiled from the cage door, groaning and clutching his chest in apparent pain, then collapsed in the middle of the stage. The audience's shrieks turned into shocked gasps. Philipsthal reappeared and moved to the front of the stage as a curtain dropped behind him, blocking the major and the tiger cage from view.

Philipsthal held up his arms in a supplicating manner. "Friends, fear not. The good major will live to continue doing his duty to king and country. I ask you to welcome back our brave soldier, Major Ellery."

The midstage curtain swept back open. Major Ellery was standing and smiling. He swept a bow to the audience, now filled with murmurs of disbelief. Philipsthal nonchalantly flicked the fingers of his left hand, so subtly that Marguerite was certain no one noticed it but her, and almost immediately the tiger's head pulled back and he roared again, this time becoming utterly still afterwards.

Ah, Marguerite thought. *The tiger is as mechanical as the Cossack.*

The curtain again came between Philipsthal and his act. Once more the spectators burst into applause.

A parade of other performances followed, including a mechanical peacock that could eat, drink, cry, and unfold its tail, but the most amazing feat was saved for last. As the midstage curtain fell again, Philipsthal moved to the very front of the stage and spoke in an exaggerated whisper, clearly heard within the fine acoustics of the theatre.

"And now, my most esteemed guests, I would like to present you with something so puzzling, so mystifying, so extraordinarily peculiar that the world's foremost men of science and reason cannot explain it." Philipsthal held an arm in the air as though summoning higher powers.

"Yes, many have known that our earthly world is inhabited by those of the spiritual realm. Desperately these spirits try to communicate with us, but they've had no means to do so until now. For, ladies and gentlemen, tonight you have the special privilege of being in contact with specters from the realm of the departed!"

Philipsthal swept his raised arm down dramatically and the curtain rose as the remaining candles on stage were extinguished, plunging the entire theatre into darkness. Marguerite could see nothing, but felt the hushed presence of the other show-goers.

Onstage was the backdrop of a cave with skeletons and other ghoulish figures glowing in relief on its walls. After being given mere seconds to view these creatures, the audience was inundated with thunder and lightning, resulting in ear-splitting cries of surprise and confusion from the audience. Marguerite shut her eyes and held her hands over her ears to block out the mayhem.

The noise and flashes abruptly stopped, and were replaced by the sight of the figures on the cave wall starting to move, their eyes and mouths opening and closing. They dashed about the wall and slowly began receding, finally vanishing in a point, only to be replaced by what looked like a cloud that got larger and larger. Out of the cloud came the figure of King Charles I, the head of which transformed into a skull. He charged forward and back over the stage. King Charles receded back into the cloud, only to be replaced by a skeleton that transformed into the visage of Lady Jane Grey. Back and forth a variety of specters went, some in human form, others as ghastly skeletons.

The audience recoiled in terror from the apparitions, but were petrified by what happened next. Instead of merely charging back and forth in the air over the stage, the ghoulish figures appeared all together and charged the audience, dashing about madly over their heads. Both men and women cried out in distress and attempted to hide down in their seats, although some of the less fearful spectators actually reached up to try to touch a passing phantom.

Marguerite could not help herself. She dug her fingernails into her hands in fright, even though the rational part of her whispered that it must all be a trick.

In a great rush, all of the figures flew speedily back toward the cave wall, and the orchestra's cymbals clanged with every visual impact made by a specter colliding with, and disappearing into, the cave wall.

With the disappearance of the last spirit, Philipsthal reappeared on stage while workers relit all of the candelabra around the theatre. The audience was still in a state of fluster over the unimaginable scenes it had witnessed.

"Esteemed guests," Philipsthal began. "I know that this evening has stretched your understanding of the world in unimaginable ways. What you once thought was ordinary you now see can be quite . . . phantasmagoric. I thank you for your kind attendance in witnessing these wonders, and do beg that you will share what you have seen with your friends. My show will not be here indefinitely, so persuade them to come right away."

And so the show ended.

Marguerite waited for Philipsthal to return to her box to fetch her, and she remained quiet and reflective until they were seated in a nearby restaurant for supper.

Over glasses of sherry they discussed whether Napoleon might invade England now that the Americans were negotiating for the purchase of a large tract of land that included Louisiana. Such a sale would replenish his war coffers.

They were served whole trout in a short crust with rosemary sprig decoration, and completed their meals with cups of chocolate. Before sipping the sweet drink from her cup, Marguerite ventured into questions about the show.

"Mr. Philipsthal, I must confess to amazement over tonight's performance. I know the spirits were some kind of trick, but I can't see how you did it."

"Ah, usually such wonders must remain the secrets of their masters. But you were so kind as to accompany me that I will tell you that my secret relies upon a magic lantern."

"A magic lantern?" Marguerite was intrigued enough to put down her last forkful of food.

"Indeed. It is a very special device that enables me to project images on backdrops. For tonight I used several lanterns to produce the effect I wanted."

"It was truly amazing. I was frightened even though I knew what I was seeing could not possibly be real."

"Every professional showman loves to hear praise of his productions. When it comes from a creature as lovely as you, the pleasure is doubled."

Marguerite mentally retreated from his compliment and sat silently nibbling her crumbs. Mr. Philipsthal had promised this outing to be free of romance.

"Mrs. Ashby, forgive me. I let my reckless tongue run away from me. I should not have offended you so. Please, tell me of yourself. How did you come to be Madame Tussaud's apprentice?"

Marguerite described as simply as she could her past as a dollmaker and the death of her husband, with her resulting stay with the Greycliffes and eventual decision to move into a related trade. She deliberately left out any mention of her shrew of a mother-in-law.

"You have suffered great misfortune. It delights me that this evening's entertainment served to divert you for a little while."

"It was very enjoyable. But I also find my apprenticeship to be pleasantly distracting."

"Is it? You don't find the wax figures to be a bit boring? How do you find it working directly with Madame Tussaud?"

Marguerite carefully considered the question with her hands around the warm cup. "I suppose some might think her abrupt, but I think that's a result of her difficulty with the language and the troubles she has witnessed in her life. She's been kind to me, and she obviously has a deep affection for her son."

"How long will your apprenticeship last?"

"I don't really know. We didn't actually establish that. Until she finds me to be a proficient waxworker, I suppose."

"And what then? Will you open your own exhibit?"

"I've honestly given it no thought. I've hardly started to learn how to even work with the figures, much less put much reflection into what the future may bring. Right now I'm happy just to be continuing on with life."

"Of course, of course. But you should eventually consider breaking away from Madame Tussaud. I could help you do so."

After Mr. Philipsthal had returned her to her lodgings, Marguerite sat quietly in contemplation. *What a strange man,* she thought. She couldn't decide if he was genuine in his friendship, or lurking about with the intent of starting a love affair.

Well, he won't get very far on that score. My devotion now is for waxworks, not love affairs.

"Tomfoolery and nonsense," was Marie's full summation of Marguerite's report of the Phantasmagoria show the next morning as they walked to the Lyceum. "Idiotic entertainment for the equally stupid. Waste of time. Tomorrow we close the show to do a special modeling. I show you how to do life masks."

Life masks! Finally, an opportunity to truly get involved in waxworking. Marguerite tried to suppress her excitement throughout the day as she stayed stationed at the entrance of the Cabinet, collecting admissions.

Exhibit visitors were charged a shilling to walk through and gawp at the wax figures. Marie was not satisfied with her clientele, desiring the more elegant members of society to traverse through the gallery instead of setting up private visits to commission figures, but her debts were high and the lower social orders were happy to spend a shilling for such exciting entertainment. Marie constantly reminded Marguerite that one day her gallery would be in demand by the upper class, and that they must constantly work toward that aim.

When the appointed hour for closing the exhibit came, the two women and young boy returned to Surrey Street, where Marie asked Mrs. Slade to watch her son for a few days while she and

Marguerite went out on a special commission. Joseph's face registered first his shock, then his complete displeasure at having been left out of whatever special sale his mother had made.

"But Maman, I am your helper. I should go with you. You need me to translate for you."

"No, Nini, this is work for the apprentice. She will help with my words. You stay here."

Mrs. Slade's offers of cakes and lemon candies could not remove the boy's scowl, and he stomped off to the quarters he shared with his mother.

Still Marie beamed with pride. "My boy is such a hard worker. Wants to be with his mother."

Inside their hired coach the next morning, along with their traveling cases, crate of modeling tools, and two other anonymous passengers, Marie explained their destination as that of Oatlands Park in Surrey. The Duchess of York was now living there, separated from her husband, the favorite son of the king. She had ventured into London some time before Marguerite's arrival and visited the exhibition after closing hours, so as not to be seen visiting with commoners. She now wished to have her own wax portrait made to amuse herself. Marie was hopeful that a royal commission such as this one would help turn her exhibition into one that was more exclusive.

Marguerite understood. As the quasi proprietor of Aunt Claudette's shop, she knew that it was receiving the royal warrant from the House of Hanover that had truly launched the doll shop into its most successful period.

During the long and bumpy ride, Marguerite assisted Marie with the practice of her English. Her mentor was slowly developing her speaking skills, but always slipped into her choppy English when upset or excited.

The coach stopped for an hour at an inn on the outskirts of Richmond to enable its passengers to have a light supper. Marguerite used some of the time to walk and stretch her legs, while Marie chatted up her exhibition with the innkeeper. Tussaud was indefatigable when it came to her business, and talked of nothing else.

The coach resumed its uncomfortable journey and it was near twilight when it finally arrived at another inn in the town of Weybridge, where the two women were met by another carriage displaying the Hanoverian seal. Their meager belongings were hoisted onto the carriage and they were soon entering the drive leading to Oatlands Park.

They approached the large, drab, gothic-style house in tan brick from the right side. Candles were already burning in many of the mullioned windows. The coach pulled up to the entrance, a stone portico with three sets of columns topped with arches.

"How curious," Marguerite remarked. "It doesn't even seem as grand as the Lyceum, and it's a royal residence."

"Hah! This is the replacement to the old Tudor house that was here. I hear that was very grand with many towers and courts."

The women were escorted into a large entry hall by a liveried doorman and were requested to wait. Within a few minutes they heard a sharp clicking noise in the distance, followed by several sharp barks. Three black, mop-haired little dogs came bounding in, stopping short to warn their mistress of the two intruders in their house. Behind them entered the exhibition's new client, Princess Frederica Charlotte, the Duchess of York and Albany.

The duchess, whom Marguerite guessed to be about Marie's age, wore an emerald green dress with white trim and a gold sash around the waist. Her matching cap with a purple ostrich feather sprouting from the crest of it covered her curled and frizzed red hair. Her nose was overly long and her eyes almost crossed, giving her a homely look, but her charm was captivating. Marie and Marguerite curtsied before her. In response, she approached both women, giving each a gentle kiss on the cheek.

"Thank you for coming to see me at my humble little residence. Would you care for some refreshment after your trip?" The duchess rang a small bell and gave instructions to the servant who appeared from nowhere.

Two more servants entered promptly to set a table near the room's enormous panel of windows set four high and six across, looking out over formal gardens and terraces, barely visible in the fading daylight.

With sharp efficiency, a linen cloth was snapped open on the table and three place settings were arranged. The women were seated and served biscuits with strawberry and apricot jams, peach fritters, nuts, and sweet wine. Two of the Duchess of York's small dogs sat expectantly at their mistress's feet and waited for nibbles to be bestowed upon them. They didn't have to wait long, as she personally slathered jam on bits of biscuit and hand-fed the eager recipients.

Thanks to the duchess's kindly charm, the three women chatted as though they were old friends reunited after a long absence, although Marie remained the quietest one of the trio. The duchess was surprisingly gentle yet candid. "I do not get many visitors from London here, although the townspeople are quite sympathetic toward me. Everyone knows of my calamitous marriage with the prince, which should have put me in the most awkward predicament. But I find I am happy to be retired here in my little home with my pets to keep me company and the affection of the locals to keep me comforted." As if on cue, another dog came scrabbling into the room, tongue hanging to one side of its small but inquisitive face.

The duchess laughed at the newcomer. "Please, Cassandra, use a more ladylike entrance before our guests." Another well-coated biscuit went to the floor.

Next to Marguerite, Marie was rustling with impatience. Marguerite smiled inwardly. She was beginning to really like her no-nonsense mentor, who was clearly becoming irritated with the canine intrusions.

"Ahem, Your Grace, would you like to talk about your model now?" Marie tried turning the conversation toward more important topics.

"Oh no. You've had such a long journey, you must be tired. I'll have you shown to your rooms and we can worry about the model in the morning."

Thus their introduction to the duchess ended and they were shown to comfortable adjoining rooms. When Marguerite crossed into Marie's bedchamber to say good night, she was greeted with the woman's usual staccato observances.

"Foolishness. Waste of time. We should be letting mask set overnight. Too much delay. The exhibition is not taking in admissions while we fritter away time here."

Marguerite grasped Marie's hand. "I'm sure that tomorrow morning we will set right to work and be on our way in no time."

"Bah. Need good light. And no dogs! Animals will spoil the plaster with their hair and drool."

"I'm sure the duchess will be sensitive to your requirements, madame. We should retire now to be sure we get plenty of rest for tomorrow's activities."

The next morning was flooded with golden sunshine and they were invited to take breakfast with the duchess on the lawn just outside the formal gardens, which were dotted with small tombstones along their perimeter. Marguerite counted seven of them. She tentatively ventured to ask about them as they finished their sumptuous morning meal of oatmeal with sweet cream, smoked herrings, and rolls with orange marmalade.

"Your Grace, pardon my rudeness, but may I inquire as to who is buried here?"

"Ah, they are the resting places for my precious ones. My pets that have gone on before me."

"Your pets?"

"Yes, a couple of my beloved terriers, my rapscallion old cockatoo, Blanche, and others. I buried them here so they could look out over the grounds they loved so much when they were alive."

Marie was fidgeting at Marguerite's side again, and accidentally kicked the case of supplies at her feet, spilling the contents. A servant was at her side in seconds to pick up the scattered tools and replace them.

"That was very thoughtful of Your Grace," Marguerite replied. "I'm sure your kindness is well appreciated by the people of Weybridge."

The duchess preened at Marguerite's words. "Thank you, Mrs. Ashby. It's a bit lonely being exiled this far outside Society. My pets and my neighbors are my only solace. And now we should attend to my portrait, should we not?"

She personally escorted them to a brick outbuilding about

twenty feet square, which she referred to as a painter's studio. Inside the structure was an assortment of chairs, chests, and other occasional pieces of furniture, jumbled together so that it seemed more like a storage shed than a place where an artist could work. Nevertheless, Marguerite jumped in to help as Marie began systematically moving furniture around to fit her needs. The two women threw open windows and used cloths covering a settee to wipe down a table Marie identified as suitable for applying the plaster cast.

The duchess protested that she would have servants rearrange the room for the waxworkers, but Marie, already annoyed by the delays, insisted that the little bit of effort to fix the room was not worth calling for help.

With the studio now set, Marie set about her first task, which was to take measurements of her subject. Spread upon the table were several types of calipers, metal instruments that looked like the pincher devices enthusiastically used by fanatics during the Inquisition.

Happily enough, their fierce appearances had no relation to the very simple task they performed. Using an outside caliper, Marie gently placed the arms of it around the princess's ankles, calves, wrists, head, and other extremities to measure their circumferences. Marguerite duly noted these numbers in the large notebook they kept to maintain a log of all their subjects.

She then used one of her several inside calipers, which measured the internal circumference of a subject, such as the spread inside of a mouth or the distance between the fingers of an outstretched hand. The princess was nonplussed at having to open her jaw as wide as she could, but acquiesced politely.

Marie then invited Princess Frederica to sit down in a simple wooden armchair whose back was to the table, and asked her to lean all the way back so that her head rested on the table. While the duchess got comfortable, Marguerite arranged the woman's skirts to ensure she remained as dignified as possible through the process. At the same time Marie spread her case of supplies on the table near the duchess's head. She handed Marguerite a jar of oil and a wide paintbrush and asked her to spread a thick layer of it over the duchess's hairline. This, Marie explained, would prevent plaster from sticking to the hair.

At the same time, Marie draped a large cloth over the front of the duchess and tied it around the back of her neck. The duchess nervously joked that even her husband's current mistress, Mrs. Clarke, would have pity on her in her present state.

"Madame," Marie began, "I must do something that will seem strange, but please do not be alarmed. I must insert one of these in each nostril." Marie held up a tiny piece of paper she was rolling up into the shape of a tube. "These will help you breathe, as once I apply the plaster to your face, you will not be able to open your eyes or your mouth. Yes?"

The duchess's eyes opened wide in the beginnings of fear. "Oh my. Oh. Well, certainly, if you say it's safe."

"Yes, this is safe. I do this all the time in France. Even Napoleon did this."

The thought that she was sharing the same experience as the infamous enemy of England heartened the duchess. "If the dreadful old Boney can do it, then what matter is it to even the weakest Englishwoman?"

Marie turned to Marguerite. "Watch closely."

This needed no telling. Marguerite gazed in fascination as Marie placed the tightly rolled paper gently into the duchess's right nostril, then allowed it to unroll until it filled the cavity. The duchess tensed her entire body at the sensation, then firmly shut her eyes.

Marie poured some water from a tightly stoppered bottle into a bowl, and added a powdery white mix to it in gradual amounts, stirring after each addition until she was satisfied with the consistency, which was thick yet workable.

She instructed the duchess to keep her eyes naturally closed, not clenched, but to not open them even the slightest fraction, for it would result in plaster in her eyes.

"Do you understand this important instruction, Your Grace?" Marie asked. The duchess looked apprehensively at Marguerite, who smiled back at her encouragingly.

"I do," she said in a small voice.

Marie used her hands to spread the gooey mix on the duchess's skin. Every inch of her face, including her exposed neck to the point where the draping started, was covered with a thin layer of plaster.

Marie then cut a two-foot section of thread from a ball and placed it from the bottom of the duchess's neck to the top of her forehead.

"What is that for?" Marguerite asked.

"You'll see."

Marie picked up the bowl of plaster again, and this time scooped a much heavier layer of it on the duchess's face. Marguerite started when the duchess grabbed her hand and squeezed it. She could imagine the woman's terror at being effectively blinded and muted and relying on two flimsy pieces of paper for breathing. Even the dead would be terrified of such a procedure! Marguerite patted the duchess's shoulder as reassuringly as possible.

Marie finished molding the plaster to her subject's face with her hands. Her fingers moved with remarkable dexterity, pushing the plaster around quickly to conform to every ridge, crevice, and imperfection of her subject's face before it began to dry. When she was satisfied with her handiwork, Marie poured water from the bottle onto her hands over the plaster mixing bowl and scrubbed them clean. Shaking her wet hands over the bowl, she said, "Now we wait."

Knowing the duchess's terror, Marguerite asked, "Madame, how long will she wait?"

Marie shrugged. "Not long. We'll remove it before it cracks."

"Madame, are you comfortable? Please squeeze my hand once if yes, twice if no."

The other woman's trembling hand squeezed hers uncertainly once. Marguerite waited for another round of pressure, but it did not come. She left her hand in the duchess's for reassurance and examined the plaster covering while Marie pulled more tools from her case.

The plaster was beginning to harden and turn a lighter shade of gray around her mouth, nose, and eyes. Already she could see the outline of a few small wrinkles the duchess had on both corners of her mouth. Marguerite was mesmerized.

But before it hardened too much further, Marie grabbed both ends of the string at her subject's chin and forehead and pulled the string evenly up through the plaster, splitting it in two.

"This makes mask easier to remove. Two pieces are easier than one."

"But won't it affect what it looks like later?"

"No, we'll make it perfect back at the workshop."

As they waited, the duchess clutched Marguerite's arm with one hand, while she clenched and unclenched the fist of her other hand on the chair's arm. Soon the plaster had developed a whitish cast to it, which Marie indicated meant it was fully dried and ready for removal. "Your Grace, I'll pull mask off now," Marie said.

Marguerite heard the duchess utter a low growl of relief from the back of her throat. Marie grabbed either side of the mask and began twisting it off the duchess's face with practically imperceptible movements.

The apprentice held her breath as Marie gently pulled each side of the ghostly wrap. The duchess's fingernails were now firmly embedded in Marguerite's wrist, but she bit her lip to keep from crying out and thereby startling the customer even more.

Finally the mask released from the duchess's face, coming off like a hinged lid from the right side to the left. Marie held up two halves for Marguerite's inspection.

"Yes, this is good casting. Mrs. Ashby, you do well with oil. No plaster in the hair."

There was no plaster in the duchess's hair, but the same could not be said for the remainder of her face and neck. Bits of plaster were stuck all over the duchess's cheeks, eyelids, and lips.

"I will wrap the mask. You assist the duchess with her wash."

Marguerite hardly knew where to begin. Sensing her indecision the duchess asked, "Am I too terrible a fright? I must have a mirror."

Marie's head came up sharply from where she was working with the mask. "No! I mean, madame, let Mrs. Ashby remove the excess particles so that Your Grace need not be troubled so much."

"It's no trouble. I'll ring for a servant."

"No no, no servants necessary."

Seeing the potential for escalating tension, Marguerite grabbed a soft cloth from the top of the pile Marie had placed on the table and dampened it with water from Marie's bottle. She touched the soft cloth to the duchess's face as she dropped her voice and began speaking in a soothing tone.

"Madame, it is my great pleasure to assist you. We know that we've put you under great stress, but we know you will be so extraordinarily pleased with the result that this will seem a trifling inconvenience to you. Imagine how thrilling it will be when London society sees your exact likeness in wax. All attention once reserved for the duke and his mistress will be refocused on Your Grace. Everyone will want to see how beautiful and gracious their maligned princess really is."

By this time, Marguerite was nearly finished with wiping excess plaster from the duchess's face.

"Your Grace, I believe you now just need a cream rinse for your hair, to take out the oil. Is there a hand mirror here in the studio?"

The duchess lifted her head up from the table. "There's probably a wall mirror among the covered pieces of furniture over there." She pointed to a large dusty cloth outlining bumpy objects beneath it in a corner of the room.

Marguerite lifted the cover and quickly found a small, gilt-edged table mirror on the floor. She wiped the glass clean on a corner of her dress as she took it to the duchess and set it on Marie's worktable. The duchess turned her chair around to look at herself and promptly burst into decidedly unregal giggles.

"Why, I *am* a frightful mess. My poor maid Sally will be hours at my toilette setting me to rights again."

"And back at the workshop we will set this to rights." Marie presented the two sides of the mask, now cradled in cotton inside a sturdy box. The mask was face up so that the Duchess could see what it looked like on her face.

"Oh, it's incredible. And you will somehow turn this mysterious lump into a replica of me?"

"Yes, you come to London in one month, it will be complete."

"How positively delightful." Now that the duchess was no longer consumed by plaster, she was back to her charming self. "You must send the bill to my steward and I will instruct him to pay you right away."

"Your Grace." Marie curtsied deferentially and Marguerite followed suit.

That evening the two women ate alone in their rooms, but the next morning the duchess was on hand to bid them farewell, kissing each of them on the cheek and wishing them a swift and uneventful journey back to London, and promising to visit the following month.

As they boarded the duchess's coach, she lifted her skirts and ran to the still-open door. "I wonder," she said. "Should we send an invitation to the duke and Mrs. Clarke to visit me in wax at your gallery? I should have smiled during the plaster session so that he would think I am the happiest of women without him."

"Never fear, madame," Marie replied. "Any lady who has her replica made in wax for my gallery is the happiest of women."

As they pulled away, Marguerite looked back to see the duchess clapping her hands in great merriment.

The duchess's wax figure occupied all of their time in the early mornings and late after the exhibit had closed. Marie did not allow Marguerite to participate in the actual finishing of the figure, but let her watch every step of the process.

Using a supply of wax bricks that were melted slightly just before use, Marie built the Princess Frederica's body on an upright stand, using her calipers and noted measurements to ensure it was close to the original. The head was secured to the torso with wire and pins.

From a stock of arm, hand, and leg molds, Marie selected pieces that most resembled the duchess's and cast them again, once more measuring for precision and sculpting to refine the figure.

While Marie worked and Marguerite learned, Joseph sat to one side, sketching a scene of the two women standing before the incomplete figure, with Marie kneeling before it as she scraped at it with a knife, and Marguerite holding the figure steady.

The final touches, which were the most detailed and complicated to execute, were to paint the head, hands, and other exposed areas to look lifelike. All of this work was meticulous and painstaking, particularly as they did the delicate work of selecting and gluing in the imported glass eyes. Wigs were coiffed and stitched down to the heads, although Marie was experimenting with inserting individual hairs directly to the figures' scalps.

The last action was to dress the figure. Sometimes Marie was given clothing by her subject, but if she was sculpting a long-dead person, or if there were other reasons she could not obtain pieces from the subject's actual wardrobe, she had to make the items herself. Fortunately in this case, the duchess had furnished her own gown, slippers, and paste jewelry, sent after their visit by one of her own servants.

During the development of the duchess's figure, Mr. Philipsthal was a frequent visitor. He appeared in their back workroom with regularity, either with foolish questions about what time the exhibit was opening on a given day, which was met with Marie's terse "We open as we always do," or how many figures the gallery now had, or how many people were stepping through the exhibit each day.

Sometimes he insisted that Marie stop what she was doing to speak with him in private, backstage at the Phantasmagoria. She returned from these private sessions blustery and irritated, snapping at both Marguerite and Joseph the remainder of the day.

But Madame Tussaud was the consummate professional before her visitors, and no one could see that she was anything other than a happy waxworker. Her typical daily dress was simple, consisting of a long, paint- and wax-stained apron over a demurely tinted gown. It was intended to show the public exactly who she was: a hardworking businesswoman. Her flaxen hair was her only indulgence, set up high with ringlets curling about her neck and topped with a white cotton cap.

Marguerite copied her mentor, having brought mostly plain dresses from Hevington anyway. She sewed both an apron and a cap to resemble Marie's, but did not go so far as an indulgence with her coiffure, opting instead for a simple pulled-back style appropriate for a widow. In her brusque way, Marie gave her approval to Marguerite's garb.

"You are beginning to look like a waxworker. This is good. But you are still a young woman. Dress your hair, rouge your cheeks a little. Young men will notice a pretty girl like you."

Marguerite shook her head. There would be no more young men for her. Instead, wax would be her life. Her apprenticeship had started very slowly in the first few weeks, but now she was beginning to visualize the art of it and that art was at least comparable to dollmaking if not more invigorating. To be able to recreate life so realistically, and then witness as visitors gasped in amazement . . . well, doll-shop patrons were never quite *that* taken with a doll.

The duchess's likeness was well received by the public and the duchess herself was ecstatic when she came to visit, again kissing and clasping both Marie and Marguerite in appreciation of the work done to bring her likeness to life.

"Indeed, I have quite forgotten the masking experience. It was certainly all worth it. Has my dear husband been by to see it?"

It was certainly worth it to the exhibition, as ticket sales doubled for the first week the duchess was on display. Patrons who had read about the duke's affairs were titillated by the sight of his jilted wife, and repeatedly asked Marie if she would be adding figures of Prince Frederick and Mary Ann Clarke. Marie had no contact with the duke and it was doubtful that he would ever model for her, but she would merely smile enigmatically at the inquiry.

One morning Marie, Marguerite, and Joseph arrived at the Lyceum to see that Mr. Philipsthal had posted a new sign.

NOW UNDER THE PATRONAGE OF THE DUKE AND DUCHESS OF YORK!
PHILIPSTHAL'S FANTASTIC PHANTASMAGORIA SHOW
A GRAND CABINET OF OPTICAL AND MECHANICAL CURIOSITIES
AMAZING INVENTIONS! WONDERS FROM AROUND THE WORLD!
COMMUNICATE WITH SPIRITS FROM THE BEYOND.
SHOW CLOSING SOON!

And once again in small print:

CABINET OF WONDERS IN GALLERY TO THE LEFT, INCLUDES FULL-LENGTH PORTRAIT MODELS

Marie's eyes narrowed as she read this, then she let off a torrent of French-sprinkled English, cursing about Philipsthal's perfidy, his low intent, and his general wickedness at claiming patronage by the duke and duchess when it had been she who obtained the custom with Princess Frederica.

"Madame," Marguerite asked, "why do you despise Mr. Philipsthal? Is he not your sponsor? Does he not have the right to do this?"

This was an unfortunate question on Marguerite's part, as it sent Marie off into another violent flow of deprecations in a dizzy blend of French and English.

The relationship between the two puzzled Marguerite. Mr. Philipsthal seemed a kind and innocuous man, but Marie was disgruntled at best, furious at worst, each time she met with him. Was she jealous of his show? And Mr. Philipsthal had insinuated that one day she should separate from Marie. Why was that? Did he want to see Madame Tussaud out of business? Hadn't the two of them shared life's ups and downs since the Revolution?

Later that day Mr. Philipsthal came to visit the exhibition once again, this time bowing before Marguerite, who was brushing the plain white busts, great attractors of dust. The exhibition typically had few people in the late afternoon and it was an opportunity to clean up the gallery from the earlier crowds.

"Mrs. Ashby, it is a delight to have an opportunity to speak with you again." Philipsthal's face was strained, his dark eyes dulled with some hidden worry.

"Thank you, Mr. Philipsthal." Marguerite set down her fine-bristled brush and folded her hands in front of her.

"I thought that if you were not occupied this evening, you might accompany me to supper. For no other purpose than to give a tired man some brief companionship. My Phantasmagoria show is of course successful beyond my wildest dreams, but such success can be quite exhausting. May I have the pleasure?"

Before Marguerite could think whether or not to accept, Marie came storming across the gallery, her invective arriving before she did.

"No! No supper! No despoiling of my apprentice. She's a good girl." Marie was waving a finger in Mr. Philipsthal's face with the fury of a countess whose daughter is being courted by a tavern keeper. Marguerite had never seen her this angry before.

"Madame, please, I am not frightened of Mr. Philip—"

"You should be. Philipsthal, you are a liar and a cheat. Go back to your Phantasmagoria and leave my apprentice alone."

Marguerite thought Mr. Philipsthal looked genuinely distressed and she attempted once more to intervene.

"Madame, Mr. Philipsthal is a friend and means me no harm. He knows I am still a grieving widow."

"Bah. He knows no friend."

Mr. Philipsthal's lips compressed into a thin, controlled line. He gave a slight nod to each woman. "I will take my leave of you now. Madame, Mrs. Ashby. Good day to you both." He left the room in a swirl of tan cloak.

Marie picked up the brush and handed it back to Marguerite, her cheeks red with displeasure. Marguerite did not pursue her point.

The following evening Marie came to Marguerite's room as she was preparing for bed.

"I must talk to you." Her employer's normally expressive face was bland, as if purposefully so. Marguerite's senses tightened. Was she in trouble? Had she offended Madame Tussaud with her interference with Mr. Philipsthal, whom she had not seen since their encounter two days ago?

"Of course, madame." She sat on her bed and invited Marie to sit at her dressing table. Marie sat only momentarily before jumping up and pacing back and forth in her darting, birdlike way.

"We must leave the Lyceum Theatre. Mr. Winsor cannot be

budged on his plans. No good for the exhibition. I've told Philipsthal. He'll pay for transport and will join us in July."

Marguerite was thoroughly confused.

"Mr. Winsor's plans? What plans? Where are we to go?"

"That fool landlord plans to install gas lighting. Throughout the Lyceum. Including the exhibition. No good at all. Dangerous for wax figures."

So they were to leave London. "Where are we going?"

"Edinburgh. We leave in a fortnight. First I must make documents with my solicitor. You will go with me? Tomorrow. Then we have to pack figures for the sea voyage. We will wait to send the Duchess of York's figure to her."

And just as abruptly Marie was gone from her room. Marguerite plumped her pillow up against the wall and sat with her legs crossed under her nightshift to continue reading a book from Mrs. Slade's bookshelves. She flipped the pages without absorbing a word. Was she ready to leave England? Hevington had been a source of comfort, and London was at least familiar. Over the past weeks she had developed some small sense of comfort in the routine of the exhibition, and was learning the craft quickly. Moreover, she had a sense that if waxworking was not permanently to her taste, she could easily return to Aunt Claudette. What would await her in Edinburgh? Would she lose her sense of security?

Tossing the unread book aside, she slipped out of bed and went to her knees in childlike prayer. Her prayers were confused, offered to both God and Nicholas. She stayed bent over her bed until her knees ached, seeking a peace that refused to come.

The next afternoon they once again left a sullen Joseph behind with Mrs. Slade while they went to see Marie's solicitor, Mr. George Wright. During the hackney ride to his office off Manchester Square, Marie explained what documents she needed drawn up.

Her husband, François Tussaud, had remained in Paris with her other son while she came to London with Joseph to try to make a success of the exhibition in England. She left François in charge of her Salon de Cire wax exhibition on the boulevard du Temple, a popular tourist area in Paris. She had inherited the exhibition from Dr. Curtius upon his death in 1795 and continued his tradition of creating wax portraits representing the most popular figures of the day. But the exhibition was in financial trouble when she inherited it, so Marie borrowed money from Madame Reiss, a woman who lived and worked at the Salon de Cire for some years. In exchange for a loan of twenty thousand French assignats, Marie agreed to pay her an annuity of two thousand livres. Now that she was in England, it was becoming quite difficult to handle this monetary transaction on her own and she wished to give her husband financial authority over the Salon de Cire as well as a house at Ivry-sur-Seine that she had also inherited from Dr. Curtius.

"This has been on my mind for some time," the older woman confided. "Now with another sea voyage ahead of me, I want to be sure my affairs are well in hand."

Marguerite pondered whether or not she had affairs remaining to be resolved. After Nicholas's death, Uncle William had stepped in to ensure their London townhome was shuttered, and gave instructions to Roger and Agnes for ongoing work at the doll shop. Aunt Claudette had ensured refurbishment of the shop and was, as far as she knew, still making periodic trips to London to prioritize orders and make important decisions. Marguerite simply hadn't given the shop much thought in recent months, but supposed that Aunt Claudette was willing to take it over completely again.

Their carriage pulled up to Mr. Wright's offices, located in a narrow town house. Mr. Wright, elderly but competent, prepared the necessary documents giving Marie's husband full power of attorney over all her property in Paris, and invited them into a back parlor for tea and refreshment afterwards. They returned to their lodging rooms before dark, where a petulant Joseph complained that he was hungry. After securing supper for the boy and themselves, each woman went off to her own rooms, Marie to write to her husband and Marguerite to send a message to Claudette.

Within a week, Marguerite received a return post from her aunt.

July 5, 1803
Hevington

My dearest Marguerite,

So you are to quit London for Edinburgh. Fear not, you may trust Marie's instincts completely. She has an unerring eye for art and theatre. Although the show may be quite successful in the city, you can be sure that she will make it successful anywhere she takes it. Have you made a figure on your own yet?

Her sponsor, Mr. Philipsthal, sounds like a strange sort. Are you certain he does not have designs on you? If Marie distrusts him, I caution you to also beware. However, I am sorry now to have missed his Phantasmagoria show, which sounds to be quite the fright!

William sends his love. The children have been pressing leaves and flowers into a scrapbook for you. They constantly ask when you are to return for a visit, but I tell them to be patient and wait for their "cousin" to become a famous waxworker. Edward wants to know if you will model him as a cricketer.

Farewell. I pray for your safe journey and hope for your return as soon as possible.

Affectionately,
Claudette

The days leading up to their departure were so busy Marguerite hardly had time to think any more about her financial affairs, Marie's relationship with Mr. Philipsthal, or how much she would miss London when she left. She was astounded by the amount of work required to prepare the exhibition for shipment.

First, Marie erected a competing sign to Mr. Philipsthal's:

DUE TO POPULAR DEMAND!!
CURTIUS'S CABINET OF WONDERS WILL BE CLOSING IN MERE DAYS FOR AN ENGAGEMENT IN EDINBURGH.
DO NOT MISS THE CHANCE TO SEE FAMOUS PEOPLE UP CLOSE.

THE LATE ROYAL FAMILY OF FRANCE—COLONEL DESPARD—THE DUCHESS OF YORK—PRESIDENT WASHINGTON
OPEN EVERY DAY FROM ELEVEN IN THE MORNING UNTIL TEN AT NIGHT
ADMISSION: ONE SHILLING

Marie grumbled considerably about the cost of the sign, which she thought was Philipsthal's responsibility.

Figures were slowly removed from the exhibition so as not to make it seem empty. Marie emphasized that they would try to collect admissions until the last possible moment, so each day one or two more figures were removed for packing and the others moved into different arrangements so as to minimize the look of disruption. The curtained-off area of ghastly heads was removed last, since it had become the most popular section of the exhibit. When the collection was reduced enough that they could no longer legitimately charge admission to see so few pieces, the exhibit was formally closed and the three of them worked furiously to pack the remaining figures, supplies, and furniture into crates for delivery to their ship.

When Marie identified a figure for packing, she and Marguerite would carry it, one at each end, to the workshop, with Joseph supporting the body from underneath. They resembled a bizarre funeral cortege, which fortunately no one else ever saw. Inside the workroom, the figure was placed inside a specially prepared crate, lined with layers and layers of cotton or linen. Gently placing the figure inside its coffin, they inserted wooden dowels of various lengths, topped with padded fabric, between the crate and a range of points on the body. The dowels were not inserted into the body, but sized precisely so that the padded end just touched the body, while the raw wood end was nailed into the side of the crate. Once the figure was surrounded by these dowels, wadded-up bundles of cotton fabric were stuffed between the body and the edges of the crate, and finally several layers were placed between the figure and the lid of the crate, which was nailed firmly in place.

Busts and their pedestals were wrapped securely in fabric and nestled two to a crate, and Marie's gory death masks were wrapped in groups of two or three. The three of them hefted each crate into stacks of four, to be loaded onto wagons later by hired helpers.

On the final day of packing up the exhibition, Marguerite was alone, sweeping debris from the gallery floor while Marie was out with Joseph finalizing travel arrangements. It had been her day of greatest exertion yet since starting her apprenticeship, and she was looking forward to finishing her work here so she could return to her lodgings for a blissful soak before packing her personal belongings.

She looked up at the sound of scuffling, and saw that Mr. Philipsthal had entered the exhibition. She rested the broom against the wall and took a quick inventory of herself. She was hopelessly dusty from her skirt hem to her hands and face, and in no condition to receive anyone, much less this kind man who had extended friendship to her.

He stepped farther into the gallery and gave her a small bow. His eyes did not have the strained, hunted look they had the last time she had seen him. "Mrs. Ashby, I am most fortunate to find you here alone."

"Good afternoon, Mr. Philipsthal. I'm afraid you must forgive my appearance. Today we packed up the last of the exhibition and I'm tidying up for our departure. I understand you will be joining us in August."

"Yes, it will be with great felicitations that I can be with you—the exhibition—in just a short while. My own show must finish up its commitment first."

"Of course. We will be delighted to see you in August."

"Is that truly so, Mrs. Ashby? Will you be happy to see me after an absence?"

"We will all be glad to see you, I'm sure, Mr. Philipsthal." Marguerite wiped a hand across her brow in exhaustion.

He stepped closer to take the hand that had just swept her face. He bent to kiss it and said, "My dear Mrs. Ashby, I was hoping that once we were all settled in Edinburgh that you might let me call upon you."

"I'm sorry, what did you say?"

"Er, I would like to pay court to you. You are a fine woman and could use a prosperous man to care for you."

Marguerite withdrew her hand.

"Mr. Philipsthal, I thought I spoke plainly when I said that I still grieve my husband."

"Yes, yes you did. I thought that perhaps with some passage of time you might reconsider."

"I've only been here a short time! Hardly enough time to give thought to any more than learning my trade, much less a remarriage."

"Has Madame Tussaud said unkind things about me to color your thoughts?"

"My employer's opinions have no bearing on my own, which is firm in the notion that I am of no desire to be paid court. I sincerely appreciate your good estimation of me, sir, but I beg you to respect my wishes."

Philipsthal's face fell, and Marguerite would have burst into laughter at his boyish look if she didn't know how earnest he was. He gave her another small bow.

"Very well. I see that for the moment your mind is made up. However, I will not leave you without impressing upon you how earnest my suit is. It is my hope that once we are in Edinburgh you may change your mind."

"I am deeply flattered by your attentions but remain resolved to maintain my widowed state."

Marguerite decided it was best not to tell Marie about Philipsthal's visit when she returned. The journey was to be stressful enough without a choleric episode from her employer.

PART TWO

Edinburgh

5

July 1803. They had to wait more than a week for the weather to clear up enough for their ship's departure for Edinburgh. The ten-day journey up the eastern coastline was rough and Marie fretted the entire time about her figures stowed away in the hold. Joseph was a good sailor, whiling away his time either pestering the crew with questions or sketching the vistas from the ship. Marguerite complimented his drawings, which pleased him enough to give her a rare smile.

As for Marguerite, she learned quickly that the sea was no place for her. The rolling of the waves unsettled her stomach for the entire passage and made her irritable. Soon even the slapping of water against the hull annoyed her and she retreated below deck for most of the voyage to sit and cover her ears with her hands. Three storms blew across them during three days of the voyage, and it was with great gratitude and prayers of thanks that they arrived in Edinburgh.

A chilly, misty rain was still with them upon entry into the Port of Leith. As they prepared to disembark, Marie said to Marguerite, "Hah! Did you see my Nini? The crew loved him. The captain wishes he had a child like him to train for the sea. Called him 'Little Horatio.' He's a good boy."

Joseph preened under his mother's praise and was so thoroughly delighted with the outcome of his voyage that he even deigned to take Marguerite's hand to help her down the ship's gangway. Marguerite and Joseph remained hand in hand on the dock, shivering under cloaks while Marie went to arrange the debarking of her crates. Within minutes Marie was back, her face a life mask of fury.

"I knew to be wary of Philipsthal! He's done it to me again. He's not to be trusted. I'll have it out with him." Hair was falling out of Marie's beautifully arranged coiffure, which she had taken great pains to maintain on the ship.

"Madame, what has happened?"

"He did not make the payment for transport of the figures. I owe eighteen pounds to have them removed from the ship."

"Do you have the full amount? I can post a letter to Claudette for the loan of the money, if it will help."

"No, I can make payment. Barely. But Philipsthal *promised* he would take care of it. Promised! He is a liar and a cheat."

"Perhaps something happened and he was distracted, which made him forget."

"Fah, he forgets nothing. Intentional."

The crates were finally transferred from the ship onto several wagons Marie hired, instructing the drivers to go to Barnard's Rooms on Thistle Street. This new location was just two blocks from the city's Assembly Rooms, making it convenient and accessible for those affluent patrons to visit the exhibition as well. Marie had earlier booked the exhibition at the Thistle Street address and arranged for quarters behind the salon for £2 per month. Exhausted from the sea crossing and the stress of getting the wax figures to their new location, they did little upon arriving at their new lodgings beyond greeting their new landlady, Mrs. Laurie, and tumbling into bed, soaked and exhausted.

The *Edinburgh Evening Courant* reported that Napoleon was in turn seizing and imprisoning British subjects in France, in response to Great Britain's declaration of war on France back in May.

Marie looked apprehensively at Marguerite. "I am a French national. Am I in danger by being here and plying my trade?"

It was the first time Marguerite had ever seen Marie express anything remotely akin to fear. Once again Marguerite's mind was flooded with the memories of how dangerous it could be to be

French—or even perceived as French—in England. She grasped the other woman's hand in sympathy but had no comforting word to offer. Was she herself safe from marauding bands of "patriots"?

But there was little time to think of it.

When they had finally unwrapped the figures at their new location, they discovered many breakages. Marguerite was relieved to see that the Duchess of York's wax portrait was undamaged, since it was her first real experience with the process. However, many others had smashed faces or broken limbs and digits. A figure of Martin Luther was ghoulishly impaled through his cheek by one of the padded dowels intended to keep him safe. Some of the crates had been crushed in transit and the figures were identifiable only by the clothing they wore.

Marie stood in the middle of the half-open crates, hands on hips as she surveyed the extensive wreckage.

"We will fix it all and be open in a week."

"In a week? Madame, the damage . . ." Marguerite hardly knew how to express her doubt.

"One week. We have to open so we can earn money. You want to learn about waxworking, this week you will learn much. Joseph will be our good helper, won't you, Nini?" She reached over to cup the face of her beloved boy, who was always in the midst of whatever was going on, although lately he was always present with a sketchbook in his hand.

"Yes, Maman," Joseph answered, without lifting his eye from his latest pencil drawing of their new salon.

So the two women worked from dawn to dusk each day, repairing gouged spots, freshening skin coloring, rearranging hair, and mending torn clothing.

Many of the aristocrats of the old French regime had emigrated to Scotland. Marie was determined to promote more of her French figures that had been popular back in Paris, so they worked doubly hard to get all of those figures ready for opening day.

In any available spare time, Marie taught Marguerite how to write advertisements for the exhibition and together they developed the handbill to be printed for their opening.

Freshly arrived from London
Dr. Curtius's
Grand European Cabinet of Figures
An Unrivaled Collection as Large as Life
Modeled from Life and Death
More than 50 Public Characters
Including
Exact Replicas of the late Royal Family of France
The Revolting Jean-Paul Marat in his Bath
England's New Enemy, First Consul Napoleon Bonaparte
and his wife, Josephine
The American Diplomat Benjamin Franklin
Open every day from ELEVEN in the morning
till TEN at night
Admittance: two shillings
Children under ten years, half price

Their new salon consisted of a small vestibule leading into two spacious rooms connected by an octagonal antechamber between them. Each room was approximately forty feet square with far lower ceilings than the exhibition in London. Marguerite estimated the windows at the end of each room to be about twelve feet tall. The walls and floors were decorated in muted golds and creams. The marble flooring had many chips and cracks throughout its surface, but they soon put that to rights by covering blemishes with scattered carpets and figures. Lighting was provided by randomly placed floor candelabra and wall sconces.

Marie much preferred this new arrangement over the one long gallery setup at the Lyceum, particularly since there was not a hint of gas lighting throughout the building. The biggest disadvantage was that they had no separate workroom, and would instead have to either work on new figures late at night, or leave unfinished compositions on the floor where customers parading through could see them. Their agreement with Mrs. Laurie provided for a cache of replacement beeswax candles per month, no small thing for an exhibit that needed to glow with varying levels of light nearly every moment of the day and night.

Marguerite and Joseph set up the admissions cabinet at the front entrance, located at one end of the first room. Marie had shipped this dark oak cabinet over from France with her. Its unique design enabled it to be collapsed for travel and quickly set back up for use. When fully assembled, it served as a three-sided booth behind which someone could stand and collect money from entering customers. Inside the booth was a small ledge where they stacked leaflets containing biographical sketches on the month's arrangement. This was a new addition to the exhibition experience. Because they now had to perform most of their sculpting work either in full view or late at night, they would no longer rearrange the exhibit on nearly a daily basis, but instead do so monthly. These exhibition catalogues gave customers information about the figures on display, and served as a souvenir of their visit. Marie's strict orders were that each customer could have one catalogue only, to ensure the exhibit did not waste any money.

A locking box was affixed beneath the ledge on wooden rails. When the box was rolled forward, money could be surreptitiously placed in it without customers noticing it. If the booth had to be unattended for any length of time, the box would be locked with a key that Marie kept around her neck, then rolled out of sight under the ledge.

From the exhausting sea voyage, to the hectic week of figure repair and set up prior to opening the exhibit, Marguerite had little time for much thought beyond the next task that lay in front of her. She rarely even stepped outside, since their rooms were located upstairs from the exhibit, and had little idea of the weather, much less of events in Edinburgh and the world beyond.

Marie was unfaltering, staying up into the wee hours after Marguerite escorted Joseph to his room, then collapsed into her own bed. After being in Edinburgh for a week, the apprentice had hardly had time to hang her dresses, much less send a note to Claudette letting her know of her arrival.

The exhibit opened as planned, a mere seven days after their arrival, on a windy day of brilliant sunshine. Joseph stood outside on the street to hawk the exhibit to passersby, while Marguerite and Marie worked inside the salon. Thanks to their well-placed advertisements, outside signage, and Joseph's winsome ways on the street, a steady stream of visitors attended the exhibition for most of the day. Those visitors who could read walked about with their pocket-sized catalogues up to their faces, devouring Marie's opinion-clouded "biographies" of famous people. Men and women alike stood before the figures of such luminaries as Robespierre, learning that he "affected to be called a sansculotte, but his clothes were always chosen with taste and his hair was constantly dressed and powdered with a precision that bordered on foppery."

Most of Marie's biographies of her figures were more commentary on fashion and style, versus any serious examination of the individuals' motives or activities in life. Marguerite attempted to persuade Marie to write more extensively about a given figure's life events, but was firmly rebuffed by her mentor.

"It's best not to comment on what they have done. It could be misinterpreted. Leads to great troubles for us."

"But do people really care just for what someone wears or how he walked down the street?"

"My dear, that is nearly *all* they care about."

Marie was right. Their opening day saw many French émigrés huddled around the figures of people they had known, commenting on the exactness of their costume.

An elderly, hunched woman pointed up, motioning to her equally aged friend. "*Non*, the du Barry never wore such brown colors. And she always had diamonds in her ears. Where are the diamonds?"

"Maybe they are still in France."

"I still think she should be wearing diamonds."

"Well, she doesn't need them now where she is." The friend drew a meaningful line across her own neck. They both tittered at the macabre joke.

Infamous figures of revolutionary France—Marat, Mirabeau, Robespierre, Charlotte Corday—mingled with European royalty, American statesmen, and infamous criminals. The effect was a bit random, as there had not been time in a week to set up sophisticated tableaux in which to set the figures. But the exhibition's guests loved the unique entertainment it provided.

Some visitors snapped their fingers in front of the figures' faces, trying to get a reaction, while others stood still for quick sketches drawn out by Joseph after he had tired of hawking the exhibition on the street. Marie heartily approved of Joseph's enterprise, which was bringing in an additional shilling per drawing.

Marie played pranks on some of the visiting children, standing utterly still in a corner, then reaching her arms out and growling at them, to their utter terror and delight.

Marguerite spent most of the day taking admissions and answering questions from patrons who had never seen such a spectacle as a cabinet of wax figures. Many of the visitors wanted to meet Dr. Curtius. Both men and women alike refused to believe that the figures were mostly made by Dr. Curtius's niece. One man even suggested that perhaps the niece had stolen them from her uncle and then set up an illegal exhibition in Edinburgh.

Overall, though, visitors left the salon bubbling with excitement and pleasure. Although to Marguerite the first day's opening was a great success, with staggered throngs throughout the day, Marie was fretting about the day's receipts when they closed the door at ten o'clock at the end of the first week.

"Not enough," she declared as her hand brushed the last of the coins she was counting back into the locking box.

"How much did we realize, madame?" Marguerite asked.

"Only ten guineas. We must have more, much more. We will have to create something more thrilling so that we can charge more."

"In London you created a curtained-off area for the more grotesque pieces. Perhaps we should do that here. We could use the back room for it, and set up separate admission in the antechamber."

Marie's eyes glowed. "Ah, my apprentice is shrewd. My dear Mrs. Ashby, you will one day be a sharp and clever businesswoman. Tomorrow we will start setting up a separate room for the more unseemly figures, only this time much better than what we had in London."

So Britain had declared war on France three months ago, the little Corsican Bonaparte now threatened invasion, and the citizenry of Britain was tense with expectation and fear. An exhibition hall of gruesome visages might be exactly what the public needed as an ironic antidote to its pent-up fear and worry.

The Separate Room was an immediate success. The two women and young boy worked long hours into the night, sleeping in small snatches, to thoroughly rearrange the exhibit to provide a chilling yet electrifying element to the show. Carpenters were hired to set up another, smaller admissions booth in the antechamber between the two salon rooms and to create props and settings for the new room. All of the revolutionary figures, as well as those of infamous criminals and their victims, were moved into the second salon and set up in several relevant settings. The heads of Marie Antoinette, Louis XVI, the Princesse de Lamballe, and Robespierre were placed on tall columns in a semicircle around the figure of Jean-Jacques Rousseau, whose writings were instrumental in his country's slide into revolutionary fervor. Shrouds of black draped the wall behind these figures.

Another tableau had Colonel Despard on a scaffold, arms tied behind his back as he stared at a hanging noose. Marguerite worked very reluctantly on that display, grateful that most of the work was done by the carpenters in the construction of the scaffold.

Initially exhausted and confused by the continual movement and rearrangement of figures in London, Marguerite now understood Marie's genius in doing so, as the exhibition stayed perpetually new and fresh. A customer could visit one week, return the following week and be able to tell his friends, "It's an entirely new show." Therefore, many customers came more than once for novelty, and some even made it a regular entertainment.

As her confusion lessened, so did her weariness. Days on end of moving figures by lifting them onto small wheeled carts and moving them to their new settings had developed her arm strength in a way that doll carving never could. This work, combined with the packing and unpacking of the precious characters, helped develop a fortitude Marguerite had no idea she could possess. Her skin regained its cheerful bloom and she found herself sleeping dreamlessly at night.

The only thing that still confused Marguerite was the state of Marie's finances. Her mentor groused continuously about the show's lack of capital. But how could this be? The crowds were plentiful, and Marguerite ended up with a full box of coins at the end of each day since admission was now double what it had been in London. Many of the supplies used were similar to dollmaking—paints, brushes, glues, carving tools—and she therefore knew that those costs could not be exceeding more than a pound or two per week. She received very little money as an apprentice—only pocket money, really—and workmen were hired on an as-needed basis. So how could the show possibly not be turning a profit?

Marguerite attempted to ask about it one evening as they applied touch-up paint to some of the figures. The constant movement to and fro in the rooms, combined with the customers fingering and brushing up against them, meant that they were in constant need of repair. Marguerite approached the subject as casually as possible while darkening the eyebrows of King John.

"Madame, how is the show faring this week? Have we made a good profit?" She kept her eyes trained on what she was doing, not daring to look Marie in the face with such an audacious question.

But Marie was not offended. "The take has been good this week. Twenty guineas. Still not enough for a profit."

"But, madame, the rental for the salon and our lodgings is only two pounds per month. Surely it does not cost much more for maintenance and creation of the figures?"

Marie put down the tools she was working with and turned to face her apprentice. Marguerite did likewise, a knot forming in her stomach. Had she completely overstepped her bounds? Would she be sent back to Claudette in disgrace?

"I can see that I teach you some things, but I do not teach you enough. Yet, the financial problems are my own doing and not for you to worry over. The exhibition has other . . . debts . . . that are not resolved, and I don't know that I can ever get them settled. I may never be successful, and may have to return to Paris a failure.

Then I will have been separated from the rest of my family for nothing. Nothing. And I will have also failed my delightful apprentice."

It was the most complete, unguarded speech Marie had ever made in Marguerite's presence.

"Oh, madame, whatever is wrong, I can help you. I had much experience with running the financial aspects of the Laurent Fashion Doll Shop, and I could assist—"

"No, Mrs. Ashby. The exhibition's problems have nothing to do with the daily management of the show. I make other mistakes, and I must live with them. Not for your worry."

But Marguerite did worry. What had happened to put the show, and Marie, near ruin?

6

London, Ash House, August 1803. "Mother, I'm a bit bored." Nathaniel Ashby tipped back the glass of sweet ruby liquid and drank the contents in two long swallows.

"My son, you'll develop gout if you continue drinking so much port. Just like Mr. Pitt."

"The prime minister likes port as well?" Nathaniel straightened up in his dining room chair. "Perhaps I should send him a bottle of the 1775 port I picked up from Croft's. Maybe that would ensure a summons to see him. Wouldn't it be grand to do some service on behalf of the Crown?"

Nathaniel's life had taken a decidedly tedious turn since his affair with Lydia Brown, the housemaid, had ended. The girl had wanted him to declare himself for her. Patent nonsense. So he had given her a bottle of perfume, a swat on the rear, and told her to find a footman to marry. Lydia cried tempestuously for several days, out of his mother's earshot but always in his full view. Sensing his weariness with it all, she had secured another posting elsewhere before Maude got wind of their affair and dismissed her without a reference.

He patted his sated belly contentedly. Mother really did make things easy for him, didn't she? But with no mistress at present, and his hope of an easy marriage with his former sister-in-law having come to nothing, he felt cagey and restless. He needed something to excite him. Some kind of invigorating exploit. An invitation to meet with England's prime minister would be very stimulating. Was Pitt a Tory or a Whig? Well, no matter. Fine liquor could be appreciated by a man of either party.

"Son, Mr. Pitt isn't in office anymore since his bickering with the king, remember? It's Mr. Addington now, although with his foolishness over the Treaty of Amiens—we wouldn't be at war had he not negotiated so badly—no doubt Pitt will build a coalition and throw him out. What sort of service do you mean, anyway?"

"Hmm?" Nathaniel had quit listening to his mother. Politics tired him. Who cared about affairs of state? Divisions in Parliament, social unrest, the devaluation of currency—how tiresome it all was. No adventure or glory in it. What would be stimulating would be a secret assignment. Ferret out French spies or something. As long as it wasn't too dangerous. Maybe he could sample a French doxy along the way. Didn't the king hand out titles for that kind of service?

"Pitt's out? Pity. Do you know if Mr. Addington enjoys port?"

An excited rapping on the door startled Marguerite as she was writing a letter to Claudette. Marie darted in, waving a letter.

"I have a nice invitation to the castle. You come with me."

"To the castle? Do you mean Edinburgh Castle? Have we done something wrong?" Marguerite had caught glimpses of the castle's commanding presence atop the hill of volcanic rock behind the Assembly Rooms. Local visitors had told her that the twelfth-century fortress was still used as a prison, having last been used to house Americans in their war of rebellion, and was now seeing reuse as the war with France was gaining a footing. Other buildings inside the castle's walls included a powder magazine, a barracks, and a residence for the castle's governor.

"No, nothing's wrong. Something's right. The governor of the castle visited here recently and liked the exhibition. He has invited me for a supper at the castle, and I would like to take you. You are a good girl and you work so hard."

"Madame, I would be honored to attend supper with you and the governor."

And so it was settled. Marguerite wore the same frock she had chosen for her supper with Mr. Philipsthal back in London. Having been sequestered inside the salon almost constantly since her arrival, she wasn't sure if it was fashionable in Edinburgh or not. But there was no time to shop for fripperies. Marie dressed in a dark green gown with a matching long-sleeved jacket. She wore no jewelry and a very simple comb with trailing ribbons. Yet her hair was in its usual perfect arrangement.

The governor, Sir Alexander Hope, had arranged for a carriage to pick them up and bring them the short distance to the castle. Marguerite realized the wisdom of this plan as the horses began straining up the steep grade from the end of the esplanade into the forbidding castle. A walk in her brocaded mules would have surely resulted in a broken heel, if not an injury to her legs, and the nippy wet weather that had been present since their arrival would have made the walk that much more unpleasant.

Their carriage lumbered patiently up the cobblestone street and through the arched opening in the Lower Ward gatehouse. The horse snuffled his relief when brought to a stop before the Governor's House, where Sir Alexander greeted them personally. He escorted them quickly through the rain and into his personal quarters to sit before a blazing fire and warm themselves with aperitifs before supper.

Sir Alexander was an unmarried man about thirty years of age, tall and gaunt. His left sleeve was pinned across his chest, and he told them proudly that he had lost his arm eight years earlier in the Battle of Buren in Holland, during the fight against French occupation. "So now I've something in common with Lord Nelson, who also sports a stump like mine."

After the battle, Sir Alexander had taken over the running of Edinburgh Castle in 1798.

He was congenial, soft-spoken for a hardened man of war, and seemed to have no other purpose in inviting them to supper other than to pass time. Once the women were sufficiently warmed, the governor ushered them into his small but elegant dining room, where another fire crackled reassuringly at one end of the room. The rectangular mahogany dining table was awash in candles and pewter plate, as was the sideboard on the long wall behind it. It was surprisingly stylish for a military residence.

Marguerite was surprised to see another couple and a man in a naval uniform already present in the dining room. Marie had not said there were to be other guests. She glanced over and saw that Marie was as perplexed as she was.

"Monsieur and Madame Fournier, may I present to you Madame Tussaud, late of London? She is the proprietress of the new wax cabinet on Thistle Street that I mentioned to you. And this is her associate, Mrs. Ashby."

"*Enchanté, mesdames,*" said Monsieur Fournier, a portly, balding man with an equally rotund wife. They stood smiling together like two blueberries beaming in a dish of cream. "Madame Tussaud, I remember hearing of your salon with Dr. Curtius before the . . . unpleasantness . . . that forced our retirement to Scotland. How fortuitous for us to meet up with such a remarkable compatriot."

His wife chimed in. "I told Monsieur Fournier that we must come to your salon as soon as possible. I hear you have a room devoted to France's recent troubles." Madame Fournier was dressed in an unfortunate blend of current and outmoded fashion, with her empire-waist dress of deep yellow and accompanying Indian shawl embroidered in reds and blues, clashing in an almost blinding spectacle with her tall black hat sprouting several ostrich and peacock feathers. Her large breasts were stuffed inhospitably inside her dress and threatened to make an unwelcome appearance at any moment. Yet she was friendly and sweet tempered, and this overshadowed her regrettable selection of clothing.

"Yes, madame, it is our Separate Room."

"Have you a figure of the Princesse de Lamballe? I never did see her, but after the atrocities committed upon her, I am curious now as to what she looked like."

Marguerite felt Marie stiffen next to her. Both Marie and Claudette were melancholy whenever her name was mentioned. "Yes, I have a figure of her I made from memory."

The governor interrupted their discussion. "And, my dear ladies, this is Lieutenant Hastings of the Royal Navy, in service under no less than Lord Nelson himself."

Lieutenant Hastings bowed to them both. He was nearly six feet tall, and what Marguerite might have called "well made" was she so inclined to express any interest. His uniform started with a cream waistcoat and breeches and was overlayed with a crisp, dark blue overcoat. The brass buttons on his coat shone from polishing, suggesting that he took more care with his uniform than his hair, which was dark and unruly and of its own mind to disengage itself from its queue. The lieutenant seemed not to notice his incongruous state.

"Lieutenant Hastings is in Edinburgh for a short time," the governor explained. "As another lonely bachelor, I thought he might find good company here with us this evening."

Hastings barely acknowledged Hope's comment with other than a quick scowl. The governor invited them all to sit down. Abandoning the formality of seating himself at the head, he pulled out a chair for Marie to his right on one side of the table. Lieutenant Hastings sat next to Marie, with Marguerite across from him and the Fourniers next to her.

The staff tending to them seemed to be a blend of regular household servants and sailors, but food and wine flowed freely and efficiently.

"Madame Tussaud," Hope began, "I thoroughly enjoyed my visit to your salon. Why did you choose Edinburgh for your highly amusing exhibit?"

"I have no wish to offend the Scots, but there are many French émigrés here, and they like to see figures of those they once knew."

"Such as the princesse," said Madame Fournier. She patted her husband's arm, causing him to splatter the soup he had just ladled into his spoon. "Monsieur, we simply must get down to Madame Tussaud's exhibition right away. Let's go tomorrow. I need to see the modiste about the bonnets I ordered and we can stop there afterwards."

Her husband grunted his assent and returned to his bowl.

"No offense is taken," Sir Alexander said. "We are all friends here. In fact, I invited the Fourniers in hopes that they might offer you friendship and a comforting link to the past while you are here. In fact, how long will we have the pleasure of your company, madame?"

Marie shrugged. "For the rest of this year. If business is good."

"Splendid." Sir Alexander speared a piece of fish with gusto. Swallowing, he said, "We must have you to the castle as often as possible."

"The exhibit is very busy. Opens early and stays open late."

Marguerite saw that their host was wounded by Marie's lukewarm response. *She is a shrewd and careful business manager, but she is too dismissive of anything that might veer her mind from the exhibition.*

"Governor," Marguerite said, "I'm sure that in every available free moment we would be delighted to attend more suppers at your residence." She ignored Marie's open-mouthed astonishment at her assertive behavior.

"Marvelous. Yes. Next week I am hosting a small dance in honor of Lieutenant Hastings's arrival here. It will give some of my officers an opportunity to meet eligible young ladies of Edinburgh. It would be a great boost to our guest list to have you here, Madame Tussaud."

Before Marie could utter the no that Marguerite was sure would follow her frown, she jumped in. "Of course, Governor. Madame and I could not think of a better way to spend an evening. I am of course still in mourning, and she is married, so there will be no dancing for us, but we should very much enjoy fine company and music."

"Married? You are married?" he asked Marie directly.

"Yes. François lives back in Paris with our other son. My son Joseph is here with me."

"Oh. I did not realize this. You wear no ring."

"Waxworking is hard to do with jewelry on hands. I forget to put it on at other times."

"But Mrs. Ashby wears her ring still."

"She misses her husband too much. But she's a good woman, a good apprentice to me."

I miss my husband too much? Truly, I thought I was getting on with the business of life. My days are so full with the exhibition that I hardly have time to breathe. Why does she say this?

Marguerite looked up to find Lieutenant Hastings staring at her curiously. *Was I thinking my thoughts aloud just now?*

The lieutenant placed his fork down carefully, revealing a significant mass of scarred tissue on the top of his left hand, which extended down the side of his pinky. The scar looked old. Whatever had happened resulted in the scarred finger being rendered useless, for it hung limply on his hand. "Mrs. Ashby, might I inquire as to your background? How did you come to be in the employ of Madame Tussaud in such an unusual profession?"

"I was widowed earlier this year, and chose to give up my previous profession to start a new life."

"And what were you doing before?"

"I was a dollmaker."

"Indeed?" Lieutenant Hastings leaned forward. "And how did you fare in such an enterprise?"

"We have the royal warrant."

"Have? I thought you said you abandoned your profession?"

"Yes, but my aunt started the shop and still sees to it."

"Hmm. Very well." Lieutenant Hastings returned to his meal.

Why do I have the feeling that he disapproves of me?

"And you, Lieutenant, how does your profession bring you to Edinburgh?"

"I serve at Lord Nelson's pleasure. I am investigating whether Edinburgh's port is secure against any potential invasion from Bonaparte. Sir Alexander is graciously offering men to help with any fortifications that might be needed."

"I see. Do you think we are in danger?"

"Lord Nelson does, and I am loyal to my commanding officer. In truth, though, Bonaparte's offer of Louisiana to America tells me he suffers greatly from a lack of funds, and his army will devour the proposed eighty million francs quickly. It is my hope that Jefferson's senate does not agree to the sale."

The rest of the table focused in on their conversation.

"Hastings, do you think that Nelson will call on you to investigate the fortifications going on at Boulogne next?" Sir Alexander asked.

"At *Boulogne?*" Madame Fournier squeaked. "An invasion must be imminent."

Hastings's reply was calm and measured. "Bonaparte is no match for the Royal Navy, madame. There is no cause for concern as of yet."

"Lieutenant," said Monsieur Fournier, "do you realize that we are in the terrible predicament of praying for the destruction of the French army before it invades, yet not wanting any harm to come to our fellow Frenchmen?"

"Yes, monsieur, I am aware of the irony of the situation here in Edinburgh. Obviously, England's priority will be the destruction of France's military might."

"How awful for us," his wife chimed in. "So much bloodshed already and now more to come. Are we safe here? Should we go elsewhere? Maybe to America?"

"Madame Fournier," said Sir Alexander. "I will do all in my power to make sure you are safe in Edinburgh, and Lord Nelson—with Lieutenant Hastings's assistance, of course—is working diligently to ensure the waters are safe. I'm sure there is nothing to fear."

"I'm just afraid we'll never be able to go home again."

"Courage, madame, we must all have courage. In the meantime, we should look forward to a little gaiety. Madame Tussaud, Mrs. Ashby, I will send a carriage for you next Saturday evening."

Marguerite jumped in before her employer could respond. "That is very generous of you, sir. We will await our return with pleasure."

"We look forward to seeing you again, too, don't we?" Madame Fournier tapped her husband's arm again, although this time his hand held no utensil, thus avoiding more gastronomic calamity.

"*Oui*, it will be our pleasure."

Lieutenant Hastings remained silent on this, seeming to have no opinion on the good fortune of the waxworkers' return for the dance.

After an offering of brandy and port, Marie stood in a silent announcement that she was ready to leave. They said their goodbyes quickly in a flurry of affection from the Fourniers. The lieutenant stood to one side, giving them a mere hint of a bow in farewell.

About halfway back to Thistle Street, Marguerite broke the silence inside Hope's carriage. "You were quiet tonight, madame. Was anything wrong?"

"No, nothing wrong, just thinking."

"What were your thoughts?"

"I wonder how a war will affect the exhibition."

7

August 10, 1803
Hevington

My dearest Marguerite,

What remarkable adventures you are having. I am breathless just to hear of them. Before I forget, William sends his love, and Little Bitty says she is naming a new kitten for you. Have I told you that that dratted mangy cat she found was a female? Kittens everywhere! It takes all my energy to keep Cicero from picking them up in his slobbery mouth and prancing about like he has single-handedly captured Bonaparte. Did I mention Cicero to you? Our bullmastiff? I'm so busy that sometimes I forget what I've said just a few moments ago. Remembering what I've written in letters is nearly impossible.

So you say Marie plans to start creating tableaux in which to set her wax figures? That sounds brilliant, really, creating scenes that put her figures in context. When you return to London again (you will return to London again soon, won't you?) we will make a special trip in to see all of your handiwork. I don't think I can spare the time right now for a journey to Edinburgh.

The doll shop is productive again. Thank heavens for Agnes and Roger, who keep things well in hand while I am home at Hevington. And for my darling William, who suffers gallantly as a courier back and forth to the shop, the bank, and Hevington. I can hardly believe how my life has been transformed over these past dozen years from my troubles in France to lady of the house.

But you, my dear, have even greater opportunities for success. Take advantage of them. And think about what I said when we were last together. You shouldn't be alone.

I send you a thousand kisses and my best wishes for you and Marie.

I do need to remember to write to her.

Affectionately,

Claudette

The day before the scheduled ball at Edinburgh Castle, Marie pulled Marguerite aside.

"I am going to teach you something new. Today you will learn how I find and buy supplies."

And so while Joseph stayed in the gallery entertaining guests, Marie led Marguerite back to her rooms to review her ordering logs.

Marie's quarters were hardly larger than Marguerite's, and a trundle for Joseph took up additional room. Everything was neat, though, other than her desk, which had several piles of letters, forms, and other documents on it. Marie pulled up a second chair to the desk, and addressed each stack of paper.

"Here are letters to suppliers. I hand copy each one to remember what I have ordered. I get paint cakes from Mr. Reeves in London. Glass is custom-made for me in Italy, but Bonaparte's occupation means I have to be careful. Fabrics and trims I always shop for locally. Always look for best price at draper shops. They get plenty of advertisement when their materials hang on our figures. Good, clean wax is always hard to find and is expensive to ship. Difficult clothing is sent out to seamstresses. One has to make good judgments about when to do it, as seamstresses are expensive."

"What is this book?" Marguerite tapped a worn leather journal lying by itself on the corner of the desk nearest her.

"*Non,* not for you. Account book, I manage. The exhibition's finances are too precarious for anyone besides me to supervise."

"Of course." Marguerite obediently removed her hand from the forbidden book.

For the next hour she learned more about the internal operations of the wax exhibit, from how to contract for salon space without seeing it first, to managing the transport of the exhibition to new locations. Marguerite's head became full near to the point of a headache.

Marie also shared with her the concerns she had for her salon back in Paris, which she feared was being badly run by her husband in her absence.

"François has no head for business. Always he is investing in dubious ventures." Marie shook her perfectly coiffed curls. "Always he is asking me to send him money. Thinks I hide money from him. I say no, I hide nothing, but he must make success of salon at boulevard du Temple. Must work hard. Must be example for our boy Francis."

"You have another son? You've never mentioned him before."

"Yes, he is younger than Nini. Was too young to come here with me two years ago. I regret this. Wish I had him here with me, too."

"I'm sure you wish your husband was here, too."

"Eh." Marie shrugged her shoulders. "Enough foolish talk. Mrs. Ashby, you look pale. A headache? We finish now. Next week I teach you how to plan a tableau. I think Nini would like to learn that, too."

Sir Alexander was as good as his word and sent around another carriage to fetch the two women at the appointed time on Saturday evening.

After a long internal struggle, Marguerite decided to leave her wedding ring behind. She had no desire to meet any gentlemen, so she could not fathom her own behavior. Nevertheless, the band stayed on her dressing table. She wore a Grecian-style gown of shimmering copper. With some difficulty she tied up her mass of coiled hair with a matching length of material. She decided that she could pass for the wife of an ancient senator.

Marie's hair was, as usual, perfect, and topped off with a petite, flat-topped lavender hat Marguerite had not seen before. Marie's dress, high-waisted and trimmed with pink flowers, was also unfamiliar. Had Marie gone shopping for this event?

As soon as they arrived at the bustling front entrance of the castle, Marguerite knew that Marie had been right to hesitate over coming. She was not ready for this sort of socializing. Not yet.

Why did I leave my ring in my room?

The castle's banquet hall was populated with a mix of French aristocrats from the ancien régime, soldiers from the castle, and important local Scotsmen to whom Sir Alexander had extended an invitation. The Fourniers were also there, chatting up their fellow refugees. The musicians were just concluding a set as they walked in, so the dancing had stopped and guests were milling about in groups.

Accepting a cup of punch from her host, Marguerite tried to blend into the Chinese wallpaper panels by herself as Marie was whisked away by their host for private conversation.

She stood leaning against the wall, debating whether to approach the Fourniers, when she was disturbed by a gentle throat-clearing next to her.

"Mrs. Ashby, I see you and Madame Tussaud have joined Sir Alexander's little . . . gathering."

"Lieutenant Hastings, good evening. Have you been here long?"

"Too long. These soirées are interminable bores."

"Why, Lieutenant, if I did not know of your youth, I might accuse you of being an old curmudgeon. Aren't you supposed to be finding an eligible young woman here tonight?"

"I'm too busy for such trifles, Mrs. Ashby. We are at war with France, in case you haven't read the newspapers."

Marguerite's fingers clenched around her punch vessel. Had she not just been standing here minding her own business? What a starched neck the man was.

"Thank you, Lieutenant Hastings, for your well-articulated synopsis of our political situation. I'm sure every Frenchman in the room right now is *well aware* that France intends to invade England, including my employer, Marie *Tussaud*. Perhaps you'd care to expand on your other obvious views, such as how pirates have disrupted trade in the Caribbean."

Hastings reddened. "I beg your pardon. I did not mean to be so impolite. My remarks were well-intentioned, if clearly misconstrued. I am not an ogre, Mrs. Ashby, and do have some sympathy for the displaced French people among us. I do not relish the task that lies before me."

"What task is that? You mean ensuring the fortification of Edinburgh?"

"Yes, among other things."

"What other things?"

He ignored her question. "May I secure you another cup of punch?"

"Yes, thank you." Marguerite waited while he took her drained cup with a slight bow and went to fetch a fresh one. *What a curious creature,* she thought, watching him. *Rather unintentionally rude, but actually a kind sort of gentleman. Decent. Might be a good match for a woman who can tolerate long absences from a seafaring husband who possesses only the barest tad of humor.*

He returned with her punch.

"How long will you be in Edinburgh?" she asked.

"Things are going well. I suspect I will be finished in a fortnight or so. What of you? Your exhibition travels, doesn't it?"

"Yes. Thus far it has been quite successful in Edinburgh, so I am sure Madame Tussaud will wish to stay as long as possible."

"And so we both wander Great Britain in service to our professions. I've not seen the exhibit yet, although the governor raves about it. Quite incessantly, I must say. Perhaps I'll come to visit before my departure."

"We are open most days from eleven o'clock until ten o'clock in the evening. You may find our Separate Room a bit thrilling."

"Undoubtedly. If you will excuse me, Mrs. Ashby, I'm afraid I have to pay my regards to others. May I escort you to Madame Tussaud?"

And, without waiting for a reply, he offered his arm to her and walked her to where Marie was cornered by the governor's enthusiastic discussion of the city's cultural offerings.

To Marguerite's surprise, Hastings gave her a nearly imperceptible wink and said lightly, "I believe Madame requires your assistance."

Marguerite did not see Lieutenant Hastings the remainder of the evening. She soon forgot about him in her quest to extricate Marie from Sir Alexander's ardent clutches.

But she remembered Hastings a few weeks later, upon hearing from their now frequent visitor, Sir Alexander, of the lieutenant's looming departure from Edinburgh for Folkestone to inspect its port fortifications across from Boulogne.

Lieutenant Hastings had never bothered to visit the salon.

Marguerite shivered as she entered the warmth of Barnard's Rooms after shopping for some stationery for a letter she wished to write to Claudette. Did the cold rain never cease in this city?

"A letter for you, Mrs. Ashby." Mrs. Laurie held out the wrinkled, smudged, well-traveled parchment as Marguerite came through the front door.

Marguerite did not recognize the handwriting. She undid her hat as she climbed the stairs to her room, puzzling over who would be writing to her besides Aunt Claudette.

She hung up her damp hat and cloak and crossed over to her small writing desk under the room's only window.

Lyceum Theatre, London
August 25, 1803

Dear Mrs. Ashby,

Although I have sent a letter to Madame Tussaud separately notifying her of my plans, I flatter myself—perhaps unduly—that you might welcome a direct correspondence from me regarding my arrival.

My ship departs London on August 31, with an expected arrival about seven days hence. My Phantasmagoria show will be situated in the Corri Rooms next door to the wax exhibition.

I expect that my show will be a beneficial addition to yours, and that the Edinburgh audiences will be awed by our combination of entertainments.

Having never been to Edinburgh before, or Scotland for that matter, it is my great hope that you will accompany me for an afternoon as I tour the city to get my bearings.

Until my arrival I remain—

Your devoted friend,

Paul de Philipsthal

Marguerite folded the letter slowly. *I suppose there can be no harm in that.*

As the two women were straightening up the Separate Room the following evening after closing, Marie broached the topic after first kissing Joseph good night and sending him to their rooms.

"Mr. Philipsthal plans to join us in a fortnight," she said as she worked Marie Antoinette's wig in her hands to separate its curls.

"Yes, I know. I have had my own letter from him."

"*Pardon?*" Marie dropped the wig to the floor and stared at her. "Why does he write to you?"

Marguerite continued at her own task, using a soft brush to remove accumulated lint and dust from the folds of the French queen's pale yellow gown.

"Mr. Philipsthal wished me to know personally of his arrival. He asked if I would assist him in learning the city's landmarks."

"What else does he want from you?"

"Nothing, as far as I can tell. He knows I do not welcome any advances and just seeks my friendship."

"Hah! Philipsthal never seeks the simple thing. Always he wants more. I tell my husband in my letters about him. He says I should abandon Philipsthal and England and go back to France, but I think one day I'll make a successful show here. It is too dangerous to go back to France anyway."

Marguerite seized the opportunity.

"Madame, what is the source of your animosity toward Mr. Philipsthal? He has always been very kind to me and seems to want both our shows to thrive."

"He is but a wolf. A wolf who devours innocent sheep in his path. He has devoured me and he will come after you if you allow it. You must stay away from him. Promise me!"

"I cannot promise such a thing until you tell me what his great sin is."

But Marie would say no more. She pressed her lips in a thin line, picked up the fallen wig, and returned to her work.

Mr. Philipsthal arrived on his scheduled day, one of rare sunshine yet still cool temperature, but without his show trunks and cases. After packing up all his equipment and settling bills with the Lyceum's owner and his temporary workers, he had entrusted an agent with the drayage and loading of the paraphernalia onto the ship. The agent had stowed it all aboard the wrong ship, a vessel headed for Inverness, and it would be another week before it returned.

"Therefore I am free to do your bidding, dear ladies, although first I must insist on an escorted tour of this delightful little town." He looked meaningfully at Marguerite. Marie caught his look and sent her own message to her protégé through a small shake of her head.

"Madame, may I persuade you to release Mrs. Ashby a few hours early today so she can squire me about?" Philipsthal's question was both pleading and softly demanding at the same time.

In response, Madame Tussaud stalked off toward the back of the exhibit.

Philipsthal offered Marguerite his arm. "I believe we have received as much acquiescence as can be hoped for."

Marguerite took the proffered arm. *What kind of strange relationship is this? Had Madame been involved in an illicit affair with him and been jilted? Why so much ill feeling?*

Inside their hired open carriage, Marguerite suggested that they take Princes Street around the perimeter of Edinburgh Castle and travel downhill on High Street toward the Palace of Holyroodhouse.

As the castle's looming presence rose before them, she told Mr. Philipsthal of their visit with the governor and subsequent attendance at a ball.

"Was the governor interested in backing the show at all?" Philipsthal asked her as they rounded the southwest corner of the castle and proceeded onto Market Street.

"I believe he was more interested in Marie herself than her show." Marguerite waited for his reaction, but his face was bland.

Would neither of these two people let her know what secret history lay between them?

Their carriage continued downhill on High Street, past St. Giles' Cathedral with its prominent tower, the old parliament building built by King Charles I, a myriad of thriving churches, candlemakers, booksellers, banks, and drapers, and all manner of taverns and inns. As they neared a pasty seller whose stand was nearly blocking their path, Philipsthal called for the driver to stop. He exited the carriage gracefully despite his towering frame, and returned moments later with three steaming, crescent-shaped, meat-filled pies, one of which he handed to a surprised and grateful driver.

Marguerite held the warm crust in her hands as they continued on, savoring its doughy aroma before taking a bite. The interior was stuffed with minced lamb, potatoes, mint, and spices. She had never tasted meat quite so savory. She did not speak again until she had finished her entire pie, and was mortified to find crumbs scattered all over her lap. Mr. Philipsthal pretended not to notice as she swept the litter to the floor of the carriage, her only possible course of action.

"Thank you, Mr. Philipsthal. It would seem the Scots have mastered lamb cookery to the point that it is impossible to talk until one has gobbled down whatever dish has been presented."

"Your pleasure is my greatest happiness," he said. "And now it looks like we are coming upon the palace."

Marguerite had not yet seen Holyroodhouse for herself. Whereas the castle grounds soared imposingly up in the air on their bed of ancient volcanic rock, dominating the skyline like a colossal, confused phoenix with its jumble of stone buildings inside ancient walls, the palace was its natural opposite. Situated in nearly a direct line about a mile down the hill from the castle, it lay on flat, bucolic grounds. The palace was shaped as a square surrounding a courtyard, with an enormous gatehouse containing three turrets at either corner of the front side facing the street. Each turret was full of arrow slits, a reminder of days gone by when the Scottish monarch first protected the Crown against usurpers of the throne, and later as a defense against the country's own internal revolts. And now it was the home of the exiled Charles-Philippe, Comte d'Artois and second in line to the nearly defunct Bourbon line, along with his longtime paramour, Louise de Polastron. King George III had granted apartments inside the palace to him as a residence. Rumors of the comte had reached Marguerite's ears at the exhibition. It was said that Charles-Philippe, seriously in debt and miserable in exile, stayed mostly within the palace's walls, gambling at cards with Louise and his entourage, and only ventured out to ride on Sundays, since Scottish law forbade the arrest of debtors on the Lord's day.

To the south of the palace lay Holyrood Park, once used for royal hunting and now just an array of pleasure grounds, hills, lochs, and ridges. They ventured down the road nearest the palace, which surrounded the gardens. Other visitors did the same and this perimeter road sometimes became congested and impassable.

Many faded aristocrats, no doubt more refugees from the revolution in France, strolled the lavish gardens pretending they were still commanding attention at Versailles.

After the full two hours it took to circle the palace gardens, Philipsthal instructed the driver to return to Barnard's Rooms. This time the driver took a different route that was on less of a direct incline back up in the direction of the castle. They instead drove past the fashionably grand façades of the New Town area surrounding Barnard's Rooms.

Marguerite checked the watch pinned to her bodice as their driver pulled up to their destination. "I believe I have been gone for longer than Madame Tussaud might have liked. I must hurry back in."

Philipsthal exited the carriage, paid the driver, and offered a hand to help Marguerite down.

"Thank you, Mrs. Ashby, for your delightful company. Our ride together was quite refreshing." He still held her hand.

"It was no trouble, Mr. Philipsthal. I value our friendship." She dislodged her captured palm and smiled. "I hope you like what you have seen of Edinburgh. But now I must be back to work."

She walked off quickly to avoid further conversation and just barely caught him saying, "Please, call me Paul."

The ride left Marguerite even more puzzled. Mr. Philipsthal seemed a perfectly pleasant man and of no threat to anyone. Yet Marie was a shrewd, calculating businesswoman. If she was leery of someone, was it not wise to heed her judgment?

Philipsthal's show trunks had been quickly transferred to another ship bound for Edinburgh, and with the help of several hired hands he was ready for his Phantasmagoria show's opening on September 20.

Marie held out the newspaper page containing his advertisement over a breakfast of biscuits, jams, and melon with fresh cream.

"He hires too many people. No eye on profit."

Marguerite glanced at the advertisement without taking it, her hands full with the buttering of bread.

"I suppose the investment in labor helped him get his show started sooner."

"Not an investment. He's lazy. Lets everyone else do the work for him. Humph." Marie took the paper back, crumpled it, and tossed it into the small fireplace in Mrs. Laurie's dining room. The previous night's embers sparked to life as they quickly consumed their own morning meal.

Marguerite saw little of Mr. Philipsthal during the first two weeks of his show's opening. He seemed preoccupied with managing all the details surrounding a new location, and Marguerite worked night and day alongside her mentor. Edinburgh had proven to be a great success for them.

As Marie had hoped, the refugee French aristocrats in this bustling town loved the wax exhibition and most happily paid the extra fee to enter the Separate Room, where they could see castings of fellow aristocrats and royalty who had been less lucky in keeping their heads on their shoulders. In the Separate Room they could also stare at the evildoers who had been responsible for much of France's destruction and eventually shared in their victims' fates.

The locked coin box was filling up daily.

When the exhibit was not particularly crowded and could be managed by the ever-precocious Joseph, Marie gave Marguerite more instructions in the waxworking craft.

"You are a good student, Mrs. Ashby, but you must learn to make sketches. We can't always make masks. For our next portrait I teach you."

Their next portrait was not long in coming, for even the Comte d'Artois and his mistress, Madame de Polastron, had heard of the show from their fellow expatriates and ventured out of the palace one Sunday to see what all the grand fuss was about.

After sweeping through the main gallery and the Separate Room, the comte—whose youthful but dominating presence could be interpreted as nothing less than royal—nearly toppled Marie and Marguerite in his exuberance before remembering that he had royal manners to maintain. He drew himself up to match his height to his own opinion of himself, then gasped in recognition of Marie.

"You! I remember you! From Versailles. But I don't recall your position. What was your relation to us?"

Marie bowed her head deferentially. "Monsieur, I was art tutor to your sister, Madame Elisabeth, for several years. Until the unpleasantness began."

"Ah yes, I recall now that you had apartments next to hers. How our circumstances have changed, no? To be exiled in this city choked with rabid Protestants. It is hard for us good, devout

Frenchmen to bear." He absentmindedly patted his mistress's hand, which was tucked in his arm. Louise de Polastron's countenance was serene to the point that the woman seemed to be elsewhere.

"I am content enough with my circumstances, monsieur," Marie replied. "I have some success with my little wax exhibition."

"Yes, I suppose for the bourgeoisie it is easy enough to earn money using your hands. But I am forced to more gentlemanly pursuits. It is difficult, most difficult. And now that fool Corsican thinks to invade England. We'll be murdered in our beds by these heathen Scots who think to curry favor with the Crown by getting rid of 'undesirable' elements. But we have more agreeable affairs to talk of, yes?"

Charles-Philippe commanded an immediate sitting for both himself and his pale, quiet mistress, assuring the waxworkers that the cost was of no importance.

Indeed no, Marguerite thought. *Of no importance when one lives off the beneficence of the Crown.*

Whether Marie agreed with her was unclear. The salon's proprietress set the price at ten pounds for both figures and arranged for a sitting in two days, at which time they would each provide the clothing they wanted their respective figures to wear.

"This time, Mrs. Ashby, you will learn to sketch as well as assist me with the masks."

"I'm afraid I have no innate talent for drawing, madame."

"I didn't, either. No, my little Nini is the natural artist in our merry little group. He needs no teaching. You have seen his drawings since we've been here? He is a remarkable boy."

"He is indeed remarkable. But how will I be able to sketch these two important patrons when I am not naturally inclined to drawing?"

"Did you not sketch dolls before carving them?"

"Honestly, no. I formed a picture in my head and from there set my hand to the carving knife. Aunt Claudette rarely sketched anything, either."

"What of their clothes before cutting fabric?"

"Sometimes, yes. But we had a very talented seamstress who was gifted at making patterns based on my verbal descriptions."

Marie tsk-tsked her wonder at how the doll shop ever produced the quality it had. Marguerite suppressed her amusement. From anyone else the comment would be insulting, but Marie was fast becoming a figure of great importance to Marguerite. Marie was sometimes secretive, and almost always oblivious to anything not concerning her show, but she was also protective of her protégé, a loving mother, and an exceedingly able businesswoman. Not to mention an artist with unparalleled talent in wax modeling.

Yes, I could have done far worse in my new life without Nicholas.

With the thought of her husband, now dead nearly a year, she waited for at least one bolt of pain to course through her. It did not come. Instead, it felt like a thin, fluttering ribbon weaving quickly through her heart, gone almost before she noticed it.

Marie and Marguerite closed up the exhibit early on the day they visited Holyroodhouse. They once again left behind an outraged Joseph, who had been chattering nonstop for two days about what it must be like to be a prince, and once again found himself left out of an exciting event.

"This is not fair to me, Maman! I am going to be a great and famous waxworker when I grow up. I have to meet the comte if I'm going to be famous." He crossed his arms and jutted out his bottom lip.

"Son, you must remain here. I want you to study the spelling book I bought for you."

"I don't need to spell! I speak English like a native. You said so! I want to visit the palace." His lower lip was now trembling.

Marguerite, thankful that he no longer aimed his resentment directly at her, felt some sympathy for the boy. Who wouldn't want to see how royalty lives? And what child can understand being too young for adult company? Especially poor Joseph, whose only playmates were two adult women and a horde of wax people.

As they finally escaped Barnard's Rooms with their two bags of supplies, Marie said, "Speaking English is not enough. My boy is getting older and needs good education. Nini needs a tutor. Mrs. Ashby, will you help me find one?"

"Of course, madame. It would be my pleasure to help you secure a tutor."

They proceeded on foot down the mile-long incline of High Street toward Holyroodhouse. Madame Tussaud rarely hired a carriage for any journey. "I can buy a case of wax blocks for the price. Hackney is a stupid expense."

The fragrant aroma from the meat-pie seller wafted upon Marguerite before she actually saw him. She made a mental note to treat Madame Tussaud to one of his delectable pasties on their return trip, which would be a welcome stop as they trudged back uphill.

At the palace gates they were greeted by two soldiers from the castle, who nodded politely to the women and let them through into the front courtyard. A large fountain sat equidistant between the guard gate and the palace's entrance. The fountain's sprays were turned off, leaving the impression that it no longer cared about greeting visitors with a happy burst of misty showers.

Two more uniformed soldiers awaited them at the palace entry. One stepped inside to seek admittance for them, while the other barred their way. The first soldier returned promptly with a servant from the palace, who led them silently through the stately, carved oak door into the palace complex. They were escorted across the inner courtyard and through another door at the back of the palace into a large reception hall flanked by tapestries on three walls and windows on the fourth. The room contained a fine writing table with matching chair, and several plush stools and sofas. The servant clanged the door shut as he left to find his master.

"Madame, I'm afraid this table is entirely at risk of damage by us if this is where we are to make the masks." Marguerite brought her voice down to a low murmur as she heard her words reverberating against the walls. The room echoed sound remarkably well, despite the immense Flemish tapestries lining the walls.

"Yes, we need a worktable. But light from the windows is good here."

Moments later the Comte d'Artois entered with an ashen-faced Madame de Polastron leaning on his arm.

Marie and Marguerite curtsied to the couple. Even Marie, typically unmindful of those around her, could see that the comte's mistress was unwell.

"Madame?" Marie asked. "Are you ailing? Have we disturbed you? Should we—"

"What do you mean, ailing?" interrupted the comte. "My Louise is perfectly well, aren't you, pet?"

The woman smiled up wanly at her lover. "Of course, my darling. As you say. I'm just a bit tired." She coughed discreetly to one side into a handkerchief tied around her wrist.

While Marie negotiated with the comte to have the elegant writing table replaced with something more serviceable, Marguerite gently took Madame de Polastron's arm and helped her to the most comfortable seat in the room.

She whispered to the seated Louise, "Madame, have no fear that you will need to submit to the masking process. Once we have completed the comte's life mask, I will instead sketch you and make your form later at the salon."

"You can do this? I confess I was a bit unsure of what to expect."

"Please, be at rest and make yourself comfortable. The only distress you will experience is from the noise of my scratching pencil."

Louise giggled and dissolved into another coughing fit before lying back against the settee to await Marguerite's attentions.

While Marie helped with the positioning of the table brought in by two uniformed servants at the comte's command, Marguerite unpacked their bags of supplies. When the table was readied, Marguerite unfurled a length of pristine velvet cloth she knew would be ruined following the portrait sitting. Marie had decided after meeting the comte that he would be more expectant that fine material be used on him, despite its purpose, so Marie had dug some purple velvet out of a trunk to use as a drape across the front of his torso.

First, though, Marie and Marguerite worked together on gathering measurements from their subject. He reacted in the same mystified way as most people did upon seeing the frightful-looking instruments bearing down upon them. Every inch the royal, though, he quickly assumed an air of disinterest.

Upon completion of body calculations, Marie gestured to the comte to be seated in similar fashion as they had instructed the Duchess of York. Marguerite lightly spread the velvet over him. Marie gently removed his wig, revealing closely cropped dark stubble underneath.

The two women worked silently but synchronously together, speaking only to tell their patron what was happening next. This time, though, Marie handed the bowl of creamy paste to Marguerite.

Today I am to apply the plaster! On such a famous person!

Marguerite took the bowl with trembling fingers and stared at it. Marie gave her an encouraging nod toward their reclining figure, whose sparse hair had been oiled and whose nose had the requisite papers rolled inside of it.

As she moved to scoop out her first handful of plaster, the comte's voice boomed out, nearly startling her into dropping the carefully blended mixture.

"Louise, my love, come sit near me so I can sense your presence."

From across the room his mistress's voice floated over, small and tired. "Of course, I'll be right there."

"Monsieur le Comte," Marguerite said, waving to Louise to remain seated, "we must proceed directly to sketching your lovely lady the moment the plaster begins to dry. Might it not be better for her to remain in the position in which we will take her likeness?"

"But I wish for her company. No one comforts me like she does."

"May I promise to send her over the moment we are done with the drawing?"

"I suppose that would be permissible. Louise, stay where you are for now, but rush to my side when Mesdames are done sketching you."

Marguerite caught Marie's beam of approval out of the corner of one eye, and Louise's gratitude wafted over to her like a palpable breeze.

Bolstered by the approval of the two women, Marguerite confidently applied the initial thin layer of plaster to her subject. He started slightly when the first of the cold, wet mixture was applied, but relaxed as she continued the process, talking to him in a low, reassuring voice all the while. She quickly laid the string down the center of his face and scalp, then applied the remaining plaster evenly over the first layer.

"Monsieur, now we will let your mask set for several minutes, while Madame Tussaud and I create a perfect drawing of Madame de Polastron. Please grab my hand if you hear me and understand."

He reached out and did as Marguerite requested. She and Marie then took a drawing pad and several pencils to where Louise still lounged on the settee.

How will I ever be able to do this without Madame de Polastron realizing I am an incompetent?

To her surprise, Marie took several sheets of paper and a pencil and returned to the fine writing desk. Marguerite looked at her mentor for guidance, but the woman merely gave her yet another encouraging nod.

"Please, madame, stay as relaxed as possible. You may even keep your eyes closed if you like."

At least then she can't watch me make a mess of this.

Louise stayed in her reclined position. The woman resembled a marble statue, so pale and still was she.

Marguerite sat on a low stool with her drawing supplies. How to begin? *Wasn't Marie supposed to teach me this in advance?* She started by attempting to sketch her subject's face, which was highly elongated.

Not a bad start.

Then she drew two eyes. But they were closed. What color were they? Oh, right, green. She wrote "Green eyes" in the bottom right-hand corner of the paper.

Marguerite's attempt at drawing a nose was an utter failure, resembling a gnarled tree branch more than anything. She turned over the paper and began again. Her second try was little better, so she added "Long, straight nose, small bump near tip" underneath "Green eyes."

Louise started to hum quietly to herself, eventually breaking out into a sweet and mournful tune. With her lips in action, Marguerite was actually able to better capture them than when her mouth was still.

"Madame, your song is sweet. What is it?" she asked, never taking her eye from her drawing.

"Ah, just a little ditty I learned while in the convent as a girl. I lived there until my marriage at age seventeen. I loved the convent. The nuns were most kind to me."

The Comte d'Artois emitted a low growl.

"But of course I adore being with my Charles-Philippe so much more. He is the kindest, most generous prince that ever lived."

Marguerite was attempting to draw Madame de Polastron's gown, a simple, cream-colored, high-waisted affair with a navy sash around the bodice. The result was a tent with a dark band drawn through the middle of it.

I am botching this dreadfully.

Giving up on actually trying to draw the resting figure, Marguerite resorted to making more notes in the corner of the page. "Ivory gown consisting of diaphanous underlay on matching silk, dark blue sash affixed by diamond closure in front, pink ribbon at neck, pink slippers with one-inch heels tied with matching neck ribbon. High cheekbones, eyebrows at least two inches from bottom eyelid, small dimple in right side of chin."

She was so intent in noting her description that she did not notice Marie's approach. The woman handed her a piece of drawing parchment.

Madame de Polastron was sketched on it, almost lifelike.

Marie looked over Marguerite's shoulder. "Hmm, we make a good pair, do we not? You have noted important features that do not make it into the drawing. Madame de Polastran, would you care to see your sketch?"

Marie left the drawing in Marguerite's hands while she went over to check on the comte's progress.

"Mrs. Ashby, you will help with the pulling, yes?" Marie called to her.

Marguerite set down her papers and pencils to assist her mentor. Once again she was surprised by Marie's easy relinquishment of activities that had been her own.

Together they started to gently pry the mask from the Comte d'Artois's face, but as it began to release, Marie stepped away and let Marguerite finish. When the entire mask was fully loosened, she pulled it away and held the two sides in her hands.

I cannot believe it. I did it. The two halves are perfect. We will be able to create a marvelous figure.

"Mrs. Ashby," Marie prodded. "You must finish."

"What? Oh, yes, Madame de Polastron, would you care to see the comte's new face?"

Louise rose to join them.

"Show it to me first!" The comte was sitting up, blinking away plaster particles. "And you will make an exact likeness of me from *this?* How can it be?"

"It is so," Marie said, beginning to repack their tools as Marguerite used a cloth to wipe down his face, which he snatched away to use himself. "Your figures will be on display in the salon in two weeks' time, and we invite you and Madame to be present for the unveiling. We transport the figures to you a month later for permanent residence here."

"And my sweet Louise will also have a perfect likeness? Even though she didn't get a mask?"

"All will be perfect. Mrs. Ashby?" Marie was already impatient to get away.

Marguerite finished stuffing the drawing implements into a bag. "I'm ready."

The comte rang a bell. A servant appeared instantaneously to escort the women from the palace. They curtsied and backed out of the room, leaving behind a chattering prince and his resigned, consumptive mistress.

☙ 8 ☙

Soon more exiled French were seeking to have their own figures made, most of which Marie and Marguerite created and dispatched immediately to their owners. Marie was gradually releasing more and more responsibility for making figures to Marguerite. Although her mentor tried repeatedly to help her improve her sketching, Marguerite was hopeless at it, so in instances where they could not obtain a mask but had to do sketching, Marie would draw while Marguerite listed the subject's physical appearance with great detail. On one thing they both agreed: only the most interesting and infamous characters were worthy of display at the exhibition. With the characters Marie had brought with her from France, combined with new creations, the collection had expanded to seventy-five pieces.

Marie decided that a worthy and interesting figure to display was her own son. Taking on the creation of this figure entirely on her own, Tussaud worked ceaselessly for many nights to create a lifelike representation of her beloved son. When finished, she placed it outside the salon on the street to attract passersby into the exhibition.

Meanwhile, Marguerite scoured the *Edinburgh Evening Courant* for advertisements from tutors. She interviewed three of them, and finally recommended to Marie a slight, quiet young man by the name of Mr. Edwards whom she thought appropriate. Marie approved Marguerite's choice without requesting to meet the young man herself, and so Marguerite hired him to come to Barnard's Rooms three days each week to teach Joseph spelling, grammar, mathematics, and history.

To her surprise, Joseph did not struggle long over the hiring of his tutor, and instead seemed to flourish under the example of an older male. Marguerite quickly noticed the boy's interests turning to other pursuits, such as mathematics and handwriting, although he still maintained a level of devotion to his mother's business and his own drawing skills.

Sir Alexander remained a frequent visitor to the salon, claiming he was forever interested in what new and unique offerings the waxwork queen had to offer. His enthusiasm for the exhibition led many of the men in the garrison to visit to satisfy their own curiosities about what had the governor in such an animated state. Some showed up drunk, and were beaten out by Marie, whose broomstick grip was fierce. She complained of it once to Sir Alexander, but after learning that the men in question were flogged for their actions she told Marguerite, "Better they feel the bristles of my broom than the sting of a lash," and never reported their misbehavior again.

More annoying for Marguerite were those soldiers who proposed marriage to her after meeting her long enough to know that she was a widow serving as Madame Tussaud's protégé. After that she took to frequently wearing her wedding ring again.

Because of their frantic pace, between taking castings, building characters, rearranging the exhibit floor, and working with customers, the women saw little of Paul de Philipsthal. In fact, Marguerite was not even sure how his Phantasmagoria show was faring. During a rare break in the tempo, Marguerite walked next door to Philipsthal's. The placard outside announced his next show at eight o'clock that evening, so his makeshift theatre was mostly empty, save for a few workers setting up for that night's performance. She found him puzzling over one of his magic lanterns, the metal parts spread in pieces on a table in a small back room. The room was crammed with all manner of stage equipment, with hardly enough room for Philipsthal himself to be in it.

She coughed lightly from the doorway to let him know of her presence.

"Ah, Mrs. Ashby, welcome. How fares the wax exhibition?"

"Extremely well. We have almost more orders than we can fill. Madame says our success here has been greater than in London."

"Greater than in London, you say? Well, that is splendid. I'll be sure to stop by to offer Madame Tussaud my congratulations personally."

"And what of your Phantasmagoria show? Is it doing well?"

"Oh, most certainly. Crowds every night. I can hardly keep up. Which is made worse now that I have a mechanical problem." He spread his hands over the heap of metal. "But never fear, Philipsthal's Phantasmagoria will be ready for its adoring audiences this evening. Please, come in. I can remove the useless rubbish from this chair in the corner for you."

"No, Mr. Philipsthal, that's quite—"

"Paul. Call me Paul."

"I only stopped by for a moment to say hello. I need to return to the wax exhibition."

"Surely you can stay a few more moments."

"Truly I shouldn't. Madame will be looking for me."

"Tell me, Mrs. Ashby, what makes the wax exhibit more successful in Edinburgh than London? Do the Scots like the figures that much?"

"Actually, it's the French refugees who enjoy our show the most. So many of them have settled here. You remember our drive past Holyroodhouse? The Comte d'Artois has had his portrait done, which led to many of the other exiled aristocrats doing the same. They love the Separate Room."

"Hmm. And Madame is able to fetch a good price for making these figures?"

Marguerite felt a prickle at the back of her neck. Mr. Philipsthal was looking at her too intently. "Madame does not discuss all of the details with me. I am, of course, just her apprentice."

"But you work with her night and day. Surely you know something about how she conducts her business."

Marguerite began edging her way out the door. "I'm afraid I

know very little. I really must be away now. I wish you success with your magic lanterns." To her own mortification, she ran quickly away from the room like a rabbit realizing it has been espied by the fox, not even turning back when she heard him call to her, "Mrs. Ashby, wait. I'd like to plan another outing together."

The next morning, prior to opening time, Mr. Philipsthal came by as promised to congratulate Madame Tussaud on her show's success. Marie led him inside the Separate Room, and rehooked the heavy velvet draping that partitioned that room and vestibule from the rest of the exhibition. Nevertheless, Marguerite could hear their muffled voices rising in heat. Minutes later, Mr. Philipsthal stormed out and through the main gallery without so much as acknowledging Marguerite.

What was the difficulty between these two?

Marguerite bit her lip as she dressed and fixed her hair in her room. Marie had suggested they go to a nearby inn for a special meal. Marie never splurged on anything not related to her show, so what was this about? Was she to be dismissed for visiting Mr. Philipsthal? Had Marguerite told him something that she shouldn't have?

Her stomach spasmed. Life was finally pleasing, and now this. Well, perhaps it was not *pleasing*, but it was at least satisfying. And challenging. And far away from her old memories.

What have I done wrong?

She smiled nervously at Marie as they left their rooms. Joseph was once more in the care of Mrs. Laurie, but he was less upset these days with taking a lesser role to Marguerite now that he had his studies and other pursuits.

Marie paused at the entrance of Barnard's Rooms to lightly pat Marguerite on the face. "You are a good girl," she said.

Marie's hand was rough and chapped. Their work was constant, and left little time for the niceties of lotions and creams to keep their skin soft. Marguerite's insides roiled and she looked down at her own hands. Soon she might be back at Hevington, doing nothing *but* creaming her hands.

Have courage, she thought, as they walked silently together.

Marie frowned at the menu, murmuring calculations softly to herself, yet still purchased a bottle of wine.

"Tonight is a celebration," she said as the golden liquid was served to them.

"It is?"

Marie laughed, an absolute rarity in such a serious woman.

"Yes. My financial worries are near their end. Thanks to our success here in Edinburgh, my debt is paid and soon I will have all the rights to my show. You helped me do this. I am grateful."

"Why, madame, I am glad of the success, but I am just your apprentice and have had no influence in your triumph." Marguerite's heart was fluttering relief.

"No no, you are more than just an apprentice. You learn fast, you help me, you care for my show as though it was your own. You help me with my English even though I will never speak properly. Claudette was right to send you to me." Marie held up her full goblet in a toast.

"But I am the one who should be grateful to you. You saved me from my own wretchedness. I might be dead by my own hand now if not for you."

Marie's laugh this time was loud enough for other patrons to notice. "You are not wretched. You are a fine companion. I write my husband and tell him about you and what I plan to do. But I don't know if my letters reach him anymore. Communication is difficult now that the treaty is collapsed."

"What do you plan to do?"

"Yes, when I have all my rights back, I will start to share some of my profits with you. You will not be owner—my dear Nini will inherit the show one day—but I will give you more than just apprentice wages. Being an apprentice is not enough for you."

"Madame . . . I am at a loss. . . . I thought that this evening you planned to . . . to . . . well, I did not expect *this* to happen." Marguerite took a gulp from her wineglass to steady her nerves, which had become fractured by equal parts fear and relief. Fortunately their goose with prune sauce arrived at that moment to distract her mentor—or was she now just a friend?—from Marguerite's trembling hand.

But by the next day it was as if the previous evening had never happened. Mr. Philipsthal arrived at their lodgings as Marguerite was waiting for Marie and Joseph to come out to walk the few steps to the gallery together. After a quick greeting to Marguerite, Philipsthal raised his hand to knock on Marie's door, but she opened it before his knuckles made contact. She asked Marguerite to take Joseph into the gallery while she spoke to Mr. Philipsthal, ushering him into her rooms while pushing Joseph out, and firmly shutting the door behind her.

Half an hour later, Marie appeared in the gallery, her hair unusually mussed. She took Marguerite aside.

"My financial obligations are not over like I thought. You are still an apprentice."

"What has happened?"

"Not for you to worry. I'll fix this." Marie's eyes brooked no further comment.

"Yes, madame, as you say."

Would she never learn what was happening behind the scenes of the exhibition?

Orders for personal wax models from local citizens continued to come in, and Marie sought out other famous or notorious personalities to model as well. By the end of September, they were working on a half dozen figures simultaneously. Marguerite noticed that their patrons enjoyed inspecting the figures in their various stages of completion almost as much as they did seeing them in their final, lifelike state.

Soon Marie decided to dedicate certain hours of the day to wax sculpting and to charge an extra shilling during that period. On Thursdays, genteel customers were invited to a special, reserved time to take tea at the salon while having a private viewing of the two women at work.

Business continued to soar, yet still Marie fussed about money.

Mr. Philipsthal once again asked Marguerite to accompany him, this time to a jeweler's shop in Princes Street, to help him select a bauble to send back to his mother in France.

"I value your good judgment, you see, Mrs. Ashby."

"Do you not fear a piece of jewelry being stolen or lost on its way to France? It seems a dangerous thing to do."

"Ah, but my esteemed mother deserves something of value."

"Then why not a small portrait of yourself?"

"A wax figure, you mean?"

"No no, a wax figure would need accompaniment to reach France safely. I mean a painting. Perhaps a miniature she can wear. I would think that less likely to be pinched in its travels."

"An excellent idea, Mrs. Ashby. Excellent."

Philipsthal approached Marguerite once again while she was alone in the salon. He had an unfailing sense of when Marie would be out.

"Mrs. Ashby, I found a painter, Sir Henry Raeburn, who has an unparalleled reputation here in Edinburgh. I insist you accompany me to visit him to pick up my portrait. I would like your approval on my choice of painters."

Marguerite wiped her hands on her apron. She had been practicing inserting hair strands into a nondescript wax head. Together, she and Marie were experimenting further with the insertion of real hair into their characters' scalps, as a measure of realism against wigs. It was difficult work, not only to obtain hair scraps from hairdressers, but to keep the hair clean, sorted, and stored properly. More complicated than any of this was the actual insertion of hair into the scalp, done by needle using individual strands of hair. Marguerite found that it took days to end up with a head like the one before her now, which merely looked to have wispy, uneven tufts dangling from it.

Surely she would not deserve the waxworker title much longer with such ridiculous efforts as the wax head she now worked on. She would have to work harder on this poor wretched figure.

"Mrs. Ashby, will you accompany me?"

Without looking up from what she was doing, she said, "What? Oh, of course, Mr. Philipsthal, although I hardly think I can offer much opinion. I have little understanding of oils."

"Nevertheless, you are certainly an artist. May I tempt you with a light supper after we see Sir Raeburn this evening?"

Marguerite wrenched her attention away from the dreadfully

coiffed wax head. Another outing might provide her with an opportunity to question Mr. Philipsthal about his relationship with Marie Tussaud.

"Why, yes, I think supper would be lovely."

After Mr. Philipsthal's departure, Marie returned from her own errands and the exhibition became busy. Marguerite had little opportunity to mention her outing to Marie the rest of the day. She finally found a moment to tell Marie of her intention to assist Mr. Philipsthal with the acquisition of his portrait for his mother, and was greeted with Marie's customary grunt of disapproval. Yet the woman did not try to prevent her from going.

Sir Henry Raeburn's studio was located in his home, St. Bernard's, just at the west edge of New Town. Marguerite was immediately struck by the overpowering mixed odors of paint and turpentine. The fumes tugged at her nostrils. She would not be able to stay long, lest a headache be the result of her visit. The studio itself was jumbled with all manner of half-finished canvases, stools at varying heights, jars of stiff brushes, and containers of paint. Sir Raeburn eyed her much as a buyer inspecting a horse for purchase.

"I could paint you, dear lady. I don't have much luck with female portraiture, but I feel quite sure it would be impossible to do wrong by an exquisite specimen such as yourself. Mr. Philipsthal, would you like me to do a portrait of your wife?"

Before Marguerite could protest, Philipsthal spread his hands, a beam of sunshine radiating underneath his serious expression.

"Alas, Sir Raeburn, although as lovely and graceful as a goddess, Mrs. Ashby is a widow who does not desire the married state again. She has merely come with me here to pick up my portrait."

"Too bad. You would make a marvelous subject."

Marguerite remained silent under the excessive flattery, uncomfortable under the gaze of these two men. Once Philipsthal had procured his painting, actually a miniature set inside a round gold frame, they stopped at a nearby inn for the promised supper. Marguerite examined the miniature more carefully at the table as they sipped brambleberry wine while waiting for their meals.

"In my limited opinion, Mr. Philipsthal, I'd say that Sir Raeburn did a remarkable job. He has captured your expression perfectly." She handed the tiny portrait back to its owner.

Mr. Philipsthal pushed it gently back toward her. "Please, it's Paul. And I must confess that this portrait is not a gift for my mother. I've hardly spoken to her in some years. I wanted to give you a token of our friendship, of your own choosing. When you mentioned a portrait, I assumed you would like it."

"But, Mr. Philip—Paul, this is an extravagant gift between friends." She looked back down at the miniature in its gleaming, filigreed setting. "I believe others may be mistaken by its intent. It is more a gift between lovers, don't you think?"

She held up the portrait once more. The odor of the lingering fresh oil paint soared sharply upon her senses and simmered under her brow, threatening a headache. She laid the piece down on the middle of the table between them.

"I'm not certain I can accept this."

Philipsthal laid his hand over hers that covered the portrait. "Please, I mean no offense. What must I do to gain your trust? As a friend, I mean."

Marguerite studied her dining partner while permitting her hand to remain secured under his. It was time to take advantage of this opportunity.

"Well, it has always been my belief that true friends don't keep secrets from one another, and I do sense a secret."

Philipsthal's face was inscrutable. "What do you mean, a secret?"

She kept her voice steady. She felt like she was about to confront the rioters again. Who knew which way this would go? Would she escape unscathed or would she be attacked? "I mean that there is something . . . disturbing . . . between you and Madame Tussaud. She won't tell me what it is, but I am determined to know. She is somehow resentful of you. Tell me truthfully, Paul. Were you and my employer once lovers? Did you jilt her after she left France to join you?"

He stared hard at her without speaking and she felt a flush creeping up her modestly exposed neckline. *If he does not say something shortly, I will look like a giant radish.*

But Philipsthal was not angry. He offered her a broad smile and patted her trapped hand.

"My dear Mrs. Ashby. May I call you Marguerite now that we are friends? Er, I see that still makes you uncomfortable. Well then, any resentment on Madame Tussaud's part is not shared by me. We were never lovers, nor have I any designs as such. I have only ever been her protector since she joined me in England. I loaned her a substantial sum of money, which she seems to have difficulty repaying. However, I've not ever called in the loan. In fact, I've continued to promote her show and advise her in her business dealings, sometimes to the detriment of my own show. It is my own great faith in her future success that causes me to let her debt mount without question, only offering ideas and suggestions for her as the circumstances warrant. I admit that she does not always take my advice well, but I wish only the best for her. For you, as well. Have my actions been less than honorable toward you or her?"

"No, I suppose not."

He leaned forward and spoke quietly. "May I suggest to you that Madame Tussaud does not manage her show properly? Perhaps she is a bit jealous of my own success?"

Marguerite felt uneasy, as though the earth were shifting beneath her. She retrieved her hand from under his and brought a finger to her brow. The odor of the miniature lingered under her skin. She would have to take a draught when she returned to her rooms. Philipsthal's explanation seemed reasonable enough, yet her skin prickled. Was Marie really jealous by nature?

"Mrs. Ashby, are you unwell?"

"No. Perhaps. I have a small pain behind my eyes. Nothing serious."

His response was solicitous and caring. "Obviously my distasteful discourse has caused you suffering. Therefore we shall never speak of Madame Tussaud's financial calamities again. And I must get you home straightaway."

During the carriage ride back to Thistle Street, Philipsthal was mostly pensive, which suited Marguerite's burgeoning headache well. But as they neared her lodgings, he turned to face her.

"You know, Mrs. Ashby, I once told you that you might choose to leave Madame Tussaud's employ when your skill grew great enough. Perhaps with her mismanagement of her affairs, now is the time."

His promise not to speak of Madame had lasted all of a few minutes. She fought the urge to roll her eyes. "Leave Madame Tussaud? First, sir, my skills as a waxworker are in their infancy. And second, I enjoy my work with her. I believe that once her difficulties—whatever they may be—are worked out, she will have a very profitable show. I am proud to be part of it."

Marguerite's head throbbed, more out of annoyance now than from the odor of paint that had precipitated it.

Philipsthal held up a hand in supplication. "My apologies. I did not wish to offend. I merely wanted to suggest an alternative to your situation. One that might bring you greater happiness."

"I gave up any idea of great happiness upon my husband's death."

"But surely you do not intend to stay shut away in this dreary little city—if it can be called that—for the rest of your days, toiling under Tussaud's sharp eyes and tongue?"

Marguerite crossed her arms. "I do not like the direction of this conversation, sir. What are you saying? Please speak plainly."

"Very well. I wish to propose an arrangement between us. You know that I have always held you in high regard, and I do not believe I am completely out of my wits when I say that you hold me in some esteem. As a friend, yes, I know. But might not friends enter into a profitable situation that might even result in a felicitous outcome for both parties?"

He shifted uncomfortably in the seat, as if buying time in order to deliberate on his next words.

"My dear Mrs. Ashby, you and I together would be a formidable force. You could manage a wax show alongside my own Phantasmagoria, and we would settle down together in any city of your choosing—London, Brussels, Salzburg—name your heart's desire and I will make it so, provided Bonaparte has not destroyed them all."

"Are you suggesting—"

"Yes, I am offering you the safety, security—and, dare I say, happiness—of marriage with me. Wait—" He held up a hand. "Do not object so quickly. Many people have married for reasons other than love, yet grew to care for each other deeply. Look at Antony and Cleopatra, Mary and Bothwell, even Adam and Eve."

"All of whom came to terrible ends!"

"Perhaps they were not the best examples. But think how many arranged marriages have ended up successful. And with no basis of friendship such as we have."

"Mr. Philip—Paul, I'm flattered, but—"

"Tell me, did you love your husband—Nicholas, I believe his name was—when you first met him?"

Without thinking, she replied honestly. "No, he was insignificant to me. Actually, he had a boyish infatuation for my mother. It was only later that I—"

"Aha! You see? You have already experienced what I am talking about. You grew to love him, and you will one day grow to love me. In the meantime, we will combine our respective talents and be rich by anyone's standards."

Philipsthal's eyes were shining now with his own fevered imagination. He took both of Marguerite's hands in his and brought them to his lips.

"Together we will be a force to be reckoned with. We might even be able to enter Society, what with your family connections and my own fame."

Marguerite jerked her hands away.

"Mr. Philipsthal!" Her voice was sharper than she intended it to be. "I am not in the habit of using my aunt and uncle to secure social invitations. Not that I have ever had a care for such things. You presume too much with me."

"How I wish I could make you see reason. You are trifling with a most agreeable offer. We've arrived. May I see you to your room?" He stepped out and offered her his hand. She took it and stepped out as well.

"I think not. I'm quite exhausted from the day and wish to just take a posset and lie down."

He grabbed her fingers tightly as she sought to disengage her hand from his. He lowered his lips to her ear and spoke in a tone that was nearly inaudible, yet his words reverberated violently in her mind.

"You may wish to think more on this, Mrs. Ashby. For it is in my power to improve everyone's lot in life. Marry me, and I will forgive Madame Tussaud's considerable debt to me. She and her son can go their own way into obscurity, and you and I will build a grand fortune together."

Was this an offer of marriage or a disguised form of blackmail?

She jerked away from him. "Since when does a friend provide such a reprehensible choice? Good night, Mr. Philipsthal."

She strode into the building as resolutely as her quaking legs would allow.

Marguerite asked Mrs. Laurie for a pot of tea for her room, intending to take it with another dose of valerian root. She entered her darkened, blissfully quiet room and heaved a sigh of relief before lighting a lamp.

She poured the contents of her reticule onto her dressing table with shaking hands, searching for her comb. Made of mother-of-pearl, it had belonged to her mother and was her favorite treasure. A thorough combing of her hair, combined with her tea and medicine, were just what she needed to calm her nerves and purge her of this headache.

She stared incredulously at the spilled contents. Mr. Philipsthal's miniature had somehow made its way into her reticule.

Is he my friend or not? Like Madame, he keeps too many secrets. Secrets that I cannot fathom. I will never marry him. I do not love him, nor would any amount of proximity cause me to love him. But do I love Madame enough to do this for her? Would he truly release her from her debt to him? This debt must be the source of her angst toward him. But again, why? Mr. Philipsthal loaned her money that he has patiently waited for repayment on, and is even still serving as her guide and promoter in whatever city they visit.

I will talk to Madame tomorrow about this, and will not permit any forestalling or evasion on the matter.

Thus resolved, she smiled warmly when Mrs. Laurie dropped

off a tea tray, and settled down to the more pressing business of relieving her headache.

By morning she had changed her mind. Surely Mr. Philipsthal's comments were borne out of a heated frustration and he did not actually mean to barter Marguerite as one does in a treaty negotiation. Her headache must have blinded her into misunderstanding his true intentions. They were friends after all. No, it would be foolish to upset Madame by telling her the events of a badly remembered evening and then demand to know what sinister secrets her employer held.

Marguerite ate breakfast with Marie and Joseph according to custom but said little. Marie must also have been lost in thought for she did not seem to mind. Joseph sat at the table dripping jam off his piece of toast while he continued working on a sketch of a flower-seller lately camped near the salon. Other than the scratch of pencil and the clinking of silverware, they were a quiet, reflective trio.

Madame Tussaud never inquired about her outing with Mr. Philipsthal the entire day, so if she was curious she concealed it well. The salon was too busy for much idle conversation anyway. Sir Alexander made another of his regular appearances, bringing along with him Lieutenant Hastings.

"Mrs. Ashby, I hear you and the good Madame Tussaud have made a figure of John Knox. I'm most anxious to see it. Lieutenant Hastings also wanted to see the exhibition before leaving for the coast, but was unable to do so. He's rejoined us for a few more days, so I insisted he come with me before leaving again, isn't that correct?"

Hastings nodded. Today he was out of uniform, and dressed in a camel-colored coat with contrasting dark brown collar and breeches. Marguerite was struck for the first time that this was actually a handsome man who had an unfortunately grim personality.

Before she could escort the two men to see the Knox figure, Sir Alexander exclaimed, "Why, there's Madame Tussaud now. I'm sure she'd like to show me the figure herself. Hastings, keep Mrs. Ashby jovial company for a moment, would you?"

Hope disappeared into the gallery after Marie before Marguerite could utter a word. She turned to Lieutenant Hastings, who had a distinct scowl on his face. This was promising to be a disagreeable encounter. And she'd had enough unpleasantness lately.

"Sir, may I show you some of the characters we have on display here? Perhaps you'd like to see our Separate Room?"

"Briefly. I have pressing business to attend to before my sailing tomorrow."

Then why for heaven's sake did the man take time to visit the salon with the governor?

But she reacted smoothly. She hoped.

"Then we will indeed be brief. Please follow me, Lieutenant Hastings."

To her surprise, his face softened just slightly and he offered her his arm. Without thinking, she took it. He kept her hand too tightly against his side, though whether it was intentional or just poorly developed manners, she couldn't be sure. And it did feel rather comfortingly secure.

Inside the Separate Room she disengaged from him, stepping over to the nearest tableau. "This is Marat in his bath. We've tried to make it as realistic as possible, with Charlotte Corday's knife still in him and his face twisted in agony."

Lieutenant Hastings's scowl had returned as he looked distastefully at the scene of the virulent Parisian writer Jean-Paul Marat in an actual bathtub set against a backdrop painted to look like a bedchamber.

"Show me another." His voice was clipped.

She showed him the various tableaux in the room, including the gruesome, but ever popular, death masks. She explained in detail the history behind each scene. Hastings's brow furrowed even deeper.

"Lieutenant? Is something wrong?" Marguerite asked. Most patrons were enthralled with the displays. She'd never experienced such an objectionable reaction before.

"Does it not strike you, Mrs. Ashby, that this is macabre in the extreme? I think it also serves to whip up sympathy for the

French, and we are trying to fight a war with them to prevent Bonaparte's overrun of Great Britain." His voice was even, but she sensed the irritation beneath his calm exterior.

"Lieutenant, our exhibition is simply an entertainment. We produce figures and tableaux that the public enjoys."

"But there are some who might think it sends a message of compassion to French émigrés, which you know are aplenty in Edinburgh. Madame Tussaud is one herself, is she not?"

"I can assure you that no such thing is intended. Everything in the show is purely theatrical. Madame and I are not insurrectionists." Marguerite heard her voice becoming slightly hysterical.

Lieutenant Hastings stepped closer to her and spoke quietly. "Have no fear, Mrs. Ashby. I am not without commiseration of the situation of the French people. I merely caution you to be discreet in your activities." His eyes were sending her a message of some intensity, but she could not fathom what it could possibly be. She hardly knew the man. She stood frozen in place by his forceful stare.

But he must have decided that he had successfully transmitted his communiqué, for he gave her a quick bow and said, "I must find Sir Alexander. It's time we were about our business. I bid you good day, Mrs. Ashby. Perhaps we will meet again one day if your exhibition returns to London."

And in moments he had secured the governor, who had Marie cornered inside a tableau of the arrest of Guy Fawkes, and they left the exhibition.

Must all men of my acquaintance be so baffling? First Mr. Philipsthal with his eccentric marriage proposal and now Lieutenant Hastings with his peculiar opinion of the exhibition. Why aren't all men like Uncle William? Or Nicholas?

The thought of Nicholas dashed through her mind like a butterfly stopping to examine a flower, then fluttering off gracefully to visit other attractions in the garden. Time stopped so that the butterfly could be admired, yet the insect was off again so quickly that contemplation was not possible.

But the number of strange men in her acquaintance was quickly dropped by one. The following morning Mrs. Laurie brought a letter to her room that had been delivered by Mr. Philipsthal personally. In it, he declared his intention of departing Edinburgh immediately for an undeclared destination, with a return by the end of the year. The note gave no indication of why he was going. It was simply signed "Philipsthal," with no courteous closing.

Madame Tussaud had received a similar letter and crowed about it over breakfast. "Good riddance to the vermin. He can take his plague elsewhere. But he not tell where he's going. Hope he goes to Russia to give Tsar Alexander a performance. The tsar is suspicious and contrary. He'll throw Philipsthal to the dogs." Marie held up her teacup in a toast. "Adieu, Philipsthal." She practically cackled in joy as she put the cup to her lips.

"But, madame, according to his letter he will return by the end of the year."

The cup clattered down into the saucer. "He might. But we won't be here for him. I have in mind to go elsewhere. Glasgow. I've made inquiries, and I think exhibition do well there. This city might not be safe long if the French invade its port. Glasgow is further inland. And maybe Philipsthal will never find us again."

Was Madame Tussaud intending to run out on her debt with her business partner? Marguerite tentatively broached the subject.

"Madame, do we not have obligations to Mr. Philipsthal?"

"Philipsthal is not an obligation. He is a parasite. I need distance from him. So do you. I see how he pursues you, plays the gallant courtier. I think you are a good girl, a wise girl, and won't give in to him, but I promised Claudette to care for you, and this I do. I'll remove you from his clutches."

Marguerite flared, a rare occurrence before her mentor. "Madame, I am no child to be ordered about. You are right, Mr. Philipsthal has paid me undue attention, but I am certainly not deceived by him. I do not require your interference."

"Hah! If you continue to see him you *will* be a child to be ordered about. I don't interfere, I maintain the good of the show. We go to Glasgow!" The teacup banged into its saucer again and a tiny chip from the base of the cup shot across the table, landing on a drawing Joseph had been scribbling on. The boy was poised, openmouthed, with his pencil midair over the page, agog at the vehement discourse between his mother and the mild-mannered apprentice.

Without another word, Marguerite fled the dining table for her room, ashamed of her infantile behavior but overwhelmingly irritated at her mentor's seeming irrationality.

Within a week Marie informed her that she had secured lodgings in Glasgow through an agent with whom she had been corresponding, which told Marguerite that Marie had long been hoping for—and working toward—an escape such as this.

And so within two weeks they had shuttered the windows of the exhibition, placed a sign outside that they were relocating to Cardiff, Wales, as a feint in the event of Philipsthal's return, and were waiting for good sailing weather for two women, a young boy, and nearly a hundred wax figures to Glasgow.

PART THREE

Glasgow

❧ 9 ❧

October 1803. The exhibition settled in the New Assembly Rooms in Ingram Street. Glasgow was larger, dirtier, and more decayed than Edinburgh, although nothing to compare with London. It was noted for its shipbuilding, which fascinated the sea-loving Joseph, so at every opportunity the three of them strolled down to the ship works to watch ships under construction.

Marie had taken a different approach to lodgings this time. Rather than focus merely on proximity to the show, she was now concerned with respectability and public approval. She rented rooms for the trio in nearby Wilson Street from a Mr. Colin, who was not only a highly respected pastry cook, but well on his way to being made a guild brother and burgess of Glasgow.

Mr. Colin encouraged them to participate in the Glasgow Fair the following July.

"Your keek show will attract plenty of folk, won't it?" he suggested.

Marie turned one eye on him in her curious, birdlike way. "Keek show, Mr. Colin?"

"Yes, you know, where people can get a look at oddities. Sometimes there are giantesses, or strange beasts from the Indies. Once I saw a learned pig there. I never saw but heard about a man who would skin rats with his teeth. Gruesome, isn't it? It's every July on the Glasgow Green. Your waxes will be much favored there, won't they?"

The Assembly Rooms themselves were their largest location yet. They were bright and cheerful and prominently located at the city center.

Marguerite engaged another young man to tutor Joseph three days each week, but this time the tutoring would be conducted at the Assembly Rooms so that the boy would be available to help with the exhibit both before and after his learning sessions.

Although disagreeing with Marie's decision to essentially run away from Edinburgh and Philipsthal, Marguerite had to admit to the woman's ruthless efficiency in ensuring that they wasted little time getting the show operating. The three of them worked tirelessly in their new salon setting up the figures, which by now were old friends to Marguerite.

Columns provided the only room partitioning, and they took advantage of them to set up their tableaux in and around the columns to break up the large expanse into the appearance of smaller rooms. At Marie's behest, Marguerite and young Joseph worked together to place a single character figure facing the street in each of the room's eight tall, narrow-paned windows. They closed the cream brocaded curtains behind the figures, both to entice passersby to enter the salon and to prevent heat from the sun from concentrating on the remaining delicate figures inside the exhibition. At night the figures were edged backward and the curtain dropped between them and the windows to discourage any night prowlers who might think it interesting to steal a human replica.

The resulting excited whispers and shuffling could be heard outside the Assembly Rooms all throughout the day, and handbills announcing the show were literally snatched from the doors by the curious public. Marguerite spent so much time replacing the posted handbills that she made a trip to a local printer to have several hundred pieces printed, and stationed Joseph outside to hand them out. Thank heavens the boy had become so agreeable and willing, his only demand that he be left with his sketching papers and pencils. Via periodic peeks through the draperies, Marguerite made note that the wax figures were attracting both the lower classes and high society. Best to recommend to Marie that they set tiered admission prices.

The two women spoke at length one day about which tableaux sets to uncrate and have erected, and what kind of workmen they would need to hire to help. Once that was done, the show would be ready to open. They decided to create a more permanent exhibit that would not be rearranged regularly but would instead provide a more lifelike experience for visitors. Also, instead of arranging their figures in topical tableaux, they decided upon a historical composition, where a visitor would enter at one end of the Assembly Rooms and step through various points of the last two hundred years of European history in chronological order, with an emphasis on Scottish events. From their characters they pulled such figures as John Knox, Robert Burns, and Sir Walter Scott, while also making plans to create new figures of legendary Scotsmen like Sir William Wallace and Robert the Bruce. Many of their figures were developed from old paintings and even their imaginations when they had no real person to work from. Marie decided upon a discreet American tableau as well, to give a prominent place to their Benjamin Franklin figure.

To enhance the patron's visit, each tableau was augmented with realistic, mood-evoking accessories, such as straw on the floor for Charles I's execution scene, and a pebbled pathway to crunch underfoot for those visitors visiting a replica of Sir Francis Drake sailing away in the *Golden Hind.*

Because their expenditures ran high in putting together such a sophisticated exhibition in a drastically short amount of time, despite all of the materials already on hand, Marie was forced to seek credit with various local merchants for supplies. Typically one to hold on to every shilling until forced to part with it, Marie was too excited about the new exhibit format to let the want of a few pounds stand in the way of success.

"We'll pay it all back quickly. Show will be grandest of all. Very profitable. Very good."

Marguerite had simply never seen her employer so relaxed and in such high spirits.

Marie let out a satisfied sigh as they returned to their new quarters, happy that the setup of most of the figures had been completed in almost no time at all. "We establish show on our own now. Without Philipsthal."

Marguerite began to envision Marie sitting in her room each night rubbing her hands together like Midas.

"Madame," she said, "if the show is to be completely independent of your partner, perhaps it would be prudent to change the name of it."

"Change the name?"

"Yes. Instead of Dr. Curtius's Cabinet of Wonders, why not call it Madame Tussaud's Wax Exhibition? After all, few people remember Dr. Curtius anymore, and the show is *yours*."

Marie pursed her lips in thought. "My name on the show? Hmm. But will the show lose respect with a woman's name on it?"

"Hardly. Everyone knows you are the real owner. Besides, what about Patience Wright? Didn't she have a wax show in London not long ago? I believe she had some success."

Marie nodded her head slowly. "Perhaps, perhaps. I guess we try here and then go back to Dr. Curtius's name in our next city if it doesn't work."

"Next city? Have you already planned another location?"

"No no." Marie waved a hand in denial. "But if it doesn't work here, we go elsewhere. Maybe Liverpool? Big trading center."

Dread spiraled slowly in Marguerite's stomach. Not another sea voyage.

"Or maybe another city in Scotland? Perth?" Marguerite tried to suggest helpfully.

"Decide later. But you have good ideas, Mrs. Ashby. You will help me with this, *non?*"

And so Marguerite engaged a sign painter for their new salon, who painted "Madame Tussaud's" and "Wax Exhibition" across two gaily decorated boards that could either be hung in the salon's windows or be propped up outside.

She also had a new exhibition catalogue made, this time with an engraving of Marie on the cover to go along with the show's new name emblazoned across the front.

For a final touch, Marguerite took out an advertisement in the *Glasgow Courier,* changing Dr. Curtius's name to Marie's, and adding a nod of deference to the citizens of Glasgow:

Newly revealed for the first time ever
For the esteemed audiences of Glasgow only
Dr. Curtius's Cabinet of Wonder is now
Madame Tussaud's Wax Exhibition
Having been managed and operated by
Marie Grosholtz Tussaud these past nine years
Across France, England, and Scotland
Engaged in Glasgow for a limited time
New character figures
The great poet Robert Burns, the explorer Sir Alexander Mackenzie, renowned professor Adam Smith, Bonnie Prince Charlie, many more
Gruesome death masks of the tragic and infamous
Robespierre, Marie Antoinette,
Louis XVI of France, and others
Curious relics, including an Egyptian Mummy
Open to the public six days each week
Admission: two shillings
Half price for working class
Children just threepence

To enhance the show's respectability, they scheduled a special showing just for the city's most esteemed members of society, a list of people given to them by Mr. Colin.

As in Edinburgh, the audience was agog at the uniqueness of the exhibition. Perfectly mannered ladies stared at the fierce, bearded visage of William Wallace without bothering to bring a gloved hand or fan to cover their open mouths. Five orders for individual figures came in that very night, with two men nearly committing to a duel over whose would be made first. Marie made a great show of disapproval of their behavior, but Marguerite could see the smile hidden behind the frown, suggesting that such fanciful antics were pleasing to her.

They held another restricted showing for Mr. Colin and the

leaders of Glasgow's guilds, in thanks for his provision of entrée into Glaswegian society.

Their new location's success, combined with the absence of Mr. Philipsthal, had a rejuvenating effect on Marie. Each evening after the salon's closing she bubbled over with new plans and ideas for improving the show, from securing a shirt claimed to have been worn by Henry IV of France, *le bon roi Henri*, when he was assassinated, to her most audacious acquisition, that of the actual guillotine blade that had severed Marie Antoinette's head. Marie had known the executioner's family back in France, and discovered through letters that he still possessed the blade. She quietly conducted the transaction to obtain it, and when the blade arrived, she revealed it to Marguerite in her room late one evening while Mr. Colin was out at a guild meeting.

Marie said nothing, but merely unfolded the blade from its layers of burlap, a new and durable fabric being employed everywhere for shipping. Marguerite gasped, recognizing instantly what her employer was showing her. The blade was rusted along its sharp edge and had obviously not been cleaned since its last use. Or had it ever seen a scrubbing?

"Madame, this is remarkable. Imagine the crowds who will come just to see this." Marguerite reached out and gently touched a heavily caked spot on the blade. Was it blood or rust? Whichever, it had seen its way through many a terrified head. And now it would live on in infamy at Madame Tussaud's Wax Exhibition.

Together they developed a plan for their grandest tableau of all.

Despite creating a historical walk inside the exhibition, they still maintained a curtained-off Separate Room. The guillotine blade became the centerpiece of the isolated area. Together they sketched out the idea to erect a guillotine site in the middle of the Place de la Révolution, where Marie Antoinette was beheaded. They worked primarily from Madame Tussaud's recollection of this location where hundreds of French citizens were executed. They hired workmen to build steps leading up to a platform four feet off the ground, less than the eight feet of the original, but allowing for accommodation of the room's ceiling height. The workmen also built an inoperable guillotine model, to which the real blade was affixed and placed on top of the platform. A basket was placed at the chopping end of the guillotine on top of a straw bale, leaving no doubt of its purpose. The walls inside the tableau surrounding the platform were eight feet tall to obscure all but the top of the model guillotine from the crowds in the rest of the exhibit. Joseph helped his mother paint the Tuileries Palace in the background and jeering people in the foreground of the scene.

The last bit of construction was a tumbrel, a small two-wheeled cart with a simple bench in it for a prisoner to sit on. They positioned their Marie Antoinette figure inside the tumbrel, looking up at the guillotine.

In her exuberance, Marie wanted to place authentic cobblestones on the floor of the tableau, but Marguerite advised against it, citing the likely damage to the existing floors. As Marguerite had become more and more a confidant in these plans rather than just an apprentice, Marie took this advice readily. So instead they scattered straw and dirt around the confines of the Separate Room.

The crowning touch was to hire a man to sit on a bench hidden underneath the platform and strike at a block of wood at periodic intervals to imitate the sound of the guillotine crashing against the neckpiece.

Marguerite could not help but share in Marie's pride and delight over the public's reaction to their newly redesigned Separate Room, for which an increased entry fee of sixpence deterred no one. Even battle-worn army soldiers emitted strangled gasps and yelps when the axman gave a resounding blow to his tree stump under the platform. After the initial fright, visitors tittered in relief and then sought to meet the owner of the exhibition.

Money was flowing in a sweet and steady stream to the show, and their creditors were repaid in just a few weeks.

Marguerite found a curious visitor—aging, balding, and bespectacled—secreted in a corner one day with Madame Tussaud. She did not interrupt their intense conversation, but instead waited until after the visitor left to see if Madame Tussaud would mention him to her. When no remark was forthcoming, Marguerite knew from her past experiences with Mr. Philipsthal not to ask about someone when Marie was in no mood to have a discussion.

I may be more than an apprentice, but I am less than a partner, and must remember my place.

They spent a surprisingly contented Christmas together with Mr. Colin. He invited several guild members who were without family to share in a feast of goose pie, plum pudding, and haggis. Mr. Colin also prepared a batch of rum-laced frumenty, and his long, planked dining room table bowed heavily under the weight of dishes, wine bottles, and elbows. All of the diners conversed congenially and even sang popular tunes together. Joseph conducted himself in a considerably adultlike way, and was praised effusively by the men there for his proper gentlemanly manners. By the end of the evening he was drowsing on the hearth next to a crackling fire lit to ward off the outside bracing wind, an unfinished sketch of the Christmas diners dangling from his lap and Mr. Colin's terrier, Angus, curled up next to him.

By the time Mr. Colin's guests rose to depart, the tallow candles around the room had burned down to sputtering stubs and only dregs were left in the bottles of rich elder wine. Joseph was sprawled out on the hearth, using Angus as a pillow.

"Well, Mrs. Ashby, I think it's time to get my Nini to bed. You look peaked, too. You need sleep."

Marguerite covered a yawn with her hand. "I can't remember the last time I feasted so well. Mr. Colin, thank you for your generosity."

Their landlord, who was brisk in manner but very good-humored under his curt exterior, wished them glad tidings and offered them both a selection of fresh pastries from his shop if they would care to visit the following day.

"Oh, Mr. Colin, right now I'm as full as that fruit-stuffed gingerbread we had tonight, but undoubtedly we'll wake up in great need of sweets tomorrow, is that not so, madame?"

But before Marie had an opportunity to weigh in on the desirability of pastries in the morning, the front door banged open and the sound of strident boot steps crossed to the dining room doorway. All thought of comfortable companionship and succulent dining fled their minds.

There before them stood Paul de Philipsthal.

He removed his brown cloak and tossed it carelessly onto a chair in the corner of the dining room. Marguerite, fearing a ferocious battle between him and Marie, jumped up quickly.

"Why, Mr. Philipsthal, may I introduce you to Mr. Colin, who is the finest pastry cook in Glasgow and quite close to a burgess of the city."

The two men shook hands, Philipsthal wary and Mr. Colin perplexed. Marie remained in her seat on the bench at the far end of the table away from Philipsthal, her face murderous.

But Philipsthal was not interested in Marie for the moment and instead focused on Marguerite. "Mrs. Ashby, I have been an utter wretch of a man looking for you. You departed Edinburgh without so much as a word left behind. It was not easy to locate you, you know."

Marguerite kept her hands folded before her, hoping it covered her mildly protruding, sated belly. Would that she could keep from retching her entire Christmas meal because of this unexpected arrival.

"But found us you have. Perhaps you would like some supper? We probably only have dried-up remains left, but I'm sure Mr. Colin would not mind if you sat down for something, would you, Mr. Colin? And the Three Foxes Inn down the street probably has some ale for sale—" She was chattering uncontrollably but unable to stop herself.

"Mrs. Ashby! I've searched for you both for weeks. You only left behind a sign saying you had gone to Wales, which was a falsehood. I had a devil of a time finding you. Why the deception? Why have you hidden from me?"

Why, Marguerite wondered, *are you directing these questions to* me?

She glanced over at Marie in time to see her rising to respond to Mr. Philipsthal. She cut in before Marie said anything antagonistic.

"Mr. Philipsthal, we simply changed our minds while en route to Wales, deciding to return and try our luck in Glasgow for a short time. We fully expected to be back in Edinburgh before you returned, but the show has been quite successful here." She kept her head held high and hoped he wouldn't notice her trembling. Deception was awfully difficult work.

"It was inexcusable for you to leave without at least sending word to me."

"May I remind you that your brief note to us on your departure provided no address where you would be staying. Writing to you would have been quite impossible."

"Yes, well, what's important is that I've found you again and we can join our shows together once again. I've made some decisions, but they can wait until morning. I'm staying at an inn nearby and will return in the morning to discuss our future plans. Good evening to you both. Mr. Colin." He nodded his head to all of them, grabbed his cloak, and was gone swiftly in a swirl of brown wool.

Mr. Colin exited from the rear of the dining room to give the women privacy. Marie's elbows were on the table, her face buried in both hands. "Ruined," she mumbled. "He's determined to ruin me. He wants to send me packing back to France. If only I'd the nerve."

Marguerite sat across from Marie and reached a hand out to cup one of Marie's elbows. "The nerve? The nerve to do what?"

"To kill him. Like he deserves."

10

March 1804. Philipsthal gave Marie a wide berth, much as a rat will do for a stalking cat, to avoid a confrontation. What worried Marguerite, though, was what would happen if the cat backed the rodent into a corner. Which one would come out still breathing?

Late one afternoon a gentle snow was falling and many of the show's visitors were disappearing back to their homes in case the snow should become fierce. The curious little man with the spectacles was closeted in a corner again with a wildly gesticulating Marie.

Marguerite shrugged. It was none of her business. And there were other, more pressing matters for Marguerite personally.

Philipsthal was avoiding Marie, but lurking about to catch Marguerite alone during off-hours of the exhibition. She was uncrating an order of wax bricks to be used in a special order for one of Mr. Colin's guild member friends when Philipsthal appeared from nowhere.

"Oh! Mr. Philipsthal, you startled me," Marguerite said, nearly dropping the ledger book she was using to record her inspection and inventory of the wax.

"My apologies, Mrs. Ashby. I will disturb you only briefly. I was wondering if you would care to join me in shopping for a special clock I intend to use in my show. You have excellent taste and would advise me well, I know. And this time there will be no gifts, I assure you."

Marguerite cringed inwardly at his obsequiousness, but despite that she saw no harm in him. Yes, he had shown up quite unexpectedly and much to Marie's dismay, but wasn't it right that he should know where his partner had gone? He was very heavily invested in the wax exhibit after all. And he had never done anything disrespectful toward her personally.

First ensuring that Marie and Joseph were not inundated with customers, she stepped into the cold winter's air with him. Philipsthal hired a hackney to take them around to three clockmakers until a suitable longcase clock could be found and a slightly modified version ordered. He did not share with Marguerite his exact plans for it, only saying that it would astound his new Glasgow audiences. Then he directed the driver to take a turn through Glasgow Green.

"Just for conversation between friends," he claimed.

As the carriage wound its way through the park, now just a depressing landscape without its summertime blooms and foliage, Marguerite became exceedingly nervous.

There was no purpose to riding through the park at this time of year. What was he planning?

It took just moments to find out.

After a long preamble in which he declared his utmost satisfaction with their friendship and his desire to ever be her benefactor and fellow showman, Philipsthal finally came around to his point.

The man simply could not stay away from the idea of marrying her.

"As I've said, my esteem for you is boundless, and I entertain the conceit that you are not wholly displeased with my own countenance."

"You have been a kind friend to me, yes."

"But I can offer you so much more, more than is actually within your grasp of understanding at the moment."

"What are you saying, sir?"

"I would be the happiest and most prosperous man alive if you would be my wife. And you will find that it will be for your own great happiness, too." He brought Marguerite's hand up to his lips, and she could have sworn his eyes were moist with emotion. She repressed a shudder.

"What is it that I don't understand?"

"Ah, my sweet Mrs. Ashby. You don't know the ways of the world, and are ignorant of how life is a series of compromises. You see, I am so desirous of a marriage with you that I would be willing to give up something else that is very precious to me. And may prove to be very precious to you, as well."

Something precious to both of them? What did Philipsthal own beyond his phantasmagoric equipment?

"Mr. Philipsthal, I beg you to speak plainly to me." She withdrew her hand, which was still clutched in his.

"Of course. As you know, Madame Tussaud has had an unfortunate time in living up to her financial agreement with me. Terrible mismanagement of the wax exhibition, really. But I've been quite patient with her, and have never called in her debt, which would bankrupt her completely. And that would be a tragedy for everyone, would it not?"

"It would. Madame Tussaud is very dear to me." Why did she feel a prickle of alarm at her neck?

"Yes, she's dear to me, too. So, you see, it would be best if I never called in that debt. In fact, I could be persuaded to be generous enough to tear up her contract altogether."

"And what would cause you to—oh."

Philipsthal clasped her hand inside his once again. "I see that you understand me. Marry me, my lovely one, and I will throw the contract onto any fire of your choosing."

Marguerite was so overwhelmed by his suggestion that she was unable to form a coherent response. What was the man saying?

He resumed his cajoling. "Just think. Not only could we live in the happiest of states together, but your friend would no longer be connected to me and free to do as she wishes. And I'm willing to make this sacrifice because of my great adoration of your person."

Great heavens, was she being blackmailed?

"Is there anything else besides marrying me that might compel you to forgive Madame's debts?" she asked.

"Nothing at all. As I said, this contract—and my relationship with Madame Tussaud, of course—are most precious to me. But you are a jewel far above price."

The price is my freedom and my own idea of happiness, is it not?

She fought the urge to flee the carriage and run back to her lodgings. Perhaps from there she could have her belongings shipped back to Hevington and withdraw back to the Greycliffe home, her place of retreat.

That would never do. What of Madame? She may have erred a bit in the management of her show, but she was a kind woman, a good mentor, and a dear friend when Marguerite was in despair. Didn't she owe the waxworker more than fair-weather treatment?

But did she owe her *this?*

Even though it was a cold day, Marguerite felt stifled inside the carriage. She needed time for a decision with such far-reaching implications.

Such permanent implications.

"Mr. Philipsthal, your offer is most generous, but I would like a little time to think on it."

"There is no time! Er, what I mean is that I'm so keen to call you my wife that I will simply expire from anxiety while waiting for your decision. And, after all, how difficult a decision is it? I will be the most generous husband in the world to you. I'll set you up in your own wax exhibition, and you can run it as you see fit. Few men would be willing to do so."

Her heart rushed back for a moment to Nicholas. *No, Mr. Philipsthal, there was one other man in the world willing to let me work at my heart's desire.*

But would Philipsthal be true to his word? Would he both forgive Madame's debt and allow her to continue in her new profession? And if so, well, life could be far worse, couldn't it? He didn't seem the type to beat or humiliate her in any way.

Still.

He just didn't have the appeal for her that Nicholas did. Even that lieutenant, Darden Hastings, sour as he was, had a rather comforting quality to him that would be attractive as a husband.

Now what in the world made me think of the lieutenant just now?

"Mrs. Ashby? What is your answer?"

What other answer was there? She could never face Madame Tussaud knowing that she held the solution to her never-ending financial problems and refused to use it.

God help me, I have to do this.

"Yes, Mr. Philipsthal, I agree to your terms."

A mixture of relief, gratitude, and lust all passed across Philipsthal's face.

"You have made me the happiest of men, my dear. The happiest."

"Remember, Mr. Philipsthal, your promise to forgive my employer's debt. I would also ask you to promise to let me continue my work with the present wax exhibition. I'm not yet talented enough to have my own wax salon, even if I wanted it."

"My dear lady, once more I insist that you call me by my Christian name, Paul. I am to be your husband now. And I will now call you Marguerite. Lovely, lovely Marguerite." He still had her hand in his grasp, and he began kissing each finger individually.

Marguerite's breathing was rapid and shallow, and she knew he was mistaking it for excitement. But she was mostly revolted. His lips on her fingers felt smooth but cold, like a lump of wax before it is heated for sculpting. All of a sudden she was not sure she could endure those same lips on her own or elsewhere upon her body. That thought led to what else would transpire under cover of darkness once she was married to him. Activities that would be his right to demand as often as he liked. This time she could not contain her shudder.

Philipsthal smiled. "My darling, I know. You are as anxious for our union as I am. Why don't we wed as soon as possible? This very night, in fact."

Marguerite pulled her damp hand away from his, pretending to be searching for something in her reticule as an excuse for disengaging from him. The first item she touched was a small mirror, and she pulled it out, feigning a surreptitious look at her hair and patting a few strands in place. But Philipsthal was so eager in his adoration he hardly noticed. She determined to maintain her composure while keeping him at bay.

"I'm sure we don't need to be as hasty as that. I would like to visit your lawyer with you to draw up whatever documents are necessary to release Madame Tussaud from her obligations."

"Of course, of course. In fact, as an added gesture of my goodwill I will turn ownership of the Egyptian mummy over to her. It's of considerable value, you know. But I intend to hold you to your promise, you little minx. I insist that we be married now, and I promise we will take care of the legal peculiarities first thing tomorrow morning."

Little minx? Is there anything remotely devious about me? Marguerite wondered. *Well, I suppose I might try something less than sincere.*

She gazed up and gave him her best attempt at a winsome smile. "Paul, you are my future husband, so of course I can trust you to do as you suggest. But I do have one more request."

"Anything, my love, just say the word."

"You once told me that we were friends and that some of the finest marriages have been born out of great friendships."

"Yes, we are the best of friends. And we will be rich and happy together. So very prosperous. Lovely Marguerite. My dear wife. You'll abandon Tussaud as soon as you see how successful you can be on your own. You'll enjoy being my partner in the Phantasmagoria, too. My delightful partner." Philipsthal's words were cascading out as a rushing stream of water in his excitement over having finally secured his goal. He was once again grabbing for her hand, this time taking them both in his now sweaty palms.

"It would make me very happy indeed if our marriage might proceed at a slower pace than normal."

"Slower? What do you mean by slower?"

"With our very short overall acquaintance, don't you think it would be a bit unseemly to engage fully in our marital commitment?"

Philipsthal's dark eyes narrowed. "My love, we will be man and wife. Exactly what marital commitments do you propose avoiding?"

She took a deep breath. *Careful, here. You must appear earnest about the marriage.*

"Naturally I don't wish to avoid anything. You will be my husband, and a fine one, I'm sure. It's just that I was an innocent maid when I married my previous husband and know little about the ways of a more experienced man such as yourself. I would wish for you to give me time to adjust to the idea of sharing a marital bed with so . . . knowledgeable . . . a husband. You must understand my fears of disappointing you."

The subterfuge made her ill. *Just imagine if I were one of those lady spies I've read about in novels. I would be snared and in a French dungeon in seconds!*

But to her great surprise the flattery worked. His eyes brightened and he was once again the ardent suitor.

"Sweetheart, of course I understand. I forget that just because you were once married it does not mean you are a woman of the world. You must forgive my devotion, which probably seems like overzealous passion to someone who has lived as sheltered a life as you have until now. We will wait a few weeks until consummating so that you have time to prepare. But I assure you the experience will be delightful." His eyes were full of amusement at his own cleverness.

Marguerite bit back a retort. She was getting her way and a caustic tongue would cost her everything. She simpered gratitude to the best of her ability.

"I knew you would understand my reticence and come immediately to my rescue. Perhaps I can continue to live in my rented rooms until I let Madame Tussaud know of my new arrangements."

"Continue living in your rooms? But how will you grow accustomed to our marriage, living apart from me? I am a patient man, my love, but also an eager husband."

She pictured once again his mouth wetly exploring her body, which only Nicholas had ever seen, and envisioned him rolling toward her deep in the night, seeking—no, demanding—her acquiescence in whatever activities he thought would be of pleasure to himself. She could not imagine that he would be gentle, but that he would be anxious and therefore clumsy. And being such a large man he would probably end up crushing her in his eager and amorous embrace. She shook her head to erase the depressing thought.

"No, Paul, of course you are right. I am entirely too selfish, when you are making me such a generous offer. You will prove to be a most competent husband, helping me to chart a proper course."

He softened once again under flattery. "You will learn that I am the most generous of men. On second thought, I see no harm in you staying with Marie a few weeks longer. After all, we have an entire lifetime together, don't we?"

An entire lifetime, indeed. What a revolting thought.

Unfortunately for Marguerite, their marriage was to be conducted in haste, since Scotland did not require the reading of banns, which would have at least delayed things a short while.

After only three days all was in order and she was duly pronounced Mrs. Paul Philipsthal. She dropped the gold band into her reticule the moment they left the church, promising sweetly to put it back on the moment she moved in with him. She did agree to wear the silver luckenbooth brooch, a traditional Scottish symbol of love, which he gave her as a wedding gift. How she would explain it to Marie if she asked, heaven knew.

The next day he cornered Marguerite at the exhibition, a lovesick expression on his face.

"My love," he whispered softly. "Since we have no opportunity for a real wedding trip right now, I will try to give you outings in snatches. Let's attend a geggy performance tomorrow afternoon. They sound to be quite amusing."

"A geggy performance, Mr. Philip—Paul? What is that?"

"My innkeeper told me about it. They're usually only held alongside the Glasgow Fair, but this troupe has been wandering the countryside for months giving shows. Say you'll come with me and see for yourself. As my dearest friend in public, of course, Mrs. Philipsthal. Besides, I am still quite put out by your disappearance from Edinburgh and my temper can only be improved by a liberal application of your delightful company."

"The delight of my company may be a matter of debate, sir, but

I am certainly interested in this geggy performance you speak of. I believe Madame and Joseph can do without me for a few hours."

"Excellent! I will come around for you around two o'clock."

The following day's frigid temperature was made more dismal by dark, cloudy skies that threatened some sort of unpleasant precipitation. Marie grumbled that the heavens should just do their worst and get it over with so visitors would come back to the exhibition.

But by two o'clock it was several degrees warmer and the skies had cleared without ever releasing a drop of moisture. Marie groused anew, this time that Marguerite was running off just as the exhibit would become crowded again.

"Madame, I shan't be gone too long. After all, it will be dark shortly. Please don't worry about my outings with Mr. Philipsthal. I assure you he means me no harm, and just seeks some . . . innocent companionship. And anyway, is it not in the best interest of the exhibit to maintain friendly relations with its investor?"

"Investor? Hah! Scoundrel, more like." But Marie's face softened slightly. "I am too hard on you, my girl. Maybe you're right. You keep Philipsthal calm. Maybe you'll even save exhibit one day, *non?*"

Marguerite smiled as she pulled her wrap around her and tightened the ribbons of her hat to keep it on securely. "I hardly think I shall ever be as important as all that."

As Marguerite passed through the doors of the salon, she came upon the little man Marie had been conversing with secretly.

"Good afternoon, miss." He greeted her politely, but with no recognition of who she was.

"Good afternoon, sir. Are you here to visit the exhibit?"

"What? No. Ah, yes, yes I am. Quite remarkable entertainment, dinna you think so? I trust you enjoyed your own visit."

"Yes, it was a lovely visit." If he did not plan to reveal himself to her, neither would she return the favor. "Good afternoon, sir."

Philipsthal waited for her nearby with a rented hackney. He wore a sturdy gray coat and thick gloves against the unpredictable Scottish weather. They rode only a short way before Philipsthal had the driver stop at the west end of Glasgow Green.

"Paul, such a short distance. Surely we could have walked here."

"Nonsense. I won't have you catching chilblains out here in the elements. Besides, it will be cold enough where we're going."

He escorted her to a large tent pitched in the middle of the field a few hundred feet away. About fifteen feet tall, the tent was made from faded canvas on a wooden frame, of an indistinguishable color, but looked sturdy enough. People in costumes milled about a large open flap in the center of the tent, and strains of music wafted out clearly through the chilly air. Numerous bonfires leaped merrily up in the air on the grounds surrounding the tent, and food and ale sellers hawked their offerings nearby. Several drunkards sang lustily.

"Go fetch to me a pint o' wine,
And fill it in a silver tassie;
That I may drink, before I go,
A service to my bonnie lassie."

Marguerite shuddered. Drunken men meant mischief, as she well knew. Philipsthal put an arm around her and led her away. The air was suddenly windy, an unsurprising event in the fickle Scottish climate, causing the bonfires to shift dramatically and singeing a few performers loitering too close to the flames. A chorus of yelps resulted in laughter from others milling about on the grounds.

"Would you care for another meat pie, Marguerite? I remember how much you enjoyed them in Edinburgh."

Marguerite blushed to recall her greedy consumption of that delightful treat. "You remember it kindly, sir. And since you choose not to recollect my appalling manners from that time, I feel less embarrassed to say that I would very much like one."

They took their piping hot treats with them in through the tent flap, with Philipsthal tossing the attendant two pennies for their entry fee. Inside the tent, Marguerite was initially blinded by the darkness, but quickly grew accustomed to the dim lighting. The interior was acrid from the charcoal fires burning in round metal braziers in several places, but it was at least warmer than it was outside. A wooden stage was set up along the opposite side of the tent, and walls along the back edge of the stage had been painted to resemble the interior of a palace. The stage was devoid of any other decoration or prop. Musicians, not uniformed but dressed in simple country clothing, sat to one side playing the lively tunes Marguerite had heard as they approached the tent. As the rising wind outside started to muffle the music, the troupe played with more gusto. Several rows of decrepit wood benches, hardly enough to fill the audience area, were positioned at angles to the stage. Beyond that, the tent contained little other than more costumed performers meandering about with cups of ale in their hands, either muttering lines to themselves or conversing with patrons.

A young boy, no more than Joseph's age, came running up to them. "Dinna you want chairs for you and the lady, sir?" he asked, his teeth already blackening in tempo with his filthy clothes. His wool gloves looked cast-off and were moth-eaten. "Only a penny each."

Philipsthal gave the boy the requested amount and he scurried off, returning in two installments to deliver the battered but clean chairs and setting them up about forty feet from the stage.

"Boy, we'd like to be closer to the performance," Philipsthal said.

"Oh, kind sir, the seats near the stage, they cost a bit more, don't they? It would be just a shilling apiece to put your chairs up nice and tight to the stage. Much better viewing there. Tonight's the last show before we pack up for Dumfries."

Philipsthal tossed another few coins to the child, who, true to his word, placed their chairs near the center of the stage where viewing could not help but be optimum. As they sat and waited, a few other guests joined them in rented chairs, but most of the people filing into the tent were content to sit on the benches, stand, or find a spot on the ground. Sitting with no activity gave rise to more chill and Marguerite rubbed her arms to warm up while they waited for the performance to start. They did not have to wait long.

A man fashionably attired in buckskin breeches, jackboots, and a wool, camel-colored tailcoat with a black top hat gracefully leaped up the three stairs on one side of the stage. He held up both hands in some kind of signal to stagehands unseen. Immediately sounds of "Hush now" rippled through the crowd, and those who could still find bench seating sat down quickly.

"Welcome, kind friends of Glasgow. I am Tavis Baird, the proprietor of this show. Thank you for visiting our humble performance on such a frightful afternoon. We trust that you will not be disappointed by what you see today. No, in fact, your senses will be awash in great emotion. From soaring heights of happiness to bottomless pits of despair, concluding with hilarity and jocularity, all in mere minutes, all only to be found inside this unpretentious pavilion. Today, you have discovered the purest form of entertainment and learning to be had in all of Great Britain. And we bring this to all Glaswegians, from the most elevated of Society to the lowest clerks and shopkeepers and even the meanest of warehousemen." He made a flourish with his arm and bowed to the audience.

Marguerite looked over at Philipsthal. He was grimacing and rolling his eyes. She leaned over to whisper to him.

"Is his introduction too preposterous even for a Phantasmagoria show?"

He bent his head down toward her and whispered back, "My dear wife, I cringe at the man's parody. I would never allow such pomposity at the Phantasmagoria."

"No? I seem to recall a certain stuffed tiger . . ."

He squeezed her hand, just a little too hard. "My love, we're missing the start of things."

". . . and now, ladies and gentlemen, I offer you now a reenactment of that most noble and tragic of lives, one that every Scotsman should have imprinted upon his heart. Prepare your minds and souls as you gaze upon that rightful queen, Mary of Scotland!"

Their host scrambled down a set of stairs on the opposite end of the stage from where he had gone up. A set of wildly made-up and costumed actors entered where Mr. Baird had done minutes earlier.

Each actor brought a prop up on stage, among which were a

chair that was presently demonstrated to serve as a throne, a long-handled ax, and a stuffed dog. After the pieces were set, the actors stood at specific points around the stage. Within moments, a woman richly clad in black velvet ascended the stairs regally. Even without the high ruff and frizzed red hair, Marguerite knew they were being introduced to Queen Mary. The musicians began playing a rousing Scottish air. First she entered a dance with one of the actors dressed in pre-Revolution French court garb. Mary whirled around happily with him. Then the actor pantomimed illness and death while Mary wept over his body. The musicians played on, and Mary caught herself up in another dance, this time with trepidation on her face before her snakelike suitor. He, too, ended in death, but this time other actors illustrated his murder by strangling, while Mary left the stage. She reentered, dressed in luxurious robes of state and a babe clearly swelling underneath her gown.

A scene of hilarity followed, as Mary's lying-in resulted first in the birth of the stuffed dog, then a head of kale, then a bottle of whisky, each one being examined by the midwife in disbelief then thrown off to the side. Finally the midwife produced a swaddled babe, holding it over her head in victory. The audience cheered wildly.

From Marguerite's vantage point, the baby appeared to be a wax figure, but she couldn't be sure. She made a mental note to check with Mr. Baird as to who supplied their wax characters. Perhaps she and Marie could secure custom with theatres like this one.

The play made another sharp turn into seriousness. A third man came to dance with the now svelte Mary. He handled her with the ease of a practiced rake, and she gazed rapturously at him while the other actors stood around shaking their heads and gesticulating their displeasure at her choice and were soon chasing him off the stage.

Next were scenes displaying the Scottish queen's fall from grace among her subjects, and her subsequent flight to England and two decades of imprisonment under her cousin Elizabeth. Whereas Mary was elegantly attired, the English queen was portrayed as a frumpy old maid in a bedraggled dress draped with jewels. The actress playing Elizabeth opened her mouth to the audience and pointed to her plethora of rotting teeth. One of Mary's male attendants walked past Elizabeth and ostentatiously held his nose while waving his hand. The Scottish audience hooted its approval.

Then came the expected denouement. Mary was brought to trial before bewigged actors wagging their fingers at her. She protested her innocence loudly in a speech worthy of Shakespeare, then was led off the stage in shackles. In the next scene she was escorted back up to stand facing the audience in the center of the stage with a rust-stained block before her. Twenty years of detention in cold, forbidding castles had had no effect on the Mary of this play, for she was as fresh and beautiful and elegantly coiffed as she was in the opening scene. Except now she was wearing a loose-fitting, martyr red gown that flowed around her like a roiling ocean of blood.

The queen dramatically ripped open her scarlet dress to offer herself up for execution, revealing a red underskirt beneath, and the crowd gasped at the ear-splitting noise it made. But it was not only the queen's dress that had torn. One of the seams of the tattered old tent had frayed open, and the wind was catching it and unraveling it further.

At first the audience clapped wildly while pointing up, and the actors tried bravely to go on, practically shouting their lines. The queen got on both knees and tried to make her farewell speech while a masked executioner got on stage with his ax and block to conduct his ugly duty. The audience booed the masked actor, but their derision turned into joy when the executioner seemed unable to make his mark. *Whap!* went the false-headed ax against the floor next to Mary's head. He tried again and struck one of the witnesses, who made an exaggerated death swoon. *Whap! Whap! Whap!* The ax could never find Mary's neck. The queen raised herself up, putting one elbow on the block with her chin in her hand, and drumming the fingers of her other hand against the block in impatience. She rolled her eyes heavenward at the English axman's utter incompetence, sending the Scottish audience into gales of laughter.

But before the Scottish queen's fate could be entirely decided, the entire roof of the tent came off in an ear-splitting slash, as if an outraged demon had brought the winds of hell with him to visit the geggy theatre. The wood and canvas walls of the tent, no longer securely supported by its roof, began to tremble.

The audience began to panic. The benches scraped and clattered as people started jumping up and running toward the open tent flap. Even the actors realized their performance was over and hopped ungracefully from the stage to join the stream of patrons who wanted out. But, as it happens whenever a crowd becomes frightened, the cluster of geggy-goers became panicked and aggressive when they could not get out of the tent fast enough.

"Marguerite," said Philipsthal, his voice remarkably calm. "I believe the performance is over. Unfortunately, we are quite far from the exit. Take my hand and I'll get us out of here."

To her surprise, he led her away from the flap and farther down the same side of the tent. The wind was screaming like a wild banshee above them now, so there was no question of regular conversation. A chill was setting in as well, since the braziers were no match for an open air theatre.

He stopped near the corner of the tent and pulled a dagger no bigger than the palm of his hand out of his coat pocket.

Whatever was he doing with that? Did he always carry it about as though he suspected attack at any minute?

But the wind would not permit a question even if she wanted to ask it.

Philipsthal firmly gripped a section of tent and used the blade to cut out a hole, enabling them to pass through. As he handed Marguerite out, she looked backward and glimpsed the bedraggled chair boy behind Philipsthal, tugging on his coat for help.

She watched, stupefied, as Philipsthal reached back in and pushed the boy away. The youngster ran to the older man again, a pleading look in his eyes, and this time Philipsthal let go of Marguerite to turn back in and use a fist across the boy's shoulder, which sent him sprawling.

A fleeting look of pure satisfaction crossed Philipsthal's face.

But there was no time for admonishment as he came through

the cut opening, grabbed her hand, and began to run from the vibrating structure. She allowed him to pull her along against the blowing wind for several hundred yards, then she slowed down, resisting his tug. Her wrap flew away from her in an angry tangle. She stopped altogether and turned to look back at the tent at the sound of cracking and popping that could be heard even over the rushing air. Wood braces were breaking and the entire makeshift building was collapsing inward. People were progressing from mild panic to absolute horror.

"Paul!" she shouted over the roar of wind, breakage, and screaming. "That young boy. He'll be killed in there! We must help him."

"No, come on. He's just a street urchin. He'll never live to see manhood anyway." Philipsthal was pulling on her arm again.

Marguerite wrenched herself away from him, the cold forgotten despite her now modest attire, determined to concentrate later on how right Madame Tussaud perhaps was about Philipsthal's character. She started to run back toward the tent, and at least now she had the wind to her back, moving her along. She had nearly reached the makeshift theatre, which she imagined had been serving its owner well for some years, when it gave a great shudder and collapsed on top of the stage and whoever was left inside.

The screaming around her was deafening. Or was she herself screaming?

She tried to lift the edge of the tent near where she thought the little boy would be. As she did so, the wind was already beginning to lift the flattened theatre and within moments it began rollicking across Glasgow Green like a woman wearing a petticoat on fire.

But it would seem that the wind, having now caught its prey, was bored of it. And in its boredom the blustering current died down as though it had never had an angry moment in its short life. The wreckage from the tent was now plain for all to see.

Other than a splintered stage and cracked braziers, the only casualty was the little boy.

Marguerite whipped around to find Philipsthal beside her once again. His normally neat appearance was ruffled, his hair moving in all directions and his face ruddy. She could imagine that she looked like a wild and demonized witch by comparison. She wished she was one so that she could curse him.

She pointed to the boy's prone figure, which was now surrounded by a weeping and costumed man and woman, presumably the boy's parents. "That poor child is dead. Why did you force him back inside? Why didn't you help him? *Why did you strike him?*"

Philipsthal looked confused at her accusation. "My dear Marguerite, he was nothing. My first duty was saving you, not that filthy creature. I couldn't risk his grabbing your skirts and pulling you to the ground. Surely you understand that."

"But that's just it. I don't understand." She pushed away the arm he was offering her and began walking back toward the road.

What have I done? Am I completely addlepated?

No. 10 Downing Street, London, April 1804. The outer room was busy with messengers, aides, and other government minions buzzing in and out of Pitt's office, now that he had regained his position as prime minister. Darden Hastings was reminded of a frenetic hive of bees, the drones all rushing in to bring food and news to the queen and thus fulfill their sole duty in life.

As he waited his own turn to meet with the prime minister, his mind drifted off to the woman whose queenly grace was stinging his thoughts far too frequently than made sense. After all, Mrs. Ashby clearly thought him a fool. Three times he had been in the lady's presence and had somehow managed to present himself as a horse's rear on each occasion.

What was he thinking, implying that she was some sort of radical dissenter while she was showing him about, *as he had asked her to do,* and appraising him with those liquid amber eyes. Her intoxicating fragrance had left him quite unable to focus on her explanation of the wax characters. Damned if he knew what the scent was. Something floral, he supposed, but whatever it was, it had the same drugging effect on him that he had seen in the East India Company sailors who succumbed to the craving for opium.

Still, no excuse for abruptly stalking off like a lout. Was he deranged?

Alfie always said he was an imbecile when it came to women. But his brother had been married to Honoria since he was barely breeched, so what the hell did he know?

And now it was too late.

Darden had manufactured an excuse to return to Edinburgh, in order to meet with the governor about future fortifications. The business was concluded quickly in a straightforward manner, and he had proceeded directly to the wax salon. The building had been relet to a wallpaper printer. The windows that once displayed replicas of the notorious now held only pattern samples. Only a sign indicating that the wax exhibition had moved to Cardiff remained as evidence that there ever was a bewitching young woman who had lived and worked there.

Discreet inquiries revealed that the exhibition was no longer in Cardiff, if it had ever been there, and he wondered for the thousandth time why the two women would be traveling so mysteriously from place to place. If only he had spent more time in Mrs. Ashby's beguiling presence when he had the opportunity.

Fool.

He shook his head. *Alfie will have plenty to say about my incompetence in handling the situation, no doubt. He'll tell me I should never have left Edinburgh, that I should have written Pitt that I was unavoidably detained in the town.*

But then Alfie doesn't understand how important my work is. That I cannot rest until I've seen things come to rights. And this female distraction was not part of the plan. No, this schoolboy infatuation would not do at all.

"Hastings! What are you about?"

Darden was jolted out of his reverie by the presence of Brax Selwyn, a fellow naval officer in direct service to Pitt. Two more different men had never been such amiable colleagues. Darden had been the last child in a family of four sons, and therefore happily seen off to His Majesty's navy. He had done well, advancing from midshipman to lieutenant in just three years. Obtaining the notice of Admiral Nelson for his coolness under fire during the Battle of Cape St. Vincent, he was quickly selected for a variety of secret and dangerous assignments.

Which suited his ultimate aims quite well.

Brax, on the other hand, was the spoilt and pampered only child of Lord and Lady Selwyn, descendants of an old and fading title. Although his father had wanted him to manage the family estate, Brax Selwyn was not content to be, as he put it, "an oafish sheep farmer." He wanted grand adventure and decided the best place for it was on the high seas.

And Brax had managed to convince his father that going off to the navy was actually in homage to his sire, since he could never live up to Lord Selwyn's deft handling of the family properties, and would spiral it into debt before the next barley harvest. Lord Selwyn had jovially agreed to the outside world that his gregarious, effervescent son would be better suited to a life of great daring, but everyone knew how disappointed he really was. Darden could easily imagine how Brax's father had capitulated to his son, because he had witnessed many of their superior officers granting Brax special favors on just a charming word or two from the young officer. His rise through the ranks had been as stellar as Darden's, and today they were both lieutenants in service directly to Lord Nelson.

But to Darden's knowledge, Brax had not been given a special assignment by the prime minister. So why was he here?

Darden stood to greet his colleague. "You know I run message errands between Lord Nelson and Pitt. But what's your business here in the hive?"

Brax grinned broadly. "To solicit Mr. Pitt's help in my next promotion. You know, to influence Viscount Melville, our esteemed first lord of the Admiralty."

Darden shook his head. "Selwyn, I'm downright stupefied by your cheek. You cannot possibly get promoted that way. How do you manage to secure appointments with men far above your station, anyway?"

Brax's face fell at his friend's implied insult, but brightened up at his own rejoinder.

"Tut-tut, Hastings. Let not your heart be troubled. I'll see to it that you pick up some scraps from me. Perhaps I'll get you an assignment as my boot boy."

"More like I'll be placing a boot up your—"

Brax threw up his hands. "Easy, friend. No need for jealousy over my superior skill and cunning."

"I can out-navigate you any day, Selwyn. As well as whip you soundly in cricket and shooting."

Brax looked up pensively. "Ah yes, quite true. But you'll never be my equal when it comes to the art of winning the fairer sex, will you?"

"I happen to be more selective than you."

"Selective? Hastings, come, when was the last time you courted a damsel?"

"I've courted plenty a lady," Darden said through clenched teeth. He did not like where this conversation was going.

"And were these ladies aplenty vaporous in nature? I've not seen one of them. Perhaps they were the ethereal spirits of real ladies from the past."

"Perhaps I should soak your head in a butt of malmsey, Selwyn. You annoy me."

Brax laughed, the sound hearty and affable. The man had the unique, and irritating, ability to infect others with his joy. It now worked as always, silencing the buzzing bees around them as the workers stopped momentarily to find out where the pleasing noise was coming from.

"Honestly, Hastings, you're such a rigid little prig. I really must take the time to teach you how to live life, not grind your molars through it."

Brax was spared Darden's scathing reply by one of Pitt's clerks, who came to notify Darden that the prime minister would see him now.

Darden nodded curtly to Brax and followed the clerk. He heard Brax call after him, "Hastings, a group of us are going to see *The School for Scandal* at Drury Lane next week. You must come with us. I insist."

Darden let the door to Pitt's inner office click behind him without answering.

Marguerite had a sleepless night following the geggy theatre tragedy. She had run all the way back to Ingram Street and secreted herself in her room without ever emerging for supper or to visit with Madame Tussaud and Joseph, even though she heard them in conversation with Mr. Colin later that evening.

The next morning she saw dark circles under reddened eyes set in the ashen face reflected in the chipped mirror on her dressing table. Well, there was no help for it. She pinched her cheeks to bring some color into them and went down to the exhibition, willing herself to be in good spirits at the same time that she prayed Paul would not show up today. She needed a day or two to compose herself, and then she would demand that he take care of the legalities that would release Marie from her obligation to him. Of her future with Paul Philipsthal she could not think right now.

As she entered the salon, she saw that bespectacled man shaking hands with Madame Tussaud, who was laughing openly with him. She held documents in her left hand. Marie's hair sported a beautiful cerulean ribbon woven through her curls. Even her coiffure seemed happy this morning. How unusual. And ironic. *Wasn't it typically Marie who needed cheering up?*

Marie caught sight of her. "Mrs. Ashby, come! I introduce you. This is Mr. Curran. He's a very important lawyer here and he has been helping me. Helping the exhibition. Look." She handed the documents to Marguerite.

Marguerite shook hands with Mr. Curran before glancing at the papers. They looked very official and had multiple seals and signatures on them.

"What is this?"

"My freedom, Mrs. Ashby. Mr. Curran likes the show and wants to see it succeed. I tell him my troubles and he agrees to assist me for no fee. I didn't know he could work so fast. Philipsthal was afraid of him—hah!"

A small clot of dread lodged itself in her chest.

"What do you mean, madame? Mr. Curran? What do these documents mean?"

Laughter bubbled from Marie again. How odd to see her mentor so cheerful!

Mr. Curran explained. "Madame Tussaud approached me during a visit I made to the exhibition, and told me of her situation with Mr. Philipsthal. Of his unfair contract with her that, had I been her lawyer at the time, I would never have permitted her to sign. You are familiar with it?"

"In fact, I am not."

Marie was apparently too joyous to care whether her apprentice knew all the details. She flapped her arms at Curran so that he would continue the story.

He removed his glasses and wiped them with a handkerchief from his pocket. "Paul de Philipsthal engaged Madame Tussaud under outrageous terms. Under the contract he signed, he loaned her a hundred pounds to transport much of her show to England and set up next to his Phantasmagoria. In return, Madame owed him fifty percent of her show's profits until she could repay him. Repay him with both principal and interest. With such an arrangement, it was very unlikely that Madame could have ever repaid the loan. In addition, he verbally promised to cover the costs of advertising her show, moving her from city to city, and generally getting her established, none of which he has honored.

"Last week I visited Mr. Philipsthal at his lodgings. I informed him in no uncertain terms that unless he considered Madame Tussaud's debt paid in full, based on the excessive amount of her profits she has paid him over the last three years, I would represent her in a lawsuit against him that would surely result in his total ruin."

Marie cut in. "He ran like the plagued vermin that he is, Mrs. Ashby. Philipsthal is no match in brains or wits for Mr. Curran. Mr. Curran is an important solicitor in Glasgow."

Madame Tussaud's laughter was infectious, but it transferred only as far as her lawyer. Marguerite felt a throbbing over her right eye, a sure sign that she would soon be taken with a serious headache. The pain was battling for supremacy over the knot of fear continuing to take shape in her breast. Marguerite's preference was for a headache.

"Mr. Curran, when did you say you first spoke to Mr. Philipsthal?" she asked.

"Just over a week ago."

"And when did he sign these papers?"

"Five days ago. I didn't have a chance to bring them to Madame Tussaud until just this morning."

Five days ago. And he agreed to it earlier.

Five days ago she had not yet committed to marrying him.

Five days ago he had already signed papers releasing Madame Tussaud from her debt.

Marguerite, you extraordinary ninny. Have you windmills in your head? How did you allow yourself to be humbugged like this?

"Mrs. Ashby, are you all right?" Mr. Curran's face swam before her.

"Come, my girl. We'll go to your room. Mr. Curran, she gets headaches, must have one now. I'll help her. Sir, my show is in your debt."

Marguerite was vaguely aware of Mr. Curran leaving the exhibition and Marie escorting her back up to her room, removing her shoes, and urging her back gently on the bed.

"Madame, I must speak with you." Her mouth felt dry and she winced at the daylight streaming in through the windows. She shut her eyes to block the strong rays.

"It can wait, Mrs. Ashby. I will go back to the exhibition while you rest. You need posset?"

"No no. I must speak with you. Need to tell you something . . ." Marguerite's voice was distant and tinny in her ears. Her tongue felt huge and awkward. "Must tell you . . ."

The pain above her eye was now radiating across her forehead and was throbbing a regular drumbeat. Heaven preserve her, this was going to be excruciating.

But not as excruciating as what she had done to herself three days earlier.

The last she remembered before sinking into oblivion was Madame Tussaud promising to bring her hot soup and some nice pastries later that evening.

As she suspected it would be, the headache was an agonizing one. She tossed and turned fitfully for nearly a full day and night before the pain subsided enough for her to rise and at least bathe herself. She had to get back to the exhibition. What was she thinking, leaving poor Madame and Joseph there by themselves for so long?

Once again she dared to sit down and look at herself in the mirror. The dark circles were still there, and she thought she noticed a pinched quality to her face.

Well, no wonder.

Her mind raced frantically over the events of the past few days. How had she been so stupid as to think she could somehow rescue her employer by such a foolish act as marriage with someone as repulsive as Paul de Philipsthal?

Only you didn't think he was entirely *repulsive until the geggy show, did you?*

Then you suspected the truth. And Mr. Curran confirmed it.

She lay her head down on her arms at the dressing table and wept until she was devoid of tears. Looking up again, she saw a distraught and frightened woman staring back at her from the silvered glass.

"Well," she said aloud to herself in the quiet room. "There's nothing for it now but to tell Madame Tussaud and make the best of the situation. But how long do you think you can avoid going to live with him?"

She stood and squared her shoulders, determined to put a good face on things with her employer. And to brave out whatever would happen with her new . . . husband.

11

Willow Tree House, London. Nathaniel sat slouched on a settee in the parlor of the Carlson family, where he was waiting to be introduced to their daughter, whom he assumed would be a saggy-breasted, mare-faced spinster, shrill and pathetic.

At least, he slouched to the extent that one could on this dratedly uncomfortable piece of furniture. A pillow on the floor would be better than this.

For once he was quite put out with his mother. She had met Mr. and Mrs. Carlson at some blasted party somewhere, and her motherly senses, as finely tuned as those of a spider sitting in her web waiting for a succulent insect to float by, unwary that it is being stealthily watched, had engaged the couple in conversation and learned that they had an eligible daughter whom they despaired of marrying off. They did not present it this way to her, merely hinting that they had increased their daughter's dowry for the *right* prospect, but Maude Ashby's sharpened focus on rising in Society was such that she knew exactly what that meant.

It meant that Nathaniel needed to pay a visit to secure the girl's affections.

So here he was, wondering how much Miss Edwina Carlson would resemble her mother. Perhaps he'd be lucky and she'd look more like her father, who was overweight but at least had the remnants of good looks about him.

He stood as Miss Edwina entered the room.

And immediately planned his escape.

On his return home, in between planning an explanation to his mother and considering whether to visit Mrs. Claire's for some gentlemanly entertainment that evening, his thoughts drifted to his sister-in-law, Marguerite. If only that had worked out. She would have been a finely crafted sculpture on his arm during the day and a warm filly in his bed at night. How interesting it would be to possess the woman his brother had treasured over treasure itself. That smug, arrogant sibling of his. Always so kind, faithful, and righteous. How nauseating. He probably never even defended himself against the invaders of his shop.

Whatever had happened to Marguerite once she ran away? Was she still in England or had she fled to the Continent? He'd have to investigate.

Now that was something pleasant to consider.

"My girl, no! I should have known Philipsthal would not let me go readily. He always plans evil. What do we do?" Far from Marie's joy of two days ago she was now distressed and wringing her hands. "I know. We'll see Mr. Curran. He will fix this. He'll fix it."

Mr. Curran appeared at the show within an hour of their pressing a message into a courier's hand. They left Joseph to deal with customers—Marguerite was still amazed at his maturity—and led the solicitor back into Mr. Colin's parlor.

"Madame, Mrs. Ashby, what troubles you?" Mr. Curran asked, breathless from his quick trip to the salon.

Marie spoke up. "It's Philipsthal."

"Again? But I took care of that. You won't have trouble over that contract again."

"No, it's worse than the contract."

In her odd blend of French and poor English that she employed when hot tempered, Marie outlined for Mr. Curran what Marguerite had told her that morning.

"So you're saying he asked you to marry him, knowing that he had already signed away his rights over Madame Tussaud's profits but promising you that he would give up his rights subsequent to your marriage? But this was not a written agreement prior to your marriage? Hmm." Mr. Curran pursed his lips and rubbed his chin. "What has happened in the intervening days since your marriage?"

"Nothing, really. We went to an outdoor theatre performance."

"The one on Glasgow Green? You know the geggy theatre there blew away. Killed a young boy."

"Yes, I know."

"Has he been cruel, beaten you? Have you committed adultery during this time?"

"Of course not! I'm not even living with him yet."

"He has permitted you to remain in your present living circumstances with Madame Tussaud?"

"Yes. I told him I needed time to, er, adjust, to our marriage." Marguerite reddened. How humiliating to have to discuss these details with Marie's solicitor.

"Forgive the indelicacy of this question, but has the marriage been consummated?"

"The marriage has not . . . progressed . . . quite that far."

"Yet he wishes to live with you. Truthfully, unless your husband has cause to divorce you—such as through your own unfaithfulness—as long as he desires to live with you, he is free to do so. The most you might be able to effect is a judicial separation if he also wished to live apart from you, but no divorce. My apologies, but this amounts to merely a wife's unhappiness, which does not entitle you to pursue legal action. I cannot—will not—take your case. I doubt anyone else will, either. I recommend that you make the best of it."

The best of what*? My life has utterly, completely disintegrated into the wax shavings that litter the floor, and all because of my own foolish decisions. I am a lunatic of the first order. Madame will fire me for certain. Who wants an unfortunate making plaster casts of respectable townspeople?*

She found that she was speechless. And shaking.

Marie shook her head. "My girl, there are other solutions. You wait here. I'll show out Mr. Curran."

Marguerite sat obediently on one of the few chairs in the room, an uncomfortably hard one in the old Queen Anne style. Marie returned promptly after showing out the solicitor and pulled up a matching chair next to her.

How ironic, Marguerite thought, *that he could so easily save Madame from Philipsthal, but he has to let me drop into the fiery pit.*

Marie reached over and patted Marguerite with her rough hand, calloused from years of plying her trade.

My hands would be honorably worn like this one day had I not jumped into this foolish marriage. Now I'll just be Paul's own personal moll, to do with what he likes. The thought is just too much to bear. It's too much.

"Mrs. Ashb—I guess now you're Mrs. Philipsthal—I have an idea."

Marguerite fought the urge to cry, which would have added weakness to her already growing list of ill-advised mistakes.

"Madame, I believe that I should now like you to simply call me Marguerite."

"Yes, I do that. And you call me Marie. After all, we're friends now, yes?" She gently chucked Marguerite's chin. "But no crying. I have idea. We'll go to Dublin?"

"We? How can I do that? I have to do what my husband wants."

"Philipsthal's an idiot. He's also terrible businessman and cannot make money without me. So I'll tell him that I plan to go to Dublin with the exhibition and will pay you double wages to go with me. I'll tell him we'll be back in a year."

"A year? But why would he agree to it? A year is a long time for a married couple to be apart."

Marie shrugged, a distinctively French gesture. "I've not seen my François for two years now. Of no matter when there are greater things to be gained. We'll tell Philipsthal that you make lots of money in Dublin. He'll like that. Will want you to go. Won't care that you're gone."

"I don't know. I don't think he'll agree." Was that another headache dimly forming at the base of her neck? "I suppose we can try."

By the next morning, Marguerite had worked through her own grief—after all, what was marrying a blackguard when compared to witnessing your dearly beloved murdered in front of you—and was feeling sufficiently angry to want to do battle with her new husband.

Philipsthal appeared at midmorning, brightly attired in a bright blue and gold embroidered waistcoat that practically sparkled underneath his darker overcoat. Marguerite thought he resembled nothing more than a strutting peacock.

She was in the process of painting rosy red cheeks on Princess Caroline, now estranged from her husband, Prince George, and in a bitter custody dispute over their daughter. Marguerite felt a strange kinship to Princess Caroline and her problems. She started so badly upon seeing Philipsthal swoop down upon her that poor Caroline ended up with a bright pink band across her nose.

"Mrs. Ashby," he boomed. "How do you fare this lovely Scottish morning? Unseasonably warm today, but that's just the unpredictability of this country, isn't it?"

"She knows," Marguerite said flatly, quickly wiping down the princess's nose and cheek.

"She? She knows what?"

Marguerite lay the cloth down on the portable worktable.

"Madame Tussaud. My employer. My friend. She knows of our marriage."

"She does? Why, that's just fine. Now we don't have to pretend, and I can call you my darling Marguerite in public."

Marguerite picked the paintbrush back up and pointed it with the brush end toward him.

"Not only does Marie know about *us*, but I know about *you*. You and your concession that predates our wedding—your proposal even—by days." Her thrusts with the brush resulted in tiny droplets of pink color splattering on his dazzling waistcoat. She hoped it was ruined.

Philipsthal at least had the decency to look abashed. "So perhaps there may have been a little overlap of a day or so between my proposal to you and my generous relinquishment of Madame Tussaud's debt. I intended to do both, so certainly I cannot be faulted for some discrepancy in timing."

"Discrepancy in timing?" Marguerite slammed the paintbrush back down on the table. She felt a small splotch of paint hit her own chin. "How dare you? You are a cretin of great magnitude, Mr. Philipsthal. Never ask me to call you by your Christian name again. You had already been run aground by Mr. Curran before you made your proposal to me. You offered to forgive Marie's debt after you had already signed away your claim. You lying, phony swindler. You cheated Marie—and me!—all the while suggesting Marie was an inferior manager. I despise you." Marguerite was now alternating between a hiss and a shrill tone that she could not even recognize as her own.

Her new husband replied with the same calm he had exhibited at the geggy performance. "Sweetheart, there is no need to be upset. You fail to see the great benefit you will receive from being my wife. You will be the mistress of two great shows—the Phantasmagoria and the new salon I will allow you to build—and you will have the respectability of marriage with a known entrepreneur. No more of this prowling from town to town. We will settle down permanently in a city of your choice. Soon you will start having children and your days will be quite full and happy. Which reminds me, I see little reason now for you to continue to live apart from me. Why not pack your things and I'll have them sent to my own rooms."

"Clearly, sir, you have not listened to a word I've said. I will *never* live with you, *never* share your bed, *and never* be more than your wife in name only."

Two female patrons that had been walking casually by hurried their steps away as they heard Marguerite's raised voice.

In contrast, Philipsthal lowered his. Dangerously so. "My dear wife, I've been patient with your coyness. And I am perfectly agreeable that you should remain in Madame Tussaud's employ for the time being. But you will respect my authority as your husband. You have one week to begin residing with me on your own, or I will drag you out of the building myself."

Marguerite stopped. She was vaguely aware of breathing heavily and knew her eyes must be flaming. But the spark quickly died. He could indeed insist on his marital rights, couldn't he? How could she possibly let him touch her? *Change your tone,* she warned herself. *Keep him at bay until you can flee to Dublin.*

"I suppose you're right that you do have that power over me. Very well, in a week I'll pack my belongings and bring them round to your lodgings."

She turned back around to Princess Caroline, lest she see any look of smug satisfaction on his face.

But Marie seemed to have rescued her, visiting her room later that night long after closing to tell Marguerite of her own visit to Philipsthal's lodging.

"I told him, Marguerite, that the lawyer Curran says there is much fortune to be had in Dublin. Philipsthal, he fears Curran but also respects him. Takes Curran's word. I told Philipsthal that I want you to come to Dublin with me for a year and I pay you double. You'll make lots of money to help support his fog-brained show while he stays here to keep it open."

Marguerite gripped her friend's hands. How remarkably close they had become over this calamity. "And what did he say?"

"He agrees. Says you both need money to start your life together. Says he will talk to you about writing him every week." Marie rolled her eyes. "Once we get to Dublin we'll figure out next steps. Tomorrow I'll courier a letter to an agent there to obtain a new salon and lodgings. Mr. Curran is returning to Dublin and will help us."

"He wouldn't help me before—I'm sure he won't now."

"Bah! He couldn't do anything because he cannot practice real law in Scotland. He's a lawyer in Ireland. He never even sued Philipsthal, just threatened him. I know he'll help you once we get to Dublin."

Marguerite's doubt must have shown on her face. "Yes, you trust me, Marguerite. I will not let you be harmed. This reminds me. I know this abominable marriage has not been fully transacted yet, but has Philipsthal . . . made any demands for your person . . . yet?"

"No, but it is uppermost in his mind. He told me this morning that he wanted me to move to his lodgings within a week or he would forcibly move me there. But if he's agreed to let me go to Dublin, what does that mean? Will he expect me there tomorrow so he can claim me?" Marguerite touched the side of her head above her right ear to quell a small throb just prickling under the surface of her scalp.

"Tell him that you have your courses."

"He won't believe me. A scoundrel knows a lie when he hears one."

"Then I'll keep you so busy and out of sight that he can't even find you."

What a staunchly loyal friend her employer was turning out to be.

"Marie, thank you, but I think I must spend tonight adjusting to the fact I will be repenting at great leisure my extraordinarily foolish action. How did I tumble down from such great heights as marriage with Nicholas to bondage with Mr. Philipsthal?"

Marie could do no more than look at her sorrowfully, hug her, and leave her alone with her thoughts.

She passed the night restlessly, but fortunately without a headache exploding behind her eyes. The following morning she choked down some dry toast points and two cups of tea before heading down to the salon to resume her work on Princess Caroline. Not thirty minutes had elapsed before Philipsthal was at her side, smiling boyishly at her as though he was once again her ardent suitor and not her new, demanding husband.

"Marguerite, has Madame Tussaud told you yet?"

"Told me what?" She did not look up from her work. Hmm, the princess's forehead seemed a bit too expansive. That would need fixing. She made a mental note to acquire some more horsehair for dyeing and insertion.

"The silly little pigeon wants to take the show to Dublin for a year. Ordinarily I would say absolutely not. Why would I want my lovely wife removed from my sight? But she proposes to pay you double wages. Think what we could do to improve my show with that money!"

"Indeed. Your show has been uppermost in my mind as of late."

"Splendid. I knew I was marrying a conscientious woman. I agreed to it, then I must confess I had a very sleepless night thinking about being separated from you for so long. It's not good for a newly married couple to be alienated from one another. Not good at all."

Drat, Caroline's left earlobe was nipped off. Had some prankster done this when no one was looking or did they have a rat problem?

"And so this morning when I arose, I realized the solution was very simple. I will come with you."

This got Marguerite's attention. Caroline's ear could stay mangled.

"Come with us? Why? I mean, how can you do so? What of your Phantasmagoria?"

He gave her the same French shrug that Marie did, a movement that suggested that such trifles were not so important. "It is far more vital that I be at my wife's side than that my show be a success in Glasgow. Besides, after Dublin we will establish a permanent entertainment in a city of your choosing. Remember my promise to you?"

"And how does this promise compare to your promises to Madame Tussaud?"

His reply was a hideous echo in her ear. "My dear Marguerite, she is nothing. But I have a duty to you."

Just like the poor chair boy. Blood roared in her ears. How blind she had been to this man.

He continued. "And you have a duty to me as well, sweetheart. As such, I will not interfere with your living arrangements as you prepare for Dublin. But upon our arrival in Dublin, that very first night, we will live together as man and wife. Don't look so downcast, my darling wife. I know you are inexperienced, but I will guide you back into your role as my helpmeet."

And so the die was cast. Marie could not change her mind now that Philipsthal had decided to accompany them, without revealing her connivance with her apprentice. Her temper grew short, leaving little camaraderie between her and Marguerite. Even Joseph avoided his mother during their final days in Glasgow.

The only member of their party who was unaffected by the move to a new town was Philipsthal himself. He popped in periodically to check on progress, chucking Joseph under the chin and kissing Marguerite's hands, but he always had a bevy of excuses for leaving when implored to assist with moving and packing the figures and tableaux.

Marguerite asked him to contribute some desperately needed cash for transport of the show, to which he replied, "Dear wife, Madame Tussaud made it perfectly clear that she wanted our partnership dissolved. Now she is spiriting my bride away to Ireland and expects me to cover the expense? Preposterous."

Marie's anger finally gave way to acceptance. "I'll never get rid of him. He spun a web around me and the harder I try to get out, the more firmly he secures me. I regret, dear friend, that you are involved."

The two women hugged one another without tears, which had dried up much like small saplings that are left devoid of moisture when a giant oak covers them with its leafy canopy and saps the surrounding soil of nutrients. Their hope of rejuvenation through transplantation to Dublin was dimming every day as the oak's branches blocked more and more of the sun and rain.

PART FOUR

Dublin

12

Great Harbour, Greenock, Scotland, May 1804. The frigid air, swollen by misty rain, was bone piercing. How did it remain so cold in Scotland this late in the spring? Marguerite's throat hurt from inhaling the freezing vapors every time she opened her mouth to speak. Next to her, poor Joseph's teeth were chattering as he hugged his arms around himself. She drew him close to her skirts and hugged him. She studiously ignored Philipsthal as he stood on her other side.

Marie was in deep discussion with the captain, evident by the frosty gusts of air emanating from their mouths. Marie shook hands with the man and gingerly picked her way back across ice patches to where they waited.

"Captain Alison says weather is not good for crossing. We must stay overnight and leave in the morning. Marguerite will stay in the room with me. Joseph, you stay with Mr. Philipsthal." Marie's tone brooked no argument, and Philipsthal seemed too frozen to care.

So they trudged off to an inexpensive inn near the docks while their six drays' worth of goods for the wax exhibition and the Phantasmagoria were loaded into HMS *Earl Moira*'s hold to await better sailing the next day. After the exhausting two days spent in a rattling carriage ride covering the thirty miles between Glasgow and Greenock, now they had to wait to complete their journey. The quartet supped silently and went to their respective rooms, kept awake most of the night by howling winds and the insistent tapping of sleet on the windows.

They returned the following morning only to be told to return again the next day.

And the next day.

And the next.

In all they waited nearly a week for the weather to settle down enough for the captain to signal for a departure. The women's nerves were frayed, Marie's because of the ever-burgeoning expenses of the move, and Marguerite's as she drew inward in contemplation of what her life was to be in Dublin.

Ash House, London. Nathaniel's search for Marguerite had been rather fruitless, but proved to be far more interesting than cozying up to whatever latest bucktoothed, pockmarked young lady of wealth his mother had dredged up from the Society papers. His first act had been to write to Marguerite's aunt. He'd received a rather curt reply from Lady Greycliffe that she had no idea where Marguerite was off to at the moment, but that she was sure Marguerite would have told him had she wanted him to know.

Damned impertinent she was.

He next engaged a private inquiry agent, but the most he learned was that the wax exhibition she was apprenticed to, Dr. Curtius's Cabinet of Wonders, had left London for Edinburgh, then disappeared. It was supposed to have gone on to Wales, but there was no evidence of it ever having arrived there.

Hmm. Now what?

Wouldn't it be a lark to go himself to look for her? Imagine the surprise on her face to see him there. And that surprise turning to great admiration when she learned how brave and clever he had been to find her. Smarter and more courageous than his idiot brother, for sure. Her shock would be better than the haughty look she had worn as Nicholas's wife.

But what would he have to show for his efforts once her initial amazement wore off? He'd need something to demonstrate that he was a better man than his brother ever was. He needed an honor, a medal, a recognition that even she could not deny. *Wait—didn't Mother say something about Mr. Pitt forming a new alliance to displace the prime minister? That would be a jolly intrigue. And one at the top levels of the government. Splendid.*

He rang for a servant to fetch him two bottles of the finest port in the Ashby cellar.

Marguerite's level of stunned exhaustion had reached a peak she had not known since the early days of her husband's death.

My first husband, that is.

The group trudged up the plank onto the ship whose tall sails still whipped about in the dying wind as they were set in place. Each carried a valise of clothing and supplies, plus Marie and Marguerite toted aboard an additional box of their most valuable waxworking supplies.

Had they only known that weather was not to be their only problem.

They boarded *Earl Moira* with about one hundred other shivering passengers and a handful of crew. The trip began well enough as they sailed calmly out of the Firth of Clyde and into the North Channel, with brief stops at Rothesay and Brodick to pick up and drop off passengers. Most passengers stayed below deck and out of the cold, but Joseph's unflinching nerve for sailing demanded that he stay above deck to watch the wind and waves. Marie and Marguerite stayed to keep the boy company, while Philipsthal followed the other passengers down below. "Good riddance," Marie mouthed to Marguerite as they watched his retreating back. Marguerite didn't respond, her mind already churning at the realization of what it meant to undergo another sea voyage. She had been so frantic over Philipsthal these last few weeks that she had given little thought to being at sea again. At least the weather seemed to have improved.

But the voyage's simple good luck was not to last.

The captain came to see what hardy souls were braving the chill on deck.

"It's my son, sir," Marie told him, a protective arm around

Joseph. "My little Nini, I call him. He's a very good sailor and doesn't want to go below deck and miss the activity up here."

"Alack! And what of his women folk? You need to consider them, don't you, my boy?" He removed Joseph's hat and ruffled his hair. "Don't one of you have a husband about? I thought I saw a tall man with you."

Marguerite spoke up. "Yes, Captain, my husband chose to go below deck."

"And leave a beautiful lass like you all alone? Why, you would charm the tail off old Lucifer himself. I 'spect my crew is off right now dueling over who will get to speak to you first. A fool your husband is, if you don't mind me sayin'."

The captain belched, loudly enough to be heard over the sails flailing above and the water slapping against the hull below.

He put a hand over his mouth. "Mmm, sorry, ladies. Must have been some spoiled beef. You best get below deck soon, though. Son, you'll take care of them now, d'ye hear me?"

Joseph nodded solemnly at the uniformed figure before him.

"Marie"—Marguerite grabbed her friend's arm as the captain disappeared from sight—"I could swear that man is in his cups. Did you smell the fumes when he blew wind at us?"

"I did, but thought it was as he said. Foul meat."

"I don't think so. I wonder if he's fit to pilot the ship. A drunken captain is a dangerous one." As though the journey itself was not enough to fret about.

"He's got crew, though, my girl. They take care of things. Not to worry."

But Marguerite was not convinced.

As the prow headed into the open waters of the Irish Sea the weather became impossibly colder, and so the trio headed into the interior of the ship, much to Joseph's protests. They did not seek out Philipsthal, but instead found companionship with a family by the name of Callum, consisting of a husband, wife, and three young girls of whom the eldest could not be more than ten years of age. They were traveling to Dublin as well. Mr. Callum was a land surveyor by trade, but had fled the Catholic persecutions in Ireland more than fifteen years earlier. He settled in Scotland, married and had children, and thought to spend his life there. But the toning down of persecution over the last decade, followed by the Act of Union in 1801, convinced him that it might be time to return home. Especially since there was now a profusion of ambitious building projects going on in Dublin that could keep him employed for many years.

The adults played cards in a common area where many passengers milled about, while Joseph and the Callums' three girls explored the ship together. Marguerite quickly realized that her innards were far more unsettled down inside the ship than they were topside. She rubbed a hand furtively across her stomach. *Please, dear God, don't let me embarrass myself in front of all these passengers.*

At least she had no headache.

But soon enough her intestinal focus was replaced by sheer terror.

In the open sea past the Isle of Man and northeastern tip of Ireland, the weather seemed to worsen. High gusts of wind blew around the ship, rocking her to and fro. Before long the rocking became violent pitching and it was plain that the ship was making no forward progress whatsoever. Silence fell over the common area, except for the scattered cries of children. Joseph and the three girls returned, all to hide inside their mothers' strong embraces. Leaky vessels, storms, and pirating were all common enough in British waters. What was this ship's fate today?

People withdrew into themselves, cards and games forgotten. The Callum family huddled together, with Mr. Callum offering them words of solace and encouragement.

Marie began muttering. "Figures . . . knocking about . . . Philipsthal's fault . . . need more wax bricks . . ."

Marguerite tried to encourage her. "Madame, we packed the figures as tightly and securely as we could. As long as the ship doesn't—oh!" The ship listed fiercely to one side then righted itself. "As long as the ship does not go down, they should be safe."

Marie raised an eyebrow at her. "Yes, so long as the ship does not go down everything will be perfect."

Marguerite could not help laughing, despite her woozy stomach and the odor of fear permeating the ship. It was so rare that her friend showed a sense of humor.

"I suppose I should go and find Paul. Joseph, would you like to accompany me?" Marguerite stood and held out a hand to him, gripping a nearby beam with her other hand. He eagerly took it.

"Yes, Mrs. Philipsthal, I will take care of you."

And even in the dim interior of the pitching ship, Marguerite could see Marie's glow of pride in her young son. As she turned to leave, she saw that some of the passengers were making their way up to the deck for air, bitter and dangerous as it may be up there. Others were retching into barrels.

They found Philipsthal in his cabin, furiously scratching away on a parchment. The room reeked of vomit and a slop bucket in the corner gave full evidence of how he had been occupying most of his time until this point.

"Whatever are you doing?" Marguerite asked him.

He turned his ashen face, usually so ruddy and hale, toward her. "I am preparing my last will and testament. I must ensure that I provide for you, sweeting, in case something happens on the ship. What say you to that?"

Provide what? Without Marie he was as poor as a church beggar. She ignored his question.

"Wouldn't you feel better up on deck? We're going up there next. Many of the passengers are doing so to get out of this reeking place."

"They're all fools to go up. They'll be washed overboard." Philipsthal returned to his scribbling.

Marguerite and Joseph stumbled their way back to his mother, whom they found busy trying to comfort an elderly couple. Marguerite could hear them chattering away in French. She waited for Marie to conclude her ministrations, then proposed to her that they follow the other passengers making their way to the upper deck. Marie grimly agreed that topside was probably the best place to be, and insisted that the old man and his wife accompany them. They clutched hands in a single line with Marguerite leading the way, the old couple behind her, and Marie at the rear with Joseph grasping her skirts.

It was difficult to even make their way to the narrow stairway with the ship continuing to pitch and roll. Marguerite had to help the wife get up from the deck twice. The woman was reduced to sobbing in French.

"Mon Dieu, aidez-moi. Dieu nous aide tous."

God help us all, indeed.

But their little ragtag group finally made it up into the open air, edging their way along beams, ropes, or other available surfaces that would help them maintain balance. Most of the passengers were clinging to rails along the outer edge of the ship. It had started raining since Marguerite went below. She and the others were soaked by the downpour in seconds, and the drenching seemed to make even her blood freeze. It was impossible to see very far off the ship at all. The only clear things were the waves, now close to reaching the deck of the ship.

What would happen then?

We should have stayed below.

She helped the old couple find seating, such as it was, along the outer edge of the ship, urging them to hold fast to ropes. She had to shout loudly to be heard, and even then the couple looked confused. So she placed the fibers directly into their hands and motioned with her own that they should stay down.

At the moment she let go of the rope, a large white wave crested up like a watery gorgon over the ship, crashing down and sluicing its snaky fingers around the deck, searching for victims. It was rewarded with a man who was trying to calm a crying child. The water knocked them both to the deck, but grabbed the man in its sodden grasp and heaved him over the side of the ship into a frothing grave.

Marguerite, too, felt herself being pulled downward, sliding in rhythm with the ship's tilt. Her head rapped sharply against the decking and she blacked out for seconds—minutes?—before she saw a stranger's face looming over her, gently smacking her face to bring her to consciousness.

She sat up, grasping his hand and sitting up, but the man disappeared before she could properly thank him. She crawled to where she saw a grate on the deck's floor, and curled her fingers into the grid pattern to keep from going overboard. The wind and rain were whipping now, too much for her to have much awareness of where she truly was. Was Marie still topside? Was that Joseph, near the stairs, going back below? The only reality was the incessant onslaught of water over the deck, combined with the ship's sharp pitching and the equally sharp cries of the people who could barely be heard over the roaring wind.

More waves crashed onto the deck, picking off passengers in twos and threes. Marguerite shut her eyes and held on to the grate as though she were clutching her dying husband again. The water felt like sheets of ice pummeling her body into submission.

But the gorgon will not have me. I will not give in to her. I will not be fodder to the sea.

For a brief moment she was transported back to the day she sat down in a tiny stream at Hevington and willed herself to lie back and be drowned. But things were different now. She had to stay alive. To help Marie. To develop her craft. Even to—God help her—help Paul with his own show and learn to be a good wife.

Her thoughts were interrupted by a tremendous jolt. The ship was no longer moving. Had they managed to anchor somewhere? No, the ship would still be bouncing wildly. But within a few moments the ship had dislodged itself from whatever had grasped it and the roiling continued.

The shrieking on deck was unbearable. Was she screaming herself? Underneath her was the distant sound of moaning, praying, and cries for help from down below. Would this voyage of terror never end?

Again the ship seemed to collide with something. Where was the captain? Was the ship steering itself while he drank himself into oblivion?

And now a great groaning noise rose above the bitter winds, sharp rain, and piteous cries of people both below deck and those under continual threat by the water gorgon.

Marguerite wasn't sure what had happened, only that the ship was once again jammed against something. But what was that deafening noise? It sounded as if the ship was complaining vociferously against the unfair treatment it had received by its captain.

And now the groaning was replaced by another noise, this one even more terrifying. The sounds of cracking and splintering could be heard—no, felt—everywhere. They must be grounded somewhere.

How close to shore are we? And what shore? Ireland or Wales? Was she to see land ever again? She shuddered in fear.

And the ship shuddered with her.

With a final moan to accompany the incessant fracturing noises, the ship began collapsing on itself. Marguerite was swept downward, grabbing fruitlessly at objects rushing past her. No, it couldn't be. The sea was rushing up toward her at a phenomenal rate of speed.

I once wanted to die. Now I want to live.

As she slammed into the rushing water, she performed one last act.

She held her breath.

What was this?

Her feet were touching something solid. Soft, but definitely solid. She reached out for a plank drifting nearby and used it to haul herself to a standing position, promptly falling down again from the effort. Dear God, but she was cold. She spit the taste of brackish water from her mouth.

Shivering, she tried to assess what had happened. They must have hit an embankment. Which meant they were close to shore. But how close? She tried to look into the distance. Was that a shadow of land or just her imagination? Ah, the rain was stopping and the wind seemed to be dying down, a small blessing of relief arriving several minutes too late.

She thrashed about in the water, calling for Marie and Joseph. A surprisingly strong voice called back to her from about fifty feet away.

"There you are, my girl. Thought you might be drowned. Nini's here with me. Is that rat Philipsthal with you?"

Even in tragedy, Marie never quite forgot her feelings for her old partner. "No, I haven't seen him since we went topside."

"Bah, he probably jumped from the ship and used his whiskers to guide him to shore."

Marguerite followed the sound of Marie's voice and found her a distance away on the embankment along with about two dozen other passengers. As the rain cleared it was easier to see that the ship had completely broken apart in the storm. Or had their inebriated captain run them aground? Debris and wreckage littered the water as far as the eye could see. Joseph was nearly blue and his teeth were chattering away. Marguerite pulled the soaked boy to her own drenched dress and hugged him in joy of his safety.

Marguerite stepped back and held Marie at arm's length. "Madame, your hair looks . . . dreadful, I'm afraid."

Marie reached up to pat her great vanity, now plastered in flat tendrils around her face, her hat long ago sacrificed to the sea's torrents.

More passengers were dragging themselves onto the bank, standing or sitting in the shallow water covering it. With the wind and rain dying down to the gentleness of bleating sheep, the sounds of crying and praying rose to full prominence again.

"Do you see your friends anywhere?" Marguerite asked Marie. "I lost sight of them not long after we got on deck."

"No, don't see the Callums, either."

"Madame, wait here with Joseph. I'll look." Marguerite wove her way heavily through the stranded passengers, seeking a familiar face from their journey. Finally she found Mr. and Mrs. Callum huddled together, but only two of their girls were with them. They all raised tearstained faces to Marguerite.

Marguerite opened her mouth to say something. Anything. What? Words of comfort?

"My condolences," she managed to squeak out. They turned back inward together, seeking the private solace that families need when a loss has been shocking.

Marguerite dragged herself around some more but did not see the elderly couple anywhere. Perhaps they were still holding on to some piece of the ship and were keeping afloat in the water. She turned to scour the water nearby but was stopped by a shout from Marie.

"Marguerite! Our cases! Broken open! Come now!"

Marguerite sloshed heavily back to Marie and followed the line of her pointing hand. She could see several of their once-securely fastened crates broken open, their contents spilled into the shallow waters.

"Must save the figures!" Marie shouted, plumes of frosty air emphasizing her distress. She stomped out toward the figure nearest her and with Joseph's help dragged it onto the embankment. Poor William Wallace looked as though he had just seen action at the Battle of Falkirk again. Marie signaled to a lone man looking for friends or family in the water nearby.

"You! Must help! Find the wax characters and bring them up here."

"Wax characters? Are you mad? There are living people we need to bring on shore."

Marie stamped a foot as successfully as she could with both legs partially submerged.

"We must save my collection, too. I'm ruined without it. I need help."

The mists of rain and water had completely dissipated now, leaving a clear enough view to see that the shore was only about a hundred yards away. Marguerite was struck with an inspiration. She went out to the man. "Kind sir, we think our wax figure collection will help save us all. If we can bring enough of them onto the embankment, everyone can use them to float to shore." She pointed so that he could see how close land was to them now.

He understood at once and gathered whatever men he saw nearby.

As Marguerite and a handful of men sloshed in the shallow waters, dragging out figures, Marie stood on the embankment like a field marshal, instructing those huddling in the cold to grab figures relative to their size and push off the other side of the embankment toward the shore. Marguerite watched out of the corner of one eye as Marie gestured to the passengers how the figures would help keep them afloat. Taking his mother's cue, Joseph demonstrated by stepping out into the water with his head and arms across the torso of some now unrecognizable petite character figure. He paddled out about thirty feet while his mother vigorously motioned toward the shore.

Soon there were more passengers wanting a wax figure than could be easily produced from the wreckage. A shout from one of the men wading about looking for them took Marguerite's attention away from what Marie was doing and her own futile search.

The man had found a crate lettered TUSSAUD—WAX FIGURES—16 CLARENDON STREET—DUBLIN. He held a piece of iron pipe high over his head to bring it down on the crate to smash it open.

"*Non!* No beating the chest! Leave it alone!" Marie was screaming as she scrambled heavily to where the man lowered his weapon. "These figures are safe. Must keep them safe."

"Sorry, mistress, we need these floaters to get us to shore. You said so yourself." The man swung the pipe up in the air again and slammed it against the crate. Several blows cracked the lid enough that with the assistance of two other men he was able to start digging out figures and dumping them into the water for the others to drag to the embankment.

While the three men worked on their found cache of "floaters," Marguerite continued wading through the debris and wreckage, trying to find other figures they might have overlooked. Several other men had taken on the sorrowful task of searching for passengers who had not survived the breakup of the ship, and two ironic groups of bodies were being placed on the embankment—wax figures, which were immediately grabbed and used to help the next person waiting to get to shore, and dead men, women, and children, largely ignored yet difficult to distinguish now from the lifeless wax characters.

She noticed a dark cape flapping in the water nearby. Another wax figure had floated in. From the looks of the attire she guessed it to be part of their Separate Room collection, either Robespierre or Jean-Baptiste Carrier. At least they would have a starting point for recreating their most popular tableau. She'd have to put this one aside for one of the brave men working to save everyone else, to ensure he had his own "floater" for getting to shore. The figure was face down so she rolled it over.

Marguerite's chilled heart managed to leap from its icy resting place and into her throat as she held the figure's cape in her hand. Revulsion mixed with a strangled desire to laugh.

It was Paul de Philipsthal.

His right hand still clutched the nib of a pen.

So what did your meaningless will document promise me? Your useless Phantasmagoria equipment?

She shook her head in dismay. No need to think ill of the dead. She must get him up on the embankment and return to work on the living. She guided his body back to where the man was pulling corpses out of the water and lining them up like a row of petrified soldiers.

Marguerite shuddered as Philipsthal was dropped unceremoniously at the end of the line. His death was not cause for grief, but it was haunting just the same. Had she somehow been granted an answer to her prayers for rescue, in this morbid way? Did Paul and the others have to sacrifice their lives so that she could escape him? Or was she to suffer herself for his sacrifice? God alone knew.

She resumed her work on recovering wax figures and was grateful that she found no more human bodies. Before long she thought she had found all there was to find, and her activity was no longer sufficient to maintain any kind of warmth. She would need rescue soon herself.

For the last time she sloshed back to the embankment, where now only a handful of people still stood next to the few remaining wax figures. She avoided looking farther down at the line of corpses.

Without a word, she joined Marie. "Where is Joseph?" she asked.

"Already on shore. My Nini escorted a group of children. So brave. I waited for you."

And together the two women joined the last stragglers from the ship with their makeshift rafts and headed for shore.

By the time they reached the shore, a handful of villagers had gathered to help the bedraggled passengers. Many of them gawped in astonishment at the number of wax corpses also floating in. But Marie took charge the minute she was able to stand on firm ground.

"You!" She pointed to a teenaged boy. "You find a wagon for hire and bring here. Need to get to Clarendon Street in Dublin."

Then she addressed a group of women. "Have been shipwrecked and need help. Tell authorities. Bring us hot tea and blankets. Go on, what do you stare at?" Marie flapped her hands at the women, motioning them to do her bidding.

"Careful! Don't hurt the figures. Put them over here." Marie moved off, issuing orders that no one at the scene thought to question in the absence of the captain or any other figure of clout.

Marguerite sank to the sandy shore, wrapped her arms around her knees, and laid her head on top of them. Exhaustion was becoming a powerful influence, quickly overcoming the cold in its ability to sap her strength.

So tired, she thought. *Just need some sleep.*

She began humming to herself to blot out the other noises around her and, despite her soaked body, began to drift off to sleep. And dreamed of nothing.

Whether she had been sleep seconds or minutes, or perhaps even hours, she wasn't sure, but she awoke, startled by a tug on her arm.

"Mrs. Philipsthal! Mrs. Philipsthal! Maman says you must wake up now or never wake up." She lifted her head to find Joseph Tussaud staring worriedly at her.

"Hello, Joseph. Yes, I suppose my work is not yet finished. But I am no longer Mrs. Philipsthal." Marguerite rose up, ignoring the question on the boy's face. She reached out her hand to him and, as they walked to where Marie was directing the loading of figures onto a wagon, said, "You know that you truly are the brave and good boy your mother says you are. I must ask her if we can reward you for your chivalrous acts today."

"What is 'shivrous'?" Joseph asked.

"It means that you have behaved far better and with more bravery than some men four times your age, and you are held in high esteem as a result."

Joseph's chest swelled in pride and he broke away from Marguerite to run to his mother to let her know that he was a shivrous boy who must be steamed right away.

Marie looked at him in confusion, but forgot him as she saw Marguerite's approach.

"Ah, dear girl, I was worried that you go to sleep for good. Would not be a happy event. See here, figures and tools are being loaded for Dublin. We'll join them later. Need to find an inn for food and rest. I think we lost about half of the collection. Half! Years of work. Our work. Gone. It will take years to remake figures. Philipsthal's fault. We wouldn't be here if not for him."

"I don't think you need to worry about Paul de Philipsthal troubling us any longer." Marguerite let her words hang in the air with no further explanation.

But for whatever difficulties Marie Tussaud had in speaking the English language, she had no trouble understanding it and its subtle nuances. Only a passing look of shock crossed her face, to be immediately replaced by relief. She wept and laughed in turns, nearly hysterical. "I would not wish this for anyone, no. But this makes you free now, doesn't it? And to be rid of Philipsthal is to be worth all the work in front of us to rebuild collection. The storm is a tragedy, yet we are blessed, dear lady. Thank the Almighty for the storm He sent us!"

Marguerite could not quite bring herself to be overjoyed about Philipsthal's death, no matter how cloying and dishonest he was in life.

And so now I'm twice a widow. Any man would be mightily unlucky to associate with me now.

And so with a heavy heart to compliment her leaden dress, she accompanied Marie and a prideful Joseph into the village to find warm food, clothing, and beds for the night before following their remaining cache of wax figures to Dublin.

She swore silently to herself. *Except to return to England, I swear this is the last ship voyage I will ever take.*

As always, Marie had secured a location well situated for attracting visitors. Their new salon was housed in the amusingly named Shakespeare Gallery on Clarendon Street. In her typical way of arranging things sight unseen, their new exhibition was positioned neatly in the center of the triangle marked by Dublin Castle, Trinity College, and St. Stephen's Green. Even without Marie's lavish praise of the locale, Marguerite knew that it was to be a successful location, as they would draw patrons from the new United Kingdom MPs, academic scholars, and from the aristocratic families surrounding St. Stephen's. Although commoners made up a large percentage of their visitors, Marie was always most pleased when the upper classes came, not only because she could charge them more, but because they increased the exhibition's respectability.

After working together in three previous locations, Marguerite, Marie, and Joseph had now established a fluid method for setting up the show in the least amount of time possible. Marie quickly took inventory of what damages had occurred during shipment—an onerous task after this voyage—and made initial notes on what tableaux to set up. Marguerite ensured their living quarters nearby were suitably furnished, hired a tutor for Joseph, and ordered whatever supplies would be needed in the coming months. Joseph, with his advancing lettering and drawing skills, worked on broadsheets and other advertisements for the exhibition, which either Marie or Marguerite would review and take to a local printer for reproduction.

The opening of their new location was delayed by the work required to repair the many damaged figures that had been rescued from the chilly waters of the Irish Sea. This time they had a large workroom in the back of the exhibition area, providing them with plenty of space to start remaking several characters at a time.

Marguerite had never been busier and she was glad for it, relieved to be too preoccupied to give Paul de Philipsthal much thought.

One of their first visitors was Marie's solicitor in Glasgow, Mr. Curran. He had heard of their planned arrival but refrained from coming round to the exhibition until they opened their doors.

"The *Freeman's Journal* mentioned a shipwreck with a number of 'false bodies' come ashore, so I knew it had to be Madame Tussaud come to Dublin." Curran's eyes blinked owlishly behind wire frames. "Mrs. Philipsthal, is your husband, er, here?"

Marguerite kept her hands clasped in front of her. "No, he was lost at sea."

"Humph, well, I see. Rather an interesting development then for you, isn't it?"

"Rather. We've been too busy since our arrival to pick up a newspaper. What did the reports say?"

"About a hundred on board, only half made it. The captain of the *Earl Moira* was rumored to be drunk and so was blamed for sailing in bad weather. He went down with the ship so there's no way to know, is there? Some of the bodies were found neat and tidy on the Wharf Bank, some floated in to shore, and some were lost to the depths. There was also an article about your scheme to get the survivors ashore, madame. Very clever. You may find many Dubliners wanting to get a look at them."

Marguerite could see Marie's mind working furiously behind her eyes as she asked, "Yes? You think we should not repair them? Leave as they came out of water?"

Curran seemed startled to be asked an opinion on it. "I don't know. I suspect they will be fascinating under any conditions."

"Marie, what if we reserved some of the damaged ones that are still not repaired and made a special tableau of the shipwreck? I'd like to do a new model of Joseph for it."

"Of Nini? Yes, yes, that is fine idea. That's what we do. Thank you, Mr. Curran, for suggestions."

Marguerite smiled at the lawyer's confused countenance as Marie escorted him out of the building so she could get to work straightaway on planning her newest tableau.

13

HMS Victory, *off the coast of Toulon, June 1805.* "Hastings, what the deuce is this?" Lord Nelson was waving an official-looking dispatch as Darden walked into the admiral's cabin.

"Sir?"

"Mr. Pitt wants me to have myself modeled by one of those ridiculous waxworkers. By a—" He squinted at the paper with his one good eye. "By a Marie Tussaud. Except she isn't in London and he isn't sure where she is. Not only does he expect me to have it done, he expects me to find her from the middle of the seas! This is a preposterous task for a vice admiral of the white. What is the man thinking? Reclaiming his prime minister's post has addled his brain."

"My lord, you *are* a hero to the British people. It seems natural that the government should want you memorialized."

"Memorials are for dead people, not the living. Anyway, I'm assigning you to find this waxworking creature. Didn't you visit Madame Tussaud's exhibit in Edinburgh?"

"Yes, sir, at the castle while I was examining fortifications of the port at Edinburgh."

"But she's not still in Edinburgh?"

"No, my lord, the exhibition appears to have left about a year ago to whereabouts unknown."

"Well, when we return to Portsmouth find her for me, will you?

I think I'll have her come to Merton to do the model. Perhaps I can convince Pitt to pay for one of my Emma."

Darden coughed politely. "Do you think he will . . . extend such an invitation, my lord?"

"No, I suppose not. Although the woman who is the source of all sustenance and life for me should be considered a national heroine." Nelson shook his head. "No, you're right of course. For Emma may be the wife of my heart, but to the world she's just a mistress. And mistresses don't get recognition beyond what is gossiped about behind cupped hands. Forget what I just said, Lieutenant."

"Yes, my lord."

"Pitt has finally conceded to giving me a bit of leave, so I'll be at Merton beginning in August. If you can find this Tussaud woman soon enough, bring her to me there."

"I'll begin looking for her straightaway, my lord, and will escort her personally."

As Darden left the admiral's cabin, Nelson muttered softly, "Ridiculous, making a wax caricature of a vice admiral of the white. I suppose it will at least be amusing for my little girl, Horatia."

But Darden hardly heard him. What unbelievable luck. Pitt had followed up on his earlier, delicately placed suggestion, and now he had an instruction to spend time finding Madame Marie Tussaud. Which really meant finding Mrs. Ashby once again.

The exhibition had succeeded well with the Irish people, particularly since the two women had employed the same strategy they had in Scotland, using national heroes as their main attractions. Writer Jonathan Swift, scientist Robert Boyle, and an imaginative St. Patrick drew crowds into the exhibition. The shipwreck tableau was also very popular.

Marguerite was cleaning paintbrushes with spirits of turpentine, the fumes making her queasy and threatening to dislodge a cluster of pain to the front of head, when Joseph burst in to where she was working on painting some backdrop scenery that Marie had sketched in pencil.

"Maman wants you, Mrs. Ashby." It was unspoken among the

three of them that the name Philipsthal should not be mentioned again, so for the past year in Dublin, Marguerite had returned to her previous name.

The boy was gone again before she could ask why. She carefully wrapped the half-cleaned brushes in a cloth to keep them damp and went to find Marie, since Joseph had also disappeared without telling her where Maman was.

She found Marie near the entrance of the exhibition, talking to a patron whose back was to Marguerite. Approaching Marie, she said, "I'm here. Joseph said you wanted—" She stopped and the patron turned around.

"You." Marguerite blinked stupidly.

"You seem disappointed, Mrs. Ashby." Lieutenant Darden Hastings gave her a small bow.

"What are you doing here?" She knew she sounded snappish, but the shock had removed her ability to think properly.

"I'm on Lord Nelson's business with Madame Tussaud. The prime minister wants a wax figure made of the vice admiral, and sent me to find your exhibition. It wasn't easy. You've been moving about quite secretively, it seems." His statement sounded largely like a question, but a small quirk of his lips told Marguerite that he was not entirely displeased with the chase. She turned her attention to Marie.

"So you are commissioned to model Lord Nelson? Why, madame, this might be your best commission ever. Imagine how a figure of the admiral would draw customers to the exhibition."

Marie's hands were clasped in front of her and she smiled slyly.

"I think I'll remain here. I'll send you to London instead."

"Me? Alone? Without you?"

"Not alone. Lieutenant Hastings will take you. You visit admiral at his home to take casts and make figures there."

"But . . . but we have no workshop in London. Where will I make the figure?"

"I will arrange a location," Lieutenant Hastings cut in flatly. "One that meets with your approval, of course."

"But I need a place to stay. I cannot sleep on the floor among chisels and wax bricks."

"I will find you suitable rooms, most likely with a widow so that you may have quiet and be in respectable company."

"Madame—" She turned to Marie, desperately casting about for a reason why this plan was unfeasible. "What of the expense? Surely we cannot afford such extravagance, even if it is for a figure of the esteemed admiral."

She felt like a hare who has been caught in a trap and is about to be nabbed by the farmer for his cook pot.

"His Majesty's government will cover the cost," Hastings continued in his even way. "Please, I beg you not to worry, Mrs. Ashby."

"I am not worried in the least, Lieutenant," she retorted, more sharply than she intended. "You will forgive me if I keep my employer's interests in mind at all times. My concerns were merely a business matter."

"Of course." He bowed again, and when he rose Marguerite could see that his lips were compressed in a thin, white line. Had she angered him? Well, what of it? He was here to take her away, when she'd only just survived a shipwreck a year ago?

Oh, Lord. Not another sea voyage. Not so soon. No, no, no.

"Lieutenant, what would be our routing back to London?" she asked.

"Why, I suppose a ship through the Irish Sea and into the channel to Bristol, and from there we will hire a coach to London."

"And how long a sea journey would that be?" Marguerite fought to remain calm.

"How long? A few days at most. What is the point of this questioning? I assure you that I am trustworthy and you will not be ill-used on the journey."

Marguerite flamed with embarrassment. How scarlet her cheeks must be! "My apologies. I have discovered that I am a poor sailor, and would prefer if we could keep our sailing to a minimum of time. Could we not cross to Wales and go overland from there?"

"Wales? Mrs. Ashby, we would have to traipse all through the hills of that country. It could take us weeks to reach London. A sailing to Bristol is far better. From there it is only a two-day coach ride to the city."

"Nevertheless, I prefer hilly ground beneath my feet to the interminable dipping and cresting of the water, especially of the wicked Irish Sea. The less time spent there, the better."

"But what you suggest is lunacy. I have to return to my post. And Lord Nelson expects that I will escort you to him with all speed, not take you on the grand tour first." He brought his hands up in supplication, palms in the air, and looked to Marie for help with his unreasonable passenger.

Marguerite was irritated that Marie did indeed intervene for the hapless lieutenant.

"Marguerite, by doing this you will greatly enhance the exhibition. We no longer have . . . the other problem . . . and this will now make us famous. I'm certain. And you get to meet Lord Nelson! The lieutenant will take you there quickly and safely. You do this for me and for the waxworks."

"But surely you would like to meet the admiral yourself?"

Marie shrugged. "Eh, I meet Bonaparte years ago. Your turn to meet a famous military man."

So Marie was against her in this, too. She sighed. "As you wish, but I shall despise every minute of it."

PART FIVE

London

14

Merton Place, Surrey, August 1805. Marguerite had to admit to herself that the journey had been uncomplicated, despite her terror of boarding a ship once more, and Lieutenant Hastings had been as affable a companion as could be hoped for. Not that she had ever indicated her appreciation to him. Solicitous after her comfort in his brusque way, he had somehow ensured a minimum of distress and worry for her while at sea. He had also arranged a private coach to take them from Bristol to London. They made one overnight stop in Newbury at a clean, comfortable coaching inn, and he had bowed graciously over her hand before depositing her in her own small but private room. How much it all must have cost!

True to his word, he had secured pleasant lodgings for her in London with a Mrs. Penny, a widow whose husband had been lost in the Battle of the Nile, and he had even gone through her trunks himself to ensure all of her equipment and supplies had arrived undamaged. After giving her until noontime the day following their arrival to rest and recuperate from their journey, he called on her for their visit to Merton, which he said was about six miles away in Surrey. His uniform was crisp and fitted him handsomely. How had he managed to look so impeccable after their long journey? She glanced down at her own gown, an old gray work dress that was dirty around the hem.

She received his bow, which she had to admit she was starting to look forward to.

"Mrs. Ashby, you look refreshed. I hope that you might find meeting Lord Nelson to be particularly enjoyable."

He held out his arm to take her to yet another waiting coach. This young naval officer seemed a marvel at managing the movement of her and her possessions. No wonder he was valued by the admiral. Drat it all, he had been kind to her and she had been as aloof as possible. Perhaps now was the time for a small concession.

"Lieutenant Hastings, I'm afraid there's something I must tell you regarding my name."

Inside their carriage, she told him everything regarding her short and disastrous marriage to Paul de Philipsthal, from his cloying way of courting her, to his devious marriage proposal, to the tragic geggy performance which made her realize his deficient moral fiber, to finally their catastrophic voyage to Dublin. Hastings's eyes blinked furiously.

In an attempt to grasp her serious lack of judgment, she assumed.

"And you say this man had already relinquished his interest in Madame Tussaud's exhibition when he made his arrangement with you to do so, if you would marry him?"

Marguerite nodded morosely. "Is there a greater fool than a woman thinking she is undertaking a rescue?"

"You mistake my meaning. A drowning was too good for such a scoundrel. If he'd been on a ship of mine, he'd have been flogged round the fleet then hung from the yardarm."

Marguerite smiled wanly at his gentlemanly outrage, even if he probably did not mean it. "You are kinder, sir, than I deserve for my cork-brained actions."

He sat back in his seat across from her, pensive. "It does present us with a problem, doesn't it?"

"What do you mean, Lieutenant?"

"Well, you are no longer Mrs. Ashby, but should I really insult you by calling you Mrs. Philipsthal?"

She laughed despite her wretchedness over the situation. "You make an excellent point, Lieutenant Hastings. For your compassion when you could have been cruel, I give you leave to call me Marguerite in private. I prefer to remain Mrs. Ashby in public so I can forget the whole unhappy episode."

He leaned forward and took her hand. "And it would give me the greatest pleasure if you called me Darden."

But by the time her visit to Merton Place was complete, Marguerite was left wondering if that pleasant interchange had ever actually taken place. Hastings returned to his stern, prim self before his superior, making as little conversation as possible with her following his introductions of the estate and its residents.

Merton was a country home that could only be described as vividly alive and effervescent. This home that Nelson shared with his mistress, Emma Hamilton, had been a small, dilapidated farm. Emma had single-handedly overseen the transformation of the existing grounds and added acreage to turn it into an estate befitting one of England's great naval officers.

The grounds themselves were a veritable wonderland of imagination, with a wide lake christened the Nile after Nelson's successful campaign there, a quaint Italianate bridge, sheep grazing in a pasture, and a profusely blooming rose garden that permeated the air with its sweet fragrance. All of this was a prelude to a charming house that was obviously fresh from renovation.

Inside, the house was cheerfully noisy with children, dogs, guests, and music. Marguerite was reminded of nothing less than the fair in Leadenhall that she used to attend with her mother. The bright colors, gaiety, and hubbub of those events always made her clap with delight. She was tempted to do so again here.

One of the house servants escorted them into a small dining room, where Marguerite recognized Nelson at once, seated among the chattering guests. He was remarkably slight for a man known to have single-handedly destroyed a large part of the French fleet. But the giveaway was his unfilled right sleeve, pinned across his chest and secured to a button by a small loop. Darden had told her during their sea voyage that Nelson had lost his arm after his elbow was shattered by a musket ball in a battle against Spain in 1797 at Santa Cruz, Tenerife, in the Canary Islands.

Less startling, but equally intriguing to her waxworking senses, was his right eye, which was milky and unseeing, and was accompanied by a rather nasty scar above it, which had nearly obliterated his eyebrow. This eye was lost earlier than his arm, in 1794 at the siege of Calvi in Corsica, according to Darden. Nelson was ironically injured not by a direct hit in the eye, but from a stone flung up by a cannonball, grazing him. In her mind she was already figuring out how to order the glass for making each unique eye.

The servant announced them and Nelson stood up, smiling in what seemed a genuine pleasure to see his officer.

"My lord, may I present to you Mrs. Marguerite Ashby, a waxworker from Madame Tussaud's, here to take measurements and castings for your wax portrait."

Marguerite performed a slight curtsy. They did not seem to stand much on formality here at Merton from what she could see.

Nelson frowned at her with his one capable eyebrow. "Why is Madame Tussaud herself not here?" he asked Hastings.

The woman seated to Nelson's left gave him a friendly push followed by a kiss on his good arm. "Nelson, she's standing right here, y'nau? She seems a well-bred lady, not one of your powder monkeys to dismiss with a wave of your hand."

"My dear, I am not dismissive of any of the men under my command, from the lowest powder monkey to the highest ranking of my officers."

Emma rolled her eyes out of Nelson's view. Then she stood and came over to Marguerite, shaking her hand and kissing her cheek in an overly friendly way.

"Mrs. Ashby, I'm Lady Hamilton, Lord Nelson's best supporter and a frequent guest here at Merton. I heard a wax figger was to be made of our dear Nelson and I've been nearly bosting at the sides waiting for you."

Marguerite felt Darden stiffen. She considered the overly enthusiastic, albeit charming lady before her. Reported to have been a great beauty in her youth, Emma Hamilton was now in her early forties and had largely gone over to fat. According to Darden, she had spent many years in Naples as the wife of the British ambassador, Sir William Hamilton, and had grown excessively fond of the food there. However, there was no denying her exquisite complexion and beautiful mass of hair, accented by a wide, guileless smile that showed off her lovely teeth. Her gown was a clever one, stylish yet loose fitting below the bodice, so that it gave every advantage to her flourishing figure.

It was in Naples that Lord and Lady Hamilton first greeted Nelson when he came ashore as part of an envoy to discuss the Anglo-Neapolitan treaty in 1793. He and Emma were smitten with one another, and although it had taken them six years to actually enter into an affair, they had burned brightly together ever since. Sir William had even turned a blind eye to it until his death over a year ago, so great was his admiration for the naval hero.

Although Darden had expressed an immense admiration for Nelson, it had not extended to condoning the admiral's affair, which he considered an insult to Nelson's long-suffering wife, Fanny. Marguerite glanced over and saw the pained expression in his eyes. Emma was oblivious.

"Y'nau, they made wax figgers of me, Sir Willum, and Lord Nelson here, when we was in Naples, to celebrate the first anniversary of the Nile victory. They was on top of tall Roman columns, though, so I couldn't see them none too well. That's why I'm fair happy to see you, and I told Nelson, too, that he should be glad for it and not as fretful as he was when Pitt commanded it."

"I shall do my best to make figures that please you, Lady Hamilton."

Emma Hamilton's eyes grew wide. "Oh, but I know you'll make just fine effigies. I'm just bosting to see you get started. Nelson, can't we show Mrs. Ashby to the room we set up so she can get to work on redoing your fine visage?"

Nelson, still smitten with Emma after so long, rose immediately to do her bidding, giving a hasty good-bye to his dining companions and urging them to remain and spend the day at cards or sailing on the Nile.

Emma left the dining room on Nelson's arm, with Marguerite right behind them. Darden followed at a respectful distance. Merton was a rabbit's warren of interconnected small rooms surging with activity. In one parlor an older woman thumped away on a pianoforte that badly needed tuning. "That's me mam," said Emma proudly as they passed through.

In the next room a young child babbled along to the music floating in the air, making up her own words.

Emma stopped to pick up the girl and kiss her. With his good arm Nelson stroked the youngster's hair.

"And that's Horatia, Nelson's child with Lady Hamilton." Darden's quiet voice next to her ear startled her.

"Did Sir William treat the child as his own?" she whispered back.

"He was tolerant of the child's real parentage."

Other people—friends, family, Nelson's cronies—packed every available space of Merton, laughing, gaming, and supping. They finally reached their destination, a sparsely furnished room at the rear of the house. Marguerite was glad to see that it contained several chairs and a rectangular table sufficient for her work. Her two carrying cases had already been brought in here. Lieutenant Hastings had thought of everything.

Emma Hamilton fluttered around excitedly as Marguerite set up her tools, and even went personally to fetch the water Marguerite needed to mix the plaster compound. While she was off on that errand, Marguerite used her various calipers to measure Lord Nelson, and wrote these important figures down in her notebook. Unlike most subjects, Nelson was completely unperturbed by the sight of the calipers, even when she timidly used them to measure the circumference of his "fin," which was how he referred to the remaining stump of his right arm.

Emma returned with the water, which Marguerite added to her plaster mix. Marguerite then invited Lord Nelson to sit in a chair she had pulled up next to the worktable, and told him the steps she would take to create his life mask. Hastings sat in a corner of the room and watched her work intently, nodding as if in approval. Marguerite felt a peculiar sense of pride in having his esteem. Strange how he could be such a sullen man at times, yet such a silent reassurance at others. It was difficult to understand Lieutenant Darden Hastings.

With Emma chattering excitedly nearby as the admiral was draped, his hair oiled, and breathing pipes gently inserted in his nostrils, Marguerite was ready to begin applying the wet plaster to his face.

She said to her subject as Marie had taught her, "Lord Nelson, please do not be afraid by what I am about to do."

"Afraid?" Nelson wheezed past the paper tubes in his nose. "My dear, I have faced cannon-shot, malaria, an amputation, and near blindness. What do you think you can do that would cause me to be fearful?"

Marguerite dropped her ladle back into her mixing bowl as she laughed unintentionally at a memory that popped into her head.

Nelson wheezed again. "Hastings, is this woman daft?"

Marguerite covered her mouth with her hand to control her amusement, then went back to mixing the plaster one final time to ensure it was of proper consistency.

"My apologies, sir, it's just that you reminded me of something Madame Tussaud once told me. About Bonaparte."

"Bonaparte! How in the name of all of the saints could that rascal remind you of *me?*" In his indignation, he accidentally blew out one of his breathing tubes, which Emma picked up and lovingly placed back in his nostril before planting a light kiss on top of his oiled head.

"When she still had an exhibition in France after the Revolution, she came under the patronage of Empress Josephine."

"Empress! Emperor! Self-styled titles, born of the little Corsican's great ego." Nelson was getting agitated. Emma knelt next to his chair, cooing in his ear.

"Yes, sir, of course. But after Josephine had her figure cast, she decided she wanted Bonaparte to do the same. He had no great desire to do so, but invited Madame Tussaud to the Tuileries to do his mask in order to please his wife.

"She performed the same preparations as I have done today, and said as I just did, 'Please do not be afraid.' His reaction was so similar to yours that I could not help my amusement. Please forgive me."

As she lifted the ladle to finally apply the plaster, Nelson's eyes flew open and he reached out and grabbed her arm with his left hand. "Well?" he demanded. "What did that popinjay say?"

And so oncc again the ladle went back in the bowl. "Oh, well, after Madame told him not to be afraid, he said, 'Madame, I should not be afraid if you were to surround my head with loaded pistols.' "

Emma burst into gales of laughter. To Marguerite's relief, Nelson also seemed to find it immensely humorous, and joined in with Emma's hearty barking. Even Darden was shaking silently from his seat.

"Bonaparte is a braggart, that is true, but I hope to be able to put at least a dozen pistols around his head one day to see what his real reaction would be. I intend to annihilate that braggart, and, praise God, I hope it to be soon. Please continue with your work, Mrs. Ashby." Nelson finally settled back with his eyes closed.

Marguerite worked as rapidly as she could to smooth the plaster all over Nelson's head, face, and neck. When she was finished and told him that he must wait patiently for the plaster to dry, she sat and thought about his fin. Should she model him exactly as he was now or, out of respect for his stature in the eyes of the British people, model him as he was before the Battle of Santa Cruz?

She knew what Marie would say. Cast him as he is. Visitors want to see figures as exact replicas of the people they represent.

As she sat with an elbow on her knee and her chin in her hand, contemplating the making of Nelson's figure to the exclusion of noticing what else was happening around her, the same servant who had shown them into the house now rushed into the room.

"Lord Nelson!" the man panted. At the sight of Nelson's head sheathed in a hardening casing with two small tubes of paper protruding from his nose, the servant started violently. However, as a good member of the staff, he quickly recovered himself and looked to Emma. "Lady Hamilton, Mr. Pitt is here. He just came up the drive. What shall I do with him?"

From underneath his plaster Nelson emitted a rumbling growl, a noise Marguerite had become accustomed to from her life-mask subjects. He began waving in a way that was senseless to Marguerite, but Emma and Darden seemed to understand him. Darden strode from the room while Emma arranged Nelson's draping more elegantly around him. As elegantly as could be had for someone who is forced to remain motionless lest his face break.

Darden returned minutes later with Mr. Pitt. The prime minister looked worn and haggard. At age twenty-four, he had been the youngest man ever to take the office in 1783, when Marguerite was merely six years old. He held this post consistently for eighteen years until surrendering it to Henry Addington, but had recently regained office through a coalition of himself, Charles James Fox, and William Grenville. Now aged forty-four, he had the look of a man well beyond his years. His face was gray and gaunt, and pronounced loudly that he was not well. The shadows under his eyes indicated a man who worried about an invasion by Napoleon Bonaparte even more than the admiral did.

Nevertheless, Marguerite could scarce believe she was in the same room with these two great men, Pitt and Nelson.

Emma greeted him effusively, yet as comfortably as an ambassador's wife would do in such a situation.

"You caught us at a messy time, Mr. Pitt. Mrs. Ashby here is from Madame Tussaud's and she's making up the life mask for Lord Nelson's figger, just like you wanted."

Another growl rumbled from beneath the hardening mask.

"Yes, so I see. I had hoped to get here in time to witness this. I have important issues of state to discuss, and it seemed more expedient to just come here myself than to ask Lord Nelson to cut his leave short and come to London."

"Issues, Mr. Pitt?" Emma inquired.

"Yes, I'll talk it over with Nelson. When he's unburied from his casing." Pitt moved over to Nelson's reclined head and peered down with his arms clasped behind his back, as if afraid of accidentally touching the admiral.

"Hmm, yes, quite interesting. When does he get . . . released?"

Marguerite approached Nelson's head as well and examined the plaster mold for the whitish cast and light crackling that would indicate it had dried.

"Soon, but not just yet. Lord Nelson, are you all right? Please tap your fingers on the chair's arm if anything is wrong."

Nelson's only response was a resigned wheeze through the

paper tubes. Emma knelt down next to him and put her head in his lap.

While he finished drying, Pitt peppered Marguerite with questions. How long did it take to complete a figure? How did she and Marie pack the figures for transport from town to town? What sort of heat could the characters take? And so on until Marguerite was exhausted from the rapid-fire interrogation. Fortunately, Nelson's mask was finally done, and she used it as an excuse to disengage herself from the prime minister.

As she had now done many times before, although always in the presence of Marie, she began the process of pulling the string and then slowly twisting and lifting, twisting and lifting, until the mask started to slowly release.

"Fascinating," Pitt breathed from over her shoulder. "What will you do next?"

"Next?" Marguerite continued working the mask from his face. "Next I shall wrap the mask and take it back to London so that I can begin working on the entire character. Lady Hamilton, it would be best if you could provide me with some of Lord Nelson's actual clothing. Perhaps a uniform he no longer wears?"

Emma looked up from her position on the floor. "Certainly. How about one of your old admiral-of-the-blue uniforms, love?" She patted Nelson on the knee, and he squeezed her shoulder in return, an apparent motion of acquiescence, for Emma then said, "I'll have it for you before you leave, Mrs. Ashby. D'ya need a wig?"

Marguerite pursed her lips, thinking about what the final creation would look like. "Maybe. I think perhaps I would like to insert real hair into the figure's scalp. Ah! There we are."

Once again she felt the same thrill she had felt since the first time she had done this on the Comte d'Artois. She held in her palms two perfectly executed halves of a mask that would be used to recreate a living person in wax. Except this time she would be making a wax version of England's national hero. In keeping with Marie's attitude toward such things, though, she tried to maintain a nonchalant composure. For Madame Tussaud's waxworkers did not get dumbstruck by their patrons. Recreating everyone from the most famous aristocrats to the lowliest infamous criminals was to be greeted with the same detached attitude.

Oh, but I can hardly wait to begin this piece.

After everyone had admired the plaster mask's likeness to Nelson's face, she wrapped it up carefully and set about cleaning the admiral. Relieved to be liberated from the smothering confines of the mask, he talked garrulously with Marguerite as she removed all traces of plaster and oil from his head. In particular, he wanted to discuss the hair for the figure.

"What is this of real hair for the figure? You want my hair?" Nelson now stood, his face and scalp red from scrubbing and his wet hair thinned and splayed weakly across his skull.

"Sir, I would not presume to such a thing," Marguerite said. "We have various types of animal hair that can be sewn in to resemble human hair. Sometimes a subject will give us his own hair that we can blend in with other fibers. We can also use a wig. It is just more realistic when we can insert real hair. But I would not think of requesting it of you."

Emma, who seemed to be forever touching Nelson as though to ensure he was still there, grabbed his arm again. "Just think. A real part of our Nelson in London where the people can 'ave him, while the rest of him is right here at Merton where he belongs. What d'ya think? Should you give her some of your locks?"

Nelson crinkled his eyes, though whether in disgust or amusement, Marguerite was not sure.

"I'll give it some thought, dear Emma. I'll give it thought."

Emma and Nelson exchanged farewell pleasantries with them and left, his good arm around her waist, to return to their guests, while Marguerite returned to packing up her supplies. Darden had moved quietly up beside her and was assisting her without needing direction.

As their bags were finally loaded on the carriage and they were about to climb in, Pitt stepped outside, using his hand to shield his eyes from the sun as though it intruded on his secret thoughts.

"Mrs. Ashby, a word if I may. Lieutenant, please hold your driver."

He offered his arm to Marguerite and they strolled over toward Merton's Nile. The prime minister did not look well, but he still carried himself as every inch the gentleman.

Pitt spoke quietly, as if the very birds themselves might be listening. "I'm actually on my way to take the waters at Bath. A touch of gout, you know, nothing serious. It fitted my plans to stop here first to see what you do with these masks. Fascinating, really. However, when I return to London next week I should like to stop by your workshop to see your progress. Depending on what I see, I—or rather His Majesty's government—may need you to create some more figures. Can you remain in London indefinitely?"

"I'm certain I can. I need to write to Madame Tussaud. The expenses—"

"Yes, yes," Pitt said, a trifle impatient. "Your expenses will be covered. Make sure you tell her that."

"Then I am at your disposal, sir, for whatever you wish me to do."

Nathaniel poured another glass of brandy for Mr. Scroggs, to celebrate their bargain. He couldn't believe how well things were working out. To have won so heavily at gambling these past few weeks was a divine indication that his carefully thought-out plan was approved by God himself. How else could he have so rapidly amassed the cash required to purchase this ship from Mr. Scroggs? Of course, it needed some repair, but that could be accomplished quickly. And he would have it renamed straightaway. Something appropriate. Like *Wax Maiden*. Ha! Now that was clever. He smiled inwardly.

The brandy was warm and encouraging as it slipped down his throat. As Mr. Scroggs blathered on about how the money from the sale of this ship and two others would help set him up in a plantation in the American colonies—and who really cared what the fool planned to do?—Nathaniel gave his own plans further consideration.

With a sleek little trading ship as was now in his possession, he could be of great use in England's cause against the French invaders. Especially since he'd thought of what he was sure no one else had. The Royal Navy was so busy already, fruitlessly chasing the French commander Villeneuve from Sicily to Barbados and back again. In addition to scuttling across the Atlantic, the navy had its hands full with patrolling the southeastern coast, where Bonaparte was amassing his forces across the Channel along the seventy-five miles of French coastline around Calais and Boulogne. So who was available to accomplish the heroic thing he was planning? His concept was inspired, really. And that realization further reinforced his recent divine confirmation.

He narrowed his eyes. Mother dared call him a fool, saying he had no naval experience. How difficult could it be to captain a small ship? The jack-tars did the work; he just needed to set their course and make the important decisions. Simple.

What had really irritated him was how she characterized his patriotic mission.

"Nathaniel. Son. What you propose to do is foolish. Mr. Pitt has never received you, nor given his approval for such activities. You will end up in grief." Maude spoke to him as though he were a mere boy.

"Mr. Pitt may have been too busy to receive me personally, but he didn't rebuff the offer I sent him."

"He didn't respond to you *at all*, Nathaniel, meaning he was ignoring you. Which means that what you are planning is tantamount to piracy without a letter of marque."

"Mother," he replied in what he hoped was as condescending a tone. "It's not piracy if you are doing it to serve your country instead of yourself."

That silenced her. He took great satisfaction in watching her walk away, head shaking. Of course, she thought his entire plan was privateering. As though he would spend his days trolling for badly armed merchant ships. What glory was there in that? No, his plan was far more . . . spectacular.

How could she have called him a fool? A pirate? Mother had never used any but the sickliest endearments on him. But that had changed of late. Maude Ashby was becoming a genuine harpy. It was his refusal to take that Edwina Carlson girl, wasn't it? Mother hated to be thwarted.

Which reminded him of Marguerite, who had soundly thrashed his mother without a single word. An absolute delight she was. He discovered she'd gone to Dublin, but it seemed too much work to travel all the way there to fetch her. No, first he'd make a name for himself at the highest levels of government and Society, maybe even secure a title like Marguerite's uncle, Greycliffe. Then Marguerite would come dashing to him. Women loved titled men.

He returned his attention to Mr. Scroggs, whose conversation was in the exact same place it was when Nathaniel drifted off.

"I'm delighted, sir, that my offer to you will enable you to make a fresh start in the colonies," Nathaniel told him. "On what date do you propose to finally quit England?"

15

After completing Nelson's mask, Marguerite's first chore on arriving back to her new rooms was to write a letter to Marie, detailing what had happened and explaining the prime minister's request. She received a quick reply, and marveled at how much better Marie's writing was than her pronunciation.

> *Yes, this of course you must do. And since we will be paid for your living expenses there will be no sapping of the exhibition's coffers. Nini and I will manage here alone. I knew this was a wise endeavor. Be sure to stay in Lieutenant Hastings's protection.*

Marguerite rolled her eyes.

> *When you return, be sure to send the figures via the longest sea routing that you can, no matter how you return yourself. You know the figures survive water better than overland travel.*
>
> *Also, you should know that I am parting ways with Monsieur Tussaud. He has heaped many an insult on me by his foolish business transactions, but his most recent dealing leaves my heart dead. I discovered that he took out a 20,000 franc loan last year, and in order to settle part*

of the debt has now sold the house my uncle Curtius left me. Furthermore, he has taken out yet another loan—for what, I ask you?—and has mortgaged the wax salon at 20 boulevard du Temple as surety. He will undoubtedly end up losing this property for me, as well. It is unforgivable.

I have written and asked him to send our other son, Francis, to me. When my dear boy is with me, I will quit Tussaud altogether.

Marguerite folded the letter thoughtfully. Marie mentioned her husband so rarely that it was easy to forget he even existed, and that he managed her original exhibition back in Paris.

She returned to the construction of Nelson's figure. Without the worries of the exhibition itself, she was able to work on it night and day, making far quicker progress than on a typical character. She savored the work, laboring happily each day from first light until the final rays of the sun slipped out of the room and returned to their celestial residence.

Her work was interrupted one day by the surprise visit of Darden, who was not alone. Accompanying him was another naval officer in a similar uniform, whom Darden introduced as Lieutenant Brax Selwyn. A man more different from Darden could not be found.

Where Darden was dark almost to the point of swarthiness, and always seemed to have secrets simmering below his stern surface, Brax was all openness, elegance, and light. His broad mouth seemed perpetually poised to laugh, and his bright blue eyes scanned the room as if seeking pleasure in its corners. Lieutentant Selwyn's hair, blond and unwigged, was tied back in a common queue, yet on him it was somehow more fashionable than on other men. He was of slighter build than Darden, but still showed a well-turned calf. Marguerite guessed he was an excellent dancer.

Even his coloring reflected his carefree bearing. His skin was as pale as any typical Englishman's, but it had an almost delicate, ethereal quality to it.

An angel sent to bring joy, Marguerite thought.

Were these men actually friends?

Brax's handsomeness was so great that she found herself looking down sheepishly at her own tattered condition. Her plain dress, although covered with an apron, was splotched with wax globules, paint, and glue. Her hair, gathered up hastily in a bandeau that morning to keep it out of her eyes, was surely as littered with debris as her gown. What a sorry sight she made!

She cleared her throat. "To what do I owe this pleasure, sirs?"

The room was silent. It was Darden's place to state the purpose of their visit, yet he was staring at Marguerite, his lips a grim line of white.

What have I done wrong?

Selwyn spoke up brightly. "Why, Hastings here has been telling me all about his most unusual assignment: to bring a waxworker to London to have Lord Nelson's portrait made. When I found out that the waxworker in question was a young lady, I insisted that he bring me to your shop straightaway, so that I could have the honor of watching beautiful feminine hands working in such dedication to the Royal Navy. He tried to deny me, but I can see already that there is to be great reward in my persistence, for it is not often that a poor jack-tar gets to behold such loveliness."

Darden's nostrils flared, but he otherwise made no comment.

Marguerite knew Brax was shamelessly flirting with her. After all, how could a man be seriously pursuing a woman as pathetic-looking as she was? But for the first time since Nicholas's death, she was actually reveling in such frothy attention. She could feel a twinge of her old saucy self rising to the surface.

She tossed her hair as well as she could from under the confines of the bandeau. "Well, Lieutenant, either you are purblind or a bit dim-witted." She tapped the side of her head for effect. "For clearly what you see before you is a bedraggled mess of a woman far beyond her first blush of youth."

Selwyn clutched his chest as if in pain. "It cannot be. Surely you seek more compliments about your devastating charms, hence why else would you tell such vicious lies about yourself? For you are unquestionably no more than nineteen. Wouldn't you agree, Hastings?"

But Darden was no longer part of the conversation, and was instead examining the scattered paints, brushes, needles, rulers, and other supplies of her trade on the worktable.

Selwyn tried again. "What, Hastings? Do you actually find worn tools to be of more interest than the divine goddess who stands before us?" He brought his forefinger to the side of his head as Marguerite had just done, winking exaggeratedly at her.

She giggled, even though she knew he was mocking poor Darden. The sound of her laughter snapped Darden to attention and he responded in a clipped tone.

"I am not eligible to judge the lady's divinity. It is not our purpose here, and I do not wish to pay so little regard to the completion of Lord Nelson's wax effigy that I stand about with my jaws flapping oafishly. As an officer of the Royal Navy, you should consider the same."

Selwyn turned his back to Darden and opened his blue eyes as wide as he could at Marguerite before crossing them and sticking out his tongue. He looked like an overgrown, naughty boy and she could hardly keep from repressing her laughter again.

Selwyn went to Darden and stuck out his hand. "You're right, Hastings. My ill-breeding has made me rude and contemptuous. Accept my apology."

Darden reluctantly took the other man's hand and shook it.

"For you see," Selwyn resumed, his attention back to Marguerite, "I was born as a result of the king's tumble in a back alley with a traveling doxy. She left me in a field to be raised by sheep and so you see before you the result. Hep, hep, what ho, eh, baaaaa."

Darden slammed a fist down on the table so hard Marguerite jumped. "What the hell are you about, Selwyn? You're the son of an aristocrat and King George would never—oh." Too late, Darden realized that Selwyn was teasing. "Damn you, Lieutenant, you're the worst rascal I've ever known. No wonder your father was eager to see the back of you when you wanted to secure a commission."

Selwyn roared his approval. "Pardon, did I hear just a bit of wit from you just now? There's hope for you yet, sourpuss."

"Gentlemen," Marguerite interrupted before anything untoward happened. "I need to return to my work. May I inquire again as to the true nature of your visit?"

Darden straightened the coat of his uniform. "Of course, Mrs. Ashby. I just wanted to let you know that Mr. Pitt will be coming by later today to check the progress of Lord Nelson here. He may also commission some other figures at that time. I thought you might like to know in advance so that you could be . . . better prepared."

So Darden thinks I look unkempt and slovenly. She flushed at the idea that he thought so little of her. *But I suppose I do, and should be grateful that he came to warn me.*

"Please accept my gratitude for this forewarning of my impending visitor. And now if you will both excuse me, I must return to my task." She nodded toward the door, and both men took her hint, but not before Selwyn departed from her with great protestations of his admiration for her person and an overly long kiss, inappropriately applied to the underside of her wrist.

Mr. Pitt did indeed return later in the day, and seemed improved by his visit to Bath. After inspecting the Lord Nelson effigy, which was nearly ready except to have hair inserted in his head—a very long task now that she had decided to go this way instead of using a wig—and to dress the figure.

"The likeness is remarkable," Pitt said. "What good luck that Hastings mentioned such a project to me."

"I'm sorry? He mentioned what project to you?"

"It was Lieutenant Hastings's suggestion that I hire Madame Tussaud's waxworks to create a figure of our national hero for the public to see. But now that I've seen the nearly completed work, there is one more figure I want."

He outlined to her his intent. Nelson would be leading a fleet to intercept Napoleon's formidable sea force somewhere off the coast of Spain. Pitt was not at liberty to divulge the admiral's specific plans. However, he had consulted with Nelson regarding his own idea: to create an effigy of one of Nelson's respected officers, Thomas Hardy, who would be captain of Nelson's flagship, HMS *Victory*.

"You will take both Hardy's and Nelson's figures on board *Vic-*

tory before she sets sail and load them into the admiral's cabin for storage. You said they couldn't take extreme heat, so they should be cool there and easily accessible for the quarterdeck. Nelson was not overly keen on having them stored with him, but agreed to it. God willing, they won't be needed."

"Needed for what, sir?" Marguerite was unsure what this all meant. Wax figures were for entertainment. What place did they have aboard a man-of-war?

"For decoy, madam. A ruse, a ploy. The French and the Spaniards fear our man Nelson. Should anything happen to him or Captain Hardy, several key officers know to have that man's figure brought up to the quarterdeck to take the place of the real man, to confuse the enemy into thinking they have not achieved the great triumph of eliminating a key naval leader."

Marguerite thought Pitt was perhaps imbibing too much port these days. The idea was preposterous.

"But, sir, the wax figures do not move. They will realize that it is just some sort of imitation statue on the deck."

"Eventually, yes. But it would work long enough for messages to be sent and a handover of authority to occur, enabling our forces to hopefully maintain an upper hand. Providing we have the upper hand at the time."

"I see." Although really she didn't see at all how this would work.

"There's one more thing. You must have both figures ready for loading the morning of September fifteenth, for the fleet sets sail that day."

Marguerite gasped. "But that's less than two weeks away! I haven't even visited Mr. Hardy yet for his measurements and his mask. It usually takes a month or more to create a figure, particularly if we are inserting real hair."

Pitt nodded sympathetically. "I know, and I regret the suddenness of my request. I had planned to wait until you were finished with Nelson before sending you off to see Hardy. We only just discovered that the combined French and Spanish fleet is in the harbor of Cádiz off the southeastern coast of Spain. We must intercept Villeneuve and all of those blasted ships before he sets off again.

It's imperative that those figures be on board when Nelson sets sail. Can you do it?"

"Mr. Pitt, for the sake of England I shall endeavor to do my part."

Mr. Pitt had a package delivered the following morning with exact instructions regarding the delivery of the figures to HMS *Victory*. Marguerite was surprised that Darden himself did not bring the message, but did not allow herself to linger further thinking about why that disturbed her. Besides, Pitt's message caused her stomach to knot as she realized that the travel from London to Portsmouth, where HMS *Victory* now lay, would trim at least another two days from her sculpting time. She took heart from one phrase in his missive regarding the Hardy figure: "It need not be of full Tussaud superiority. Just finish it quickly."

Accompanying the letter were both a woodcut engraving of Captain Hardy and a small painting of him on a folded piece of canvas. Pitt had scrawled some approximate height, weight, and size measurements on the back of his letter. They were surely not accurate, but would have to do for this hasty mission.

Marguerite's days and nights became a blur of activity. During every moment that the sun was up, she was molding, carving, painting, and reworking wax mistakes. At night, she sat by candlelight studying her best route to port and writing letters to Marie, Claudette, and a drayer who could haul the figures to Portsmouth. She even had bedding moved from her rooms with Mrs. Penny into the workshop so she would not waste time traveling back and forth. She was grateful there was no mirror in the workshop, certain that her condition was deteriorating daily.

Despite Marie's admonition about always transporting the figures by sea, Marguerite could find no good way to do so in this situation. The map she examined in her room at night showed no decent river route from London to Portsmouth. To dispatch them out the Thames and through the Channel past the coast of France was unthinkable. Few vessels would be willing to do it, and the risk of her precious cargo falling into the hands of the French was too great. No, it would have to be an overland journey.

Brax Selwyn and Darden Hastings both tried to visit individually, but she was so frantic with her work that she refused them more than mere seconds at the doorstep before shutting the door in their faces again.

But by September 12, she had put the final touches on Mr. Hardy, whom she hoped was a good representation of the man himself, and sent a message to Darden that the figures were ready for transport the following morning. Pitt's instructions stated that he wanted Darden to personally oversee their loading and to have an understanding of their routing.

Marguerite then set about the task of properly wrapping and packing the two figures. She could hardly wait for her final activity, which was a return to her rooms to bathe and work out the bits of wax and paint from her tresses.

To her surprise, both Darden and Brax showed up early the next day, with Brax holding a small box wrapped with twine. At least she was finally presentable. Anticipating Darden's arrival, yet knowing she needed to be dressed for rough travel by coach, she wore a pale green dress with two subtle stripes of pink around the hem. She tucked her now glossy hair up into a straw bonnet also edged in pink, and carried with her a shawl of deep, burnished yellow, almost gold. Over her arm was an embroidered reticule Claudette had given her for her birthday at Hevington two years ago. How long ago that seemed!

Brax's eyes exclaimed his admiration of her, but Darden's face was inscrutable and he greeted her stiffly. The man vacillated between kindness and priggishness, didn't he? Why, then, was she so disappointed that he didn't seem taken with her fetching outfit today, after the care she had put into her appearance?

But Darden's attention was upon her workshop, not her. "Mrs. Ashby, if I'm not mistaken, your personal trunks are here, too. Do you intend to leave London for good?"

"My work for Mr. Pitt is complete, so there is no reason for me to stay. I was planning to meet the figures in Portsmouth and arrange them on board *Victory*, then return to Dublin."

"Via water from Portsmouth?" Darden asked. "As I recall, sailing is not your preferred method of travel."

"In fact, Lieutenant, I was planning to return much as you brought me. Overland to Bristol and then I will brave a ship to Dublin."

"I'm not sure your planning is wise, Mrs. Ashby. You may want to return to London until—"

"Until what?"

Darden pursed his lips and went quiet.

Brax jumped in. "What is all this chatter about travel back to Dublin, Mrs. Ashby? Why, we've only just met. Does this mean you won't be waiting for me when I return?"

"Return, sir? Return from where?"

"Didn't old stiff-neck Hastings tell you? We're off to war, with Nelson. I'm joining *Royal Sovereign*, which is already out to sea, while Hastings got the plum. He'll be on *Victory* as part of Lord Nelson's staff. I've no idea why the admiral or Captain Hardy wants the buzzard. He's no fit companion for anyone."

"Watch yourself, Selwyn," Darden growled.

But Brax was not to be deterred. "My heart is utterly shattered, Mrs. Ashby, that this is the last time I'll be in your flawless company. You've not yet had an opportunity to see my serious side. I can be quite captivating, you know. Why, when I'm glum and despondent it makes old Hastings here look positively delirious with joy. You will be weeping copiously, mistress, when I tell you all of my tales of woe and anguish."

"Your next tale of woe will be about the thrashing I give you if you don't be quiet," Darden said.

"But already I'm woeful because you won't let me properly court the lady, yet you won't declare her for yourself." Brax turned down the corners of his mouth in an expression of great anguish. "He wants to, you know, but hasn't the daring."

"Enough, you idiot."

Marguerite found the two of them quite amusing together. Serious and strong Darden Hastings coupled with the effervescent Brax Selwyn made for an extraordinary diversion. But she didn't have time for such leisure. She needed to get her precious cargo and her own person to Portsmouth quickly.

"Sirs, although I would much rather remain here in your delightful company, I really must be on my way."

"Of course," Darden said. "As soon as the figures and the rest of your baggage are loaded we will see you off. May I suggest, though, Marg—Mrs. Ashby, that you unpack a heavy cloak to take with you. You're a woman traveling alone and it might be best if someone with your, ah, charms, appeared as nondescript as possible. In fact, I've half a mind to accompany you myself and let Selwyn travel with the other officers."

"Oh, no you don't, Hastings! What a sly devil. By my arse will you do any such thing. You know you're committed to go with the rest of us. If you decide to desert your duty, well then, you'll have me along, too. Besides"—Brax winked at Marguerite—"I couldn't live with myself if I found out later that Mrs. Ashby never made it to Portsmouth because she died of boredom on the trip."

"Gentlemen, I thank you both for your kindness, but I assure you that I will be quite cautious on my journey. Although, Captain Hastings, I do appreciate your suggestion about my cloak and will unpack it now. But then I really must be on my way."

She put down her reticule and retrieved a heavy woolen cape from her luggage, and the three of them went onto the street where the drayer Marguerite had hired was waiting. Darden took over instructing the man and his crew on loading particulars, while Brax hailed a hackney and helped Marguerite with her personal bags onto it. She planned to go to the nearest carriage stop, where she would pick up a public coach to Portsmouth.

Darden returned, his forehead glistening with perspiration for his efforts, just as Brax was about to hand Marguerite into the hackney.

"Mrs. Ashby," Darden said, "may I thank you on behalf of Lord Nelson and Mr. Pitt for the service you have done in the war effort?"

Marguerite smiled. Darden was always so stiff and proper. "It was my pleasure and honor, sir, to do this small thing for England. And I pray you will both be safe and well and return to England whole."

"Oh pish," interrupted Brax. "You're such a stuffed hen, Hastings. Mrs. Ashby, I know I will personally slash the throats of a hundred French sailors to hurry the war to a close so that I might see you again. But, alas, you will be far away in Dublin, so after dispatching all of the Frenchmen, I might have to turn my sword on myself in my grief."

"Indeed, Lieutenant? Then you will have no ability to try to find me, will you?"

"Ah, the lady speaks truth! Therefore I will endeavor to save myself after saving England from the French, so that I might spend the rest of my life searching for my fair maid Marian."

Brax handed Marguerite into the carriage. Just as it was about to lurch forward, Brax called for it to halt. He opened the door and jumped in, taking the seat opposite her.

"I nearly forgot. I brought this for your journey. Fare thee well, Mrs. Ashby." He lay the twine-wrapped box on the seat next to her and took her hand, kissing it while looking up at her face with large doe eyes.

He leaped back out just as nimbly, to where Darden remained glowering at the curb.

As she pulled away, she saw Brax offering Darden his hand with a broad grin and Darden turning away to walk in the opposite direction.

Marguerite's traveling companions changed throughout the day as the coach stopped at various points. At midmorning she finally opened the box Brax had given her. Inside were a variety of biscuits and treats, which she shared with the other salivating passengers. Buried at the bottom of the box was a little parcel, which she unwrapped to find a tiny purple porcelain violet. The flower of lovers' potions. She hurriedly dropped it into her reticule before any of the other passengers noticed it. As she closed the bag she noticed the corner of an envelope inside. What was this? Had Brax also managed to slip something into her reticule when she wasn't looking? She pulled out an unsealed letter with her first name written across the front.

Dear Marguerite,

Please allow me to express my appreciation for what you are doing in the English cause.

I hope you will indulge me as I explain myself over something. Mr. Pitt told me that you expressed surprise that it was my idea to have Lord Nelson modeled in wax. I pray you did not consider it brazen of me to do so. Mr. Pitt sought a way to memorialize Lord Nelson for the people and I remembered fondly my tour of the waxworks with you. It seemed an ideal way to accomplish this and to enable me to make the acquaintance of both you and Madame Tussaud again.

I apologize that the figure is no longer intended for its original use, but may instead be destroyed in its new purpose.

It is possible that I will see you again briefly in Portsmouth before we sail. I will certainly look for you to ensure that everything is stowed on board as planned.

If I do not return from this sailing, please accept my utmost regard for your person.

Your servant,

Lt. Darden Hastings

What a touching letter. Did he really care so much what she thought, or was he merely seeking correspondence with a woman prior to sailing for war? She had heard it was common for a sailor to find an unattached woman to whom he could pledge his heart, just to give him courage and a reason to survive his trials. But Darden Hastings did not strike her as a desperate man. Well, she might not see him again anyway, so it was best not to worry on it.

By the time her public coach stopped at an inn for the night, just outside of Guildford, she was exhausted and immediately fell into a deep sleep. Her sleep was interrupted in the early morning hours by her bedmate, Mrs. Chudderley, who was in the coach headed for Portsmouth. The woman's snoring was enough to waken a dead man, despite the fact that the woman was lying on her stomach. Marguerite shook her head. Impossible. Unable to sleep any longer, she rose and got ready for the day's journey in the dawn's light. After brushing her hair and getting dressed again in her green dress from the previous day, she sat at the room's small table to read a page of a week-old newspaper that someone had left behind. Mrs. Chudderley still rattled the walls.

The paper talked only of Nelson, Nelson, Nelson. The entire hope of the nation was on this man. Would that he have success and beat the French once and for all. She thought of Darden and Brax, too, both on their way to join Nelson's fleet. She said a quick prayer for their safety and bravery.

Finally, Mrs. Chudderley was rolling over and snorting herself awake. She helped the woman get ready herself, then they joined the rest of the passengers to finish their journey.

PART SIX

Trafalgar

☙ 16 ☙

Portsmouth, September 15, 1805. Marguerite was now grateful for her woolen cloak, as drab as it was in faded sepia tones from its once rich chocolate color. It was not only very chilly at the harbor this morning, but it was crawling with every manner of man, some respectful and some leering. She pulled the cloak closer to her. Between it and her three traveling bags surrounding her, she felt some modicum of defense against the dockyard's assault of noise and stench.

How would she ever find the cart bearing her figures in this chaotic melee?

Before her loomed HMS *Victory,* at least four stories tall and gleaming from fresh bands of paint in ochre and black around the entire hull. The admiral's pennant flapped gaily from the topsail, a sign that Nelson was here. Atop several other masts waved the Union Jack, the new flag created to recognize the formation of the United Kingdom upon Ireland's official union with Great Britain.

Hanging down the bow of the ship was a rope thicker than Marguerite's body, suspended from pulleys. Surely such enormous coils of rope must be connected to an anchor hidden below the surface of the water. Sailors scrambled on and off *Victory*, carrying foodstuffs and barrels of beer and brandy on board, as well as dragging cannonballs, grapeshot, and other materials of war on carts across the gangplank. From far up in the air, sailors crawled about on the masts like little monkeys, coils of rope in their arms as they unfurled and adjusted sails. The smell of hot tar permeated the air.

Sailors of many nationalities, ranging in age from mere boys to grizzled old men scurried about, dressed in what could hardly be called uniforms, given the extent to which no man's clothes entirely matched another's in style or color. They yelled at one another in English, Dutch, Portuguese, and Italian as they sorted through the stocks of supplies on the quay, determining what was to go aboard and where it was to be located. The tense excitement was palpable, and Marguerite shivered.

But she was not the only female at the docks. A few wives and sweethearts had come to say good-bye, and several women had set up lean-tos, selling items that the sailors would not receive from the navy on their journey, like small wheels of hard cheese, and warm blankets. A man of the cloth sought out the faithful and unbelievers alike and pressed Bibles in their hands.

Conversely, a handful of prostitutes sauntered about, offering their wares as well, catcalling to the men hastening about their business. Marguerite watched as one of the sailors threw his arm about one of the prostitutes and led her around the back of a small, orange brick building, returning less than two minutes later, whistling. The woman followed him shortly thereafter, straightening her shabby skirt and calling out to another jack.

Marguerite shivered again.

Who could help her deduce where the wax figures might be? She shielded her eyes from the sun and looked up to the topmost deck of *Victory*. There was practically no chance she'd see Darden up there, so why bother? She could see what looked like officers up there, but it was hard to tell.

"Miss, can I help you with something?" a gentle voice said from behind her.

She whirled around in surprise. It was the minister, a kindly smile on his face.

"No, thank you anyway. Well, maybe you can. A wagon of goods was supposed to arrive here today for loading on *Victory*, and I'm not sure how to go about looking for it."

"A wagon of goods? Nothing unlawful, I hope?" His smile was still intact, but his voice had a harder edge to it.

"No no, it's something special for Lord Nelson."

"Of course it is, my dear. Of course it is. Well, you may want to check over there." He pointed to the brick building where the sailor and the doxy had just emerged from the back. "Someone at the storehouse should be able to help you with anything that's been delivered here at Pompey."

She managed to pick up all three bags herself and take them with her. The inside of the building was another beehive of commotion, except that the stench of too many unwashed bodies in close confinement, with their jabbering and shouting to clerks behind a counter, added a particular urgency to her mission. She managed to jostle her way past a bulk of people up to a counter where a harassed and flustered man with dark circles under his eyes stood over a large ledger with a quill pen in his hand. His fingers on both hands were stained with black ink.

"Yes, miss?" he asked. "Were you next?"

"Yes. No. I mean, I'm looking for a cart that was supposed to be delivering some goods to *Victory* in my name."

"Which is?"

"Oh. Marguerite Louise Ashby."

He examined his ledger, flipping pages backward and forward several times and running a blackened finger down the columns. "Here it is. 'Marguerite Louise Ashby of Madame Tussaud's.' " He started in surprise. "Madame Tussaud? How do I know that name?"

No need to tell him she was delivering wax figures to His Majesty's fleet!

"She's an artist."

He scratched his head. "Don't know why I'd know her, then. Well, here you go." He sketched out a rough map for her. The figures were several blocks away.

She thanked him profusely and scurried as fast as she could with her baggage out of the crowded building.

The wagon and four horses were left untended exactly where the clerk told her they would be. She did a quick visual survey of what was loaded on it. Everything appeared to be there.

Now what? Do I stand here until the driver decides to return, or should I walk this to the gangplank of Victory*?*

As she stood with one hand against the side of the wagon, debating with herself, the driver came running up, wiping crumbs from his mouth, the smell of beer strong on him.

"Sorry, miss, is this your load? I was getting around to taking your stuff to the ship. Truly I was. My crew's off somewhere spending money, I 'spect, so there's no one to help you unload your crates."

"What about you?"

"Oh no, miss. I'm just a driver, not a laborer."

Marguerite refrained from muttering an oath, instead saying, "Please, just take me back to the ship as quickly as you can." She threw her bags on top of the load and climbed up onto the seat next to the driver.

He gave her an appreciative look. "Never did see a woman scramble up here before."

"Please, sir, I just need to get to *Victory*. It's very important to Lord Nelson."

He winked. "Sure it is, miss, sure it is."

And with a cluck of his tongue he started his horses moving forward.

As they rolled up as close to the ship as possible, Marguerite half slid, half jumped out of the driver's seat. She didn't dare look down at what her dress must look like at this point.

"Now, sir, what will it cost to have you help me load these figures?"

The driver opened his eyes wide. "Why, miss, I told you. I'm just a driver."

"How much?"

He scratched his chin, which was sorely in need of a shave.

"Well now, I s'pose a crown would enable me to help you get everything taken down from the cart. And for another half crown you can have a little cart I've got back there. But I'm not going aboard. No, sir. Next thing I know I'll be pressed on, and I'm not going to be part of no stinking navy and certainly not part of any war with the French."

"You are kindness itself, sir," Marguerite replied.

He dropped his reins on the bench as he climbed out himself. "That indeed be true, miss. My mother always said so."

Twenty minutes later, Marguerite stood alone with a pile of personal belongings, waxworking supplies, and two crates holding the figures of Nelson and Hardy. Supposing that her personal effects and tools would be safe enough on the dock while she loaded the figures—and what choice did she have anyway?—she struggled to lift one of the crates holding a figure onto the wheeled cart the driver had left her. She was soon perspiring mightily from the effort despite the nippy air, but managed to get the crate plus a small bag of tools on it securely enough to walk it to the gangplank. Before stepping on, she looked up one more time, hoping to see Darden on the quarterdeck, but it was no use. With the sun in her eyes it was impossible to see anything, much less identify a specific man in the pandemonium of the upper deck.

She rolled her cargo up the gangplank but was stopped at the entrance of the ship by a fierce-looking man with an even more ferocious knife strapped to his side in a leather sheath. His white trousers had wide legs, and he wore a short, rumpled, tight-fitting waistcoat. His uniform was finished off with a black felt hat with a matching neckerchief.

"Where would you be going, little one?" he asked.

"I've got two crates to bring aboard for the admiral's cabin. They're for Lord Nelson."

"A pretty miss like you is bringing cargo on board for Lord Nelson? Now that is very interesting. And what might this cargo be?"

Trouble was about to start. "I can't tell you. It's private."

"Of course it is."

Did every dratted man in Portsmouth have only the same four words in his vocabulary?

She gritted her teeth and plastered on a smile. After all of her exertion to get the figures made and to the ship on time, they were damned well going to make it to their final destination. "May I suggest that you tell Lord Nelson that Marguerite Ashby is here with the items he requested?"

He bowed exaggeratedly. "Why, of course, miss. How rude of

me. I'll just hop right on up to the poop deck myself and tell him his lady friend is here. After all, the admiral is, I'm sure, sitting on his breeches waiting for the likes of me to barge in on him and let him know."

"Very well, what of Captain Hardy? He should also be aware of my arrival."

The sailor looked at her with something akin to amusement.

"I'm imaginin' the captain is with the admiral, if you understand, miss."

"Yes, I do. What is your name?"

"My name's Reginald, though most call me Gin."

"All right, then, Gin. *Please.* Please do as I ask. I assure you I am expected."

He looked Marguerite over again. "All right. I 'spect you're probably telling the truth."

He disappeared for several minutes, while Marguerite waited at the entrance to one of the lower decks. Sailors ran past her in and out of the ship, some cursing her for being in the way, others swallowing her with their eyes, knowing there would be no female companionship in their near future.

Gin returned, a small hint of respect in his eyes. "Cap'n Hardy said you're to be permitted to bring your goods aboard. To the admiral's cabin. Let me help you, miss." With powerful arms that were hidden under his shirt, he grabbed the cart and finished hauling it into the ship, shouting for another of the mates to help him get the crate up the stairs. Marguerite stayed poised at the entrance, unsure whether to follow or not.

Gin and his companion came back, looking hardly winded from their exertion. "What else, miss?"

She pointed to where the rest of her belongings were. "See that long crate there? It matches the one you just took on board. Please bring that one."

While the sailors took care of the crate, she tentatively stepped inside *Victory* to try to find the admiral's cabin herself. She almost had to crouch, the ceiling was so low, and it took several moments for her eyes to become accustomed to the dank darkness, pierced only by a few lanterns hanging from nails around the deck. Surely the admiral's cabin was not on this level, which seemed to be living quarters for the men. Hammocks were slung from battens fixed to low overhead beams in very narrow intervals, and there were what looked like dining tables hanging by ropes from the ceiling. It might have been an orphanage, if not for the bustle of men preparing for their sea departure and the serious weaponry on this deck. Incongruously situated at intervals between sections of hammocks and tables were gleaming black cannon, each mounted on a wheeled carriage and already positioned out open ports that provided some additional dim light.

Did the sailors seriously sleep, eat, and conduct warfare in the same place?

Thank goodness I'm not pressed into service.

She saw a set of stairs in the center of the deck and fled as quickly as she could to them. Since surely the admiral's cabin was not on the same level as where the rest of the soldiers lived, it must be farther up. Besides, the admiral would not have cannon in his room!

Would he?

The next deck was much like the previous one as far as she could tell as she passed through quickly, except that it seemed to be divided into many rooms instead of a single large common area. But the hanging dining tables interspersed by cannon were all there.

She dashed to the next set of stairs and climbed up as rapidly as her skirts would allow. More cannon. But there was a little less activity on this deck. The central part of it was uncovered and open to the air, making it much less confining than the other two decks she had been on. A man could stand up straight here. Perhaps the admiral's cabin could be found on this level. She espied a highly polished and darkly stained wood door and hurried to the rear of the ship toward it.

Pushing the door open gently, Marguerite saw that she had found the right place. The splendor of this cabin, which seemed to be roughly divided into a living area, a dining space, and sleep quarters, contrasted so sharply with the other two decks below that she gasped. A beautifully polished mahogany dining table, flanked on each side by a dozen red velvet chairs and topped with five multi-armed, silver candelabra, dominated one half of the long room that spanned the entire width of the ship.

On the other side were inlaid chests, tables, and settees that would be more fitting in a great country estate. A round table, surrounded by more velvet chairs, was heaped with well-worn maps, notebooks, quills, and silver inkpots. A jacket was thrown carelessly across one of the chairs, as though its owner would be back to claim it at any moment.

Hanging from the ceiling off to one side was a great cot. Compared to the hammocks she had seen below, this hanging bed was lavish. The sides of it were covered in white silk, a seemingly inappropriate material for the rough seas. Embroidered hangings draped over the rod suspending the bed and cascaded around the cot like a shroud. They were simply magnificent.

The floors were, unbelievably, made of marble, and luxurious Aubusson carpets provided serene colors and warmth to the room. Marguerite wondered how such carpets could survive the salt-drenched air at sea. She bent down to touch the carpet, and a closer inspection of the floors revealed that they were not marble, but that black-and-white squares had been painted on large sheets of canvas, and the canvas sheets covered the deck from edge to edge.

The sloped walls of either side of the palatial room were dominated by windows surrounded by wainscoting. The room was flooded with bright sunshine through the paned windows. Inset benches, topped with cushions and also decorated with wood paneling, followed the line of windows. She knelt on one of the benches and peered out the window. She hadn't realized how far up she had climbed. Marguerite shook her head. Enough idleness.

Standing upright near the door of the enormous cabin was the object of her search. The crate itself was undamaged, and was hopefully not upside down. The bag of tools had been tossed onto the floor next to the crate and some of her implements had fallen out. As she went to the bag to begin gathering the spilled contents, Gin appeared alone with the second crate and set it upright next to its mate.

"Here you are, miss. Just as you asked. You'll tell Cap'n Hardy I did as you asked, right?"

"Why, certainly, although I'm sure I won't see him, since I—"

But Gin was gone again, undoubtedly to return to whatever he was doing in preparation of sailing before Marguerite interrupted him.

Darden Hastings was third lieutenant aboard *Victory*, made so because two other lieutenants had earlier commissions than his. Nevertheless, his ranking was a good one, and if they engaged the French and Spanish fleet he would have great responsibilities. But he considered his greatest responsibility to be ensuring the wax figures were brought topside if they were needed. Darden was decidedly pleased with this task.

He looked over the side of the quarterdeck for the hundredth time, scanning the dockside. Still no sign of Marguerite. Had he somehow missed her? He needed to check with someone to see if her cargo had been brought aboard.

"Lieutenant!" A red-faced sailor puffed up to him. "There's a bit of a scrap going on down below. Can you come help sort it out?"

"Fighting already? We haven't even left port yet."

"Yes, sir, I know."

"Do these ignorants know they'll end up in irons?"

"No telling, sir."

Darden followed the sailor, regretting his inability to maintain watch for the wax sculptress.

Marguerite set about dislodging the figures from their coffins right away. She unlocked each crate still in its upright position, carefully pulling the hinged lids away so as not to rub them too harshly against the fine carpet underneath them.

"Well, my lord Nelson and Captain Hardy, it looks as though the first part of your voyage has ended, and the second is to begin. Without me to accompany you, praise be. Now, where would you be most comfortable on this part of your journey?"

She looked around the expanse of cabin again. They needed to be easily accessible should they—heaven forbid—be required, yet be well protected from the tumult the ship was sure to endure. Knowing that the admiral had been less than enthused about having the figures made, she knew they should also remain as unobtrusive as possible.

She could hear distant whistling, not quite a piper's tune, yet not a distress signal, either. Probably *Victory* signaling something to its crew. She must hurry and finish. If only Gin were still here to help her move the heavy pieces.

While contemplating where exactly to position the figures, she made quick work of assembling the special stands she had developed for them in anticipation of turbulent ship movements. Looking much like a post jammed upright into the center of a thick wooden disk on the floor, the stand would be a platform that the figure could be lashed to, using buckled straps. The buckles could be easily undone in case the figures needed to be released in a hurry. Packing the stand pieces inside each respective crate had made the boxes far heavier than normal, but the work and the weight were worth it, since the figures would be much more accessible than if they remained lying flat in the crates.

As she was discovering now that she was trying to pull poor Mr. Hardy out of his compartment. The figures were dreadfully heavy under any circumstances, but always worse when they had to be picked up from the floor. Even in their current upright position it was difficult to extract them from their snug lodgings. Even Joseph would be a welcome help right now.

Did she dare step out of the room and seek help from one of the men? Not all of them would be quite as respectful as Gin was, would they? No, better to do this herself and get off the ship as quickly as possible.

With an arm around his waist, Marguerite gave one more gentle pull. "Ah, Mr. Hardy, there you are. Let's put you somewhere safe, shall we?"

She slowly walked the deadweight figure to its stand. She gave it a little lift to get it onto the large round base and leaned it against the thick wooden pole, breathing heavily as she did so. Grabbing several straps from one of her bags, she tied him to the post around his shoulders, waist, and thighs.

She stood back and surveyed the figure. "Not a very dignified position, is it, Captain? My hopes are that you stay lashed like this for the entire voyage."

Moving the wax character was now easier because she could get on her hands and knees and simply slide the round platform disk across the carpet, instead of attempting to walk with her arms around the figure. She maneuvered the Nelson figure out of his crate and tied it to the second stand. Now both figures were ready for positioning.

But where?

I suppose they're best at the back of the cabin.

It appeared from the round table that the admiral conducted meetings in here.

No need to startle his officers.

She finally decided on a location behind the far end of the elongated dining table, underneath another bank of windows. Under the windows behind the table stood a sideboard inlaid with fanciful marquetry. She would place a figure on either side of the serving chest, as though they were servants standing post for the admiral's supper. That would probably be less shocking for Nelson's officers, who might be used to having servants attend to them.

On her knees, Marguerite pushed Captain Hardy down the length of the cabin and around the near rounded edge of the dining table to position the figure on the left side of the sideboard.

She returned for Lord Nelson and pushed his figure in the same way, this time going all the way around the end of the table to place his figure between the right side of the sideboard and a wainscoted window.

She sat back on her knees, her skirts jumbled around her, surveying her work. Yes, this positioning would do nicely for the figures. Lord Nelson should be pleased. Or at least not displeased.

Marguerite moved to stand up, not realizing that her right foot was on her skirt. The resistance of her clothing pulled her backward and she fell, her head cracking loudly against the polished edge of the dining table and jostling it. She yelped, crouching down again in pain and surprise. Seconds later, the silver candelabrum nearest that end of the table came rolling off and hit her square on the back of the head in the exact spot where it had just made contact with the table.

Her last thought before blacking out was for the dreadful headache this was sure to cause.

The sailor named Gin scanned the quay and was ready to report that all cargo had been brought aboard when he noticed the lady's bags still remained on shore. *She musta forgot.* Cursing the troubles a woman brought to a ship, he stomped off to retrieve them and deliver them to the admiral's cabin.

"Miss?" he asked as he knocked on the door. Getting no answer, he opened it and entered. "Miss? I brought your bags. Where d'ya want them?"

No answer. She wasn't here. Where was she? The crates stood empty where he had left them, so she musta been here doing her work. Eh, not his problem. Gin dropped the luggage inside the room near the door without bothering to look farther into the cabin. She could figure out what to do with her belongings. He turned to leave and paused.

The admiral probably wouldn't want his cabin left unlocked once they were underway. Best if he found the first lieutenant and asked him to come back with him with a key to latch the door.

"Are we ready to weigh anchor?" Nelson asked.

"I believe so," replied *Victory*'s captain, Thomas Hardy. He reviewed his lists. "The magazine is full of shot, the surgeon has his tools and bandages, and the hold has over five hundred barrels of water, fifty tons of beer, and enough salted beef and pork to make the Prince of Wales scream for mercy."

"Indeed." Nelson repressed a smile. "What of those dratted wax figures? Has that Ashby woman stored them in my cabin?"

"Yes. One of the men reported her arrival to me, suspicious of course as to why a woman wanted aboard."

"Is she done? Has she left the ship? Make sure of it."

Hardy had Gin summoned.

"Seaman, did you get the two crates aboard and in the admiral's cabin?"

"Yes, Captain."

"And did the woman accompanying them get them opened?"

"Yes, sir."

"Is she gone?"

"Gone, sir? She wasn't in the cabin when I was just there a few minutes ago, but—"

"Thank you. That will be all."

And so Gin returned to his post, and, with Nelson's approval, Captain Hardy gave the signal to pull anchor.

Nathaniel had no idea how difficult it would be to drum up a crew for his ship, now rechristened *Wax Maiden*. Press gangs took most of the able bodies, and it was difficult to persuade the willing with mere money to spend an indefinite amount of time at sea. He'd resorted to offering extra rations of beer, free clothing, and bonus money on top of a promise of spoils for completing certain types of missions. All in all, a degrading business for him. But he'd finally rounded up a crew of men who claimed to have good naval experience. He worried briefly that they might be a crew of misfits instead of a complement of hardy sailors, but dismissed the thought as one that did not take into account his own skills as a leader.

He was also surprised by the cost of victualing even a small ship such as his. The price of a single potable barrel of water was positive thievery. Not to mention the amount of food Mr. Scroggs said he must have aboard even for a small journey, plus guns and shot for protection. Fortunately, he had good credit with the bank.

Or at least his father did, and Nathaniel had no compunction in borrowing on his father's name.

But most of his difficulties were behind him. Just a few more repairs and *Wax Maiden* would be ready to do her duty, a duty that would ultimately result in great glory and recognition for one Nathaniel Carter Ashby.

This accomplishment deserved a celebratory glass of port. He decided to send for one of his father's finest vintages from the cellar right now.

Maybe he'd offer a glass or two to the new maid, Polly something-or-other, Lydia Brown's replacement. She was a saucy-looking thing who might enjoy a brief dalliance with a man poised to be quite famous, indeed.

And when he was that famous, why, Marguerite Ashby would come scampering back to London, now wouldn't she?

☙ 17 ☙

Marguerite woke slowly, all of her senses coming back to her individually. Where was she? What had happened? As her eyes became focused, she saw Nelson and Hardy in wax, standing before her like sentinels.

Dear God, did her head throb. She tentatively reached up a hand and touched the back of her head. The pain was excruciating and she withdrew immediately, holding her hand up in front of her. Was that blood? Why was she bleeding?

Right. The table. She'd clumsily fallen, something she'd never done before when working with wax figures. How embarrassing. Well, she just needed a bit of tidying up and she'd be on her way now that the figures were set in place. Her hand flopped down to her side again.

She lay still for several minutes, willing the pain away. Surely this was the worst headache she'd ever had, although it wasn't every day that she crashed into a heavy mahogany table, now was it? The boisterous noises of the crew outside the cabin as they prepared for the journey were magnified inside her tender skull.

She again attempted to get up and at least this time maneuvered into a seated position. While sitting motionless to again regain control of her pulsing head, she felt a gentle movement beneath her. Sort of as though she was floating. Surely that was just her mind playing tricks in her weakened state.

Wait, there was the feeling again. Motion forward. Dear God, no, surely the ship had not pulled anchor. With as much rapidity as she could muster, Marguerite pulled herself up by the edge of the table and stood, wobbling. She stepped gingerly to the cabin's rear windows and saw nothing but a receding coastline.

Even through her muddled wits, she realized she was trapped aboard the ship. But they weren't too far away from shore yet. If she could get someone's attention quickly enough, then without a doubt she could be put in some kind of launch and sent back to Portsmouth.

Marguerite groped her way to the front of the cabin and pulled down on the entry door's handle. The door would not open. She rattled and pulled on the handle, yet it wouldn't budge.

She was locked in. Who did this?

Now overcome with a panic that overrode her throbbing head, she pounded on the door with her fist, calling out for someone to help her, release her.

She could hardly hear herself over the din of the sailors working. Why would she expect them to hear her weak voice from the other side of the door?

A banging fine accomplishment, Marguerite. You, who loathes sailing more than anything, are now trapped on a hulking beast headed for battle. This couldn't be happening. Surely someone will find me soon and send me back to shore.

She continued rapping on the door and crying out until she was hoarse and her smarting head had her near to blacking out.

Perhaps I should rest a moment.

She stumbled back across the room to one of the leather-cushioned benches along the wall of windows next to the dining table.

She felt better as soon as she sat down. The pain receded only a little, but it was enough that she began to feel drowsy. The rhythm of the ship slicing through the water added to her lethargic feeling.

Perhaps I should lie down for just a few minutes.

Marguerite lay down on one side, facing the interior of the cabin, her knees pulled up toward her chest and her skirts in a jumble around her. She was fast asleep in moments.

* * *

"What in blazes are you doing down here?" Nelson's agitated voice pulsated in her ears.

Marguerite slowly opened her eyes. How long had she been asleep?

She blinked her eyes, trying to get her bearings again. So many blurry faces above her.

A familiar voice drifted over from somewhere in the room.

"Admiral, I believe Mrs. Ashby is injured. Her hair is matted with blood. May I suggest we have Mr. Beatty have a look at her? There's no sense in incurring a casualty so soon."

Another voice interceded calmly. "Mrs. Ashby, can you hear me? What happened to you?"

Marguerite mumbled that she had fallen while setting up the figures but had been locked in and couldn't leave the ship before it departed. Meanwhile, she was trying desperately to fully wake up despite her throbbing head.

That second voice spoke up again. "Admiral, it would seem the woman has had an accident and should not be blamed. Once we catch up to the rest of the fleet, I recommend we transfer her to a ship at the back of it. Lieutenant, she's in your charge. Keep her out of the admiral's sight until we reach the rest of the fleet."

Squinting her eyes, Marguerite could just make out the shape of what must be Captain Hardy's long, dour face.

Nelson spoke again, and his perturbed tone made her wince. "As though Pitt's idea wasn't idiotic enough, now we have to deal with an injured woman creating a predicament for us. Can you imagine what would happen if it was put out that I *forgot* an unauthorized woman was aboard?"

"Yes, Admiral," replied Hardy in a soothing voice. "I imagine I should also be castigated soundly as well."

"Quite. Make sure the crew knows its duty with regard to this."

Marguerite attempted to apologize for the trouble she was causing, but couldn't quite form the words. Besides, didn't they realize she might have died? Instead, she closed her eyes to block out the light and the faces, and sank back into quiet oblivion.

When she awoke again, she was still lying on a window bench, only now she had a thin blanket tossed over her. It smelled faintly of grease. Darden was on one knee next to her and peering into her face with concern.

"Marguerite, do you know me?"

She nodded her head slowly. Her headache was still excruciating and the movement made it worse.

Darden clasped one of her hands in his damaged left one. "Everyone else is gone. You were shivering so I covered you. I apologize for taking that liberty. The ship's surgeon has been in to see you and doesn't think there is serious damage. He wanted to bleed you to release ill humors from your brain, but I thought you'd had enough trauma to sustain you for one day. I must admit your hair is a bit frightful, though. Fortunately, you're on a man-of-war and mirrors are a scarcity here."

Marguerite laughed weakly. "Why did Captain Hardy say he would put me off the ship once they meet the fleet? Why doesn't he put me off before we leave sight of the shoreline?"

Darden looked at her, baffled. "Marguerite, do you know how long you were sleeping?"

"Not more than a few minutes, I'm sure."

He shook his head. "We were at sail for two hours before Nelson called his officers together for a meeting in his cabin. That's when you were discovered."

"That's not possible!" she gasped.

"I'm afraid it is. Do you think you can take some tea?"

He gently helped her up into a seated position and put her hands around a warm cup before slipping into a dining chair nearby. She gratefully sipped the hot liquid.

Keeping her eyes down on her cup, she said, "I suppose Lord Nelson and Captain Hardy are furious with me."

"I suppose it's not every day that a beautiful widow stows away in the admiral's cabin." He looked away, embarrassed, when her eyes met his.

An uncomfortable silence ensued.

Marguerite swallowed the last of her tea. "So how long before we reach the fleet? A day?"

"I'm afraid not. Captain Blackwood has blockaded Villeneuve

and the combined French and Spanish fleet at Cádiz. Vice Admiral Calder's fleet presumably arrived there today to join him, and Nelson's plan is to get there as soon as possible to take overall command. I expect it to take another couple of weeks."

"Two weeks! You must be joking. Darden, you know I cannot possibly survive in a ship that long. Besides, I have no change of clothing or any personal belongings."

"That's actually not true. All of your personal bags that I loaded onto the carriage in London are here." He nodded to a pile of luggage near the door.

"I don't understand. I left all that on the dock while I was setting up the figures. A sailor helped me with the crates after getting approval from the captain, but that was all."

"Well, somehow your belongings got aboard *Victory*. So hopefully you have a book or two to keep you company for the journey. My intent is to put you in the sick berth, since it's empty right now. You'll need to stay as inconspicuous as possible. Promise me that you will do so."

She nodded obediently, feeling like a chastised little girl. "You know, I didn't do it on purpose, Darden. And I worked dreadfully hard to fulfill this order for Mr. Pitt."

"I know. And when we catch up to the rest of the fleet, we'll put you in a launch and deliver you to a ship at the rear of our columns. You should be quite safe. How does your head feel?"

"Rather like it made contact with an anchor, but the tea helped. By the way, is Lieutenant Selwyn aboard with us?"

Darden's face darkened. "No, you may recall that the lieutenant was headed for the *Royal Sovereign*. It is doubtful that we will have the pleasure of his company for the foreseeable future."

"Yes, I remember now. How foolish of me to ask."

Darden stood and offered his arm. "Are you ready to go to your new quarters? The sick berth won't be as glamorous as the admiral's cabin, but you'll be on the same deck near the figures and it's as private a place as you'll find in the ship."

She attempted a feeble joke. "Will my bed be as sumptuous as the admiral's over there?"

Darden smiled in return. "I'm afraid not. That cot was specially made to fit Lord Nelson's frame. If something happens to him, he'll be wrapped in it with two round shot at his feet and buried at sea. Lady Hamilton made the hangings herself."

"He loves her greatly, then?" Marguerite's question was more a statement.

"Unfortunately, yes. Although most of the Royal Navy and the government find their relationship scandalous, given that both were married when Lord Hamilton was alive, it does have its supporters. Captain Hardy thinks Emma is good for the admiral."

"And you? What do you think?"

Darden shook his head. "I don't think anything at all. Not on this topic, anyway, should I like to retain my position. But I will say that when I am married there will be no room in my life for a mistress, because I'll be too busy loving my wife."

And on that very interesting comment, Marguerite allowed herself to be escorted to what would be her new home for the next two weeks.

Time passed slowly for Marguerite. Although her head wound bled, the surgeon decided it did not require sewing up, so after a biting cleanup with saltwater, she was left to mend on her own. Her headache lasted nearly as long as the large knot on her head, although it did get progressively better with each night of sleep.

She was provided with a hanging bed in the farthest corner of the sick berth, which was still in view of the admiral's cabin. Darden told her this was the upper gun deck, an undesirable-sounding place, but the cannon pointing out through the open ports reminded her that it was an accurate term. At least her bed did not hang directly over one of the guns, a decidedly unpleasant notion. The flat beds with their raised cloth sides in the sick berth were infinitely better than the rough, rope hammocks the regular sailors slept in on the decks below, but the conditions made her dream at night about the glorious four-poster bed Aunt Claudette had provided during her time at Hevington. She made a mental note to visit Claudette and William the moment her feet touched English soil again.

She quickly grew used to the noise, comprised of both the wood creaking and groaning, and the men constantly yelling in a variety of languages and moving about. Most of the sailors avoided her, whether because of some superstition about women aboard a ship or because Darden had let word out that she was under his care, she couldn't say.

Marguerite spent most of her time sleeping or reading. She had packed a few books for her journey to Portsmouth and she was very grateful to have them now to pass the time.

She was even more grateful that the weather had been cooperative. She was beginning to feel like perhaps she could overcome her fear of sailing.

Marguerite took her meals with the officers on the middle gun deck, one level down. The officers' quarters, which Darden called the wardroom, had four cabins with a shared dining table in the center of them. Darden personally escorted her down there to eat with him during his appointed meal times. After witnessing the ordinary seamen on her deck eating in shifts with their messmates, she realized that officers were treated much differently. Unlike the routine of salt pork, dried peas, thin stews, cheese, butter, and bread, to be washed down with eight pints of beer each day, the officers lived in relative luxury.

If the confined quarters anywhere in the ship could be termed luxurious.

But they did have fresh meat whenever the captain ordered goat, or goose for his afternoon dinner, as well as fresh eggs from the chicken coops. An entire area above the galley was reserved to keep the animals confined in pens. And the officers partook of sweet wines not available to the rest of the crew.

She was also granted the right to use the officers' quarter gallery, a private toilet that Darden assured her was vastly superior to the six "heads" the rest of the sailors used, which were located in the open air at the foremost point of the ship, and through which waste was dropped directly into the sea below. Some of the officers looked at her askance or with questioning eyebrows, but most left her alone.

Under the same orders as the rest of the crew, I suppose.

Still, it was a fine thing to be able to share with the officers on board the man-of-war, and she was grateful for Darden's intervention, which assured her better status while she was trapped here.

The ship's surgeon, Mr. Beatty, a surprisingly young man with wire-rimmed glasses who looked more like a university student than a medical man, exercised deliberate contempt for Marguerite's presence in the sick berth. He perpetually muttered about the bad luck women bring to a ship and what it meant to lose even a single precious cot that could be used for tending to a sick seaman. "Ill-advised, I say. Sure to bring about defeat," he would say for Marguerite's benefit when no one else was around to hear. Fortunately, his disdain for her company meant he spent as little time in the sick berth as possible unless there was a call for his services, instead spending time training his assistant surgeons, Messrs. Smith and Westemburg, or staying hidden away in his own cabin several decks below. Marguerite made it a habit to hold her breath when he came near, and to finally expel it with relief when he disappeared again.

Marguerite observed that most men who came to the sick berth had been injured in their daily work routine. Fingers were routinely sliced by men cleaning the pistols and cutlasses that seemed to be stored in plenty aboard the ship.

But the primary recipients of injury seemed to be the men working the sails. On more than one occasion, a man was carried in by two others and heaved into a bed, moaning about the pain of a broken leg, arm, or worse. Marguerite soon learned that these men deftly scurried across the yardarms to furl or unfurl sails, but with no protection against falls onto the deck or into the undulating ocean. The men were experienced, but the combination of wind and waves resulted in more than one fall.

She cringed one day when a sailor was brought down, looking more battered than most and crying piteously for relief. Mr. Beatty gave him some beer to gulp down while he examined the man's injuries. The man wiped his mouth with his sleeve and fell backward onto his cot, as if unconscious. The surgeon put a small piece of glass to the man's mouth and shook his head, gesturing to one of his assistants.

Mr. Smith rolled the nearest cannon away from the gun port, while the other hurried off the deck and returned shortly with a sailmaker carrying a rolled-up piece of cloth. The sailmaker unrolled the fabric on the ground into what looked like a large sack and, with the help of Smith and Westemburg, hauled the expired man from his bed and placed his body into the bag. The sailmaker grabbed two small cannonballs from a rack of them nearby, and put one at the man's feet and the other at his head. From there, he quickly made loose stitches to close the sack around the man's head. Marguerite could have sworn the sailmaker made a stitch across the dead man's nose but shook her head to clear the thought.

Silly goose, why would he have sewn across the poor man's face?

The sailmaker departed as quickly as he had arrived. The surgeon's assistants picked up the wrapped man and unceremoniously tossed him through the exposed gun port. Mr. Smith looked through the opening, as though to make sure the man had made it down to the waves.

Marguerite gasped and broke the unwritten rule of not communicating with the crew. "What did you just do? Was that a proper sea burial? Isn't the chaplain called before someone is . . . is . . . sent down like that?"

Mr. Smith lifted a shoulder. "Sorry, miss, not everyone gets it done up all nice and pretty. He was just an ordinary seaman. He probably didn't even have anything his messmates could sell to raise money for his family. The captain will write to his wife, though."

Marguerite clutched her stomach after the men left. *How horrid the life of a sailor could be!*

Whenever Darden had a free moment, he would slip down to see her, inquiring solicitously after her head wound and wanting to know what else he could provide for her.

Of Nelson she saw nothing, as her view from the sick berth to his cabin was blocked. Captain Hardy actually came down once to let her know that he intended to have her rowed to HMS *Pickle*, a small sloop already waiting at the rear of the assembling fleet.

"*Pickle* is armed, so you'll be protected, Mrs. Ashby."

Somehow that information was of little comfort in the face of potentially witnessing serious fighting between the navies of her homeland and Madame Tussaud's. But hopefully *Pickle* would be far enough away that she wouldn't see or hear much.

Although that meant she also wouldn't know whether Darden was safe. Strange how fond she was growing of him. He was a curious mixture of rigid politeness and some kind of hidden, burning obsession. He expressed no blatant desire for her, though, leaving Marguerite to assume that he was merely taking his duty toward her very seriously.

Brax Selwyn, though, was as far from serious as the bright sky was from the darkened night. What levity he brought to a room! And how he plagued poor Darden! How did the two of them ever become friends? Were they really friends?

Together, the two men reminded her of nothing more than Nicholas, who combined Brax's light and humorous spirit with Darden's grave sense of devotion and duty. She smiled with the pleasant recollection of her husband, gone almost three years now. Whatever would Nicholas think of her situation now?

"Damn you, I'll have you lashed, you insubordinate whelp." Nathaniel's face was mottled with rage. How dare these drunken, ill-tempered, overpaid buggers cross him with complaints about his orders? He was the captain, wasn't he?

The unshaven man stood defiantly before him, stocky legs spread apart and arms across his chest.

"You're not likely to find anyone to do it for you. Unless you propose to do it yourself." The man's eyes flashed his scornful challenge. "As I said, the other men and I have been talking, and we've decided we won't go along with you. You lied to us about what you're doing. We don't plan to go to the scaffold for the likes of you. We're taking the ship back. You can pay us the wages you owe us and we'll forgive the rest."

"*You* will forgive *me?* This is mutiny and I can have you hanged for it." *Couldn't he?*

"You ain't the bleeding Royal Navy, *Captain*." The man spat the title out like an overly chewed bit of tobacco. "You'll have to look for some other dumb boobies to follow you on this dunderheaded mission."

"I'll spread word around that you can't merit a farthing's worth of hard tack, and none of you will ever get jobs again," Nathaniel said. Maude Ashby had used this technique many times with great success on the household servants.

"As you wish. But I'd be sleeping with one eye open every night if you do that, *sir*." The hired hand stalked off.

And without even a salute. The cheek of him.

So the ship returned to shore and Nathaniel was forced to pay the men before starting over. His face flamed with the humiliation of it. Obviously he had to look elsewhere for more *cooperative* sorts of workers.

At least all of the salted and pickled barrels of food and his store of beer would not go to waste. He'd keep them aboard until he got a new crew.

As the days stretched out, Marguerite realized that the men were never left idle. Strict routine seemed to be critical to maintaining morale. She noted that each day of the week required specific activities, whether it be washing decks, performing drills, mending clothes, or submitting to inspections. On Sundays a church service was held on the quarterdeck and the men had free time in the afternoon. The schedule of activities was so unchanging that Marguerite hardly need look at the watch pinned to her dress anymore.

September 28, 1805. An unusual commotion roused Marguerite from her book. Skirting quietly around the sailors busy at work on the deck, she slipped in next to one of the cannon and peered above it through the open port.

They were plowing straight toward a large gathering of ships. Terrified at first that the enemy had found them alone on the open seas, she realized that the ships were flying British colors. She expelled her fearful breath. Soon she would be transferred to HMS *Pickle* and be out of the way. She had survived yet another potentially fatal sea journey.

Darden stood next to her bed where she was sitting up reading again a few hours later. "Nelson has officially taken over command of the British fleet from Captain Collingwood. I expect in the next few days you'll be put on a launch over to *Pickle*. The captain's first priority will be to wood and water not only *Victory*, but the other ships that have been out to sea awhile."

She flipped the open book down on her lap. "Thank you, Darden. Truly. For everything you've done for me."

"I was happy to perform my duty toward you," he replied stiffly.

"Duty or not, you were kind to me in a situation where you had many other obligations to attend to. I should never have survived this journey if you weren't here. I guess that's twice now you've escorted me, isn't it?"

Was that a hint of red in his cheeks?

Darden shifted uncomfortably from foot to foot. "Marguerite, I won't be able to escort you in the launch to *Pickle*."

"I understand perfectly. I've no doubt it would be difficult for you to leave your obligations for any period of time."

"Yes, well, ahem, it wasn't my choice. Captain Hardy thought that perhaps I was attending to my duty with you a bit too well, so another of the men will escort you. I'll handpick the man, so you needn't have any fear on that account."

Marguerite reached out and patted Darden's arm. "Lieutenant, I have no fears whatsoever with you around."

He took her hand and bent over it, kissing it lightly. He rose again and stared at her with those dark, penetrating eyes. They whispered everything and said nothing.

"Fear is something you should always leave in my care, Marguerite." And without releasing her hand or giving her warning, he bent down and kissed her full on the mouth. His lips were powerfully comforting, and the scarred hand he raised to cradle her neck was warm and work-roughened. He massaged her open neckline with a hidden message of desire, and she could barely suppress her own sigh of longing. He smelled of the coarse shipboard soap that all the men used, as well as the ubiquitous odor of tar that clung to everything. Yet his scent was intoxicating, and she could taste the tang of the ocean, combined with a strong flavor of cloves, on him. She brought her free hand up to cover his, hoping he would not notice her quaking. He stiffened as she lay her palm on the roughened bulge of his scar but relaxed when she demonstrated no repulsion.

Darden moved from her lips to her cheeks, nose, eyebrows, and forehead, planting feathery kisses everywhere before returning once more to draw from her mouth, this time more hungrily, as though he had just realized he was drowning and Marguerite was his life preserver.

He tore away from her as suddenly as he had pulled her close. "Please, forgive my impertinence. It was inexcusable. Good day, Mrs. Ashby."

"But I wasn't—" Marguerite tried to stop him, but he had turned on his heel and strode off, taking the staircase two steps at a time back to the quarterdeck.

She put two trembling fingers to her lips. *What had just happened?*

Darden berated himself over and over. What a complete fool. An idiot. He was letting Marguerite steal her way into his soul. This was completely unacceptable. He couldn't fulfill his duty and take care of other matters if he was going to allow himself to be befuddled by a woman.

But you did this to yourself, didn't you? You had to seek her out in Edinburgh, and this is the result of all your mischief. You should have managed it so that Selwyn handled the details of the wax figures—there would have been no harm in it—but you let jealousy override your common sense, didn't you?

"Lieutenant? Are you all right?" A midshipman looked at him in concern. "You've been at that quite some time."

The sailor nodded down to where Darden sat on a stool, repeatedly knotting and unknotting a length of rope.

And now you look a fool in front of your men.

"I'm perfectly fine. Just working out a small problem."

The sailor nodded and moved on without a second thought or care as to what his superior's problem might be.

Enough. I need to have my wits about me, especially if we're to engage in battle.

Darden resolved that he would not see Marguerite again before she disembarked from *Victory*. Furthermore, he wouldn't seek her out ever again. Not while he still had so much to do that could potentially go so very wrong.

18

Hevington, October 10, 1805. "William, I think something may be very wrong." Claudette looked up from her letter to her husband, who had just entered the library. Little Bitty lay at her feet in a most unladylike fashion, making a sketch of her most recent acquisition: a tiny red squirrel whose front leg had been injured by one of the dogs. Bitty had stuffed a pillowcase with old rags and perched the little rodent on it as though it were Cleopatra on her barge.

William Greycliffe smiled indulgently at his favorite daughter before kissing his wife and settling down in the King James Monstrosity next to her.

"Has Edward dashed another ball through a window? My poor boy has never quite learned how to manage a stick properly."

"No, nothing like that. It's Marguerite."

"Is that another letter from her? How is she? How was her journey to Portsmouth?"

"That's the trouble. This is from Marie Tussaud. She says Marguerite hasn't returned to Dublin yet, but it's been more than three weeks since Marguerite wrote and told her she was headed out to deliver the figures."

William gently took the letter from his wife's hand and scanned it, frowning.

"Is it possible that she decided to visit friends in the south?" he asked.

"Her whole life was in London with the doll shop, although I suppose it's possible she knows someone down that way." Claudette was doubtful.

"Or maybe she decided to have a rest along the coast. Or perhaps she decided to return via Bath, to take the waters there. Didn't you say Mr. Pitt recommended that highly to her?"

"Yes, but it's not like Marguerite not to send word. William, I'm worried that something happened to her. Maybe her coach was attacked before she reached Portsmouth and she . . . she . . ." Claudette couldn't finish the thought.

"We don't want to assume the worst just yet." William went to his desk and searched through a stack of old newspapers. He selected a couple of them and brought them back to his beloved chair.

"Let's see," he mused as he scanned the papers. "Nelson departed Portsmouth on September fifteenth. What was the date of her last letter to you?"

"September tenth. A month ago."

"And she left after that? She must have flown on the back of a falcon to reach him in time. Hmm, looks like Nelson was planning to take command of the entire British fleet somewhere off Cádiz."

"Where is that?"

"On the southwestern coast of Spain, near the entry to the Straits of Gibraltar. I believe our brave lads in the navy have been blockading Bonaparte's French and Spanish ships ever since they stopped at port there to obtain more supplies." He shook his head. "Did the Spaniards learn nothing from the Armada?"

"Well, if Nelson has sailed off to Spain already, either Marguerite never made it to Portsmouth, or something happened to her on her return. I remember how vile the port of London was when I came here from France. If Portsmouth is the same, maybe she's been robbed, or maybe even forced into prostitution." Claudette heard the terror in her voice but couldn't help herself. "William, we must do something."

"The first thing we must do is not panic. I'll write a letter to the

Admiralty office to see what I can find out. Actually, why don't we go to London directly and visit together? I'm sure we can find someone who can help us."

"That's an excellent idea. I'll have Jolie prepare my things immediately. And I don't plan to return until we've seen Marguerite with our own eyes."

And so Little Bitty remained behind in the library, feeding the little squirrel mashed up bits of fruit as a reward for being such a good model for her drawing.

Fourth lieutenant Brax Selwyn stood almost alone on the deck of *Royal Sovereign* with his right hand on the ship's wheel as he guided the ship on its southward course toward Cádiz. He enjoyed taking on the quartermaster's job at nighttime. Three other men were stationed around the great wheel, which reached from deck to ceiling, and could require great strength and coordination of movement to steer. But the other three were in as little mood for conversation as he was. Brax threw perfunctory glances toward the lamp-lit compass set in its wood post mount, but otherwise stayed preoccupied with his own thoughts.

The clear sky was brilliant with stars and the air was breezy and crisp. The moon, hanging low on the horizon, was full and glowed so bright it seemed to reflect celestial glory. This ship sliced easily through the water. Most of the activity on the ship was finished hours ago, so the only sounds came from the few men on duty, most of them on a watch shift.

Brax sniffed the air cautiously. Men had tarred the masts again yesterday to ensure protection against rot and salt, and the pungent odor lingered. The smell of tar was the only thing about navy life Brax didn't like. Unfortunately, it was a major part of sea life, since masts and most other exposed areas of a ship were tarred regularly. Some of the men even tarred their pigtails to keep them waterproof. But he would never complain. Not when there were opportunities like tonight to be at peace with nature.

It was a perfect place for a man to be in private to reflect on things.

Tonight his thoughts had started with his duties and the upcoming engagement with the French and Spanish fleet. But, inexplicably, his mind drifted off to the clever little waxworker, Mrs. Ashby. She was obviously not married, so why the deception? Even if she was widowed, she was too young to still be so reserved. So stately.

He couldn't quite understand the woman, and that made her a puzzle. And Brax Selwyn enjoyed nothing more than solving an amusing puzzle.

She was full of spit and fire underneath that matronly facade, he was sure of it. He was equally sure that Hastings knew more about her than he let on.

Brax wanted to know more, as well. He shook his head and the breeze lifted his pale, rope-colored hair. His thoughts shifted with the gentle wind.

What was Hastings's true knowledge of Marguerite Ashby? It was obvious from her familiarity that they knew one another well. Brax would have wagered ten pounds that his fellow officer was pursuing the lady, except that Hastings was so clumsy and grim all the time that any woman's interest in him would by definition be short-lived. And he hadn't spoken a word about her since they left her lodgings to get her settled in her coach. Hastings had simply resumed his customary scowl and continued about his duties in preparation for departure to Portsmouth.

Duty.

Hastings perpetually blathered about his obligations and duties. A parroting, miniature Nelson the man was. Brax knew Hastings thought him a wastrel and not serious about his responsibilities, but then Hastings didn't really know Brax Selwyn and his own considerable commitment to grave and vital matters, did he?

But do I really know Lieutenant Darden Hastings?

More importantly, do I really trust him?

Marguerite hadn't seen Darden in several days now, but didn't attempt to find him. Between Nelson's irritation, the surgeon's disdain, and the crew's detachment, she deemed discretion to be her best strategy. And that meant staying put as much as possible, no matter how agonizingly bored she was becoming. She decided it was best to forget what had happened between them the last time they were together. Clearly he regretted it, else why did he stay away from her?

But why hasn't anyone come to transfer me to Pickle*?*

Her thoughts were interrupted by the rare appearance of Mr. Beatty. Employing his usual grace, he scowled at her. "All of this going on and we've got a bed occupied by the most useless individual ever to sail with the navy." The man began gathering bandages and other supplies from a small locker bolted to the deck and stuffing them into a small canvas satchel.

Marguerite's boredom overrode her discretion, so she ignored the surgeon's derision.

"Excuse me, what exactly is going on?"

The surgeon seemed so surprised by her ignorance that he shared the news. "Ten sailors are getting lashed in the morning for drunkenness. Thirty-six lashes each. Most likely they were just in high spirits over our impending engagement with the enemy, but order has to be kept, doesn't it?" The man narrowed his eyes at Marguerite. "Even if the rules aren't *always* followed."

"Why are you emptying your supply box?" she asked.

He rolled his eyes at her unwanted pestering. "I have to be present afterwards, don't I? The men will be a bloody mess."

"Yes, I see." Marguerite retreated back to her book, revolted at the thought of such a vile punishment, no matter what the crime. Well, it was no matter of hers to say what proper discipline for the navy was.

But curiosity got the better of her the following morning. She awoke to a hoarse cry of "All hands ahoy to witness punishment!" from the boatswain, and the ship's bell pealed mournfully.

Noticing that the deck emptied out in a solemn procession at the boatswain's call, she quietly slipped out of her cot and padded up two sets of stairs to the quarterdeck. She poked her head out through the opening while continuing to clutch the stairs for support. No one noticed her. The scene before her was grim. What looked to be the entire crew stood at a distance from a section of grating that had been removed from the deck and securely fastened upright. Their mood was tense and an air of dread permeated the silence of the morning fog. The thick, sour odor of fear wafted from the crew's unwashed bodies and encircled Marguerite in her hiding place.

Ten sailors, presumably the offenders, stood stripped to the waist, heads bowed. One poor lad was trembling, and Marguerite found herself shaking sympathetically.

Captain Hardy was in attendance, but Marguerite did not see Nelson. She swiveled her head, looking for Darden, but instead caught sight of Mr. Beatty, holding his sack of supplies. The man had a hint of anticipation on his face, as though he would now finally have something truly useful to do.

As she turned her head back to where the punishment scene continued to unfold, her eye caught a flash of blue coat. Ah, there was Darden, standing off to the side. He was ramrod straight in his focus on what was happening. Although his eyes were bright and alert, the lines around them were deeper than usual. Funny how not too long ago those same eyes radiated heat and desire for her. Now they conveyed his worry and pain.

Over the lax discipline? Or maybe . . . for her?

Don't be foolish. The lieutenant has far more important things to worry about than you.

But her attention was diverted back to the disciplinary action. Two of the ill-fated sailors were motioned to step to the grating with the sides of their faces against it. Their wrists were pulled overhead, spread apart, and strapped to the grate.

Two boatswain's mates stepped forward, each holding a curious-looking lash. It looked like a whip, with a stiff handle of extra-thick rope, and multiple strands of thin rope protruding from the head of the handle. Each of these strands had about three evenly spaced knots in it. Marguerite held her breath.

Each of these men would take thirty-six lashes from that? Her own back prickled in trepidation.

Really, I should go back down below, away from what is sure to be—

On a hand signal from the boatswain, each of the mates swung his lash over his head and bent his body back to give it full force. The mates then brought their lashes down upon the sailors' backs.

The sailors grunted but did not cry out. The lashes came down again.

And again.

And yet again.

Always in unison with one another.

By the tenth blow, the sailors' backs were raw and bleeding, and one of them was whimpering. Marguerite could watch this no further.

She inched her way quietly back down the steps and retreated back to her swinging bed, pulling her thin blanket over her head to block the sequence of blows, grunts, and cries that accompanied the floggings. The covering did little to protect her from the noise, even though it was two decks away.

How had she managed to get herself trapped in this stink-hole of commotion, boredom, and malodorous men?

Still the lashings went on.

She covered her ears with her hands and hummed a French ditty her mother had taught her as a child.

And still the blows penetrated her ears and her mind.

What good was such extreme punishment? These men would be dead by the time it was all over and of no use to the ship's crew at all.

Thwack. Grunt. *Thwack.* Whimper.

At an unexpected silence, she pushed the covers away. Was the lashing over this quickly for so many men? But the quiet was shattered by the clattering of several men coming down to the upper gun deck. It was the surgeon, followed by the two flogged sailors. Each sailor was supported by one of the surgical assistants.

Mr. Beatty caught sight of Marguerite, and scowled as though seeing her for the first time.

"Dratted woman. Be off with you now. I need to treat these men's wounds."

Without thinking she said, "I can help."

"Help? You? How would that be? You haven't done much but be in the way, have you?"

"I've not had much of a chance, have I?"

The surgeon crossed his arms in front of him. "And just how is a delicate little missy like you going to help these bleeding men?"

She looked around desperately and caught sight of one of her bags.

"I can make masks!" she exclaimed triumphantly.

"Are you daft? They're not going to a ball."

"No no, I mean that I know how to mix plasters. Surely you will apply a plaster of some sort to their backs. I can help you. Give me the ingredients and I will make it for you. Then the three of you will be free for more important duties."

Mr. Beatty stared incredulously at her, as though she had asked to be allowed to amputate a leg or dig shrapnel out of a man's chest.

One of the flogged men groaned and slumped down out of his helper's grasp, falling forward and hitting the floor with a thud. Marguerite went and knelt before him to examine his tattered back, full of countless bloody welts. They would not heal easily.

Without waiting for approval from the surgeon, she opened his locker and whisked out a large wooden bowl and ladle.

"Tell me your recipe so I can make a poultice for him. Hurry. This man is in pain." When he didn't respond, she added, "*Now*, Mr. Beatty."

The surgeon shook his head and reached into the locker, pulling out a ragged notebook. He flipped through it until he found what he wanted and handed it to her without a word, then turned away to issue instructions for lifting the flogged men into beds. The last she saw of him he was headed back up the stairs, shouting upward to have the next two flogged sailors set aside for him to check.

Marguerite ran her finger down the list of ingredients and began poring through the locker looking for them. She lifted out a buckled case and opened it. Inside were vials, bottles, and boxes of various creams and liquids. From the case she pulled a corked bottle of olive oil, a wrapped paper of flour, and a small box marked "Litharge of Lead." She put all of these items in the bowl and scurried off to the officers' galley with her supplies, but not before stopping off at each of the two occupied sick beds and offering the men a word of comfort.

Since most of the crew was on the quarterdeck witnessing the punishment, the galley was empty. She spread her things on top of an upright barrel in the middle of the area. A kettle boiled merrily on its hook atop the iron stove. Using a nearby rag, she lifted the kettle from its perch and poured some water into her bowl. She blew on the scalding water until it cooled enough for her to taste it with her finger. Fresh water, excellent. She allowed it to cool a few moments more, then added the proper amounts of oil and lead, stirring after each addition. When she felt the plaster was of a proper consistency, she sprinkled in some of the flour. She stirred again until the powder was blended into the rest of the mixture, and returned to where the injured sailors lay.

Marguerite went to the swinging bed of the man groaning the loudest, bending over and saying quietly, "I won't ask if it hurts, since that would be the question of a knave. I've brought you something that will help you. It's cool and should make you feel better."

The man nodded his head weakly. With the expert hand of a waxworker, she scooped some of the plaster out of the bowl and gently applied it to his back. The man's groan this time was one of relief. It did little to block out the noise of the continued floggings two decks above them.

Out of habit, she passed a fleeting thought to how she would re-create the man's back as part of a wax figure. What an interesting character it would make for the Separate Room.

When she considered his back to be sufficiently coated, she moved on to the second man, who looked up at her fearfully with one eye.

"What's your name?" she asked as she gave the poultice another stir to keep it from hardening.

"Wynn. What's that you got?"

" 'S okay, Wynn," called the first man from his bunk. "Feels good. Makes me want to sleep. Guess we're lucky we didn't have to go right back to work."

Marguerite lifted a full ladle up for the man to see. He nodded and she applied it in the same manner as she did the first. Soon both men were snoring comfortably.

By the time Mr. Beatty and his assistants returned with the second set of lashing victims, Marguerite had prepared another bowl of the plaster and was ready to tend to those men right away.

There weren't enough sick beds, so some of the patients were laid on pallets around the deck. While Marguerite continually prepared new batches of plaster and applied them to their flayed and oozing wounds, Mr. Beatty went from man to man, checking on his overall state and making determinations as to which patients had priority on plastering, who needed to be bled, and who needed to be dosed with a pint of grog, which the assistants served up. Nothing could be done to block out the noise of the punishment itself, as the lashes continued with their ruthless exertions.

Hours later, Mr. Beatty declared Marguerite's work finished and gave her a sort of grudging apology. "Not bad work for such tender hands," he mumbled.

Marguerite put away all of the supplies and sat on top of the locker to rest her feet. Her bed was now occupied by one of the men, so finding a place to curl up and sleep would be no easy task. She wiped a hand across her brow and looked down at her dress. It was hopelessly encrusted with dried plaster and oil splatter. Undoubtedly her face looked the same. Thank goodness Darden had told her there were few mirrors on board. No need to frighten herself to death.

She slipped to the deck from the top of the locker, leaned upright against it, and pulled her knees up, arranging her dress around her as modestly as possible.

This will have to do, I suppose.

She leaned her head back in exhaustion. Deep, dreamless sleep came to her, despite the resumed cacophonous activity of the crew.

Word of Marguerite's work reached Darden's ears with the speed of an unfurling sail. As though there wasn't enough to admire in the woman, now he learned of her selfless care of the flogged sailors. He contemplated Marguerite smoothing her hands over his own bare back and could well imagine why the men in the sick berth were now resting comfortably.

But he had to resist going down there on some contrived mission of thanking her. Until everything was finished, he couldn't let his mind get entangled in thoughts of her. Could he? He hoped none of the other men would do something rash, like fall in love with her.

Or worse, that she would fall in love right back.

❧ 19 ❧

"I simply cannot believe she has disappeared like this."

Claudette sipped her tea nervously. The Greycliffes had learned nothing from the Admiralty office. William had even been able to secure a meeting with Mr. Pitt, who offered his condolences on their situation, but offered no help other than to say he knew the wax figures had been delivered to *Victory,* therefore Marguerite must have made it to the ship.

Which was no more than they had learned at the Admiralty office.

William reached a hand across the table at the inn where they had stopped to rest and have a meal during their journey back to Hevington. "My love, we don't know that anything untoward has happened to Marguerite. We must be patient. I'll hire a private agent to look into matters."

Claudette tilted her head to one side as she put down her teacup.

"Like last time?"

William had hired a private agent to investigate Claudette's own disappearance inside Paris many years earlier when she was tricked into traveling there. That agent had proved useless, and William charged into France himself to take care of matters.

"Well, certainly someone different. Why are you staring at me that way? I do believe there is a dangerous thought percolating under your frilly new bonnet."

"My lord Greycliffe, my thoughts are never dangerous. They're just . . . a bit persistent. I say we go to Portsmouth ourselves to see if we can find out what happened to Marguerite."

"Ourselves?" William considered this. "I suppose it's better than doing nothing. We'll stop back at Hevington to collect more clothing and to send for my cousin Arabella so she can come and keep an eye on the children."

"Don't you think they'd be fine with the servants? I'd like to get to Portsmouth as quickly as possible without detouring through Kent. We could make it there so much more quickly if we left directly from here." Claudette fidgeted in her chair, ready to depart the inn at that very moment.

William squeezed her hand, knowing that she must be anxious indeed to be willing to leave the children indefinitely without at least saying good-bye. "Persistence is fine. But there will be no impetuosity. We'll go to Portsmouth, but via Hevington."

Claudette sighed. She got her way most of the time, so it was difficult to argue when William put his foot down. If only this wasn't one of those rare occurrences when he said no. She shook her head in resignation and held up the watch pinned to her breast.

Across the table, William smiled and pulled out his own pocket watch.

"Do you fancy a race back to Hevington, sweetheart?"

So once again Nathaniel Ashby sought out a crew for *Wax Maiden*. But this time he was much smarter about his financial investment in outfitting the ship. No sense in risking so much this time. At least not until Mr. Pitt recognized his great contribution to England's success and began showering him with rewards. An appointment as some kind of foreign envoy would be appropriate for services rendered, wouldn't it? With the necessary title to go along with it. And funding for future ventures would be his topmost requirement. No negotiation on that point.

But the biggest prize would be Marguerite's return to him. He imagined it perfectly in his mind. So eager to greet the incoming hero that her hat had flown off, exposing all of those waving tresses of lavender-scented hair. Her cheeks flushed with excitement and her eyes burning bright. And her heart beating so fiercely with pride that it was nearly visible beneath the mounds of her—

"So where d'ya want this?" asked his new assistant.

"What? Oh, put it in my quarters."

Nathaniel had indulged himself in the purchase of a small desk for his cabin. The desk took up most of the floor space in the tiny cabin, tucked as it was below deck in the stern of the ship. But it made him feel more like a real captain to have a private place to study charts and letters and to write out his daily log.

The man did as he was told without the merest peep of rebellion. What a brilliant idea it was to scour the rolls at the Marshalsea prison for minor debtors who could never pay their way out. He swept in and offered to pay monies owed for nineteen men who had been rotting away for over a year.

There was no better way to ensure loyalty than by making a man obliged to you for his freedom. Better yet, Nathaniel had learned his lesson and was not about to reveal his plans to the crew, so this new group of men was led to believe that the journey was to deliver supplies to the fleet, which reports said had now reached the coast of Cádiz.

Finally. He was manned and victualed and ready to carry out his mission of greatness.

The mood aboard *Royal Sovereign* was one of tight anticipation. Brax and his shipmates had been bored to the point of exhaustion when the first signal had gone out.

The nearest ship watching the port of Cádiz, the frigate *Sirius*, hoisted a message in the stilted code of naval semaphore flags: "Enemy's ships are coming out of port." This was it. They were planning to run.

Their long wait to engage England's long-standing adversary was over.

The message was hoisted from *Sirius* to *Euryalus* to *Phoebe*, to *Defence*, and so on until it passed through *Royal Sovereign* on its way to its ultimate destination, *Victory*, which was still fifty miles out to sea.

Nelson's return message through the chain of ships was clear: "General chase, south-east."

And so every ship in the British fleet was in the process of obeying the admiral's order. Brax felt almost joyfully anxious. A battle would bring relief from the mind-numbing monotony of the daily life of patrol and blockade, even though the idea of a confrontation in which many men were sure to die was sobering.

Yet there was a great possibility of promotion to post captain if he performed well, and everyone had the chance for prize money, which would be distributed to the men of the ship or ships that captured a prize.

To earn both a promotion as well as a share of treasure would be a fine pairing indeed. Every lieutenant sought the elusive advancement to post captain; a difficult achievement, but once made nearly ensured eventual promotion to admiral. His father would then be quite proud to have given his son to the navy.

For although Lord Selwyn had graciously released Brax from his duties to the estate, Brax knew his father well enough to understand his hidden disappointment.

And hidden doubt in his son's ability to rise on his own.

An officer could rise through the ranks in three ways. Someone important on the outside could influence the promotion process, or a man's sheer ability could get him through the ranks. Nelson had risen through ability. The third, and riskiest, path to promotion was through a singular act of heroism, usually in a time of battle.

Brax was anxious to earn his promotion himself, preferably through a fearless act of valor.

"No need to be ashamed of me yet, Father," he whispered to himself as he helped a gun crew strap down its platform. "I'll marry a fine woman one day"—his thoughts flickered over Marguerite—"and settle down to have a bevy of strapping sons to carry on the Selwyn name. Just be patient until I can establish for myself what sort of eminence I can bring to the Selwyn name before I think about passing it along to heirs."

The boatswain shouted some orders from the new captain, Captain Collingwood, who had transferred over to *Royal Sovereign* from his flagship *Dreadnought* several days earlier after Nelson had taken command. Collingwood was now Nelson's second-in-command, which meant that Brax was now on a very important ship in the Royal Navy's fleet. He mentally cast aside his personal dreams and angst.

Be a man, Selwyn. This battle will prove to be your death or your most glorious moment to date.

Mr. Beatty's attitude toward Marguerite improved dramatically after the floggings. The men were returned to duty after several hours in their care. Afterwards, he spent time talking about various remedies he had developed and experimented with, and shared with her his particularly favorable impression of Nelson's insistence that citrus fruit be available on board any ships under his command, thereby greatly reducing the incidence of scurvy. The fruits were expensive, so many officers skipped purchasing them. Crews noted that few officers took such good care of their men as Nelson did.

Marguerite could feel the admiration for Admiral Nelson pulsating through the ship beyond Mr. Beatty's words. She often overheard sailors bragging of their honor at being on Nelson's flagship. Even some of the sailors who had been flogged were less concerned with their wounds than they were over the thought that Nelson would be personally disappointed in them.

Does Darden feel proud to be on Nelson's flagship?

Mr. Beatty even invited her to sup with him, an invitation she gratefully accepted, since the man Darden had sent to tend to her rarely spoke more than two consecutive words to her and reminded her more of a shriveled, salted side of beef than a breathing human being.

Why did Darden abandon me, then send me such a colorless companion? And when will I be transferred to a ship at the rear of the fleet?

At least Mr. Beatty's friendlier attentions gave her some company, especially since she had read through all of her books. Twice. And, truth be told, she had rather enjoyed the excitement of tending to the wounded men. It wasn't fun, exactly. More like she had been *useful*.

Something she had not been since the moment she cracked her head on Nelson's dining room table.

Her mild pleasure turned into amazement when Mr. Beatty reported his recent conversation with Captain Hardy to her.

"You want me to *stay?*" she managed to squeak out.

"Yes. I told the captain about what you did with the men and that you might actually be of some value to me. He says you can stay if you want, but there's no pay in it for you since you aren't a member of the crew. What d'you say?"

There was no question for Marguerite that she wanted to do it, if for no other reason than to escape the sheer boredom of lying around all day with nothing to do. A transfer to another ship would not improve her conditions. Well, except to keep her away from the line of fire. But to stay on *Victory* also meant to be near Darden, even if he had abandoned her. She pretended to consider Mr. Beatty's offer.

"Well, I suppose I would be willing to do so."

"Good, good." He beamed happily. "The enemy has come out of hiding so we're giving chase and will be engaging soon. Come, let me show you more of what I do. You need to learn quickly the kinds of injuries that result from a naval battle, and you can help me set up the hospital."

"The hospital? What do you mean? Won't we treat them right here in the sick berth?"

And did he just say the fleet would be engaging *soon?* What, exactly, did *soon* mean? Her stomach fluttered uneasily.

"My girl, look around you. See all of the cannon pointing outward? This is a gun deck, and soon Captain Hardy will want to take over the sick berth for fighting. We'll lay canvas down on the orlop deck for the wounded, and have the ones needing surgery put on the midshipmen's mess tables and chests. Besides, it's safer for us below the water line."

And so Marguerite followed the surgeon to the orlop, where Messrs. Smith and Westemburg were scooping sand out of sacks and sprinkling it on the deck.

"What are they doing?" she asked.

"The sand absorbs blood and other fluids from the injured so it doesn't soak into the deck. There's more being spread on the gun decks."

"I see." What other response was there?

Once the sand was fully distributed, she and the surgeon spread out canvas, also intended to capture blood flow and to put some sort of layer between the wounded and the rough deck. Like the other lower decks she had passed through, this one was not tall enough for an average man to stand straight. Even she had to duck to avoid many of the beams spaced at regular intervals along the ceiling. After that, they cleared off the few tables in the midshipmen's mess on the orlop and spread more canvas sheeting on them.

Unlike on the upper gun deck, these tables rested on the deck on legs, instead of being suspended from the ceiling by ropes. She asked the surgeon about them, and he told her that tables are suspended from ropes to get them stowed out of the way quickly in a time of battle. The orlop had no guns, therefore the furniture was placed more or less permanently. Dim lanterns dangled above each table, providing little light for what was sure to be intense work.

Mr. Beatty showed her what instruments and supplies needed to be distributed on the tables, and she helped him and his assistants with getting them all laid out properly. One particular instrument, which resembled a miniature saw with a smooth blade, made her particularly queasy, and she hoped she would not have to watch it in use.

Afterwards, the surgeon showed her his own cabin on this deck, as well as the locking dispensary next to it. Looking at the crowded shelves in here, Marguerite realized that the small trunk of powders and potions in the sick berth were but a sampling of the treatments Mr. Beatty had at his disposal.

She slept fitfully that night, her mind swirling with thoughts of Darden, the wax figures stowed in Nelson's cabin, and the myriad of formulas and procedures Mr. Beatty had stowed into her head.

And there was to be little sleep for her again anytime soon.

* * *

"Lieutenant!" Nelson commanded as Darden passed by the admiral on the quarterdeck. "I need you to take a message to Captain Hardy. Tell him I want *Victory* to be at the head of my division and he's to raise a message for the other ships to slow and wait. Collingwood will have *Royal Sovereign* leading his division."

"Yes, your lordship." Darden abandoned his previous task to obey Nelson immediately. Much of a lieutenant's life was consumed with the bearing of messages between decks or even between ships. When confidential messages had to be passed, the process was made tiresome by repeated scrambles into launches to row quickly to the designated ship, board the ship, deliver the message, row back, and scuttle aboard his original ship. All instead of using the more common flag signals from atop the deck.

Darden didn't mind, though. He knew he was fortunate to be on board *Victory* and to be considered part of Nelson's staff on his flagship. A few inconvenient treks to find Captain Hardy, or even to the captain of another ship, were just part of the duty and honor of serving Lord Horatio Nelson.

But this reminded him that he needed to have Marguerite set into a launch bound for *Pickle* as soon as they pulled close enough to her. After delivering his message to Hardy, he sought out the midshipman whom he had assigned to look after her. The man was undoubtedly shirking that duty to the greatest extent possible, but as long as she was eating, being escorted to the wardroom for private necessary activities, and getting some opportunity for bathing, that was all that could be hoped for.

He addressed the sailor. "I need you to prepare Mrs. Ashby for transfer in a launch to *Pickle*. We should be meeting up with *Pickle* within a few hours."

And in the same way Darden dropped anything he was doing to obey Nelson, so did the midshipman instantly obey his command.

20

Claudette ground her fists in her eyes in frustration as she and William left the inn at Guildford in their carriage.

"So they have a record of Marguerite staying overnight here with some other female passenger, but they don't know that she was necessarily going to Portsmouth the next day."

Across from her, William patted her knee. "It's not likely that an innkeeper cares much about his guests beyond their ability to pay and not cause trouble. I'm sure Marguerite paid her bill promptly and was no nuisance, so why would he notice her?"

"I know. I'm just frightened out of my wits as to what could have happened to her." She reached out and took her husband's hand for comfort.

"We'll learn more at Portsmouth. You need sleep. Come over here with me." He pulled his wife over to his cushioned bench, wrapped an arm around her, and with his other hand pulled her head to his shoulder. "Rest, sweetheart. We'll find her, I promise."

But now even William was becoming concerned. How could Marguerite have simply disappeared like this?

Brax was energized. *Royal Sovereign* and *Victory* would be entering battle together. So he and Hastings would be side by side until they split through the French and Spanish fleet. The two divisions of ships were racing parallel to one another in order to smash the enemy's line in a perpendicular cut. Nelson's goal was to slice through and damage the enemy's fleet beyond repair before it had a chance to begin tacking its ships around to point its guns at the British ships.

And everyone knew Nelson was a naval genius beyond compare. His plan would work.

And surely, being at the front of the line, Brax would get an opportunity for derring-do. Captain Braxton Charles Selwyn. Perfect.

Was Hastings also made of the substance necessary to earn a promotion? Brax's competitive spirit whispered the question softly as he issued an order to an underling.

"I haven't noticed a launch depart yet. Has Mrs. Ashby been removed from the ship?" Darden was tapping his fingers impatiently on the outer rail of the quarterdeck. He needed to know Marguerite was out of danger before he could focus on the tasks ahead. It was past dawn, and engagement with the enemy would occur today. Soon.

"No, sir, she said she was staying." The man was sweating from the exertion of battle preparations, as they all were.

"She *what?* What do you mean, staying? I issued an order and I expect both you and Mrs. Ashby to follow it."

"Yes, sir, Lieutenant, but she was quite insistent that she had permission to stay."

"*Permission?* From whom? For God's sake, why would she want to stay aboard this floating arsenal?"

"I'm sorry, sir, but she refused to come with me to the launch. She said the surgeon would vouch for her, but I couldn't find him at the moment and, sir, I've got my hands full with other duties. I didn't know the woman meant that much to you."

"Well, she does!" Darden slammed his fist down on the rail. "I mean, she doesn't. Only in that Nelson will have my guts for garters if I don't see her off this ship."

"Yes, sir." The midshipman waited expectantly for further instruction.

"Never mind. I'll deal with the woman myself."

The sailor scurried away gratefully, far more interested in preparing for battle than worrying about some random female trapped on the ship.

Darden gritted his teeth for the confrontation ahead. He took the steps to the upper gun deck two at a time, not stopping to acknowledge any of the men who tried to ask questions of their superior officer. All of the sick berth hammocks had already been stowed away and the deck made ready for battle. He went farther down and found Marguerite standing on the orlop, already at work. She was examining the contents of a stoppered bottle among a collection of several such vessels on one of the makeshift surgical tables. She looked up at him and smiled warmly.

"Why, Lieutenant, it's nice to see you again."

Damn the woman. Her eyes sparkled mischievously as though at some secret knowledge. And he knew that knowledge was of his absurd weakness for her. And her hair was still full and unruly, even after weeks of washing it in buckets of sea water. He wanted nothing more than to dig his fingers into that mass of curls and pull her to him—

Enough.

"Mrs. Ashby, I gave my midshipman specific orders to have you taken to *Pickle*. Yet somehow you are still standing here, playing with the surgeon's potions. May I ask why?"

The light went out of Marguerite's eyes. "Mr. Beatty asked me to stay aboard. I helped him care for the men who were lashed for drunkenness—"

"Yes, yes, I heard about it."

"—and he thought I might be of some help to him during the battle."

"Mrs. Ashby, have you any idea of the danger involved on a first-rate man-of-war like *Victory*?"

Marguerite put the bottle down slowly, as though gathering up her temper and storing it away in the container before it reached the table.

"Actually, I do have some idea of it, based on my experience with those poor men's flayed-open backs." The new, dark glints in her eyes should have warned him that this was not going to go well for him, but he was too angry to care.

"You know nothing. Those injuries were like flea bites as compared to what happens in battle. Men were brought down in simple pairs. They had wounds that were easily treatable. The ship was not under attack and the noise deafening. You don't have a man screaming and begging for you to take a knife to his throat so he can avoid the pain of the three-foot wood splinter protruding from his chest. Or his leg. Or his eye."

"I assure you, Lieutenant, that I am fully capable of managing myself and assisting the surgeon."

"The only thing I see you to be fully capable of is disobeying me."

"Disobeying you?" she gasped, incredulity on her face.

He knew he had gone too far, but he couldn't help it.

"Yes. I told you that I was arranging for you to be transferred to *Pickle* at the soonest possible moment. You deliberately defied me by telling my midshipman some ridiculous story about how the surgeon wants you to stay aboard. Now it's probably too late to shift you over."

Marguerite folded her arms across her chest. "Well, since you haven't given me a moment's thought in quite some time, thinking so little of me that you delegated me to others, I hardly think it's any of your concern what I do."

"Believe me, Mrs. Ashby, what you do is very much my concern. And I now have to figure out what to do with you so I don't have to report a dead woman under my care."

"I hereby absolve you of that responsibility. Besides, Captain Hardy gave his permission for me to stay."

Darden grunted. "Not likely. Nelson wants you off, therefore Hardy does, too. Except you're not gone, and you're my responsibility, so I have to do something with you to keep you safe."

"You're not listening to me. Captain Hardy did say I could stay on board to help the surgeon. Ask him. Ask Mr. Beatty."

"I knew I should have escorted those wax figures to Portsmouth myself. You've been nothing but trouble for me since you came aboard."

Marguerite froze before him, and he knew she was remembering their last encounter.

Nothing but trouble? Hastings, is this your best romantic line? And I'm accusing Marguerite of appalling conduct?

"Well. Lieutenant. It would seem there's nothing you can do about it now, since we're too far from *Pickle* and the fighting will start soon."

Darden's sense of duty washed over him in a wave, followed by another bursting dam of anger at this stubborn, willful, heavenly woman.

"You think so? My dear Mrs. Ashby, you have no understanding of how much I can do."

And with that, he strode over to her, bent down, and swept her up in his arms before she had the wherewithal to react.

She was as light as a hammock. The weeks of ship food had taken their toll, despite her inactivity. But it hadn't reduced her obstinacy.

"Where are you taking me?" Her eyes glowered as she hissed the question. At least she had enough sense not to struggle against him.

But just as quickly as her temper flared it simmered down again. He nearly stopped in his tracks when she wrapped her arms around his neck and nuzzled him.

"Where have you been?" she asked, plaintive and beseeching.

He nearly came undone at her words.

"Busy," he replied gruffly. She remained buried in his neck as he stayed bent over, carrying her across the deck and to the stairs to the next deck.

He maneuvered, as gently as he could with her in his arms, down to the hold and straight into a room full of bags stacked at various heights and marked "Hardtack." It served as storage for the ship's biscuit, a tasteless but rot-impervious blend of water, flour, and salt that was baked until all of the water had been removed. The biscuits were a commonplace part of everyone's shipboard diet. The dim lighting from behind them through the open door provided the only illumination.

"What is this place?" Marguerite asked.

"It's the bread room. It's lined with tin to keep the rats out, which means it will also help to keep the shot out. It's also way below the water line, so that you will be safe. And drat you, Mrs. Ashby, you have to be safe at all costs, do you hear me? I couldn't bear it otherwise."

She reached up and cupped his cheek. "Am I no longer Marguerite?"

And at that he was broken.

"You are," he said hoarsely, and did exactly what he knew he shouldn't, his mouth seeking hers with the desperation known only to the condemned. In just a couple of hours he would be in the throes of a battle. Anything could happen. He could be directly hit by cannon-shot, or torn apart by a splintering deck, or fired upon by a French sharpshooter. Marguerite responded in kind, sliding both hands around his neck again and pressing against him as though to meld into him and thereby derive some of his essence into her own body.

But duty murmured to him.

He tore himself away from her yet again. "No," he said. "I cannot. This is too . . . much. It ruins everything."

He averted his face from the bewildered look in her amber eyes and set her down atop a stack of hardtack bags four feet high. He disengaged from her, but she grabbed his injured hand. He jolted at her touch.

"Ruins what, Darden? Why am I a cause of your distress? I did not mean to get caught on board *Victory*."

"It's not that. I have a specific future, and it doesn't contain—doesn't have room for—an entanglement."

"An entanglement? I see. I didn't realize how inconvenient I was to you, *Lieutenant*."

She dropped his hand and crossed her arms over her chest again. She was back to being defiant. "You are the strangest, most inconsistent man I have ever met."

Her words sliced through him like a freshly sharpened cutlass. Duty and loyalty were what he valued most, and to be accused of unpredictability was a deep blow. But there was nothing to be done for it now. He lit the single lantern hanging from the ceiling.

"Perhaps one day I can explain it to you. But for now, you must remain here. Promise me you won't try to leave the bread room until I come for you. Or until someone does."

She stared at him steadily, giving him no response.

He put a hand on her shoulder. "Marguerite, promise me."

She wrenched away from him, distaste evident in her flaming eyes and the grim line of her lips. He let his arms hang limp at his sides.

"Promise me. Promise me, you rebellious little minx." He hoped an attempt at humor would soften her.

No such luck. She cocked her head to one side, pursed her lips, and gave him the briefest of nods.

"Blast you, Marguerite, you've no idea what you've done to me." Without waiting for what was sure to be a scathing response, he left the bread room, slamming the metal-backed door behind him.

Marguerite spent nearly an hour nursing her fury. Fury at Darden for locking her away in this dark, cramped room. Even more angry at herself for her own self-imprisonment on this ship. At least the weather had been mostly calm so she hadn't experienced any seasickness. And her only headache had been the one brought on by her fall in the admiral's cabin.

But at her first chance to be useful, she was thwarted by the one man on board she assumed cared about her. What was wrong with that man? He floated capriciously between admirer and adversary. And what were these secretive "plans" he seemed so obsessed with? Why couldn't he share them with her? Was he up to something illicit?

It was time to build the wall around her heart again. It would not do to expose it any further to Lieutenant Darden Hastings. No, he was simply not to be trusted.

Having spun through her anger and concluded that Darden was no longer to be a part of her own future plans, either, she set about to more thoroughly disobey him by escaping from the bread room to join Mr. Beatty back on the orlop.

She stood up with resolve. Her first move would be to try to break through the bread room door. She turned to one side and ran against the door, intending to slam into it with as much force from one side of her slender frame as she could, in hopes of loosening the door's hinges. Her body made impact with the door and it flew open effortlessly, sending her hurtling to the floor and landing on her shoulder. The shock hurt her more than the impact. What had just happened? Why, Darden hadn't even locked the door. She laughed despite herself. Her captor had done little to confine her.

No, he'd merely asked for her promise that she wouldn't leave and had taken it for granted that she would do as he asked.

She got up and smoothed her skirts. There was no advantage to thinking upon Darden's baffling nature now. Her mind was made up. She returned to the bread room long enough to blow out the lantern, then scurried back to the orlop to find the surgeon. She *would* be useful on this voyage, no matter how hard the good lieutenant tried to thwart her.

The orlop deck was fairly quiet, although she could hear the echoes of men shouting and cannon being rolled into place on the decks above her. What a melee it must be already.

She found Mr. Beatty inside the dispensary with his assistants, counting bottles and performing other last-minute preparations. His look of relief upon seeing her instantly gave way to irritation.

"Where have you been, Mrs. Ashby? You committed to a responsibility to me. Have you lost your wits or your nerve?"

After her encounter with Darden, the surgeon seemed a tame kitten to her.

"Neither, Mr. Beatty. I was unavoidably detained. I'm very sorry. But I'm ready to work now."

The surgeon accepted her apology and gave her further instructions. She was to stay posted where the canvas was laid out for the wounded. He expected her to come up with a way to keep track of who had come down first, so the men could be treated in order of arrival. She would also offer water, succor, and comfort to the sailors while they waited their turn for a surgical table.

Any further instructions the surgeon may have had were forgotten as a blend of shouting and cheering above them reached the pandemonium level. Marguerite could have sworn she heard the sound of a band striking up a patriotic tune.

"What is happening?" she asked.

"I do believe we have met the enemy."

But the surgeon was wrong. A wild-eyed sailor flung himself into the orlop, bursting with excitement. "Lord Nelson's giving us the go-ahead. We're about to engage. He's sent up a signal: 'England expects that every man will do his duty,' and followed it up with another one for close action!" The man scurried away to the other decks with his news.

Marguerite held her breath as she and the surgeon stared at one another helplessly while waiting to see what happened next. She looked down at her timepiece. It was just before midday.

They didn't have long to wait, although it seemed an eternity.

Brax was standing on the quarterdeck of *Royal Sovereign*, taking stock of how close they were to the enemy's fleet so he could report it down to the gun captains on the decks below. Other officers were translating flag messages drifting by on frigates whose sole purpose was to run up and down the line delivering these missives.

Nearby, Vice Admiral Cuthbert Collingwood shook his head at the other officers standing about on deck. "I wish Nelson would stop signaling, as we all know well enough what we have to do!"

Brax sympathized with the admiral's sentiments. Nelson was not one for autocratic control of his fleet, and typically gave simple, general direction and extended his vice admiral's flexibility in how to carry out those orders. A message about performing one's duty was akin to telling crew members how to breathe properly.

Collingwood's irritation extended to those around him. "Lieutenant Selwyn! What the devil are you wearing?" The admiral strode angrily to where Brax was standing. Collingwood's uniform of blue jacket with tails, white waistcoat and breeches, and large cocked hat was impeccable, almost as if he were preparing for a formal ball rather than going into battle. By comparison, Brax was similarly attired but was not sure he carried off his superior's stiff and ceremonial look.

"Sir?" Brax asked.

The admiral gestured at Brax's feet. "What is that?"

Brax looked down to where his superior officer was pointing. "Sir? My boots?"

"Exactly! You know my policy. Get those things off. If you're wounded it will be impossible for the surgeon to remove them. Stockings only. Quickly, man." Collingwood pointed down at his own unshod feet for emphasis before moving off to deliver other orders.

Brax sighed. He didn't think the surgeon's convenience should trump a man's dignity—God only knew how ridiculous an officer looked gliding about like a half-dressed girl, and besides, boots provided protection against rolling cannon and wreckage on the deck—but he would obey the order without question. It would be foolish to anger the one man he planned to valiantly impress today. Brax shucked his boots off as quickly and gracefully as he could before dashing down to the decks below to store them away and give his report to the gun crews and the ship's captain, Edward Rotheram, who was busy in his cabin at his log books.

Brax rejoined Collingwood on the quarterdeck as soon as he was done, taking care not to slip in his nearly bare feet. He intended to stay as close to Collingwood as possible, in case an opportunity for bravery showed itself. Brax was convinced that this day, this battle, was his one opportunity for glory and he would not waste it.

Even if it meant risking his life.

For it would do him no good to return home empty-handed, so to speak, without having laid claim to a rightfully deserved promotion. Such an unthinkable occurrence would mean seeing great disappointment in his father's eyes, and would give him little to commend himself to a potential bride.

"Lieutenant!" Collingwood's voice exploded from behind him. "Look in front of you, man. A sharpshooter could pick you off easily while you stand there like a sack of barley. Get below and have the gun captains line up a simultaneous broadside. Tell them to fire as soon as we are centered there, on that frigate that looks to belong to those devil Spaniards. Quickly. And tell Captain Rotheram what I intend."

Cursing his bitter luck that the admiral was forever sending him away from his side, Brax flew down to the ship's upper gun deck and relayed the message, instructing a sailor to carry it farther down to the other gun decks, and returned once again to the captain's quarters. Brax then scurried back to the open air, determined to keep his eyes open for an opportunity.

Nelson's division of ships was running parallel to Collingwood's to the port side but lagging behind a little. Because *Royal Sovereign* headed up Collingwood's line, that ship would be the first to smash through the line of French and Spanish ships that were frantically trying to shift their perpendicular position to the British fleet. The enemy was starting the battle in a seriously compromised position. Since gun ports were in the sides of the ship only, a ship needed to pull up alongside another in order to fire at it properly.

But Nelson's genius plan called for the British fleet to separate into two lines and dive directly through the enemy's fleet, splitting it into three sections and firing on the aft and stern of the ships it passed by. The British ships would have all of the advantage while the French and Spanish ships spent time tacking around to a new position.

As they neared their first target, Brax used a telescope to just make out the words *Santa Ana* on her stern.

The Santa Ana *has no chance,* he thought.

But to the starboard side of *Royal Sovereign,* a French–flagged ship was tacking quickly around, and to his surprise, fired a broadside at them from what was obviously too far a distance to cause any damage. Most of the shot fell short into the ocean.

Admiral Collingwood stood nearby and unfurled his own telescope to better see the ship that had fired upon them.

"*Fougueux.* Why would any naval officer give an order to fire that far back?" He shook his head. "Damned waste of rounds, it is. *Fougueux* will regret its stupidity."

Royal Sovereign continued on its single-minded path straight into the enemy's fleet, with *Victory* about a half hour behind it. As the man-of-war inched its way toward the line, more enemy ships joined the *Fougueux* in firing on it, but their aim was too high and their ships were not positioned well to conduct a direct attack.

Brax stood alongside Collingwood and Rotheram, who had joined the admiral on deck. Both the admiral and the captain wore enormous grins at their impending engagement, Collingwood's irritation with Nelson, Brax, and anyone else entirely forgotten. Collingwood clapped the captain on the shoulder. "Rotheram, what would Nelson give to be here!" he said, nodding back to where *Victory*'s line trailed theirs.

Royal Sovereign steered its way through the narrow gap between *Fougueux* and *Santa Ana*, and at a command from Captain Rotheram, unleashed a thunderous broadside into the *Santa Ana*, sending over one hundred cannonballs plus grapeshot ripping into the whole length of the gun decks of the Spanish ship.

From a pocket, Collingwood pulled a shiny apple and casually took a bite.

It was eleven minutes past noon.

The battle had officially begun.

21

From the poop deck of *Victory*, Nelson and Hardy, along with a contingent of several other officers including Darden, watched the engagement unfold before them.

Nelson shook his head. "See how that noble fellow Collingwood carries his ship into action. Not an ounce of cowardice in the man. Our turn next, eh, Mr. Hardy?"

"Indeed yes, sir, and none too soon."

Royal Sovereign disappeared in a cloud of smoke from guns firing not only from its own decks, but from those of *Fougueux, Santa Ana,* and other ships that had gathered round the British man-of-war.

Nelson's ragged column of ships was slowly pressing its way into the enemy line about a half mile north of where *Royal Sovereign* had broken through. As she neared shooting range, several of the enemy's ships had turned to position and opened fire. Most of the French and Spanish gunners were aiming high, causing damage to *Victory*'s sails and rigging and not to the ship itself, but the growing sea swell soon made their aim wildly inaccurate and they decided to focus on another, smaller British ship pulling up to join *Victory*.

Victory, however, had already sustained some damage without firing a single shot herself. One of her topmasts had been completely shot away, and parts of other masts had been brought down or were bouncing across the upper decks. Further compounding the ship's problems was a shot that smashed the wheel, leaving the ship out of control.

"Lieutenant Hastings!" Hardy barked. "Organize a team of men to control the tiller by hand down below. Coordinate for messengers to run my directions down to them."

Darden saluted, his tar-stained palm turned toward his face. He soon found himself assembling a team of forty men to haul the enormous tiller beam in accordance with instructions that were raced down minute-by-minute via messengers. The tiller turned the rudder, which was the source of the ship's precise steering. They could see nothing, buried down inside *Victory*, so the timing of messages from above was as critical as the men's ability to obey the commands instantly. Fortunately, when crisis came to a man-of-war, few men had the temerity to disobey any superior officer's orders.

Darden stripped off his jacket and shirt, already soaked with sweat, and joined the team of men in their hot and heavy work until he thought they were working well in tandem. One wag modified a sea shanty, and soon all of the men were singing a new version of "Spanish Ladies" in rhythm to the tiller's movement.

"Now let ev'ry man drink off his full bumper,
And let ev'ry man drink off his full glass;
We'll drink and be jolly and drown melancholy,
While Hastings rests flat on his arse."

Darden rolled his eyes and laughed at their mocking of him. Although discipline was strict, most officers didn't mind sailors poking fun at them in song. It usually prevented other, more serious rebellion.

Once the tiller crew was in good working order, Darden sought out the ship's carpenter and issued orders to have the ship's wheel repaired straightaway, then raced back to the upper deck.

Nelson and Hardy had moved from the poop deck jutting over the rear portion of the ship down to the quarterdeck. The enemy's fire was still being directed chiefly at the rigging, but was pointed so high as to be basically unnoticed on the exposed decks. Only two men had been wounded up here, and as they were carried, bleeding, past Darden to the orlop, he could see that they had been wounded by musket fire from an opposing ship, not cannon-shot.

Thank God Marguerite is safely ensconced in the bread room, and will have no reason to witness not only these two wounded men, but the carnage that is sure to ensue. Assisting the surgeon, what a notion!

Far below Lieutenant Hastings, Marguerite and the medical men waited wordlessly in the dimly lit operating theatre. An eerie period of silence passed, punctuated by the distant, muffled sounds of cannon fire. Then, the sound of hurried steps preceded two men brought down in the arms of comrades. Marguerite ran forward to inspect them. Both were bleeding so profusely that Marguerite couldn't quite tell where their wounds originated.

Not that it mattered. Mr. Beatty's assistants stepped in front of her and instructed the men to deposit the wounded sailors on two of the three operating tables that had been set up. She sighed and sank down on a stool. Perhaps she was to be of no use after all.

But the grunts and cries of the injured men piqued her concern and she quietly approached one of the operating tables. The patient lay there, groaning, moving his head back and forth in delirium. His wrists and ankles were held down by the sailors who had brought him to the orlop, and they were offering words of encouragement such as were possible to a man in extreme pain. Some of the blood had been smeared away, but what was left was combined with sweat and grime, and made for an ugly, muddy-looking trail across the man's bare torso that emitted a sharp, acrid smell. At least it was now obvious that the injury was in his left shoulder.

Mr. Beatty gave instruction to Mr. Westemburg on how to fish for the bullet. The assistant plunged his index finger and thumb into the poor man's gaping wound, eliciting a great cry of agony as the patient struggled against his restraints.

"I don't feel it, sir," the assistant said helplessly to Mr. Beatty.

"Let me try," Mr. Beatty said, not unkindly.

Westemburg removed his fingers, now bright red and dripping, and wiped them on his trousers.

Now Mr. Beatty thrust his large index finger into the man's shoulder and attempted to feel for the musket ball. By this time, the sailor was howling and begging to be shot in the head to end his misery.

"Aha!" Mr. Beatty raised his own soiled hand and proudly showed off the nugget now lodged between his thumb and forefinger. "I have it! Simple bit of surgery, that."

The injured man raised his head to see that the ball had indeed been removed from his shoulder, groaned, and fell unconscious.

"Sew it closed, put a bandage on it, then put him off to the side," Mr. Beatty instructed. "Mrs. Ashby can point out a place for recovery."

Mr. Beatty moved to the next table where Mr. Smith was, but the assistant there just shook his head.

The surgeon looked around, irritated. "Where's the sailmaker?" He gestured to the dead man's companions. "Go find him. Tell him to send someone to stay down here for the duration."

Marguerite stood rooted to her spot. Not another sea burial! She didn't think she could watch another one. She was just beginning to realize that Darden was right. Assisting the surgeon was going to be much more grisly work than mixing plasters and applying ointments to men who had merely taken a lashing on their backs.

"Miss? Where do we put Pearce?" One of the sailors had tapped her shoulder.

"What? Oh, lay him on the canvas over in that corner. I'll tend to him."

Unfortunately, the man's compatriots carried him over and dropped him rather clumsily, stirring him out of unconsciousness and resulting in more cries of anguish. Marguerite brought him a tin cup of beer and lifted his head so he could drink it. Tears leaked from the man's eyes as he fell back from slaking his thirst. He grabbed Marguerite's hand with his right one.

"Can you scribe?" he asked.

"Yes, I can."

"I need you to write to my wife, tell her what happened. Tell her I love her and I'm right sorry about the wench from the Fox and Hounds Inn. Tell her my messmates will raise money from my belongings and send it to her."

"But, Pearce, you're not going to die. The surgeon removed your bullet."

" 'Course I'm gonna die. Nobody leaves the ship's surgeon without a missing arm, leg, or eye. And since I've got all of those, it means I'm done for."

Marguerite thought the man was becoming delirious and tried to comfort him as best she could. But he refused all encouragement shy of having his letter written. Even the sound of cannon fire from far above them did not seem to penetrate his determination. So Marguerite ran as quickly as she could to the other end of the deck to find Mr. Burke, the purser, to buy some stationery, a quill, and ink, with a promise on Darden's name that it would be paid for later. To her great surprise, using Darden's name got her a large sheaf of parchment, several quills, and a pot of ink.

She wrote Pearce's letter according to his dictation, and he seemed to settle down and rest after making her swear to send it off once they returned to England.

"I promise, but it's a better chance that I'll be handing this letter back to you, and you can deliver it to your wife yourself."

"Maybe." Pearce drifted off to sleep and Marguerite went back to join Mr. Beatty. Before she could open her mouth to ask him a question about the selling of a sailor's belongings, a series of massive explosions occurred in a way that seemed to hurtle straight over them. Had they been struck already? Was she to die so quickly?

Marguerite grabbed the edge of a table, her ears ringing. "What's happened? Are we sinking?"

The surgeon smiled. "No, my dear, that's just *Victory* giving the enemy a taste of what's to come. Captain Hardy must have ordered a rapid broadside."

"What's that?" Marguerite massaged her neck under her ears. They were completely stopped up and she could hardly hear the surgeon's reply.

"All of the guns on one side of the ship are timed to fire in quick succession down the line. It creates confusion for whatever enemy ship is fired upon, because its crew can't react quickly enough to it. That's the only one you'll hear, though, because by now it's too chaotic on the gun decks to coordinate it again. But I think it's time for these." He picked up a wrapped ball of linen strips, tore one off, and tore the strip into smaller pieces, handing Marguerite two of them and more to his assistants.

"Put these in your ears. Crew members who don't plug their ears often end up deaf."

Marguerite took the proffered pieces of cloth, wadded them, and put them in her ears, wondering if the damage had not already been done. The surgeon plugged his own ears before turning to stare at the steps leading to the lower gun deck, waiting for more casualties to arrive.

Darden had to admire Nelson's resolve and bravery. The admiral stood straight, his right sleeve pinned across his chest, just below the paste replicas of his honors and marks of command. The real ones stayed stowed safely away. Wearing these decorations made him an easy target for enemy sharpshooters, but still the admiral stood boldly on deck, as though he had not a care in the world.

It was even more impressive given Nelson's apparent determination to break the enemy's line by colliding with one of its ships. His rapid-fire steering orders were accepted by Hardy and relayed down below nearly instantaneously by the communication chain Darden had established, enabling *Victory* to maintain precise steering despite her lack of a wheel.

Thank God I have done my duty well thus far, he thought.

As they neared closer to the enemy ship that Darden was certain they were to collide with, he could see activity on that ship's deck. A man who appeared to be its commander held the French imperial eagle over his head, shaking it and shouting something to his men that must have inspired courage in them, for they cheered, picked up their muskets, and began firing at *Victory*'s deck.

Darden responded without needing direction from Nelson or Hardy, signaling to one of the countless marines on deck to open fire at will. Darden watched as the red-jacketed men quickly loaded their muskets with gunpowder and shot, took aim through the hail of bullets coming in around them, and fired almost concurrently with one another. The simultaneous flash of flame from their muzzles blinded Darden for a moment, but he blinked away the light and went to a gun chest to pull out a pistol and tuck it into his waistband.

As close as they were to that ship, it was likely that *Victory* would be boarded. He had no intention of succumbing without taking two or three Frogs into the watery depths with him.

But his attention was taken away from the thought of the enemy boarding *Victory* by a more immediate problem. Although the enemy was lobbing shot far and high, and generally missing the deck completely, the masts and sails were under vicious attack. He grimaced as he saw the fore-topsail break away, which was followed by great shouts of joy aboard the enemy ship.

"I'll personally cut that imperial eagle up and feed it to them as their prison rations," he growled to no one in particular.

The loss of the fore-topsail was followed in quick order by three mast sections, putting *Victory* in jeopardy of not being able to pick up speed or tack easily.

Sections of mast lay broken on the deck, although thus far it didn't look like the debris had injured anyone. He searched for Nelson through the acrid smoke gathering from both the marines' musket fire and the cannon fire from the enemy ships. Spotting the admiral in conference with Captain Hardy across the deck, he went to him.

"My lord? Orders?" he shouted above the whizzing bullets and the creaking of tottering masts.

An enigmatic smile crossed Nelson's face. "Now, Lieutenant, we will show the enemy what the British navy is made of. The *Bucentaure* over here on our port side, and the *Redoubtable* to our starboard side, are to be very surprised, indeed." He issued Darden a puzzling steering direction, one that would shift them at the last moment from its collision course with one ship and practically into the stern of another.

But Darden knew the genius of Nelson, so however disconcerting the change might appear, he knew it came from sound judgment. He sent the order down and returned to Nelson's side. Captain Hardy had disappeared again.

Nelson raised an eyebrow at him and Darden nodded in return. The admiral smiled again, in remarkably good humor aboard a ship whose masts and sails were being shot to bits.

Victory was now tacking toward the stern of the ship Nelson had identified as *Redoubtable*. "Hardy is taking care of the next step of our little plan. Have a care, Lieutenant." Nelson cocked an ear expectantly.

In seconds, the plan was executed. As they passed *Bucentaure*, one of *Victory*'s carronades unleashed a barrage of shot onto the enemy ship's upper deck. Even through the confusion created by the smoke, Darden could see that the attack had devastated the crowd of men on *Bucentaure*'s deck. Screams of shock and pain accompanied the sounds of sailors falling against the deck and into the swirling waters below.

But before Darden had a chance to congratulate Nelson on the surprise attack, *Victory* opened up her ports and fired into the stern of the French ship. *Victory* was so close by that Darden, Nelson, and other officers on deck were covered in dust blown from shattered woodwork on *Bucentaure*'s stern.

Yet still there was little time for Darden to react, for another French ship immediately to the east of *Bucentaure* fired a broadside into the bow of *Victory*, returning the same kind of destruction. But there was no time to check for damage, for Nelson's new target had been reached.

With a colossal jolt, accompanied by the sound of splintering wood and the roaring of men whose pent-up boredom is about to be satisfied in a fierce and bloody way, *Victory* collided with the *Redoubtable*.

❧ 22 ❧

Above her, Marguerite could faintly make out the sounds of men shouting, weapons firing, and heavy items being dragged across decks. Her ears cleared after a few minutes and she took the plugs of cloth from her ears, but Mr. Beatty shook his head no at her, so she replaced them.

The lull in activity did not last long. Soon there was a trickle of men being carried down to the operating theatre and the trickle rapidly became chaos, with half-naked, sweating, wild-eyed men scrambling down the stairs to deposit their fellow crew members mixing with the cries and groans of the injured. In between pointing out dropping spots for wounded men and those who had been through surgery, she tended to those in the queue as best she could. A cup of water for a gasping man here, a rough blanket for a shivering man there, and the wiping of blood off everyone. So much bleeding. The smell of it as she wrung it from rags into buckets was nauseating, and she was soon wearing a mélange of every injured man's blood on the front of her dress, which had been none too clean to begin with, since it was only one of three changes of clothes she'd had in weeks. But compared to these seamen, she was dressed regally, so she took a deep breath and smiled as she bent down, took out an ear plug, and listened to the next man's request.

If the influx of wounded men was not enough to tell her that fighting was in full force on *Victory*, the rising heat on the orlop and the perpetual blasts and jarring thuds of cannons on their carriages on the gun decks was indication enough.

And where was Darden? Did someone in his position fire cannon? Was he with the captain, or with Admiral Nelson? Was he even safe?

Please, God, don't let me see him down here.

She focused on putting Darden and the battle raging on above her out of her mind, and soon she was even able to block out the cries of men on the operating tables and the exploding cannon above her head as she concentrated on succoring the injured men within her care.

But her constitution was about to be tested further.

"Mrs. Ashby, quickly, I need you here!" Mr. Beatty shouted.

She patted the hand of a man whose cheek had been torn away. She could see that the wound was already festering and would become infected if he wasn't treated soon. She counted. He was seventh in line so he shouldn't have to wait too terribly long.

She scurried over to Mr. Beatty's table and nearly retched by what greeted her there.

It was Gin, the sailor who had brought her things on board *Victory*. He lay on the table awash in blood. His mouth was clamped around a thick, filthy piece of rope. His eyes were darting everywhere but seeing nothing, and he was sweating profusely. He wore the same trousers and shirt he had when Marguerite first met him, only now they were tattered and stained, and the left leg of them had been knifed off. What lay below the cut line threatened Marguerite's stomach with total upheaval.

The leg that had so nimbly supported Gin on the gangplank while carrying her wax figures aboard was a shattered mess.

Bone protruded jaggedly in two places, and the muscle and sinew around the bone had been reduced to a pulpy mass. Marguerite averted her eyes from the man's misfortune, which could in no way be called a mere wound.

"Everyone else is busy. Get on the other side of the table and hold down his right leg and arm. Can't do anything for this leg and it will have to go if I'm to save him."

Marguerite blindly followed his order without question, putting one hand on Gin's right thigh and the other against his shoulder and pressing down, but not before giving his arm what she hoped was a comforting squeeze. Gin looked at her in terror and desperation, and, like the sailor Pearce before him, began crying uncontrollably.

She had no idea how to further console him, especially since her role was that of restraining him.

The surgeon took no notice of Gin's fear or pain. "We have to do this swiftly and surely. The key to his recovery will be to take the limb in as few cuts as possible. You need to hold him so he doesn't jerk and impair my ability to do that. Do you understand?"

Marguerite nodded grimly, knowing her face was probably as pale as Gin's by now.

First the surgeon wrapped a tourniquet above the location where he planned to amputate. He twisted the knob that tightened the tourniquet as much as possible. Gin groaned under the pressure of it. Then, in a move so fast Marguerite was not quite sure she had even seen it, Mr. Beatty sliced through Gin's leg, using a dark-stained knife with a very long blade. Tossing the knife down between Gin's legs, he picked up one of the saws she remembered seeing earlier when they had set up the operating tables. With three interminable, crunching movements back and forth through his leg, the surgeon had separated most of the man's leg. The saw was tossed down and the knife picked up again, and Mr. Beatty neatly sliced through the remainder of skin beneath the bone. He pushed the leg aside. Gin's screams were muffled behind the rope stuffed in his mouth.

"Now hand me that pail there. It was brought down from the stove a short while ago and should still be hot."

Marguerite looked where his finger was pointing to a pail hanging from a large hook in a beam. She removed it, and the now-familiar odor of tar assailed her. Funny how it no longer made her sick.

Or so she thought.

Inside the steaming pail of tar was a thick baton of oak. Mr. Beatty pulled out the baton, which was thickly coated with the hot substance, and slabbed it over the bottom of Gin's leg stump, covering the just-cut fusion of bone, muscle, and nerves.

Gin's howling was akin to a fox in a trap. The rope fell from his mouth, and Marguerite hurried to pour him some rum from a bottle stored nearby. With her hands trembling uncontrollably, she sloshed more of it over the sides than actually made it inside the cup. She put an arm under his neck and lifted him up to take the liquor. He gulped it greedily and lay back down.

Less than two minutes had passed since the surgeon had first picked up the knife.

Mr. Beatty took Gin's stump and tossed it into a short barrel Marguerite had not noticed before. Inside the barrel was a macabre assortment of arms, legs, feet, and fingers. The movement of the ship made the blood draining out of the limbs and into the container slosh up and over the rim onto the floor around it. It looked like an oversized soup pot full of mutton bones waiting to be cooked down.

Don't be hysterical, Marguerite. You don't want to end up a babbling patient down here yourself.

Mr. Beatty nodded to the barrel. "See to that, Mrs. Ashby. It's almost full."

"See to it?" She felt her heart quicken and swallowed to quell the panic again.

"It needs to be dumped overboard. Get someone to take it up one deck and put it through a porthole not being used by cannon. Go on, don't just stand there gawping at me, woman. And hurry—there's more to do here." The surgeon shouted to two sailors rushing by to clear Gin off the table.

Marguerite was more sickened by this task than by assisting in Gin's surgery. For at least Gin was put out of his misery quickly and was now lying unconscious on the floor with a blanket over him. Finding two men willing to carry the grisly container of body parts proved very difficult, and she finally had to bar entry into the orlop until two burly sailors holding a fallen messmate grudgingly agreed to do it as long as Marguerite moved their fellow seaman to the top of the queue. She agreed and the deed was done. Marguerite wiped a hand across her sweaty brow and returned to work. From then on she knew how to get the limb buckets emptied quickly.

After what she thought was a temporary duty as Mr. Beatty's assistant, she found herself recalled again and again to his operating table, since his assistants were overwhelmed with their own work now. Marguerite dashed back and forth between succoring the injured and helping the surgeon with whatever incision, removal, or stitching he needed to perform.

It was impossible to know from down in the hot, stinking, windowless orlop what was happening in the battle. Marguerite caught bits of news from injured men and those who were carrying bodies back and forth. Her interest was piqued to hear that *Royal Sovereign* had been the first to engage. She wondered fleetingly if Brax was unharmed.

Other comments penetrated her plugged-up ears as well, and she pieced together that *Victory* had become quite disabled thus far, although she was placing some well-landed shot.

She threw up a silent prayer for Darden's and Brax's safety, but all thoughts of the two lieutenants disappeared while she washed a man's wounds with vinegar. She could tell this poor soul would not make it. His gun crew companions had brought him down shortly before. The man had been injured by splintering wood from enemy cannon-shot. He was pierced in several places by the sharp wooden projectiles, but the largest piece had inserted itself in his abdomen. His mates unceremoniously yanked it out of his stomach before bringing him down. It looked as though his friends had done more damage than the enemy. Their coarse work resulted in the some of the man's entrails being pulled out. They were now lying on top of his skin.

She smiled encouragingly at the man, another one who seemed near to delirium. She suddenly remembered an old verse Claudette sang to her in the dark days following Nicholas's death. They would sit in a darkened room together and Claudette would wrap her arms around Marguerite, rocking her back and forth and singing softly.

Marguerite now did the same in an attempt to comfort the man.

She knelt next to his head, put an arm under his clammy neck, and looked directly in his eyes as she sang.

"Lavender's blue, dilly dilly,
Rosemary's green.
When you are king, dilly dilly,
I shall be queen."

She wasn't sure if he could actually hear her over all the din of the ship, but he smiled gratefully at her before closing his eyes to sleep. Within seconds his breathing became shallow, and then he breathed no more.

Marguerite removed her arm from around him, patted his head with a whispered, "Farewell, friend," and went to find the sail-maker's assistant, a useless boy of about seventeen who was utterly terrified of his job. She found him cowering in a squat near the dispensary, his bag of materials slung over a shoulder. She yanked him to his feet and dragged him to the expired sailor.

"We're all frightened," she shouted so she could be heard. "But we all do our duty. Do yours now."

How peculiar that she had only been down here a short time and already she was becoming numb to the carnage and gore.

She left the boy there and turned to go see if Mr. Beatty needed her. Penetrating all of the chaos and noise was the sound of a great *thud* and almost instantly she found herself lying flat on her stomach on the deck.

What happened? Did she trip over something?

Two falls in a very short time. *Really, Marguerite, you are quite clumsy.*

No one else seemed to have taken the same tumble she did, although she saw some men looking upward with concern. But they immediately returned to what they were doing. She got to her knees and looked down. More blood, now combined with sand and bits of flesh, made a messy pattern all over the front of her dress.

She made a halfhearted swipe at it all, then resigned herself to it. No time for cleaning up—there were wounded men who needing tending to. She returned to Mr. Beatty's table, where he had obviously been waiting impatiently for her. He took no notice of her disheveled condition, merely giving her instructions for the operation he was performing next.

After yet another surgery accompanied by howling and gore in the immense heat, Mr. Beatty threw down his knife and looked at Marguerite in despair.

"There are too many, too fast. We need more help assigned to us, instead of just grabbing someone nearby and convincing him to help us. I want you to do something, Mrs. Ashby. Something difficult."

Marguerite nodded her willingness to do as he asked.

"I want you to go find Mr. Hardy and ask him to send us anyone who can possibly be spared. He'll be on the quarterdeck somewhere, managing things with Nelson."

"But wouldn't Mr. Smith or Mr. Westemburg have more sway with the captain, Mr. Beatty? Why do you want me to do this?"

Mr. Beatty looked uncomfortable for the first time that day. "Listen to me. It requires great risk to go up to the quarterdeck right now. I cannot imperil my assistants, for I need them the most. Do you understand?"

She did indeed.

She was more expendable in the event that she was wounded or killed in the attempt to go on deck.

But Darden's principles were a drumbeat in her head.

I must do my duty.

Just as I made that poor boy do with the dead sailor.

She attempted a salute to the surgeon, imitating what she had seen other sailors do dozens of times. His amused bark was incongruous as they stood there in the middle of their horrific situation.

"One more thing, Mrs. Ashby. See the purser. Get a uniform. I don't want you on deck dressed like that. You'll be too . . . conspicuous."

She dashed off to Mr. Burke again, who cocked an eyebrow but did not question her request for a uniform and merely added it to her bill. She locked herself in the dispensary to change. It was blessedly more quiet in here, although the confined space meant it was even hotter than the rest of the orlop. Her dress was nearly impossible to remove, as it was so thoroughly encrusted with blood and grime that it stuck to her skin. She finally got it peeled off, removed the watch to pin it onto her new uniform, and rolled the dress up and stuffed it in a corner for retrieval later. Or perhaps burning.

Her skin underneath was stained everywhere from blood. A couple of hours ago she would have been mortified, but now it seemed quite normal.

Marguerite quickly threw on the jacket and used the neckerchief to tie her hair up in as small and inconspicuous a bundle as possible. The sleeves were too long and required rolling up, and her torso practically swam in the jacket, but its loose fit would help with the heat. She enjoyed the odd sensation of pulling on the white trousers and tying them around her waist with rope. She walked back and forth across the dispensary twice in her bare feet, getting used to her new uniform, then took a deep breath and opened the dispensary door to embark on her deadly mission.

Marguerite took note of the time. It was 12:45.

She ignored the cries of men in the queue pleading for water or help, averting her eyes as she dashed past them. She scrambled up the steps to the lower gun deck and very nearly lost her nerve before she even got started.

The milieu of the gun deck made the orlop seem like a barge ride along the Thames on a mild spring day.

She could hardly believe it. The slaughter was actually worse here than below.

The fifteen or so cannon that lined each side of the deck were manned by crews of varying number. It looked as though most had six members, each performing a different job in the complicated process of loading and firing his cannon, but it was difficult to see for billowing clouds of eye-stinging smoke emitted each time a cannon fired. Some of crew were obviously injured, with blood trailing from their noses, ears, and other locations, but they ignored it and kept at their assigned tasks. The noise of the cannon firing at differing intervals made for one long, cacophonous stream of explosions. As each cannon fired, it jolted backward several feet on its carriage, and that cannon's gun crew hopped back to avoid being crushed by the massive weapon. The sailors took their jobs seriously, and despite the soul-numbing danger, kept at their jobs relentlessly.

The stench here was so bad that she practically longed for the simple filth-and-blood mix in the operating theatre. Not only was there the sickly smell from blood spattered everywhere, but the putrid odor from the firing cannon made her gag. It was as though the eggs from a thousand dead and decaying chickens had been smashed everywhere, and were releasing their noxious fumes in an all-encompassing miasma.

But the enemy's cannon wreaked havoc on deck, as well. The impact of shot hitting the side of the ship added a different kind of terrifying noise to the ongoing, deafening racket. Some shot bounced off *Victory*, but some made it through open gun ports, splintering the wood around the port and sending shrapnel flying into whatever was nearby, mostly sailors who screamed in agony when they were hit. Marguerite knew they were screaming only because their mouths were open as wide as their terror-filled eyes. Most fell and were kicked or shoved out of the way by their crewmates. Some valiantly stood and continued to work.

Next to firing cannon, it appeared that the second most important job was repair. Whenever there was mutilation done to the deck, a carpenter would rush forward to try to patch the damage the best way he could. So most of the crew worked to inflict destruction, whereas some crew members' sole job was to fix things.

Several of the youngest men scampered past her on and off the deck, delivering shot and gunpowder to each of the cannon and avoiding the rolling carriages as well. She presumed the supplies came from somewhere in the ship's hold. A few of them scowled at her when going past, and one sailor yelled something at her. Although she wasn't sure what he said, she was certain it was not flattering and probably referred to her shirking her duty as a crew member.

She clung to the rails of the stairway, too terrified to move. How could anyone survive this? And how much worse was it on the quarterdeck?

Was she meant to die on *Victory*?

Do your duty, Marguerite.

Another man carrying shot scrambled past and knocked her in the shoulder with his load. He kicked her shin and shouted at her. This time it was clearly an insult.

It was time to pluck up her courage and head farther up.

The middle and upper gun decks were identical scenes to what she saw down below. She now desperately wished for the relative safety and calm of the orlop.

One more set of steps, Marguerite.

She poked her head out again in the same location where she had witnessed the flogging just a few days before. How different it all was now. She could see the feet of men stomping past her on their way to carry out their orders. There were the ubiquitous cannon on their carriages firing and jolting backward, and through yet more smoke she caught glimpses of men in red uniforms poised around the perimeter of the ship, firing muskets at targets she couldn't see. She could hear return fire whizzing over the deck and striking various points.

And the smell was little better up here than down below.

How would she ever find the captain, even if she could make it past the hail of bullets?

But luck was with her. The captain came into view, strolling calmly with another officer whose back was to her as he turned to speak to Hardy. They paraded about as though completely unaware of what was going on around them.

Were they brave or foolhardy? No time to think on it now.

Marguerite said another quick prayer, then leaped out of the hole, running headlong toward Hardy.

Victory was now locked together with *Redoubtable*, and the momentum of *Victory*'s impact on the other ship carried them both out of the line of the other ships. The ships were so close together now that Darden could actually see through the continuing musket fire into the faces of his opponents.

We could board Redoubtable *and take her*, Darden thought.

As though his thoughts had been transmitted to the captain of the other ship, he saw that the gun ports on the side facing *Victory* were being rapidly closed.

They fear us gaining access.

He joined Captain Hardy, who was pacing the deck in front of Admiral Nelson. Nelson still wore his faux decorations that singled him out as an important naval officer, even though they were practically in hand-to-hand combat with the *Redoubtable.* Nelson even wore his peculiar green eyeshade that was made specially for protecting his good left eye while in the sun.

Does the admiral have a death wish? he wondered, but tamped the traitorous thought down. He knew the admiral was the bravest man alive. If only he understood that he needed to be protected. Without Nelson, English morale would be lost just as French morale would be boosted. A completely unacceptable state of affairs. But what could be done?

And then something utterly horrific happened that gave him the most magnificent idea.

Marguerite nearly collided with the captain.

"What ho, sailor? Why have you left your post?"

"Pardon me, Captain Hardy. It's me, Mrs. Ashby."

Hardy bent down to peer into her dirty face. "Why, so it is! What are you doing up here? In a uniform, yet. I thought you were assigned to the operating theatre."

"You were *what?*" burst the man next to Hardy.

Marguerite turned to see who it was. Darden. Naturally. His eyes were filled with a thousand questions, most of which she was certain would result in a tongue-lashing after she answered them.

She decided to ignore him for the moment.

"Yes, sir, I've been helping Mr. Beatty. He sent me up to ask you for more men down in the orlop to help. Sir, there are too many injured coming down for us to handle."

"Why didn't he send one of the men? It's entirely too dangerous for a woman up here."

"Yes, Captain, but I volunteered to do it. I got a uniform from Mr. Burke so I could move about more easily and now here I am."

"*Volunteered?*" Darden roared, his detonation as earsplitting as one of the cannon below deck.

Even in the midst of battle, Hardy was amused by the lieutenant's obvious concern for his charge, a concern that clearly went way beyond duty. Thus he was agreeable when Darden suggested that he take care of both getting Mrs. Ashby to safety and resolving the shortage of men in the operating theatre.

Darden took Marguerite's hand and yanked her across the deck back down to the next staircase, where she nearly fell down to the next deck because he was pulling her so hard.

She yanked back to get his attention through the battle madness around them. Seeing her practically sprawled on the deck, he slowed and helped her descend the staircase a bit more gently.

From there he took hold of her elbow and led her down one more level to the middle gun deck. Marguerite shut her eyes reflexively against the turmoil that lay before them. Darden squeezed her elbow so she would open her eyes and gestured to her that she was to hide under the staircase for a few moments while he took care of getting her more help. He pointed down at the floor under the stairs and then waggled his finger in her face sternly.

Do not disobey me this time.

If she wasn't so terrified, she would have found his expression quite funny. His flashing eyes and humorless lips were set inside a scruffy, unshaven face with his dark hair thoroughly soaked from sweat, undone from its queue, and hanging limply down the sides of his face.

But she was indeed terrified. She crouched under the stairs as directed, and watched his retreating figure as he bent over and ran through the gauntlet of horror to the stern of the ship. Before he disappeared from view in the smoke and press of bodies, she saw him limp once as though he had stepped on a small stone.

Hopefully that's all he stepped on.

For once, Marguerite obeyed Darden completely and did not so much as twitch an eyebrow while he was gone. He returned shortly with two men who looked none too happy with their new duties. They took the staircase down toward the orlop and Marguerite moved to follow them, but Darden had grabbed her elbow again. He shook his head no and motioned for her to follow him.

Taking his hand willingly she went up with him. Were they going back to the quarterdeck? She hoped not. To her surprise, she realized he was leading her to Nelson's cabin. Except that most of Nelson's cabin had been turned into a battleground. The beautiful settees, tables, and chairs were gone, as well as his exquisite bed, the paintings, and other décor. Instead, cannons were firing out gun ports, and the exquisitely painted canvas floor was obliterated by sand, blood, shrapnel, and gunpowder. Darden wrapped an arm around her head and tried to cover her body with his as best he could as they raced down to the back of the admiral's cabin. Against the back wall of windows stood the wax Nelson and Hardy. They were remarkably untouched, although their faces were melting a bit and their uniforms were stained with drops of paint and wax. Still, they had survived well.

Darden flattened her against the windows between the two figures, pressing his body against hers. He pulled the cloth plug from her right ear and bent down to speak quietly to her.

"Listen to me. I want to take at least one of these figures on deck and set it up as a decoy."

"But I thought they were to be used only if the admiral or captain was injured."

"Yes, but they're both strutting about the quarterdeck as though nothing will ever happen to them. *Victory* is jammed into the *Redoubtable* now, and their sharpshooters can take easy aim at us. I want to deflect their attention. I want you to help me position the figures."

She nodded her comprehension.

He cupped her cheek in his roughened hand as he continued speaking in her ear. "I despise myself for asking this of you, because it will be treacherous work. But you know the figures and will handle them properly. And it's my obligation to do what I can for Lord Nelson and the captain. It's more important than anything else. Do you understand me?"

She nodded again. Despite the miserable heat and noise, she

couldn't help but be contented to have him enveloping her in his arms, even if it was to basically issue her battle orders. Hopefully no one else had noticed him pressed up against what looked like a young boy in the admiral's cabin.

He placed the cloth plug back in her ear. Just as she thought he was turning away from her to dislodge one of the figures from its stand, he turned back to her and kissed her with the same hungry passion he had shown when she was a mere accidental passenger in the sick berth. Except now they were pressed entirely against one another, under the threat of imminent death. She clung to him, fearful that this would be their last embrace. Ever. His body was hard and taut and powerful from shipboard life, yet she knew this was a man who would never intentionally hurt her.

Unless it interfered with his duty.

As though he had just had the same thought about his responsibilities, he broke away from the kiss.

He mouthed something at her, but he said it softly and she couldn't hear him. It looked as though his lips formed the words, "I'll love you always." Or did he merely say, "Time to lug the figures"?

But he really had turned away this time and the moment was gone.

They decided on taking the Nelson figure, simply because it was a bit smaller and was therefore easier to carry. What a sight they must have been to anyone who was watching: the lieutenant and a young seaman, carting an effigy of their admiral up to the quarterdeck.

But the crew was too busy to pay attention to anything that didn't concern firing upon the enemy.

Getting "Nelson" up the staircase to the quarterdeck was difficult work. The figure had become slippery from the softened wax, and they had to handle it gingerly to avoid damaging its limbs. Not to mention evading the maelstrom of flying debris and enduring the copious clouds of smoke threatening to suffocate them.

But they finally hoisted it out flat onto the quarterdeck, and both Darden and Marguerite popped out behind it. Marguerite followed Darden's lead as he stayed crouched next to the body, looking around as though waiting for something. At some optimum moment that she didn't understand, Darden nodded to her and they dragged "Nelson" forward toward the bow. Even through the confusion Marguerite could see that *Victory*'s bow had collided with the other ship's, and fierce hand-to-hand fighting was going on in the intersection. Knives and cutlasses flashed in a blur, and thankfully she could no longer hear screaming for the booming of cannon on board *Victory*, the *Redoubtable*, and other ships nearby.

How close did Darden plan to go?

Together they stepped down a gangway onto a lower section of deck, even closer to the personal fighting. Marguerite began to sweat not just from the heat, but from fear. She was certain she was very close to death now, yet Darden showed no fear, just caution.

They had now crept up next to a launch boat that was kept stored in the middle of this deck. Surprising, since she'd previously seen others lowered into the water as the crew prepared the decks for battle. Darden nodded to her and pointed at the launch. Once again she nodded her understanding of his hand gestures.

They propped "Nelson" up next to the launch, putting one of the figure's arms over the side of the tiny craft to hold him up, however temporarily that might work. Marguerite jumped as a ball ricocheted off the launch and sent a shower of wood chips spraying around her.

Was that a random shot, or is someone aiming at me?

But this was no time to allow fright to take over her presence of mind. She casually brushed the debris from her head and shoulders as though she had hardly noticed anything.

But Darden had certainly noticed. He grabbed her hand again, and together they hurriedly made their way back up the gangplank to the quarterdeck and down that deck toward the staircase. Darden helped her down to the upper gun deck. At the bottom of the staircase, he pointed to himself and back up to the quarterdeck, then put a finger to her chest and pointed down. Apparently they were not going back for the Hardy figure.

Yes, Lieutenant, she thought as she brought her hand up in a salute as she had watched other sailors do. Like the good seaman she had become, she knew now that it was imperative to obey orders.

Darden laughed and kissed her forehead, surely taking away a puddle of filthy sweat on his lips as he did so. He saluted her in return and scrambled up the staircase as nimbly as a monkey.

As she made her way back to the dimly lit orlop and the distinctive horror that awaited her there, Marguerite pictured in her mind the real Nelson with the wax figure, and thought with ironic pride that the wax figure's decorations looked much better than those on the admiral.

But would Darden's plan work?

23

As the first ship to enter the fray, *Royal Sovereign* had been engaged in heated battle with the Spanish man-of-war, *Santa Ana*, for hours. Or had it been days?

Both *Royal Sovereign* and *Santa Ana* were badly battered, although the British ship was finally prevailing over her enemy. But for Brax the news was disheartening: No specific moment had arisen during the hours of battle in which he could distinguish himself before either Captain Rotheram or Admiral Collingwood. Collingwood had even taken a bad leg wound from a splinter, but Brax had been off on some errand or other, and so had not been on hand to help the admiral. Or to somehow take the shrapnel for him.

He'd nothing to be ashamed of, for he'd fought as valiantly and with as much courage as every other crew member. There just wasn't a decisive moment of heroism on his part.

Was his time in the navy worth it?

Marguerite's sojourn away from the operating theatre had felt like hours. She lifted the watch from where it was pinned onto her jacket to read the time. The face was completely encased in dust. She wiped it with the sleeve on her other arm to check the time. It was fifteen minutes past one o'clock.

At least the noise on the orlop was reduced to a dull roar as compared to the decks above. She even removed the plugs from her ears as she moved back and forth between helping wounded men get positioned around the deck and assisting Mr. Beatty with his sweltering, messy work.

An unusual clattering on the stairs accompanied raised voices that could be heard above the din. On seeing who had just been brought down, all activity ceased on the orlop; the only sounds were those of the battle raging above, punctuated by the groans of the wounded who did not realize what was happening.

Several wild-eyed members of the admiral's staff clambered into the orlop, including a man in chaplain's dress. Behind them, and supported by a marine and two seamen—Darden and a man she'd heard referred to as Sandilands—was Nelson, drenched in blood. His green eyeshade was askew, and his face was completely drained of color. Nelson greeted the surgeon. "Ah, Mr. Beatty! You can do nothing for me. I have but a short time to live. My back is shot through."

The surgeon quickly recovered from his own shock and signaled to have his table cleared of its patient and a clean piece of canvas laid on top of it. Darden and the other two attendants gently lifted Nelson and laid him on the table. Mr. Beatty then motioned for Marguerite to join him.

She passed Darden and searched his face for an explanation, but it was as pale as Nelson's and only reflected his abject misery. The other officers glanced curiously at Marguerite in her uniform but were too preoccupied to make comment.

"Quickly, Mrs. Ashby, we must make the admiral comfortable," urged Mr. Beatty.

Together they worked to strip him of most of his uniform, working carefully not to move him too much. Nelson didn't seem to care much. Marguerite retrieved as clean a blanket as she could find and spread it over the admiral.

While she and Mr. Beatty worked, Nelson continued to talk in a calm and composed tone.

His good eye first landed on the chaplain. "Dr. Scott, I told you so. I am gone." Nelson paused briefly and added in a low voice, "I have to leave Lady Hamilton, and my adopted daughter Horatia, as a legacy to my country."

Before the good chaplain could respond, Mr. Beatty interrupted. "Your lordship, I'm afraid I must examine your wound to discover the course of the ball. I will endeavor to do so without putting you in much pain."

"Go ahead, Mr. Beatty, but assuredly my back has been shot through."

Marguerite watched as the surgeon worked to trace the ball from its deep penetration into Nelson's chest. "Your lordship," Mr. Beatty said, "tell me of all the sensations you feel."

Nelson grunted. "I feel a gush of blood every minute within my breast, but no feeling in the lower part of my body. Breathing is difficult."

Mr. Beatty looked up at Marguerite as though Nelson had said something quite significant, but she had no idea what it was.

"And what of your back, sir?"

"I have very severe pain in my spine where the ball struck, and I felt it break my back."

The surgeon probed Nelson's chest and side a bit further. "My lord, I believe I've discovered the path the ball took. Please rest while I confer with my assistants over the best way to proceed."

Marguerite rolled the blanket up over Nelson's shoulders to warm him while Mr. Beatty stepped away, and placed two more rolled-up blankets under his shoulders to prop him up. To her surprise, Mr. Beatty didn't confer with Messrs. Smith and Westemburg but instead motioned to Nelson's staff members, including Darden, and the group of men huddled together out of Nelson's sight. Activity on the deck resumed, with ambulatory men staying respectfully away from Nelson's makeshift bed.

Marguerite focused on her patient. "Sir, would you like some water?"

"Yes, yes, water. Need a drink."

She helped him take the cool liquid, which revived him a little.

"My thanks, madam." He gazed up at her with his good eye, as though just seeing her for the first time. He gasped, but she wasn't sure if it was in pain or recognition.

"You're the waxworker, aren't you? Why are you still here? And why are you in a uniform? Weren't you transferred to the *Pickle*?"

"No, sir. Mr. Beatty requested that Captain Hardy let me stay to help out in the operating theatre. I obtained this uniform so I could move around easily on the quarterdeck. I came up to see the captain and to help Lieutenant Hastings move your wax figure on deck. Did you see it?" Marguerite added another blanket to Nelson's shivering body and patted his face with a cloth dipped in water. She wished she had a lemon nearby to squeeze into the cup, which would make it more refreshing for the admiral.

"Yes, I saw it." Nelson grunted again. "I nearly tossed Hastings overboard when I saw it. The fool thing was supposed to be brought up only if something happened to me. Hastings thought it would be a good decoy. I thought it an assault on my dignity." Nelson went silent for a moment, as if thinking about it.

"Hate to admit he was right. *Redoubtable* focused her energies on that wax figure and off the other men on deck. Shot it to bits. Her crew stopped firing and began cheering. Thought they had conquered His Majesty's navy. Gave us a chance to reestablish our dominance in the fight."

Nelson screwed his face up in pain and touched his chest. "I feel another gushing. No matter. I'll be done soon enough. Once we had the advantage again I stepped down to the fo'c'sle, and someone perched up in the *Redoubtable*'s masts realized they'd been mistaken in their impression of my demise. I'm certain my death ball came from a sharpshooter up in her mizzenmast."

Nelson sighed. "I suppose Mr. Pitt must be told he was right about the wax figures. He'll have a laugh at my expense, won't he?" He grabbed Marguerite's arm with his good hand in a viselike grip that belied his weakened state. "You'll take the message to him, won't you? Tell him I concede to his tactical brilliance on that one matter only."

"Of course, my lord," she replied.

Nelson released her arm. "But are we won for the day? I pray

God doesn't take me until I know. I must know if we're victorious or not."

Marguerite had no idea how to respond. She patted his forehead again with cool water.

"Fan, fan," Nelson muttered. Marguerite ran and found her sheaf of stationery bundled up with her dress in the dispensary and waved it on his face, which seemed to bring him comfort.

The wait for the surgeon's return was endless, even though only a short time had passed since Nelson was brought down. She glanced at her watch again. It was forty-five minutes past the hour of one.

Mr. Beatty finally broke away and returned, and most of the admiral's staff that had crashed its way down the stairs, including Darden, came to stand watch at Nelson's side. Marguerite thought Darden looked sickly, but her energies were concentrated on her patient.

After moments of quiet, Nelson became agitated again. "Where is Captain Hardy? Why hasn't he come to see me?"

Mr. Burke, the purser, had joined the staff gathered round the admiral and spoke up. "He is commanding a great victory topside, sir, and will be down as soon as the enemy is defeated."

"Nonsense, all nonsense." Nelson was quiet again. His breathing was labored.

Messages were repeatedly sent up to Captain Hardy to come and attend on the admiral, but thus far the captain had not come down himself, merely sending a return message that he would avail himself of the first favorable moment to visit his lordship.

Minutes later Nelson's eyes flew open again. "Where is Hardy? Will no one bring him to me? He must be killed. Surely he is destroyed."

Dr. Scott, the chaplain, tried also to comfort the admiral, but to no avail.

Hardy at last came down at almost two-thirty to pay a quick visit. He and Nelson shook hands affectionately and Nelson said, "Well, Hardy, how goes the battle? How goes the day with us?"

"Very well, my lord," Hardy replied. "We have got twelve or fourteen of the enemy's ships in our possession, but five of their vanguard have tacked, and show an intention of bearing down on *Victory*. I have therefore called two or three of our fresh ships round us, and have no doubt of giving them a drubbing."

"Ah, excellent. I hope," said Nelson, "none of *our* ships have struck their colors, Hardy."

"No, my lord, there is no fear of that."

"Then I am greatly encouraged." Nelson closed his eyes again.

Soon Nelson was calling fitfully for Captain Hardy again. He seemed to derive comfort only from the presence of his friend and colleague. Hardy stepped back into Nelson's view.

"I am a dead man, Hardy. I am going fast. It will be all over with me soon. Pray, let my dear Lady Hamilton have my hair so she can make a memento, and give her all other things belonging to me."

"Your lordship, does Mr. Beatty hold out no prospect for your life?"

"Oh no! It is impossible. My back is shot through. Beatty will tell you so."

Hardy looked to the surgeon, who nodded sadly.

"Nelson, you may trust that I will follow your requests exactly, although I will never give up hope of your recovery."

The two men clasped hands before Hardy returned to the upper deck to resume his duties.

Out of her perpetual habit, Marguerite looked at her watch again. It was three o'clock.

Mr. Beatty signaled Marguerite away from Nelson's side and escorted her to the dispensary to speak privately.

"You must know, Mrs. Ashby, that nothing can be done for Lord Nelson."

"Nothing at all?"

"No. When he told me of the gushing he feels in his chest, I checked his pulse. I believe that he is hemorrhaging such that his entire body cavity is being filled. Some months ago there was another man on *Victory* with similar complaints as Nelson's after a spinal injury. He expired in a short time. I'm certain Nelson remembers the man, thus why he knows he's finished." Beatty's voice broke. "I cannot save him."

Marguerite tried to contain her shock and remain calm. "But . . . what will happen to the fleet? To our likelihood of victory?"

Mr. Beatty wiped an eye. "Lord Collingwood is next in command and is surely able to carry out the day. But I must caution you. Only the captain and those of the admiral's staff down here now, plus Smith and Westemburg, know that the admiral's wound is fatal. No one else must know. It would be devastating for the crew to learn that Nelson was not long for the world."

Marguerite herself felt the walls of the ship crumbling in on her. The navy without Nelson? Impossible. She mustered a smile. "Thank you, Mr. Beatty, for your confidence in me. And now we should return to the patient."

The surgeon escorted her out, but she didn't get any farther than Darden's side.

"Lieutenant! You look ghastly." Darden's face had gone from pale white to a greenish cast, and he was weaving back and forth. Mr. Beatty left her to cope with the lieutenant while he went back to make Nelson as comfortable as possible.

She put Darden's arm around her shoulder and escorted him to one of a few free spots on the deck, under the stairs and well away from Nelson. He fell to the floor heavily.

"Darden! What happened?" She dropped to her knees and quickly began loosening his clothing.

"I don't know. I got a little light-headed standing near Lord Nelson. Perhaps it's just too confined down here." Darden cocked himself onto one elbow. "Listen!"

Marguerite stopped. "I hear nothing."

"Right. Our cannon have stopped. I pray we haven't struck our colors. We can't both lose Nelson and lose to the French."

"Nor can we lose you, Lieutenant. My, but this boot is wedged onto your leg."

Darden gasped in pain. "What are you doing to me, woman?"

"Just trying to make you comfortable."

"Well, you're not. You're tearing my foot off at the ankle."

"Perhaps you shouldn't be wearing boots. Perhaps you should be barefoot like the rest of us." She brought one stained foot forward to show him.

Darden laughed despite his pain. "Most impressive, sailor. You should be instructing crew in proper dress. Ahhh!" He winced as Marguerite finally yanked his boot off with a great sucking sound.

Blood spurted everywhere.

"You're injured! When did this happen?"

"I don't know. I don't recall anything."

Marguerite threw the boot aside and inspected his foot. She found a gash near his ankle. Grabbing the boot again, she scrutinized it and found a tear near the bottom. She turned it upside down and shook it. A sharp, bloodied piece of wood shrapnel tumbled out. She held it up for him to see.

"You didn't feel this slice your foot?"

"I felt nothing." Darden began shivering.

She threw the boot and the projectile aside to get him some water and a blanket. She sought out one of the surgeon's assistants, but they were both busy with other patients, and she didn't dare interrupt Mr. Beatty's attendance on Nelson. She would have to take care of this herself. Adding a roll of bandages and scissors to her collection of goods, she returned to Darden.

He drank the water greedily, then eyed thc bandages and scissors. "You don't intend on removing my foot for its small offense, do you?"

"No! I mean, I wouldn't know how to do that. Forgive me. What I really mean is that I'm going to look at your ankle again, but I don't think there is any shrapnel left in it, which means I'll just bandage you up tightly to try to staunch the blood flow." She cut away the lower part of his stocking to fully expose his foot, snipped a length of bandage, and wound it firmly and repeatedly up and over his ankle, securing it at the top of his foot. Marguerite's ministrations seemed to have some good effect, for the color was already returning to his face.

"Lieutenant, I'm afraid you're going to survive."

"My mother will be ecstatic. And now you'll need to put my boot back on."

"You'll recover much better here without your foot confined in it."

"That would be true if I planned to stay here recovering. But

Captain Hardy will need me more than ever without Lord Nelson. He'll need every available officer."

"But you're not really in any condition to—"

"Please put my boot back on."

"I really think you should lie here for at least—"

"My boot."

Stubborn, dutiful Darden had returned to the scene, and she knew better than to continue arguing with him. With a sigh, she gently replaced the torn boot on his bandaged foot.

She helped him to his feet, where he wobbled unsteadily before regaining his posture and straightening his soiled, sweat-encrusted jacket.

Marguerite shook her head. "You are completely impossible, Lieutenant Hastings."

"Feel free to chastise me after we've won the day. For now I must take my leave of you. I've rested long enough." Darden stepped gingerly on his newly wrapped foot, but, realizing he could put pressure on it easily, was soon making his way off the orlop back to the quarterdeck, where the great cannon had resumed firing.

Meanwhile, Nelson continued to decline. "Fan, fan. Water," he continued to request, and Marguerite took turns with Dr. Scott and Mr. Beatty to comply with his wishes. Marguerite also found some pillows and used them to bolster him up into a near sitting position.

Nelson seemed more content now. In fact, he now gave his attention to other wounded sailors in the orlop, insisting that Mr. Beatty and his assistants return to the wounded and let him be.

"For," he said once again, "you can do nothing for me."

The surgeon obeyed and for a few minutes he, Smith, and Westemburg busied themselves with other patients while Marguerite stayed close to Nelson to tend to his needs.

But soon Nelson wanted Mr. Beatty again, to emphasize once more his imminent mortality.

"Ah, Mr. Beatty! I have sent for you to say, what I forgot to tell you before, that all power and motion and feeling below my breast are gone, just as happened to that midshipman not so long ago, so *you* very well *know* I can live but a short time."

Nelson's emphatic manner left the surgeon nodding his head miserably. "My lord, you told me so before. I had merely hoped . . ."

Mr. Beatty pulled the blanket down in an attempt to examine Nelson again, but the admiral stopped him. "Ah, Beatty! I am too certain of it. Scott and Burke have also tried to hope on my behalf. You *know* I am gone."

The surgeon replied in utter dejection, "My lord, unhappily for our country, you are right. Nothing can be done for you," and withdrew out of Nelson's line of sight to conceal his emotions.

Nelson put a hand on his left side. "I know it. I feel something rising in my breast which tells me I am gone."

Marguerite and Mr. Burke resumed fanning the admiral, who was sweating profusely once again.

"God be praised. I have done my duty," he said.

Nelson and Darden could have been birthed from the same mother. Duty was their only focus.

Now composed, Mr. Beatty came back to Nelson's side. "Is your pain very great, my lord?"

"Indeed, Beatty, it is so great I wish I were dead presently. Yet, one would like to live a little longer, too."

The orlop went silent except for the occasional, distant boom of cannon from somewhere in the fleet.

Nelson added softly, "What would become of Lady Hamilton if she knew my situation!"

Marguerite saw that the surgeon was losing his poise again. "Sir, why don't you attend to the newly wounded, and I will stay here and make the admiral comfortable?"

Mr. Beatty nodded, willing to let Marguerite guide him in his despair over his inability to help the navy's most highly regarded member.

With Mr. Beatty out of view, Marguerite boldly reached for Nelson's hand and squeezed it while still fanning him. "My lord, what else can I do for you?"

"Who's there?" he asked, confused.

"My lord, it's me, Mrs. Ashby." When he didn't respond, she added, "The waxworker, sir."

"Ah, yes, Hastings's charge. That figure of yours worked, you know. For a short while. Long enough." Nelson's breathing was labored.

"Yes, sir, you told me. I'm proud to have done my part for the navy."

"Quite right. Water."

She helped him take some more sips from a cup. "My lord, how else can I make you comfortable?"

He responded in agitation. "Anchor, we need to anchor. A storm is brewing."

What did he mean by this? Was the admiral delirious? She whispered innocuous words of comfort.

"Hardy needs to know. You'll tell him?"

"Sir, you may tell him yourself. The captain has returned."

Nearly an hour had passed since Hardy's first visit, and the incessant pounding of *Victory*'s cannon had gone nearly silent, although fighting could still be heard raging in other ships in the distance.

Once again she stepped aside so that Captain Hardy could speak to the admiral, then stepped up a few moments later to continue fanning Nelson at his request.

The captain and admiral shook hands once more.

"My lord," said Hardy. "I've sent someone to tell Admiral Collingwood the lamentable circumstances of your being wounded."

"Quite right to do so, Hardy. Quite right," Nelson said.

"His reserve failed him, my lord, and he shed tears to know that you have come to such grief." Hardy held on to Nelson's hand. "But, sir, you should know you've had a complete victory over the enemy. The crew of the *Redoubtable* boarded us briefly, but we annihilated them, and many of the enemy's ships are striking their colors."

Marguerite's heart lurched. *Was Darden safe?* He'd not been brought down as wounded, but that didn't mean his body had not been thrown—

She shook the thought out of her mind and concentrated on the meeting between Nelson and Hardy.

"How many of the enemy ships have been captured?" Nelson was asking.

"I'm not certain at present. At least fourteen or fifteen have surrendered."

Nelson disengaged his hand and dropped it back to his side in a disappointed motion. "That is well, but I bargained for twenty." He shut his eyes briefly before becoming restless. "*Anchor*, Hardy, we must anchor. We must ride out the bad weather."

Hardy looked at Marguerite with puzzled eyes. She shrugged lightly while continuing to fan her patient.

He replied gently, "I suppose, my lord, that Admiral Collingwood will now take upon himself the direction of affairs."

"Not while I live, I hope, Hardy!" Nelson exclaimed, and that moment attempted to raise himself on his makeshift bed. "No, you anchor."

The captain, overcome by the failing condition of his friend and leader, gave in. "Shall we make the signal, sir?"

"Yes, for if I live, I'll anchor. And while I retain my faculties, I'll retain command of the fleet, and thus, Hardy, you must carry out my orders. Although in a few minutes I shall be no more."

Nelson sank down again, the labor of sitting up too much for him.

Marguerite offered the admiral another cup of water, which he refused.

Nelson grabbed his friend's arm. "Don't throw me overboard, Hardy."

"Oh! No, certainly not."

"Then you know what to do with me. Take care of my dear Lady Hamilton, Hardy. Take care of poor Lady Hamilton."

Hardy nodded and assured him that he would.

"Kiss me, Hardy," Nelson commanded, to which the captain bent over and pressed his lips to his revered friend's brow.

Nelson sighed. "Now I am satisfied. Thank God, I have done my duty," he repeated.

Nearly in tears, Hardy stood silent in contemplation, then kissed the admiral's forehead again.

"Who's that?" Nelson voice was plaintive.

"It is Hardy, my lordship."

"God bless you, Hardy!"

Unable to control his emotions, the captain withdrew to the quarterdeck.

Everyone in the admiral's presence held a collective breath, knowing that with his good-byes said to the captain, he would not last long.

His remaining time was spent pleading for the country not to forget Lady Hamilton and his daughter Horatia, as well as steadily repeating his great sentiment, "Thank God, I have done my duty."

He soon grew speechless, so Marguerite called the surgeon back over from his attendance to other wounded sailors. Mr. Beatty felt Nelson's forehead and declared it cold, but almost as if to deny his unstated prognosis, Nelson opened his eyes and quickly shut them again. So the surgeon moved on again to take care of other patients.

Marguerite was certain she had stopped breathing herself, as she watched the great admiral's breathing grow more and more shallow. After not seeing his chest rise and fall whatsoever for several moments, she employed Mr. Beatty's technique of putting a small mirror to Nelson's mouth to see if it would fog the glass.

Nothing.

"Mr. Beatty!" she called, although it was unnecessary. The cries of anguish from the men gathered about their commander were enough to bring the doctor back and officially declare that Nelson had expired.

It was half past four. It had been less than five hours since the start of the battle and it was already concluded. England's greatest victory had brought with it her greatest loss.

24

Mr. Beatty assumed leadership in the care of Nelson's body. "Mr. Smith, Mr. Westemburg, we'll need to find Lord Nelson's hammock and wrap him in it."

"Mr. Beatty, excuse me," Marguerite said. "His lordship specifically asked Captain Hardy not to throw him overboard."

"But he has one with hangings made by his mistress. It's his special shroud."

"Yes, sir, I know. But he and the captain seemed to have a special understanding about it."

The surgeon grunted his disbelief in Marguerite's assertion, yet still sent Smith topside this time—since most danger was past—to find out the truth of the matter.

Mr. Smith returned with a confirmation that Marguerite was correct: Nelson was not to be buried at sea but instead taken back to London for a state funeral. A special coffin, made from a piece of the mainmast of the French flagship at the Battle of the Nile, had been presented to the admiral after the battle. Nelson had left the coffin in keeping with agents in London but, before leaving for Trafalgar, had had the history of it engraved on the coffin's lid. He told Hardy mere days ago that he thought he might have need of the coffin upon his return.

Mr. Beatty deliberated only a short time, while tapping his glasses against his own bloodied shirt, before deciding what to do, and enlisted Marguerite and both of his assistants to help him.

Since there was no lead on board to make a coffin, he decided to use a leaguer, the largest size cask on the ship, to hold the body. He had Marguerite cut the admiral's hair off so it could be sent to Emma Hamilton, and also asked Marguerite to dress him in whatever clean shirt she could find. She performed this task with greater melancholy than anything else she had done thus far. The mood on the orlop was somber at best, and few men were even speaking, much less laughing, singing, or shouting over their victory.

Meanwhile, the assistants were sent off to find an empty leaguer.

Once they returned with it, the four of them lifted Nelson's body and put it in the cask as gracefully as possible. The two assistants were then sent to the hold with two other sailors to find some casks of brandy, which were used to fill the leaguer and so preserve Nelson's body. A sentinel was posted next to the leaguer night and day to guard it.

Their grim task finished and the battle as good as over, Mr. Beatty invited his workers—including Marguerite—to his cabin to share some ale and rest awhile.

But there were more troubles brewing for the crew aboard *Victory*. For Nelson was not delirious when he so anxiously fretted about a storm.

And it was not just any storm.

It was a hurricane.

Nathaniel fancied he was a born pirate, given his success at capturing a small French merchant ship. She was carrying luxury items—magnificent fabrics, casks of fine wine, and a fine collection of rococo furniture—and was slowly making her way to parts unknown with her trove. *Wax Maiden* crept up out of a morning fog onto the unsuspecting ship and took her with little trouble. After plundering the ship, they shot through her sails and masts to disable her, and left the French crew aboard to drift until one of their allies could find them.

Nathaniel's men were overjoyed by the take, which would keep them all in ale and the gaming hells for a year, even with Nathaniel taking the lion's share.

A smart thing it was, not telling his new crew that he didn't actually have a letter of marque authorizing him to do any privateering. Now the men were so sated by their fresh kill that they'd do anything he asked of them.

He stood at the bow of his ship as it plowed along, his eyes closed against the considerable wind.

Finally, he was approaching his destiny.

"Mr. Ashby?" Nathaniel was interrupted in his reverie by his quartermaster. Mr. Watson was his only crew member who actually had sailing experience. He'd seen action years ago at some tiresome old battle with the French.

"Yes, Mr. Watson, what is it?"

"Sir, I think there's a storm brewing."

"So? Don't ships like this just ride them out?"

"Sometimes. I think this is a big one, though. Maybe even a hurricane. Sir, with this kind of load we're carrying, we should probably head back to shore. It'd be a shame to lose what we worked so hard to get."

Nathaniel would normally be outraged by an inferior telling him his business, but tonight was different. He *had* coordinated a great victory for his men, so he could afford to be magnanimous.

"Very well, tell the others. We'll dock for a few days to revictual and let them expend some of their exuberance, then we're off again. Tell them there's a bonus of a sovereign each for everyone who comes back."

Yes, Nathaniel Ashby was on the verge of a great, heroic adventure that would make the capture of the French merchant ship look like a meager fishing expedition. As Mr. Watson departed, Nathaniel was already imagining medals being looped over his neck.

❧ 25 ❧

Portsmouth, October 20, 1805. Claudette and William had been in Portsmouth more than a week. Daily they made visits to various naval officials and the local hospital to inquire about their missing niece, but no one knew anything. Their task was made doubly hard because they had no portrait of Marguerite to show anyone.

In a stroke of inspiration, Claudette suggested they visit nearby churches. Perhaps Marguerite had sought refuge at one for some reason.

"Refuge?" William questioned. "Refuge from what? Or whom?"

Claudette looked at him helplessly. "I don't know. But it's worth exploring."

"You realize it could take weeks to visit all the churches in the vicinity?"

"Whatever it takes, William. We have to find her."

So the pair rode from church to church during the day, inquiring of ministers and groundskeepers about their missing niece, and in the evenings pored over newspapers for some article that might give them a clue about her disappearance.

Even Claudette was on the verge of admitting defeat when they came upon yet another small parish church, a dilapidated structure about two miles away from Portsmouth Harbor. Storm clouds were gathering in the distance, promising a soaking rain later in the day.

The parson, a kindly man by the name of Langdon, furrowed

his eyebrows in thought. "You say she was bringing something for Lord Nelson on *Victory*? In fact, I do remember seeing her. I visit the docks regularly, you know, to spread the gospel to the lost who come in and out of England's harbors. Your niece was standing on the quay with her bags about her, trying to figure out how to find her wagon of goods. I recommended that she visit the storehouses at the harbor."

"Yes," Claudette interrupted. "We've been there, but no one remembers her."

The parson smiled gently. "No, I suppose no one would be remembered in the lunacy of that building. However, I saw her come back out. She disappeared briefly, then returned on top of what I presumed was her wagon of goods. She paid the driver, and one of the sailors standing about helped her carry everything aboard. I'm afraid I must tell you that she never left the ship."

"Never left? What do you mean?"

"She never came out. I believe *Victory* sailed with her still aboard."

Claudette gasped, and William put an arm around her to steady her.

"Impossible! Are you sure? Might you have turned away or been focused elsewhere and missed seeing her depart?"

Langdon's eyes were kind but certain. "No. I pay close attention to those who enter and depart ships, to be sure I get a chance to speak with everyone. Besides, your niece was very noticeable as one of the only females at the dock who was not a sailor's wife or an . . . unfortunate woman. Your niece sailed on *Victory* and is presumably still there."

Claudette sat down on one of the church's pews to fan herself. The parson quietly excused himself, murmuring that he would pray for Marguerite's safe return.

William sat next to her, stroking her hair. "At least we know now that she wasn't abducted or murdered by a highwayman somewhere."

"Small comfort, William. I promised Marguerite's mother I would always look out for her. And now she's off to *war* with England's greatest enemy. Possibly hundreds of miles from here."

"Marguerite is a grown woman. She chose her involvement in Pitt's scheme. There was nothing you could do."

"I know, I know, but now the agony of waiting is even worse. She's all alone in a ship full of rough sailors, with not a soul who cares about her. What must she be going through?"

"Come." William tugged on her hand. "Let's go back to the inn before it begins raining. We'll think overnight about what to do."

But that night their thoughts were preoccupied with the fierce storm that raged up against the coast. It didn't rain so much as it flooded to nearly biblical proportions. The cacophony of howling wind and gyrating water was deafening, punctuated only by the periodic crashing of uprooted trees and loose objects outside being flung furiously against the building. It was as though God had initiated a second flood, but they had not been chosen for the ark.

"William," Claudette whispered deep in the night. "Is Marguerite in this storm as well?"

William rolled over and kissed his wife's forehead. "I don't know, love, but you can be sure that Lord Nelson has things well in hand."

Claudette snuggled against him for warmth and comfort. "I hope so. For now he's not only England's greatest hope, but Marguerite's. And ours."

By morning the storm had reduced its wrath, but the rain continued to pour steadily for the next two days. During a break in the tempest, William took a drive to inspect damage. He returned with his opinion that the roads surrounding Portsmouth would probably be impassable for days.

"And I suspect the storm was of such magnitude that what we experienced was just a glancing blow. For anyone out in the ocean . . ." He let his words drop.

Claudette was too exhausted from sleeplessness and worry to respond, and went back to the letter she was writing to Marie Tussaud to let her know of their progress. But wordlessly the couple was of the same mind.

They would remain in Portsmouth until *Victory* returned with Marguerite. Alive or dead.

* * *

There was no rest for either the victorious British, or the defeated French and Spanish ships, the hulks of which were being lashed to British ships for towing in. Unfortunately for the fleet, Admiral Collingwood overrode Nelson's final command that they anchor in anticipation of the brutal storm, and so for three days they endured another battle, one to keep their ships out on open water without colliding into one another nor riding inland to be smashed against the shoals.

For Marguerite, the chaos of the battle paled as compared to the turmoil and fear that coursed through *Victory* in dealing with the heavenly outburst. Many of the ships in the fleet, including *Victory*, were badly damaged, with masts blown off, holes blown into their sides, and inoperable steering mechanisms. The storm not only pummeled the ships further, but prevented any repair work from occurring.

During and after the battle, carpenters and sailmakers alike had been frantically trying to repair their ships while afloat, but most of the sea craft needed dry docking to effectively restore them. All of the crews' focus was now on simple survival: keeping the ships on course and avoiding more damage. Marguerite overheard a sailor say, "A beady-eyed Spaniard I can face, but God's fury makes me weep like a baby."

As she prayed for safe deliverance, she reflected with irony on the rough voyage from Greenock to Dublin in which Philipsthal had been killed. My, how that now seemed like just a pleasure voyage compared to this. As she sat huddled in the sick berth, changed back into a set of her own clothes once again, she resolved that if she survived this storm, she would never, ever, *ever* board another ship as long as she lived.

Not even at Darden's insistence, if he was even still alive.

26

"Sir, I insist that I'm not deserving of this honor." Darden stood at attention in Captain Hardy's quarters, where his superior was dashing off multiple memoranda, letters, and ship's log entries at his writing table, which had been placed back in the center of his cabin once they were through the worst of the storm.

"Nonsense, Hastings. Your quick thinking preserved Nelson for us a little longer, and was absolute brilliance in drawing fire away from the other men until we could get our bearings after our ships collided. The nation is grateful. A promotion to post captain is the least that can be done. That will entitle you to a medal, and a greater share of prize money, too." Hardy added his signature to a document before him and scratched some notes on a page already filled with scribbles. "Although I admit that I would have never thought to bring those silly figures topside prior to anything happening to Nelson or me."

Darden continued to stare straight ahead, his mind awhirl at the reward being given to him. He'd no thought of promotion when he boarded *Victory* to chase down the French and Spanish. He needed time to think about how such a promotion would affect his other crucial work.

More importantly, what will Marguerite think?

"Sir, it was my duty to help England win this war, and I'm thankful that I could be present for her glorious triumph."

"And you did your duty. Thank you, Lieutenant. By the way, Collingwood is sending *Pickle* back right away with the news of our victory and our unfortunate loss of Nelson. I'll have the schooner drawn up alongside *Victory* to pick up mail and some other papers. See to it that Mrs. Ashby is aboard *Pickle*, will you? No sense keeping the poor woman on board any longer than we have to. It's too bad she can't be counted as crew. For her work with the wax figures and her clear head down in the orlop, the woman deserves promotion to captain as well." Hardy laughed at his own joke.

Darden knew his grin was foolish, but he couldn't help it. "I'll be sure to extend your felicitations, Captain."

"Right. Now in the meantime we need to repair *Victory* as best we can. I'd say she's been very much mauled, eh? I want you to ensure she's got enough mast to get us home."

Darden saluted again and departed, still amazed by his stroke of good fortune.

He sought Marguerite out at the first opportunity to tell her of her impending transfer and Hardy's admiration of her. She blushed prettily and demurred at the captain's praise.

"But I was there, Marguerite, and saw with my own two eyes what you did. You'll not play modest with me." He brought his scarred hand up and cradled her cheek. Marguerite closed her eyes and brought her own hand up to cover his, running her palm over the weals and hardened tissue.

"What is this?" she asked.

"Isn't it obvious? An old injury." He pulled his hand away, but she held fast to it, bringing it to her lips and kissing it gently. She used the fingers of her other hand to trace the raised ridges down around his hand and alongside his little finger.

"But how did it happen?"

"A foolish accident, really. I managed to get burned while assisting with the firing of a cannon at the Battle of Cape St. Vincent."

"I see. I find it hard to believe that Lieutenant Hastings would ever act foolishly in the heat of battle." She smiled at him, lightly tapped his foot with her own, then brought his hand to her lips again, placing feathery kisses along his disfigured finger.

The all-consuming heat that overcame him when he was around her began radiating upward from where her foot had met his. He never felt as undisciplined as he did around this splendid creature.

And what would happen now? Was her ardor for him just a result of shared hardship? Soon she'd be aboard *Pickle* and returning to her previous life, whereas he had just taken the next step in his naval career and had much to accomplish that would only be complicated by a woman waiting for him.

She must have been of the same mind, for although she still held his hand she stopped kissing it to say, "I suppose we are saying farewell now?"

"I believe our paths are different, yes." Was he mistaken? The brave and fierce Marguerite Ashby wasn't about to cry, was she? The woman had not spilled a single tear since he found her in Nelson's cabin.

She lowered her face so he could no longer read her expression. "Yes, Lieutenant, I suppose you're right. We're on different paths. I'll return to my comfortable life modeling wax with Madame Tussaud, and you'll continue riding the high seas as a gallant officer. How many more ladies in distress will you comfort, I wonder?" She looked up at him with a smile, but tears were running down her face.

He knew he shouldn't, but Darden folded her in his arms one last time, the unwanted heat be damned.

Brax's grin at his good news also bordered on idiotic.

"Lieutenant Selwyn, I have a special assignment for you," said Admiral Collingwood.

"Sir?"

"I need to send someone back to deliver the news about our success, and of course about our great loss, to the Admiralty Board in London. I've decided to send *Pickle* with this singular honor." Collingwood grimaced in his chair and shifted his injured leg into a more comfortable position.

Brax said nothing and remained impassive. This was a great honor indeed, and one that would surely result in a promotion for the lieutenant in charge of *Pickle*, John Lapenotière. But Lapenotière was extraordinary only in that he was so unremarkable. A feeble officer at best, he had little skill in commanding a ship. And why entrust this mission to a schooner that was the second-smallest ship in the fleet? Why not a larger frigate?

As if reading his thoughts, the admiral said, "Lieutenant Lapenotière once saved a ship I was on, and I promised to do him a service if ever the opportunity arose. That time is now. However, although I am giving Lapenotière this mission, I'm not convinced that he has the sailing skills to return to London as quickly as possible. That is why I've called for you, Selwyn. Although Lapenotière will have the credit for delivering the news, I want you to have overall command of *Pickle*, to ensure it gets back with all speed. Assuredly, Lieutenant, the Royal Navy will be deeply indebted to you for this quiet service. I will see to it myself."

Brax was stunned. Would he get his promotion just by conducting a single-ship race back to England? The simplicity of it all left him speechless. Slowly, a grin stretched across his face.

"One more thing, Lieutenant. There are prisoners aboard *Pickle*. I want them sent to the *Revenge*. You'll also need to go around the fleet and pick up letters from men to their families. And finally, there's a woman aboard *Victory* who needs to be escorted back. See to it that she returns safely. Captain Hardy asked me for this special favor."

Brax saluted Collingwood smartly and left the admiral's cabin.

He ignored his fellow officers who asked why Collingwood wanted to see him and set about preparing to transfer to the *Pickle*. So overjoyed was he that he sang at the top of his lungs for hours until *Pickle* pulled up alongside *Royal Sovereign* to pick him up.

"Rule Britannia!
Britannia rule the waves.
Britons never,
never, never shall be slaves."

Yes, Britannia ruled the waves, and Brax was now ruler of his own destiny. He didn't need anyone else's help. Captain Braxton

Charles Selwyn. He'd have to write to his father about it the minute they landed in Portsmouth.

Brax was anxious to begin the journey back to England. He had ensured the transfer of prisoners to *Revenge*, including survivors who had been picked up from the French ship *Achille*, which exploded late in the battle four days ago. *Royal Sovereign* was a mile away when the ship combusted, but the booming noise could be heard even over the lingering fighting going on. And of course the leaping flames drew every eye from both fleets.

The survivors had been a sorry lot, half-naked and badly burned. But one survivor in particular was wearing on Brax's nerves. This was one Jeannette, who had followed her husband on board the *Achille*. She lost him in the fire that raged on the ship. Unable to find him, and finding herself trapped by flames, she eventually divested herself of her clothing and tumbled into the sea through a gun port. The woman found a piece of cork and was floating there when Lapenotière and his men found her.

Brax admitted to a certain admiration for the woman's pluck, but the crew on board *Pickle* adopted her as a kind of mascot, offering her silks, muslins, stockings, and other goods they had obtained from a Spanish prize ship, so she could fashion herself a more becoming costume than the uniform a purser could provide. All the men doted on Jeannette now, to the point of neglecting their own duties.

Why would a man lead his wife out into battle? Brax wondered in disgust. *And this woman is distracting the crew beyond reason.*

Although Brax delighted in a woman's company in almost every conceivable situation, he was most disapproving of a woman being trapped inside a man-of-war with hundreds of other men. He was happy to see the back of Jeannette as she and the other French survivors were relocated to the *Revenge*.

So after the *Revenge* transfers, he'd led the ship around to collect as much mail as possible from other ships in the vicinity, finally stopping at *Victory* to pick up yet another cursed woman for the men to lavish attention on.

He watched from topside with arms folded across his chest as the launch from *Victory* was winched up to *Pickle*. At least this was the last errand and he could finally get Lapenotière off on his mission.

As the launch drew even with the ship and the crew helped the woman and the bags of mail onto the deck, Brax blinked in disbelief.

It can't be.

But it was. He'd recognize that proud and erect carriage anywhere, even if it was clothed in a dress that belonged in a burn pile. Once she was on board with her bags around her, he strode over and stopped the sailor who was picking them up to stow.

"I'll assist the lady."

This time it was Marguerite's turn to blink in surprise.

"Lieutenant Selwyn? Is that really you? How wonderful! But I thought you were aboard *Royal Sovereign*."

"And I thought you were headed back to Dublin." He lifted her rust-stained hand and put his lips to it.

Marguerite threw back that mass of hair, still stunning even if it was a bit unkempt, and laughed.

"Lieutenant, if I told you my story, you would never believe it."

"I am ready to believe anything you say, Mrs. Ashby. I insist that you have supper with me in my quarters so I can hear this amazing story."

And so every evening of the journey back, Brax invited Marguerite to his quarters to dine. She was weary from her ordeal, but he admired her pluck for having volunteered to stay aboard *Victory* to help the surgeon. Although if she had transferred to *Pickle* as originally planned, he'd have had her company sooner. And Darden wouldn't have had it at all.

She mentioned little about Lieutenant Hastings, other than to say he'd made extra effort to ensure the journey was as comfortable as possible for her, but Brax didn't like the glow in her eyes as she said it.

But Darden was on *Victory* for the foreseeable future, and the lovely Marguerite was with him here on *Pickle*. Their journey passed swiftly for Brax, not only because they were physically racing to shore, but because he was enthralled to have the little waxworker almost completely to himself. She gradually relaxed in his company, and soon they were bantering like old sea dogs, swapping stories about the battle and about their own personal lives. She shared with him deeply personal stories about her twice-over widowhood, and he was enthralled with her unstated bravery in both situations. Combined with what must have been a serious well of intestinal fortitude in the battle, Brax couldn't help his high regard for Marguerite, despite his objection to women aboard ships.

Brax loved all women in his light and easy way, but this woman was . . . different.

For certain he could see why even taciturn Hastings was attracted to this woman. He was, wasn't he? Hard to tell what was going on behind that scowling visage.

Well, Lieutenant Hastings, you got the glory for being in the heat of battle aboard Nelson's flagship, but I'm the one who earned a captaincy. And I also plan to win the lady's hand. She's more worth fighting for than a thousand French and Spanish ships.

Within a couple of days of Marguerite's departure, Darden was already cursing his mulishness. The importance of all his future plans seemed infantile now that Marguerite was gone. He should have done something. Offered to escort her back to Dublin. Told her he'd request a shore posting. Asked her to marry him, for heaven's sake.

And now it was too late. She'd forget him as soon as she returned to her old life, and some country squire would come along to claim her hand, move her to his estate, and that would be that.

Well, there was nothing to be done for it now. Best to try to forget her, too. If Horatio Nelson could hold fast to his sense of duty until the very end, well then, so could Darden Hastings.

PART SEVEN

London

❧ 27 ❧

Portsmouth, November 4, 1805. "Sweetheart, come quickly. There's a ship docking. It's not big enough to be *Victory*, but it's definitely a naval ship. We should be able to get some news." William rushed into their room after taking a walk.

Claudette dropped the letter from Marie Tussaud she was reading and scrambled to put on shoes and a bonnet. By the time she and William reached the sloop, goods and crew members were spilling out of it. To one side, an officer was already jumping into a post chaise and shouting orders for the driver to take him to London without delay.

In no time, they heard the news from men milling about. A great triumph had been had over the French and Spanish combined fleet, yet woe to England, for their great leader, Nelson, was gone.

"Where is *Victory*?" William demanded of a nearby sailor.

"She'll be in soon. A few weeks, maybe. She took a lot of damage and had to make a stop at Gibraltar. Torn up terrible she was." The seaman moved on.

Claudette trembled. "A lot of damage? What do you think that means? I can't bear to wait weeks to know what happened, William. My nerves are frayed as it is. We must—"

William grabbed her elbow and pointed at the gangway. "Look. Do my eyes deceive me?"

Strolling onto land on the arm of a neatly uniformed officer was Marguerite. Her dress looked like it belonged in a charity box, but other than that, she seemed healthy and whole. She was gazing at the young officer and laughing at some joke he was telling.

"Marguerite! Marguerite!" Claudette couldn't help shouting across the quay like an ill-bred hoyden.

Marguerite heard her name and turned her head to find the source of the shouting. Seeing Claudette and William standing together, she tugged on the officer's arm and dragged him over. She dropped his arm to throw herself at them. Claudette grabbed the girl in a mix of tears, hugs, kisses, and laughter. William maintained better composure, and shook the hand of the officer.

Claudette held the young woman out at arm's length. "Marguerite, we've been frantic with worry over you. How in the world did you end up staying on *Victory*? Did you meet Lord Nelson? What a sight for worried eyes you are. Were you frightened much? Did you sail through the hurricane? We've got to get you changed into better clothes."

"Aunt Claudette, I've looked far more dreadful than this over the last few weeks, believe me. May I introduce my friend, Lieutenant Brax Selwyn, to you? Lieutenant Selwyn captained the ship that returned me home, and was very good company for my weary soul. Were you not, Lieutenant?" Marguerite looked at the officer fondly.

"My dear Mrs. Ashby, to the contrary, it was *you* who provided the delightful companionship. The voyage was pure bliss with your niece aboard, Lord and Lady Greycliffe. She's told me much about you, and she is indeed fortunate to have you waiting for her."

"We thank you, Lieutenant, for taking care of our niece. We are greatly indebted to you. But now it's time to take her home." William was swiftly concluding the meeting.

Marguerite offered Brax her hand, and he bent over it gallantly. "Mrs. Ashby, I do hope we have an opportunity to meet again. Will you be going straightaway to Dublin?"

"No. I know Uncle William and Aunt Claudette will want me to spend time at Hevington, and besides, I need a rest before thinking about another sea voyage, short as it may be from Bristol to Dublin." Actually, she didn't plan to return to Dublin at all, and had an idea in mind for how to avoid it, but that could wait.

"Hevington, then Dublin. I'll remember." He shook hands warmly with William again and walked away, whistling the national anthem.

"Aunt Claudette, I have so much to tell you, but first I would truly like a genuine bath. One with fresh, warm water. Oh, and I have a letter to post from one of the sailors on *Victory* to his wife. I could have put it in *Pickle*'s mail bag, but I wanted to take care of it personally. I owe the poor soul that."

Within a week Marguerite was settled back at Hevington as though she'd never left. The servants, glad to see her so confident and in high spirits since the long-past days of her bereavement, welcomed her warmly and fussed about her constantly. The Greycliffe children were in awe of her adventurous tales, which were so fantastic they could not quite believe they were true. Little Bitty followed her around with a sketch pad and pencil to capture a drawing of their very own heroine.

Soon friends and families from neighboring estates heard the news of Marguerite's escapades, and Hevington was filled every evening with guests hanging on her every word over the dining table. It made the Christmas holiday tolerable, given the nation's general melancholy over Nelson's death, and Marguerite's new status was a far cry from the days when the neighbors considered her a bit of an unfortunate.

It was inconceivable to everyone that she had served practically as a crew member aboard *Victory*, alongside the great but lamented Admiral Nelson. Marguerite's story soon made its way into local newspapers, and eventually into a tiny corner of the *London Gazette,* next to an article about Napoleon repealing the calendar of the French Republic that had been instituted by Robespierre during the Reign of Terror.

The papers also reported on Nelson's funeral, which was held on January 9, 1806, with great pomp and circumstance in London. A procession of royalty, nobility, politicians, and military men stretched all the way from Whitehall to St. Paul's Cathedral, where he was to be buried. He was carried from Greenwich up the River Thames to Whitehall in the coffin given to him after the Battle of the Nile. At Whitehall the admiral was transferred onto an elaborate, open funeral carriage, carved and decorated to look like the bow and stern of *Victory*.

People traveled to London from across the country to line the route to St. Paul's Cathedral. Many of them, eager to catch a glimpse of the hero's passing hearse, paid handsomely for viewing positions inside the upper floors of homes along the way.

As was customary, the funeral itself was attended only by men, with not even Nelson's wife, Frances, nor Emma Hamilton, present.

The nation had already been in mourning for the past month, ever since Lieutenant Lapenotière had arrived in London on November 6 with his sorrowful news. The king declared December 5 to be a national day of thanksgiving for the victory at what he formally declared the Battle of Trafalgar. And although Marguerite and the Greycliffes joined their fellow countrymen in this day of gratitude to the Almighty, it was tinged with grief.

But life in England had to resume, for, after all, Bonaparte was still anxiously sniffing at her shores, despite the thrashing he had received in the open waters.

And Marguerite knew it was time for her own life to resume. Two months had passed since she'd last been held in Darden's tight clasp, and not a single letter had arrived from him. She wondered if he had attended Nelson's funeral. Surely Brax had. Was Darden back out to sea? She hadn't spoken of him at all to her family, even to Claudette, in an effort to keep his memory sealed away in her heart where she wouldn't have to share it.

She tried to muster up some righteous anger toward Darden for turning her aside so easily, but found she couldn't. After so many weeks aboard *Victory*, she now understood the man's passion for duty, and how it could override everything else.

Marguerite sighed and picked up her pen again, looking at the crumpled pieces of parchment on the desk around her. She returned to her fifth try of a letter to Madame Tussaud.

I am happy to tell you that I am well and have no cause for complaint as to my health or constitution. Whatever you have heard in Dublin with regard to the great triumph on the seas by Nelson is probably true. And if I know you well, madame, you already have in mind a tableau to mark his great achievement.

We were able to use the Nelson wax figure to deflect the attention of the Redoubtable*'s sharpshooters long enough for* Victory*'s crew to gather sufficient strength to repulse the enemy entirely after our two ships collided. Captain Hardy said the figure probably preserved Nelson for the nation a little longer, and I am grateful to have performed this small service for England.*

As for my return to Dublin, I confess that I am heartily sick of ships, storms, and oceans, and the thought of any of the three is a revolting one indeed.

However, dear friend, I do greatly miss you and my life in wax portraiture. I pray Joseph has been your good assistant, as always, and also that the exhibition continues to do well under your good management. I should like to put forth a proposal to you: What would you think of shipping some figures to me and letting me start a permanent location to display whichever figures you have no current use for? I can send them back to you when you wish to use them again. I can make additional figures by your direction. Both collections would stay fresh and updated, and you could simultaneously collect entrance fees on both sides of the Irish Sea.

What would Marie's reaction be to her proposal? One thing was certain—Marguerite couldn't endure another sailing.

The last month had been a bit of a setback for Nathaniel. After returning to port he'd gone home to present his mother with a considerable length of heavily embroidered linen, a plum from the merchant ship. She'd looked at him as though he'd offered her a dead rat.

"No letter of marque and still you took a ship? Nathaniel, had you not been fortunate enough to overpower the other ship's captain, he could have cut your throat and the Admiralty Board would have looked the other way. Son, you're behaving without even the sense God gave a rooster. You should be following my guidance and looking for an appropriate young lady to marry."

Not even Nathaniel's presentation of the value of his share of the take had impressed his mother, although at least his father ran an appreciative eye over his account book.

Fortunate enough? Nathaniel fumed later over a glass of port. Why didn't the woman understand that it was his skill that had landed him the French ship? And that small victory was another divine sign that he was meant for his other, greater purpose.

He had been further taken aback when his mother shoved a newspaper under his nose, and he learned that Marguerite Ashby was a local heroine in Kent, having provided a wax figure of Nelson to the navy, putting it up on deck herself to deflect sharpshooter fire away from the men on *Victory*.

How had she gotten aboard a man-of-war? he wondered. Well, the article explained his mother's stormy mood.

He read further that Marguerite had returned to her relatives at Hevington.

Wait for me there, my sweet, while I attain my own momentous success. Together we'll be crowned with laurels and live together in perpetual bliss.

Before departing Ash House, he'd made a quick and satisfying visit to Polly's room, and afterwards gave her the linen he'd initially intended for his mother. The wench showed proper appreciation by kissing him deeply, which aroused him yet again, so he gave her another hour to continue paying her respects to him.

After docking, it had taken him longer to round up his new crew than he'd thought it would. At least Mr. Watson was loyal. A couple of the men had died in drunken brawls, some were back in jail again on other offenses, while others had simply run away with their take, figuring they'd met their obligation to Nathaniel Ashby.

He and Mr. Watson secured as many of the men as they could, then Nathaniel made another trip to Marshalsea prison. He'd found men by not only paying their debts, but by also convincing them they'd be following in the footsteps of the lately departed Lord Nelson.

Fortunately, once again no one asked him about his letter of marque.

So now they were stealthily approaching the area between Dunkerque and Calais, looking for an obscure garrison he'd heard was tucked away here. Nathaniel told Mr. Watson that he was actually working secretly for Mr. Pitt, to destroy enemy morale by picking off its smaller garrisons one by one. So carried on the tide of Nelson's victory against the hated Frogs was Mr. Watson that he never questioned Nathaniel's story.

See, Mother? My men believe in my great genius for seamanship, and you should have, as well.

Which reminded him that he was several days behind on his journal, the one he planned to show Marguerite when they were finally reunited. It detailed all of his mind's workings, from his various plans and ideas, to his triumphs over his scoffers. He kept the journal locked up in a secret drawer away from his regular ship's log. It wouldn't do for just anyone to come across it. He was saving it for Marguerite, to help increase her devotion to him.

The December night air was frigid as they approached the coastline of France. He could swear the same temperature felt at least twenty degrees chillier out on the sea. His men grumbled a bit, too, but not enough to give him cause for concern.

Surely the freezing weather would assist him in his element of surprise, for the French wouldn't expect a lone English ship to creep up on them. A surprise ambush had worked perfectly well on the French merchant ship, and so it should work equally well on a poorly manned garrison. And one Englishman was worth ten Frogs, anyway.

Mr. Watson motioned toward what looked to be their target. They stayed hidden in a nearby cove until just before daybreak, then sailed out at full speed toward the garrison's dock. A lone, rumpled-looking soldier came out to greet them, rubbing his eyes and yawning.

"*Bonjour, monsieur* Englishman, 'ow may I 'elp you?" the soldier called up to where Nathaniel stood on his top deck.

This was not a proper reaction at all. France and England were at war. Didn't the fool see *Wax Maiden*'s British colors flying off the stern? Where was his fear? Why weren't the other soldiers dashing about in panic? Perhaps he'd not heard of their crushing defeat at Trafalgar yet to realize their imminent doom.

The cold air carried Nathaniel's voice readily, so he barely had to raise his voice as he replied in French. "We're claiming this garrison for Great Britain. I'm sending a deputation down to accept your captain's surrender. Do not try to escape. All of our cannon and guns are trained on your barracks, prepared to destroy you if you resist." There, that was a courageous speech that should show them just who they were dealing with.

Instead, the soldier stood there, blinking as if making a calculation, then threw his head back and laughed in the sarcastic, condescending way that only a Frenchman can.

"Oh, *oui,* monsieur, we tremble like *petites filles* tied to their mothers' apron strings over your—what is it, five?—great cannon. I shall wake my commander instantly to let him know that the entire British navy has arrived to secure its prize."

The soldier turned casually on his heel back to his commander's quarters.

The insolence, the utter cheek, Nathaniel thought angrily.

He heard some of the crew on deck begin to mumble uncertainly about their mission. He curtly told them to keep their silence until he had negotiated the garrison's surrender.

He didn't have to wait long for the soldier to return. He did so along with his commanding officer and ten other soldiers armed with carbine rifles.

The commanding officer was even more haughty than his subordinate.

"*Mon capitaine*, I am *le commandant* here. My lieutenant says you've arrived to capture our humble little camp. Is this really true?"

The men with him sniggered.

Nathaniel raised himself up to full importance.

"It is indeed true. And you would do well to watch your impertinent tone before a representative of the British navy."

The garrison commander rubbed his chin as though considering Nathaniel's words.

"I see, I see. Tell me, *mon capitaine*, does the British navy give its ships such fierce and battle-worthy names as *Wax Maiden*? For we French do have a way with soft and supple ladies. Are you sure you're not carrying a shipment of—what do you English say—*doxies*, to visit us?"

The men behind the commander now burst fully into laughter. This was not going according to plan. Not at all.

"I've no time for your brilliant Gallic wit, sir. Do you plan to surrender peacefully, or should we take you by force?"

"By force, monsieur? And how do you and your dainty ship and your equally effeminate crew propose to do this?"

"Are you perchance blind? Do you not see my ready cannon waiting to fire upon your garrison?"

The French commander slowly turned to look at his quarters, then turned back just as leisurely toward Nathaniel's ship.

"Perchance it is not me who is blind. What do you have there, measly little six pounders? You could hardly hit us standing here, much less reach all the way to the buildings. However, *mon capitaine*"—the commander gave a signal to the men around him—"these soldiers are highly skilled sharpshooters, and at my command they will each pick one man off your deck. I suggest that you run along home now, and leave fighting to real military men."

The commander's soldiers raised their guns in unison, rested them on their shoulders, and peered down the length of the barrels.

Without waiting for Nathaniel's orders, Mr. Watson instructed the men to turn the ship around and flee.

No, this had not gone according to plan at all.

☙ 28 ☙

Marguerite's filthy clothing from *Victory* was ceremoniously burned on Hevington's front lawn, and now her room at Hevington was filled with new dresses, hats, gloves, and shoes. Claudette had insisted on providing her niece with a yet another whole new wardrobe, rather than asking Marie Tussaud to ship her things to Kent.

"Besides," Claudette told her, "you deserve a reward for what you've done and what you've been through."

After hours spent with dressmakers, who plied her with bolts of exotic fabrics, making her nostalgic for her dollmaking days, she and Claudette decided upon designs for several day dresses, a negligee, and two fancy dress gowns, as well as an assortment of hair ribbons, hats, and chemises. Claudette was insistent on the ball gowns, certain that Marguerite would be much in demand in London when she returned.

For Marie Tussaud had approved her plan to start a new exhibit there, sending her letter after letter of instructions on what to do in setting up a new location. Marguerite shook her head bemusedly, for hadn't she helped Marie with the setup of Dublin? Nevertheless, it was Marie's property, and she followed her mentor's directions exactly.

Marguerite sat at the chinoiserie desk in her room, which was stacked with piles of papers and plans regarding the new exhibit.

The desk's messiness complemented the heaps of clothing bursting forth from trunks and her armoire and hanging from every available hook in the room. A multitude of apparel bags and boxes, some filled and some empty of their garments, were scattered across the floor.

Claudette's personal maid, Jolie, tapped on the door and entered, her disapproval of Marguerite's disheveled quarters plain on her face. "Mistress Marguerite, Lady Greycliffe sent me to find you. She's in the parlor, entertaining a visitor she wants you to meet."

"Thank you, Jolie."

Jolie lingered at the door, fidgeting. "Mistress, may I help you?"

"Help me? I'm not sure what you mean." Marguerite knew exactly what she meant. Jolie was meticulous in maintaining Claudette's wardrobe, one of the primary reasons Claudette had hired the maid away from her previous position at a hotel in the city of Versailles prior to the Revolution.

The condition of my room must be making her deranged.

"Your room, madame, is very . . . ah . . . is in some disarray. Your lovely gowns should be wrapped in tissue. Perhaps I can tidy up for you."

"Is it that bad? I hadn't noticed, Jolie. But I suppose if it really bothers you, I could really use the help." She winked at the maid. "Besides, I'll be leaving for London soon so I suppose I need to put an eye toward packing."

Marguerite left her room in Jolie's competent hands to organize while she hurried to the ground floor to find Claudette. As she entered the parlor, she saw Claudette talking to a man in a uniform. A dark blue and white uniform. The sight of the uniform with its gleaming brass buttons momentarily blinded her, and sent her stomach fluttering.

Darden? she thought tremulously.

"Mrs. Ashby, how delightful to see you again," said a warm, familiar voice.

Not Darden's.

It was Brax Selwyn bending over her hand.

"You seem disappointed to see me. I hope that's not true." Brax was at his charming best. "I should have to jump into the River Medway if I thought the sight of me caused you distress."

Marguerite mentally quelled her jellied innards and produced a weak smile. "No, of course not, Lieutenant. How lovely of you to visit. I suppose you and Aunt Claudette have gotten reacquainted?"

Claudette's face was pensive, as though she were trying to figure out the state of things without revealing her own confusion.

"Yes, Lieutenant Selwyn was just telling me about Lord Nelson's funeral, which he attended. I suppose he'll want to tell you about it himself. Edward! Darling, no! Not in the house."

Her son came scampering into the room, a trail of mud tracks behind him and one of the family's bullmastiffs at his heels.

"But, Mama, look what Cicero found!" The boy pointed at the dog's jaws, which held a wildly frightened squirrel in them. The dog sat down and thumped his tail, pleased to present his gift.

"We don't allow wild animals in the house. You know that. Take Cicero outside."

At that moment Little Bitty entered to see what all the commotion was about. At the sight of Cicero's trophy, she emitted a screech at a volume with which only little girls are gifted.

"Mama! That's my pet squirrel, Baby! He's hurting him!" The girl burst into loud, noisy tears. Edward tried to deny it over her sobs. Cicero looked confused.

Claudette had gone from elegant lady of the house to harried governess in mere seconds. With a quick apology to Marguerite and their guest, she hastened out of the room with children and dog to resolve the crisis outdoors.

With the door closed, Marguerite was alone in utter silence with Brax. Even the floor clock's subdued ticking seemed clamorous in the stillness between them.

Brax cleared his throat. "Lovely children. How many do the Greycliffes have?"

"Three. It's not always like this. Wait, what am I saying? It *is* actually always like this. Hevington is a home of great joy and . . . enthusiasm."

Brax laughed. "So I see. You must take pleasure in living here."

Marguerite sat down, inviting Brax to sit in a nearby chair.

"I've always thought of Hevington as a retreat. A place to clear my mind during the more tumultuous periods of my life."

"And is this one of those times? Even with Trafalgar behind you?"

"It was, but soon I'll be heading for London."

"London? Not Dublin?"

"No, Madame Tussaud and I have agreed to establish a second waxworks, which I will operate in London."

A smile slowly spread across Brax's face. "Well, that is just splendid, indeed. How fortuitous for me that I will be posted at the Admiralty while waiting for my promo—while waiting for my next posting. My heart can barely contain itself to know that you will be nearby. Already it's as if I'm floating on air."

Marguerite permitted a small smile in return. "Brax the Light-hearted, I suppose?"

"From your lips, any name sounds sweeter than the mellowest of wines, madam."

She shook her head and changed the subject. "What brings you to Kent, sir? Have you Royal Navy business here? On your way to Dover, perhaps?"

"Alas, no, I am a free man on leave at the moment. I went to my parents' estate near Chichester since I haven't seen them in some months, and remembered you mentioning your own family's estate. Since we spent so much companionable time together on *Pickle*, I didn't think you'd mind a visit."

"Of course I don't."

"But more importantly, I was rather hoping you might be happy to see me."

"And I am, Lieutenant."

"Brax, please."

"And I am happy to see you, Brax."

He pursed his lips. "Your eyes said something else entirely when you first saw me."

"Don't be silly. I was merely surprised to find you at Hevington."

"All right, I accept your explanation, mostly because I want desperately to believe you are enraptured by my arrival, and not because I'm actually convinced by your explanation. No no"—he held up his hands against her protest—"please, no more clarification necessary. We've far more important matters to discuss."

"Such as?"

"Such as when do you plan to depart for London, and have you yet secured an escort for your trip? Someone who understands and appreciates your fine artistry? Who would personally run through any greedy highwaymen?"

"Well, I hadn't realized I needed an escort, since I was planning to go by public coach if Uncle William did not have time to take me. But you're perhaps suggesting that I need a personal bodyguard who appreciates my person as well as my safety. Would you happen to know where I can find such a man?"

Brax stood and placed his right hand over his heart. "Madam, I am your most devoted servant. Never will you find a man more willing to lay down his life to protect your exquisite and charming perfection." He made a bow with his hand still over his heart, adding a flourish with his left hand.

"Nor, Sir Brax the Lighthearted, will I find one more passionately absurd."

He looked up from the bowed position he still held. "It is your presence that makes me so."

How difficult it was not to like this man! Full of mirth and not a care in the world. And his attentions were obviously exaggerated and thereby not intimidating. Unlike Paul de Philipsthal's professions of love. She shuddered inwardly.

Of Darden she refused to think.

"Sir Brax, I accept your offer. However, I don't plan on departing for London for another week. Will you still be available for service then?"

Brax stood up. "My dearest Mrs. Ashby—may I call you Marguerite now that we are to travel together once more?—at your command I will ask the Royal Navy to cease all its maritime maneuvers against Bonaparte, until all assistance can be rendered for your own personal mission."

"How highly the first lord of the Admiralty must think of me."

"Yes, of course he does. You must hold this in the strictest confidence, but I've been told that he thinks more of you than he does his own mother."

"Well, that makes me highly regarded indeed. Tell me, Sir Brax, since you plan to serve as my personal knight, have you found any lodgings in town?"

"Not yet, but I'm sure there's an inn nearby, run by a lonely widow who will have pity upon a poor officer of the Royal Navy. Especially one who has seen such recent action with Lord Nelson."

"She won't be able to resist your considerable charms, I'm sure."

"Alas, it is only the dear person before me now who seems immune to my earnest supplications."

Before Marguerite could respond, the door to the parlor banged open again. Claudette entered, mud spattered on the front of her dress and tendrils of hair falling from her coif. "Edward, I told you I wouldn't—oh! Lieutenant, I didn't realize you were still here. My apologies." Claudette attempted to prod some of her unruly curls back under her hair ribbon. "It does seem to be getting on in the afternoon, doesn't it? Lieutenant, won't you stay for supper? I'm sure my niece would be pleased with your company, if she hasn't asked you to dine with us already?" Claudette looked at Marguerite expectantly.

Marguerite bent her head and bit her lip, trying not to laugh at her aunt's obvious attempt to discern what her relationship was with Brax.

"No, Aunt Claudette, I'd not gotten around to it yet."

Brax piped up brightly, "I've no doubt that was where our conversation was turning next, Lady Greycliffe, and I accept your kind offer with great happiness."

And so Brax supped with the Greycliffes that night, and every night until Marguerite was ready for departure. Brax's utterly charming nature even won over William, and each night the two men would leave the women after dining, to retreat to his study for brandy and to discuss Napoleon's troop movements against Russia and Austria, which had culminated in his recent decisive battle victories against both countries at Austerlitz. Great Britain was part of an alliance involving these two nations and Sweden, and the defeat meant the collapse of their coalition.

Sometimes Marguerite and Claudette joined the men for political conversation, but more often they moved into the library to read or embroider. Marguerite refused to be drawn into questioning by Claudette, saying only that Brax had been present to see the Nelson and Hardy wax figures onto a wagon for shipment to Portsmouth, and he had escorted her safely home.

"But, darling," Claudette protested. Again. "He seems a nice young man. And very taken with you. Are you sure there's no hope for a courtship with him?"

"Brax is mostly taken with himself, I'm afraid. And I'm certain that all he wants is a flirtation."

Claudette shook her head once more. "I don't know. I think he has serious intentions toward you. But you know him best, I'm sure."

The night before their departure the topic of conversation at the table was Prime Minister Pitt's death from liver disease at the age of forty-six.

"The man was too liberal with his port glass," William decided.

"Yes, sir," Brax said, always deferential to the older man. "But I venture to say that Napoleon's win at Austerlitz hastened his death. He was counting on the coalition to ensure our nation's defense against Napoleon. Now we're vulnerable again."

The two men stayed up far into the night, discussing who would be declared Pitt's successor and what it would mean for Britain's approach to rapidly unfolding world events.

The next morning, clear and crisp with a light remainder of frost on the ground, Hevington's footmen had piled all Marguerite's belongings—consisting mostly of her new wardrobe—atop the Greycliffe family's carriage. William shook hands warmly with Brax, admonishing him to care solicitously for Marguerite, while Claudette used her final moments for one last piece of advice.

"Keep an open mind, dear. See how things progress with the lieutenant. He seems both ambitious and kind. You could do far worse." They stood together, wrapped in warm capes, while Uncle William and Brax made their good-byes nearby.

"Aunt Claudette, my mind was open to someone aboard *Victory*. But it resulted in nothing. I'm not sure I care to expose my heart again for dissection."

Claudette's mouth stood open as Marguerite reached over and patted the older woman's shoulder.

"Don't fret for me. I'll be fine."

"What do you mean, there was someone on *Victory*? Who? Why didn't you tell me?"

Marguerite was spared having to answer as Brax came to assist her into the carriage and and sat across from her. The carriage lurched forward, and Marguerite blew Claudette a kiss as she departed for London.

While Marguerite settled into her new location, she gave little thought to national events, Brax, or the Greycliffes. There were walls to be painted, carpets to be laid, tableaux to be designed, and handbills to be printed. The arrival of thirty figures from Dublin kept Marguerite and a hired hand busy for days. Brax stopped by a few times, but she dismissed him quickly, unwilling to waste precious time in a social visit. Even letters from Claudette remained unopened on the writing table in her rooms, located about two blocks away from the exhibit.

A month after her arrival, she was ready to open her doors to Madame Tussaud's London Wax Exhibition. She settled down in her rooms the night before with a cup of tea and a newspaper, and was surprised to find how much had happened while she remained shut away from the world.

After Pitt's death, a new Ministry of All the Talents was formed, a coalition between William Grenville, Charles James Fox, and nine others. Grenville became leader of the House of Lords and first lord of the treasury, whilst Fox was made leader of the House of Commons and secretary of state for foreign affairs. Other members of the eleven-man coalition were given plum assignments. Marguerite ran her finger down the list of positions and saw that Charles Grey, Viscount Howick, was named first lord of the Admiralty.

Darden did work for Mr. Pitt. Will he now be on staff for Lord Grenville, or maybe Lord Grey?

And don't forget that Brax performed services, as well.

Mr. Pitt was laid to rest on February 22, 1806, inside Westminster Abbey, with a public funeral and a monument, despite the opposition to such special treatment by Mr. Fox, Pitt's political opponent for decades.

How foolish and childish men could be in their political gamesmanship. Hadn't Pitt saved England's finances after the American rebellion? Wasn't he greatly esteemed by the king? Perhaps he was not the hero Nelson was, but surely he deserved recognition in death.

29

Charles James Fox was the complete opposite of William Pitt in most ways. Where Pitt was a slight and fair-complexioned man, Fox was dark, corpulent, and hairy. Even his father referred to him as a monkey.

Furthermore, where Pitt was well beloved by King George III, Fox was less than enthusiastically received by the sovereign, who blamed Fox for the debauchery and many failings of his son, George Augustus Frederick, one of Fox's associates. Fox further distanced himself from the king when he attempted to put the king's son on the throne when the monarch went through a bout of insanity in 1789. Pitt championed the idea that the king's illness was only temporary and, curses on the man, Pitt was right. Fox's defense of the bloody revolution in France—again in complete opposition to Pitt's hostile stance—made him more of a pariah with the king, who would have despised Fox for his dissipation alone.

Indeed, Charles Fox led a notoriously profligate life, in a society known for the licentiousness of its upper classes, as opposed to Pitt's somewhat more austere mode of living. Now, though, Fox was gratified in his choice of a wife, Elizabeth Armistead, whose steadying hand had been curbing some of his cavalier behavior. No matter that she was previously a courtesan and he hadn't publicly revealed the marriage in its first seven years.

But he was more like Pitt in his affinity for liquor than he cared to think. Fox looked at the glass of scarlet liquid in his hand, a port sent to him in a presentation box by some fortune-seeker in London who wanted a letter of marque. The port was probably a fine vintage, but Fox's palate had lost much of its discernment over the years. He sat back in the tufted leather chair behind his desk and tipped the rest of the glass's contents down his throat.

A knock on the door was followed by the entry of Charles Grey, Viscount Howick, holding a small packet of papers.

Fox got up and stepped around his desk to greet the first lord of the Admiralty. It was so much easier these days to simply move into the room to shake hands with someone, rather than try to reach over his desk—and his extended belly—to do so.

"Lord Howick, greetings to you, sir. How fares your lovely wife? Just had your—what is it—sixth child?"

"Seventh, actually. Mary and I lost an infant boy a few years ago. But Frederick William is, at six months, full of spit and fire, and I'm sure will take over for his own father at the Admiralty one day."

"Indeed. The boy can but hope to have his father's illustrious career."

The two men sat at a round, inlaid mahogany table on the other side of Fox's desk.

Grey wasted no time in coming to his point. "I need your sage advice on an idea. No one knows how to maneuver through a difficult political situation like you, eh, Charles?"

"I do admit to some expertise in cunning and daring." Fox leaned back and folded his hands together over his considerable stomach.

Grey laughed politely at Fox's self-conceit.

"I've come to you with two peculiar issues, Charles," said Grey.

"Peculiar? Is there anything happening in and outside the government that *isn't* peculiar?"

"True, but these may be of particular significance." Grey slid his finger under one of the previously broken seals on the top document, then did the same to the next one, laying the two documents side by side.

"As we already know, with their staggering defeat at Trafalgar, combined with dismissive treatment by the French, the Spanish are secretly negotiating with us." He tapped one of the documents. "This was picked up by one of our naval couriers. The Spanish gentleman in question is still interested and requests a meeting with us."

Fox picked up the document and scanned it. "Excellent. I'll have this most fortuitous opportunity arranged. But what makes this odd?"

Grey pushed the second paper forward. "This. I suspected that there might be a spy among us who just might ruin our ability to keep these negotiations secret. But I wasn't sure and didn't want to be an alarmist."

Fox put aside the first document and read the second one.

Now Grey had the foreign secretary's interest. Fox sat up straight.

"Hmm. This seems to confirm your misgivings. How good is your intelligence?"

"Good enough that I'm worried it could be true."

"Then this is indeed a problem, Lord Grey. I don't need to remind you that with Spain committed to remaining neutral, we can open a second front against Napoleon, and we can also provide stronger fortifications for our ally, Portugal."

Fox folded the incriminating document. "This is very serious. We can't have our plans destroyed by a traitor. Do you have specific evidence linking this purported spy to any revealed information?"

"Only what is described there." Grey pointed to the folded sheet Fox had just put down.

"What do you propose to do?"

Grey sat back in his chair, elbows on its brown leather arms, and folded the fingers of both hands into a temple in front of his chest.

"I believe our fabled waxwork stowaway may be the locksmith who can make the key to solve our little problem."

"You mean the woman aboard *Victory*? The one who made the Nelson figure? What could she possibly have to do with this?"

Grey explained his idea, which Fox considered for several long moments. "You know, Grey, I had no insight before now as to how well your mind worked. You're quite clever, really. And I believe I could be of some use to you, given my position. I can, shall we say, bring some influence to the parties in question."

"Which cxcccds my highest hopes. I'll arrange things immediately."

The two men shook hands over their private agreement.

Marguerite was surprised by two noteworthy visitors to the exhibit a week later: Charles James Fox and Charles Grey. The two men looked like caricatures of one another, with Grey's tall, lean, and dapper stature in direct contrast to Fox's short, rotund, and decidedly sloppy appearance. Fox's breath reeked of spirits, but he was articulate nonetheless.

They made a special point of introducing themselves to her and admiring her collection of figures, stating that her work at Trafalgar was well known to them. Marguerite was flattered but told them frankly that most of the exhibition was part of Madame Tussaud's collection, currently being shown in Dublin.

A look she couldn't interpret passed between the foreign secretary and the first lord of the Admiralty. She was even more puzzled when they asked to see what figures she might personally have in progress.

Putting the exhibit in the charge of her new assistant, a young medical student trying to fund his education, who cared for the figures as well as Marguerite did herself, she led her esteemed guests to the workroom.

She showed them her current works in progress, re-creations of both Nelson and Hardy, which she was working on from the mask she still retained from the Nelson sitting and the portraits she'd been given of Hardy.

Fox and Grey circled around the partially completed figures, murmuring their appreciation of the artistry in them.

Fox patted his stained waistcoat. "We know, Mrs. Ashby, that Mr. Pitt engaged you to make these figures originally. I'm no fan of the late prime minister's, but must admit that he was rather a genius in his decision to employ your talents."

"I'm deeply honored, sir. My mentor, Madame Tussaud, deserves most of the credit for whatever talent I might have."

"To the contrary, madam, you clearly have natural skills for this sort of work. Even the facial expressions are so very . . . accurate."

Charles Grey brought the tips of his fingers together in front of his chest. "I must echo Mr. Fox's assessment. No wonder the French were momentarily confused. A pity, almost, that we don't recognize women's contributions aboard ships. Thank you, Mrs. Ashby, for an enlightening visit."

The two men departed with promises to call again at the next available opportunity. Marguerite's only regret was that they had not commissioned any figures during their visit.

"What do you think, Charles?" Grey asked once they had left the exhibition.

"I think you've concocted a brilliant plan. I doubt the slightest suspicions will be aroused regarding our little scheme."

"Excellent. Care to stop by Admiralty House for a drop of brandy?"

"Yet another masterful idea, Grey. I knew including you in the Ministry of All the Talents was one of my more profound decisions."

Brax praised Marguerite's new salon effusively. "A superlative rival to the Dublin exhibition," he said.

Pure flattery, she knew, since he'd never even seen the Dublin salon.

But Brax had more on his mind than mere flattery.

"Would you honor me with your presence to dine at my parents' town house this evening?"

"Your parents live in London?"

"Just during the Season. I've told them all about my dear friend, Mrs. Marguerite Ashby, the incomparable waxworker, and they're in an absolute pother over meeting you."

"Really? Well, I hate to disappoint them with my extreme ordinariness, so perhaps I should decline."

"And spiral them both into a complete knot? I won't hear of it. Besides, their cook, Mrs. Kenyon, makes an extraordinary partridge à la Burgundy. A soul is poor indeed without having tried it in his lifetime."

"I see. I really did intend to just retire to bed early this evening. I'll be tired after a long day—"

Once again, Brax assumed his pose of wounded suitor, with one hand over his heart. "Dear lady, I shall not be able to eat another morsel of food myself until I know you've had the pleasure of Mrs. Kenyon's culinary temptations. Do you intend to starve me to death?"

"Sir Brax, you are quite . . . *incorrigible*, I believe is the word."

"You are absolutely correct. Why, my father asked the headmaster of my school to cane me every day just for good measure. All to no avail. I've no manners, no civility, and can never take no for an answer."

"Very well, then. If I say yes to your invitation, will you let me tend to my customers for the rest of the day?"

"Madam, I am your servant." He bowed to her. "I'll return for you at seven o'clock."

Conversation flowed easily with Brax's parents. Lord Selwyn especially doted on his son. His parents expressed great interest in her waxworks, having heard of Madame Tussaud during her earlier tour in England. Marguerite was surprised by their interest, given her status as a tradeswoman, but if they were accepting of their adored son's decision to pursue a life in the navy, why wouldn't they accept his friendship with her?

They promised to visit Marguerite's exhibition at the earliest possible moment, and invited her to return to tea when she found it convenient. Brax was at his genteel best before his parents, and indeed Mrs. Kenyon's tender poultry was superb, especially topped with its exquisite burgundy sauce and finished off with a nice bottle of claret brought up from the family's estate in Sussex.

It was a lovely evening in general.

The hackney ride back to Marguerite's rooms in the dark that February night was frigid. Marguerite kept her arms tucked in a muff, while Brax put a heated brick taken from his parents' kitchen beneath her feet and covered her with a blanket.

Brax was solicitous in the extreme and Marguerite felt nearly drowsy in her comfort, between the full meal, the bundling up, the rhythmic clip-clop of the horse's hooves, and Brax's warm attentions.

He also seemed content to sit back languidly. But upon arrival at her rooms he revived to his spritely self, elegantly helping her from the hackney, paying the driver and sending him off.

"Won't you have him wait for you?" Marguerite asked.

"Another will be along soon. In fact, I see the lantern of one in the distance." He pointed back the way they had come.

He escorted her into the entry of Mrs. Grove's home, where she had taken rooms. Marguerite had specifically sought out a widow from whom to rent, in silent deference to Darden's earlier admonition that she would be in respectable company that way.

Brax relieved her of her wrap and muff, setting them both on a chair in the entry. He took her hand and bowed over it, placing one of his typical lingering kisses atop it. Except this time he didn't let go, instead twining his fingers through hers and stepping closer.

"My parents liked you, you know. And they are very discerning people. After all, they chose me for a son."

Brax's voice was light, but Marguerite felt an air of purpose about him. It was discomfiting, and she intended to keep things airy.

"They were probably just intrigued by a woman who lives among wax people. Much as they are probably intrigued by their son, who is always merry and never has a solemn moment." She disengaged her hand from his to playfully swat him on the arm and thus release his hold on her. "They probably named you Sir Brax the Lighthearted long before I did."

But Brax imprisoned her hand again between both of his own.

"I am solemn now, Marguerite. My life is changing. I'm about to earn a promotion to captain."

"Why, Brax, that's wonder—"

"You're the first person I've told. And I've been engaged by Grenville's new government on a sensitive special project. The reward for my success will be considerable, not to mention my chances for eventual promotion to admiral. My life is finally becoming commendable. I lack only one thing."

I know what he means, but I don't want to hear it.

"Oh, come now, with all these honors, how can you possibly lack anything?" she asked.

"My life could only be complete if you had a permanent place in it."

Oh dear. He said it plainly. He wants me. *And I'm indifferent to his offer. Why?*

You know why.

But Darden is gone now, forever, off on his personal quest. I was mistaken about his feelings on Victory. *For heaven's sake, he would have at least sent me a simple letter by now if he cared for me. Brax is here, and he's kind, pleasurable company. I could do worse.*

You could do worse? What makes you think you deserve better? You've seen what happens to men who fall in love with you. First Nicholas, then Philipsthal. Protect Brax by sending him on his way.

But I didn't feel that way about Darden.

That's because you were thinking like a simpleton about him. Besides, your emotions were muddied because you were trapped on a ship with him in the throes of a dangerous sea battle.

True. I let my good sense get away from me. I suppose I could at least try *with Brax. I'm certainly fond of him.*

"Marguerite?" Brax's voice interrupted her woolgathering. "Where are you?"

"What? Oh, I'm sorry. I was just thinking about the exhibition. What I need to fix before opening it again tomorrow morning," she added lamely.

"Ah, my heart is pierced once again by the fair maiden, whose mind cannot concentrate on her devoted knight." His words were weightless, but his voice was dense with emotion.

"Marguerite, most women are easily drawn to me, and I love them easily in return. But your shell is a difficult one to break open and it intrigues me greatly. I want to beseech you for something that I would never bother to ask of any other woman—I would simply take it."

I don't want him to ask me.

"Sir Brax, so serious? What could you possibly have to ask me that is so gravely exceptional?"

"I would like to kiss you. May I?"

No! I'm not ready for this. Isn't there still hope for Dard—

You're being a fool again.

I'm not! I just don't want to hurt Brax in case Darden should—

He's not coming back.

No, he's not. So I've no reason to say no.

She swallowed and laughed nervously. "Sir Brax, how gallant of you."

He met her lips with his gently and with great reverence, still holding her hand between both of his. She felt like a fragile piece of Wedgewood that he was afraid of dropping if he handled it too roughly.

He pulled away slowly, opening his eyes and smiling with delight. "Thank you, my sweet," he breathed.

What response did she really have for him?

She was silent as he left Mrs. Grove's, whistling. She watched from behind a curtain in the parlor as Brax hailed down the hackney he promised her would be available when he wanted it. She brought her fingers to her lips as she watched the carriage rumble away, the horse's snuffling resulting in great clouds of mist she could see reflected in the light of the hackney's lanterns.

Brax was handsome, amusing and mild mannered. He didn't seem to care that she was a tradeswoman, either. He would probably be a fine husband. Why didn't she feel the same with him as she did with that dark, high-minded, exceedingly frustrating lieutenant aboard *Victory*?

If only she could come up with a reason to hold Darden in contempt, she might be able to move on with Brax.

There just didn't seem to be any great reason to hate Darden Hastings.

Brax reappeared at the exhibition late one evening shortly after their visit to his parents' home, whistling and carrying a large, flat, wrapped package.

"I've something very important for you. Can we speak privately?"

Marguerite asked her assistant to tend to the show's final customers, and escorted Brax to her workshop. "Why all of the mystery, Sir Brax?"

"I've been entrusted with a rather delicate matter, and interestingly enough it involves you. Grey and Fox think you have proven yourself to the Crown once before as a patriotic woman who keeps good counsel, so they wish to rely on you once again."

"Brax, if they are seeking someone to join in another battle against the French, let me assure you that I will not—"

Brax laughed and held up the wrapped package as though defending himself. "Heavens, no, it was never the government's intention to deliberately send a lady out to sea to serve in war. What a thought! No, they have a more . . . subtle . . . idea in mind. You see, they would like to have a figure cast of the king of Spain's son, Ferdinand."

"For what reason?"

"They have a secret deception planned, much as what you assisted with on *Victory*."

"Is the prince going to war?" Marguerite was confused.

"Something like that." Brax laid the package on her worktable and unwrapped it. Inside was a framed painting of a dark-complexioned man in a military uniform, with a sash denoting some sort of honor proudly draped over his right shoulder.

"Meet Ferdinand, son of Charles the Fourth of Spain. The government proposes to pay you handsomely to create a figure of him."

Brax explained that Fox and Grey wanted her to create a likeness of Ferdinand, which would be shipped to Spain, and Ferdinand's people would use it to create the appearance that the heir to the throne was enjoying some leisurely time away in the Valencia countryside.

Meanwhile, Ferdinand would travel to a covert location for a clandestine meeting with Lords Grey and Fox to determine the best course of action for preserving Spain's sovereignty without alerting Napoleon.

"What do you think?" Brax asked.

"Certainly I can do this for His Majesty's government. I'll just send Madame Tussaud a note to let her know—"

"No, no communications with your employer. This is a delicate matter and you are only the fourth person being brought into it. This has to be conducted in total secrecy."

"I see. All right, I suppose there's no harm in that."

"Oh, and I forgot to mention that after you've finished the Ferdinand figure, they wish for the two of us to load it aboard a ship that will be specially docked on the outskirts of London. Obviously, since we four are the only ones privy to this plan, we cannot have anyone else entrusted to do it."

"This sounds terribly dangerous."

"You'll be perfectly safe with me. And of course I will ensure that you won't accidentally be trapped aboard the ship. A grievous calamity it would be to His Majesty's navy for it to happen twice. With the same woman."

"I see. Why do I suspect there is far more to this than you're telling me, Brax?"

"Truly, I've told you all I know. It's an excellent opportunity for both of us to achieve notice inside the government. Aren't you pleased?"

"Making myself known at the upper ranks of His Majesty's government has not exactly ever been a plan of mine."

"But still . . . you'll do it?"

Brax stood in silence, his face an expression of eager anticipation.

Marguerite smiled. "I'm a loyal subject of His Majesty's, aren't I? Of course I'll do this."

She escorted Brax out to the entrance of the exhibition. The building was clear of visitors, and only her assistant remained behind, sweeping up in a remote corner.

Before leaving, Brax bent gallantly and lifted Marguerite's hand to his lips. "My greatest dreams have been fulfilled, you know. To perform such an enormous service for the government, and to do so working alongside the loveliest woman I have ever encountered, far exceeds any expectations I may have ever had in this lifetime."

Marguerite withdrew her hand, laughing. "Sir Brax, you never stop being the gallant, do you?"

He clutched his chest. "Dear lady, how you persevere in wounding me. How can I ever convince you of my deep sincerity?"

"I believe in the depth of your sincerity, Brax Selwyn. The depth of your sincerity matches that of your grave and serious mind."

A look of confusion passed over Brax's face, but he let Marguerite's comment pass.

He turned back as he was ready to leave and said casually, "Incidentally, you may want to stay away from Darden Hastings."

"I've not spoken to him since Trafalgar. Why do you mention this?"

"Grey told me he has reason to believe our friend Darden, who has unbelievably been promoted to captain in the Royal Navy, is not the most loyal of His Majesty's subjects. You must have had some sort of contact with him aboard *Victory*. Did you notice any unpatriotic sorts of behavior while out to sea?" Brax's voice could not hide its tone of hope.

What?

Darden? Disloyal? The most duty-bound Briton in the country, next to Nelson himself?

"Nothing whatsoever. He was utterly steadfast in his duty to both Captain Hardy and Admiral Nelson."

"Hmm. Yes, of course. Well, unfortunately, Lord Grey has it on good authority that he is profiting handsomely from certain deeds, courtesy of the French government. Such activity is, as you know, treasonous."

Marguerite's mind whirled in confusion. This just couldn't be possible. They simply didn't know Darden the way she did.

I just need to tell Brax more about his character.

Or perhaps they know more than you think. Remember Darden did *tell you he had a "different path."*

Yes, but that had to do with his naval career.

Did it?

Of course it did! And didn't Brax just say he was promoted to captain? Why would a suspected traitor be promoted?

To convince him he's not under a cloud of doubt. Remember also that he abandoned you for a time on Victory. *Why did he do that?*

I don't know.

Still, it was impossible. "I can't believe the lieutenant—I mean captain—would do something so odious as to turn his back on his country."

"I know. It does seem a terrible shame, doesn't it?"

"Why do they suspect him?" She hoped she didn't sound as though she was pleading for him.

"I don't know. Grey said he couldn't discuss his information. My condolences to you at having to learn this dreadful news. It distresses me, as well, to know a fellow officer has behaved thus."

Brax's voice lacked the regret that his words declared.

Marguerite drew a deep breath. How could she have been so utterly witless about a man, once again?

More importantly, how could Darden have cared so much for his duty while intending to betray his nation?

That's what traitors do. Pretend one thing while doing another.

Was I so completely mistaken in what I thought was his intense and guileless feeling for me?

But surely Fox and Grey knew what they were about, and if they thought Darden was a traitor, there must be truth in it.

I believe I just developed a reason to hate Darden Hastings.

30

Marguerite immediately had a lock installed on her workroom door and did not give her helper a key, telling him it was just temporary without telling him why. If her assistant was curious, he kept it to himself. Each evening after the exhibition closed, she retreated to the workroom to continue her work on the Ferdinand wax figure, which she had decided to sculpt in a seated position, since he would be shown most often riding about in carriages across the Valencia countryside.

Brax had delivered several good likenesses of the Spanish king's son, which made her job easier. But either Fox or Grey was sending a message nearly every day through Brax inquiring about her progress. After a week of this, she became peevish.

"Please tell Mr. Fox and Lord Grey that the figure is being completed as quickly as I can possibly construct it. It takes time to find the right color eyes and get the hair arranged properly, not to mention sewing a costume for a member of royalty. If they wish it to be produced instantly, they may both come down here themselves and work on it."

"Ah, Marguerite, I have distressed you. Please accept my apologies." He swept a bow. He hadn't attempted to kiss her again since the evening after dining with his parents, evidently unsure of his status with her now that they were involved in an intrigue together.

"I'm not angry at you, Brax. It's just that, honestly, Mr. Pitt never plagued me like my new masters do. He just let me do my work. I do know that swiftness is critical."

"You are certainly the most intelligent of women. Never fear, I will convey your assurances that the figure is being worked on expeditiously and will be completed in the shortest time possible."

Without Fox and Grey pestering her, the work progressed faster. She held thoughts of Darden at bay as she worked far into the night, reminding herself repeatedly that a traitor cannot be countenanced.

No matter how the man I thought I knew contradicted the man the government had unearthed.

You've been a poor judge of wickedness and dishonor these past few years. And remember that you are playing your part to bring a Judas to justice.

Yes, but it's little consolation.

Once this task is finished, you should think about Brax. He obviously wants to marry you. You could have a happy life with him, especially since you will undoubtedly grow closer after this.

I suppose. I'd just hoped to feel what I felt with . . . Darden.

Yes, yes, I know. The traitor.

Marguerite wrinkled her nose. The whole business was so distasteful and upsetting. Thank God, though, she was at least doing her duty.

But she should have known that doing one's duty generally meant involvement in distasteful and upsetting events.

She was nearly finished with Ferdinand, and one evening was applying additional flesh-toned paints to his face to increase his natural qualities. Marguerite stepped back to observe her work. She thought she had captured his features well and that he could easily pass for the real man, especially passing by crowds in a carriage.

Even locked in her workroom she could hear the insistent knocking on the exhibition's front door.

Drat it all, she thought. *The building is dark. Why do customers think they can have the exhibit opened up especially for them at all hours of the night?*

She considered ignoring the rapping, but its continued repetition was too vexing to be disregarded. She sighed, put down the paintbrush, and wiped her hands on a rag before picking up one of the candlesticks positioned around the workroom to illuminate her work.

She hastened through the exhibition, calling out, "I'm coming!" which at least ceased the infernal racket the visitor was making. She unlocked and opened the front door, and held up the light to see who her visitor was.

Darden Hastings.

He looked considerably better than he had the last time she'd seen him. Well, she supposed she looked a bit more polished, too. Although she was undoubtedly wearing paint across her nose and under all of her fingernails. She self-consciously wrapped her hand tighter around the light to hide her work-worn fingers.

Darden wore a crisp, new uniform that bore his captain's insignia on the sleeves, over which he wore a long, woolen cape. His own dark hair was neatly pulled back in a queue. He no longer smelled of sweat, blood, and gunpowder, although the faintest whiff of tar still lingered about him. And it was not an altogether unpleasant smell. In fact, she felt rather nostalgic about it.

Silly goose! A traitor stands before you and would slit your throat if he knew what you were up to, and you're feeling sentimental about his scent?

Darden cleared his throat. "Were you going to let me in, or must I remain out here, chilled to the marrow?"

Marguerite debated. Why was he here? Did he know about the wax figure she was finishing up in her workroom? Was she in any danger?

Please, dear God, they must be mistaken about him.

But they have evidence.

Quiet! I won't listen to this.

You know your duty. Pretend nothing is wrong.

"Of course." She held the door open to allow him in, then shut it against the cold. The single taper's light kept them together in an intimate, warm glow. It was unnerving. "I was just a bit surprised to see you. Especially so late in the evening. How did you know I was here?"

"Your landlady said you've been keeping late hours at the exhibition. I'm glad to see you remembered my advicc about lodging with widows." Darden removed his cape and hung it on a hook near the door.

Marguerite gritted her teeth. Whereas she had been proud of following his advice mere weeks ago, now it seemed like she'd been blithely following the devil.

"What brings you to London, Captain Hastings?"

He self-consciously touched his insignia. "What, am I no longer Darden?" he asked with a crooked smile.

She wanted nothing more than to rush into his arms, cover his face with unladylike kisses, and assure him that he was her Darden and she was his Marguerite.

You know your duty.

Shc ignored the question. "I suppose you're on some leave? Or are perhaps surveying some strategic fortifications?"

"Yes, among other things. I'm sorry for the lateness of my visit, but I'll be leaving soon on a mission and wanted to see you, since I'm not sure when I'll return."

"All of a sudden? You've been absent a long time."

"Yes, well, *Victory* didn't get into Portsmouth until November, then I had many duties surrounding Nelson's funeral in December. I spent time on leave with my family in Somerset, and only just came back to London in recent weeks to receive my promotion and a new assignment."

"And where will you be heading on your new assignment?"

Darden shifted his weight to one foot, the one that had been injured at Trafalgar. A full recovery, apparently. "I can't really speak of details. It's confidential, you might say."

"Yes, I see."

"After you left *Victory*, I realized I was most unhappy with our parting, and just wanted an opportunity to convey to you my . . . regret . . . over things."

"Your regret, Captain?"

"Yes. That further association was not possible at the time. Given our circumstances."

"Our circumstances? What are those? I'm just a simple wax-worker's apprentice trying to ply her trade."

Darden laughed. "Simple? To the contrary. You're as complex and varied as a blustering headwind." He reached out a hand to touch an errant curl that had slipped out of her bandeau. She jerked away from his touch.

He held his hand in the air as if confused by her reaction, then dropped it back to his side. "I suppose I deserve your disdain."

"Why, Captain, you deserve neither my disdain nor my appreciation. I believe things are very clear between us."

He sighed. "But they aren't. There are events occurring you cannot possibly understand. Which brings me to another reason for my visit. To caution you. Certain national affairs could place you personally in great danger, and I want you to promise me you'll be as careful as possible. I'm afraid it's my fault you're in this position."

"This is all very mysterious, Captain. Please speak plainly, or not at all." She set the taper down on a nearby stand and crossed her arms in front of her. It provided a physical barrier that brought her comfort.

"I can't. I shouldn't be here at all. It was wrong of me to come. I just couldn't let events unfold as they might without seeing you one last time."

So he's admitting to it all.

The Darden Hastings she knew aboard *Victory* was a sham, a fake, a forgery. Standing before her now was the real man: a scoundrel who was gladly trampling on his honor to fill his pockets with French livres.

She could almost hear the metal cage slamming shut around her heart.

"Well, then, I must certainly thank you for the notable risk to your livelihood you undertook to warn me against persons and events unknown. Is that all, Captain?" She picked the taper up and moved toward the door to let him out.

Even in the soft reflection of the candlelight, she could see that his face was red, though from embarrassment or anger she couldn't tell.

Without a word, he plucked his cloak from the hook, threw it about his shoulders, and stepped back out into the freezing night air.

Marguerite shut the door softly and locked it. Setting the taper down again, she put her forehead against the door and let the tears stream according to their own undisciplined will.

Once the wax figure was complete, Brax brought delivery instructions from Fox. They were to move the figure in the middle of the night one week hence.

"And so our little adventure will be concluded, Marguerite. At least your part in it will be finished. I have further, private instructions with regard to Darden." Brax was practically standing on the balls of his feet in his excitement.

"Please, Sir Brax, I've no wish to discuss this further. Once we stow the figure, let's not ever talk of it again." She hadn't confided in him about Darden's visit, since it would serve no purpose—Darden would be arrested soon enough anyway—and the thought of his visit still pained her with excruciating force.

"You're right. You know, I have an idea. What say we go to the theatre together to celebrate Ferdinand's, shall we say, rebirth? It seems to be the most popular activity in London since we entered hostilities with France again. There's a young actor, William Betty, whom everyone raves about in his Shakespearean roles. They call him Young Roscius."

"Who is Roscius?"

"Some actor who rose from slavery to fame in ancient Rome. I guess Betty comes from the lower classes. He's playing Hamlet at Drury Lane. It will be a night of entertainment away from all of the exertion you've been at these past few weeks."

Wasn't it absurd to sit down for lighthearted entertainment when the very outcome of the alliances against France might depend on the figure now wrapped in layers of muslin in her workroom? But what else was there to do?

"I suppose you're right. A theatrical performance might be wonderfully distracting to attend. With a friend."

"A friend. I am, of course, ever your devoted friend."

Marguerite's last act the day of their planned cargo transfer to the ship Lord Grey had arranged was to send a letter to Claudette. She said nothing of her planned intrigue, only that Brax had been assisting her and the exhibition had thus far proven successful. She hating being so deceptive with her beloved aunt, but hopefully soon she'd be able to tell her everything. And presumably there would be no need for Claudette to come looking for her. She waited anxiously after closing the exhibition for the evening, tense, if not necessarily fearful, of what lay ahead.

Brax tapped quietly at the same door Darden had nearly pummeled down just a week prior. Together they carried the bundled wax Ferdinand into a waiting carriage provided by Fox, and sat him up as a third passenger. Marguerite giggled in nervous tension at their fellow traveler, who looked as though he had been swathed in bandages from very serious burns.

The night was clear and not quite as chilly as it had recently been. Spring was sure to arrive soon. The moon hung full, low, and bright in the sky as it made its descent on the horizon. They would have to work quickly before the sun rose.

Unable to see much beyond the carriage's lanterns through the vehicle's smudged windows, she was only able to know they were arriving at their destination by the crunch of pebbles under the wheels and the nearby sloshing of water after nearly an hour's journey. She stepped out of the carriage and back into the moonlight. The ship sat anchored out in the river, and a small launch was lodged on the shore, waiting for them. Brax and the driver silently lifted Ferdinand out and Marguerite followed them closely to the launch. A man sat inside, oars in his lap. Brax and the driver hoisted Ferdinand into the launch, then the driver saluted Brax before heading back to the carriage.

"He'll wait for us to return," Brax whispered to her. She nodded her understanding.

The man rowed them to the merchant ship without a word, the

only sound his oars slicing through the water as he maneuvered their craft as quickly as possible. The ship's crew lifted up the launch, and another man, who was obviously the captain, silently escorted Marguerite and Brax, the figure balanced between them, down into the ship's hold. As soon as it was positioned to Marguerite's satisfaction, they returned to the launch and back to the shore. The edges of Marguerite's dress were soaked and heavy, so she leaned on Brax's arm as they made their way across the loose pebbles and stones of the shore back to their carriage.

He helped her back into the carriage and said, "Wait here," slipping back out himself. Moments later he reentered the carriage and sat next to her as the driver urged the horses forward.

"How very interesting our night has just become," Brax said.

"More interesting than stowing a wax figure on a ship in the dead of night?"

Brax laughed quietly. "Yes, Marguerite, even more fascinating than that."

Brax rapped on the ceiling of the carriage so the driver would stop. He opened the door and called out, "Please, Captain, permit us to give you a ride to your destination. You shouldn't be out so late at night."

To Marguerite's surprise, Darden's scowling face appeared in the doorway. He leaped into the carriage and sat across from them.

"Where to, Captain?"

Darden growled out an address, after which complete silence ensued. Marguerite could sense Brax's exhilaration over their extra passenger, and knew he could not remain quiet for long.

"So, Captain Hastings, what do you think of the weather tonight? Or should I perhaps say this morning?"

"It's mild, as you well know."

"Yes, yes. I see you are out alone on this mild night. No lovely lady to keep you company, hmm?"

"No."

"No. Well, perhaps your duties as a new captain prevent you from enjoying the companionship of exquisite damsels, such as Mrs. Ashby here." Brax brushed a finger across Marguerite's cheek. She refrained from her desire to jerk away.

"I suppose you're right." Marguerite could hear the strangled note in Darden's voice.

What was Darden doing in the same place as she and Brax in the middle of the night? Dear God, this confirmed everything Brax had told her. Darden was spying on them. He really was a traitor to the Crown.

Oh, Darden, how could you?

She could feel his penetrating stare on her, even inside the dark carriage. She kept her face averted.

But Brax was thoroughly enjoying himself.

"I've had the pleasure of working closely with Marguerite—I mean, Mrs. Ashby—lately. To some extent, I must thank you. For not being in the way of our courtship."

"Right."

"You probably don't know that she granted me the pleasure of having dinner at my parents' town house. They adored her. A man likes to know that his intended is well loved by his family, eh?"

Darden rapped on the ceiling of the carriage, and it slowed to a stop.

"I'll take my leave here." He opened the door and stepped out.

"But, Hastings, we're nowhere near your address."

"No, but I want to hasten the moment in which I can be as far from you as possible." Darden slammed the carriage door and stalked off into the waning darkness.

Marguerite flinched at the slam, which seemed to symbolize a shutting of the door on whatever there had ever been between her and Darden Hastings.

She touched Brax's arm and tried to maintain a steady voice. "What was Darden doing at our seaside location?"

"Watching us, I suppose. And isn't that just very interesting?"

Nathaniel Ashby was also watching from atop the deck of his ship inside a nearby cove. He rubbed the week's worth of whiskers on his plump and sunburned face. How very interesting. Two people—and one looked to be a woman!—carting off a large bundled package to a ship under cover of night. Surely they were up to evil intent. Smugglers, probably. Although the package had an unsettlingly familiar outline. What did it remind him of? Well, no matter.

Finally, this was his opportunity to do a service of undeniable value for the government. He would accost the ship, capture its valuables, and present them—along with the smugglers, of course—to Mr. Fox.

Mr. Fox had never responded to his letter that accompanied the bottle of vintage port he'd sent. One of the loathsome rascals working in the parliament offices must have pinched it for himself.

Nathaniel had never stopped applying to the government for a letter of marque, but his requests had gone unanswered. He bemoaned to himself the incompetence and prejudice of the government that kept him from achieving recognition.

After the debacle at the French garrison, he'd licked his wounds by sailing around the Kentish coastline to Faversham and joining his men in whoring and gambling for a week. Once he was refreshed and his mind cleared of the humiliation the cursed French had inflicted on him, he was able to devise his next plan: to continue on around and into the Thames toward London so he could scour the banks of the Thames for any suspicious, unpatriotic activities.

How gratifying to have found something so quickly. Now he'd finally receive the laurel wreaths he deserved.

Nathaniel turned to his able assistant, who was watching the activities with his master. "Mr. Watson, I do believe our hopes for glory have just been realized."

Late the next night, under his own dreams of glory, another man stood along the shore of St. Margaret's at Cliffe, a continuation of the chain of cliffs at Dover, but far enough away from the reinforcements so as not to be seen. He held a lantern in one hand and a small valise in the other.

He held up the lantern as he picked his way across the pebbly coast and stepped quietly into the small skiff he had earlier rented from a local fisherman who was finding it difficult to ply his trade in the navy-infested waters. The man rowed quietly out into St. Margaret's Bay. He faced the white, chalky cliffs as he glided silently away. They glowed in the predawn sky like the apparitions in Philipsthal's Phantasmagoria Show Marguerite had talked about.

When he was about a mile from shore, too far away for anyone there to see his lantern, he stopped rowing and looked up in the sky toward Calais, France.

Where was the promised signal?

He waited patiently in the boat as it sloshed rhythmically in the water. Was he doing the right thing? He was risking everything for this. His honor, his position. Was the recompense worth it? More importantly, what if Marguerite found out? That seemed worse than any penalty for treason.

The twinkling of a light from above the Calais landscape caught his eye.

The signal.

A hot-air balloon had been arranged for this day and time to pick up his message. The occupant dangled a light down, indicating his presence.

The man in the boat opened his bag and pulled several flags from it, using them with naval precision to convey his message to the balloon's occupant. He hoped that between his own lantern and the slowly emerging sunlight, the balloon's occupant would be able to read it. When he was finished, he extinguished his lamp, his signal to the other party that he was done. Moments later, the balloon did the same.

His work was finished.

The only questions that remained were what would Napoleon do with the information, and how would he be rewarded?

Marguerite's trepidation was palpable as she arrived at Admiralty House. Why this summons? She'd done her work and been paid. Did they plan to tell her of Darden's capture?

I don't want to know. I just want to be left alone.

A scowling lieutenant stiffly greeted her at the entrance and escorted her to Lord Howick's office. The lieutenant stepped aside to permit her in and followed behind her to salute his superior before shutting the door on his way out. Fox was sprawled on a settee; Brax and Lord Grey stood to welcome her formally.

Fox smiled. "Mrs. Ashby, a great delight to see you again."

"Thank you, sir. To what do I owe the great honor of being here? I presume you were pleased with the Ferdinand figure and that it is adequately doing its job?"

"Not quite. Actually, that is why we wished to see you. Please sit down."

Marguerite sat in a tufted, leather chair while Fox rose and turned his back to splash some amber liquid into a glass from atop a nearby sideboard.

He proffered the glass to her. "I believe, Mrs. Ashby, that this will be a brandy visit, not a tea visit."

Marguerite believed that wholeheartedly. She took a brief swallow, letting the powerful liquor melt her insides, which were nearly frozen with fear. Grey and Brax stood by mutely.

"We've had a rather interesting occurrence. Something we weren't expecting in our plan. We thought at first that someone arranged this intentionally, but it appears that you, Mrs. Ashby, may have some involvement."

"I, Mr. Fox? I've done nothing since helping Lieutenant Selwyn with the Ferdinand figure except work in my exhibition." She looked to Brax for explanation, but he avoided her eyes.

"Yes, I see. Nevertheless, we've apprehended a man, little more than a pirate, really, who temporarily captured our ship as she was heading down the Thames toward open water. Some of her crew were able to escape and reported to us right away, so he didn't hold the ship more than a few hours. However, he had unwrapped the figure and presumably it scared him, for he threw it overboard and we were unable to recover it.

"Odd fellow. Kept bellowing about his letter of marque. We have no record of one. But what's even more interesting, Mrs. Ashby, is his name. Which he shares with you."

"I beg your pardon?"

"The man claims to be a Nathaniel Ashby. Do you know him?"

Nathaniel! What was that slothful, preening, pompous son of Maude Ashby's doing?

"Unfortunately, I do. He's my brother-in-law. Or rather, I suppose he *was* my relative, until I lost my husband in 1803."

"And did you know he had purchased a ship and was trying to terrorize both the English and French coasts? We now have reports that he attempted to take a French garrison on his own. I might applaud his bravery if he hadn't been so abominably stupid about it."

Marguerite held her tongue, despite wanting to ask what Nathaniel had done. If he was involved, then of course it was done in a brainless way.

"Because that idiot assaulted our ship and lost the figure, we wasted precious hours in reaching Ferdinand's followers on the Spanish coast. They waited at the appointed time, but naturally our ship did not show. Suspecting some kind of trap, they left before we could arrive to tell them what had happened. Now our credibility is ruined and our secret alliance will more than likely crumble.

"We're holding him at Fleet Prison. We plan to charge him with treason. Or at least piracy. But I find it decidedly interesting that he is your relative by marriage. When was the last time you spoke to him?"

"Just after my husband died. He and his mother decided that I should move to the family home with them, where they could supervise me."

"Supervise you? Weren't you a mature widow?"

"Yes, but it was possible that I was a mature widow carrying my husband's son, and they wanted to make sure I wasn't."

"Fascinating. And did you go live with them?"

"Certainly not. I became Madame Tussaud's apprentice shortly thereafter and went to stay with her in London, then Edinburgh, Glasgow, and Dublin."

"So you haven't had contact with him since entering Tussaud's service?"

"No."

"Very well. We didn't truly think anything was amiss with you, Mrs. Ashby, but you can understand that we needed to ask you about the man."

"Yes, sir. Tell me, what will happen to him now?"

"He'll rot in prison for a while until we can bring him to trial.

Whether we charge him with treason or piracy makes no real difference, I suppose. The penalty is the same."

Marguerite shook off Brax's offer to escort her home and hired a hackney to take her to the Fleet, stopping along the way to purchase a small basket of oranges from a fruit vendor.

"Yes, madam, he's being held here," said the warden. "You can visit him, but I just took someone else down there to see him."

A guard led the way with a lantern through a maze of dark, dank, crumbling brick hallways. Foul water seemed to be oozing from every crack and crevice in the building. Marguerite put one of the oranges to her nose and took a deep breath of its sweet, citrus smell to try to block out the revolting smell of the prison. With her free hand, she lifted her skirts to keep them from trailing over the grimy, wet floors, which were far worse than any London street.

"Here." The guard stopped in front of one of many barred iron doors inset in the hallways. He unlocked it and threw the bolt back. The clang echoed in the hallway. He opened the door to let her in, saying, "I'll be back for you in fifteen minutes, miss."

When she saw what was waiting for her in the cell, Marguerite momentarily considered turning on her heel before the door shut behind her.

In the tiny cell with its straw pallet, chair, and a small wooden table with a lone candlestick atop it, stood Nathaniel Ashby. He had a scraggly beard struggling to fill in, a bruised eye, and the dried remains of blood below his lip. He was downright filthy. But it wasn't Nathaniel's appearance that made her want to flee the room.

It was Maude Ashby.

Marguerite hadn't set eyes on either of them in several years, but her mother-in-law still set her teeth on edge. Maude was as regal and brittle as ever, but was dressed in widow's weeds. Mottled spots of color rose in her cheeks at seeing Marguerite.

"You!" was her former mother-in-law's first word to her, spat on the ground with venom. "Well, if it isn't the unsung heroine of Nelson's great victory. How dare you come here! Did you come to see poor Nathaniel in his sorriest state? I'm sure you're simply rapturous over my poor boy's misfortune."

"That's not true. Actually, Nathaniel nearly caused *me* great misfortune."

"How ridiculous. You've had no contact with him whatsoever since you ran off like a servant girl in the face of my kind invitation to live with us. And didn't you go traipsing off to Edinburgh?"

Marguerite ignored the irrational barb. "I've been to many places, but now I reside in London. And apparently one doesn't need to have contact with Nathaniel Ashby to be troubled by him." She turned to the prisoner and held out the basket.

"I've brought you some oranges. I thought you might like some fresh fruit."

Nathaniel took the basket and inhaled its scent. "Heavenly. Thank you, Marguerite. I knew you'd eventually come to me. I just didn't plan for these deplorable circumstances. But now that you're here—"

"Nathaniel, did you know what was on that ship when you took it?"

"What? No. I was merely patrolling the shores, saw some suspicious activities, and decided to investigate. Two people were loading a suspicious-looking package aboard, and I thought they might be smugglers."

"Patrolling the shores? Were you invested with that responsibility?"

"No. At least, not yet. I was waiting for my letter of marque to come through."

Maude screeched her way into the conversation. "Son, what did I tell you about that? That you'd come to no good. I lost your brother thanks to his marriage with this strumpet, and I'm not even out of grieving over the loss of your father to his weak heart. Now what will happen to you?"

"Mother, I tried to explain to them that it was a mistake. They just didn't listen to me."

"Of course they didn't listen to you. Sailing about like a pirate. Whatever is wrong with you? You're lucky they didn't shoot you outright. Your conduct is probably treasonous. Do you realize what the punishment is for treason?" Maude's voice was turning into a wail. "What would your father say if he was here right now? What will Society think?"

"Mother Ashby," Marguerite began. "I hardly think Society's opinion is of first priority."

Maude turned her rage on Marguerite. "And do you think you're of some significance in this debate? Had you done as I asked after Nicholas died and moved into Ash House, you and Nathaniel probably would have married and then he wouldn't have gone off on this . . . this . . . adventure."

So I've gone from detested daughter-in-law to the reason for all of her other son's problems.

Marguerite turned her attention back to Nathaniel. "I believe I can help you, but you must listen to me very carefully."

"Oh, certainly, Nathaniel, I can help." Maude was mimicking her now. "I am the sorriest excuse for a relative ever, but I will now wave my hand and rescue you from the terrible trouble you're in."

Maude's behavior was too much, even for Nathaniel. "Mother, do shut up and let Marguerite speak."

Her indolent son's irritated outburst stunned Maude into silence. Marguerite was certain only seconds were available before Maude's storm clouds gathered again, so she'd best speak hurriedly.

"Nathaniel, I was one of the people 'smuggling' the package on board. When you saw that it was a wax figure, didn't it occur to you that there are very few waxworkers in England?"

"No, I just thought it was gruesome. Since it wasn't of any value, I had it tossed overboard."

"But it was of great value to the British government in the war effort. That's why you're in such a bad predicament."

"How could a wax figure have any importance? And are you saying that you've been serving as some kind of spy since Trafalgar?" Nathaniel's voice was full of admiration.

"I can't say. But I may be able to speak to certain officials on your behalf to convince them that you were acting quite unintentionally when you stole the figure from them."

"Oh yes, I always have little knowledge of what I'm going to do next when I'm on my ship."

And Marguerite knew that was probably true enough.

Maude's face was a mixture of confused emotions. Marguerite could understand it. A woman Maude disliked more than most might hold the key to her son's freedom.

Through tightly clenched teeth, Maude said, "I suppose we must thank you for your generosity. If you truly think you can bring influence to bear in getting my son released."

"I will do my best. But hear me, Nathaniel. You must make me two promises if I'm to do this for you."

"Anything. Name it."

"First, you must give up whatever it is you're doing on the seas. It's dangerous and foolhardy."

"Yes, yes, I was ready to give it up anyway."

"And second, you must promise never to contact me in any way. As of this moment, I hereby repudiate the Ashby family entirely. I don't want to know anything about any of you ever again. The best part of you died with Nicholas."

Nathaniel's face fell. He spread his hands in supplication and one of the oranges tumbled out of the basket and onto the soiled, stone-paved floor. "But, Marguerite, surely you don't mean that. We're kin. I had always hoped we might . . . reconcile to one another and be friends. Very good friends."

Without looking at her, Marguerite knew Maude was probably ready to thrash her son.

I'll save you the trouble, madam.

"Unfortunately, I cannot risk my work and my reputation by association with your tainted past. I'll take my leave now. And remember, do not ever attempt to write or see me ever again."

Thankful that the guard had reappeared, Marguerite followed him without looking back at whatever odious expression Maude Ashby might be wearing. She headed back once more for Admiralty House to plead Nathaniel's case before Lord Grey and Mr. Fox.

The next afternoon, Brax reported to Marguerite that Nathaniel had been released that morning, upon the government's reconsideration of his actions.

In a strange way, Marguerite was pleased to have done Nathaniel this service. He was just a pitiful idiot, after all, without the wherewithal to plan out an act of treason. And as a result she could wipe the Ashbys from her mind forever.

The man read the coded message in dismay. He'd worked so hard to get to this point, and everything was going awry.

Napoleon was furious with him. The wax figure that he'd signaled was headed for Valencia had never been seen, and Ferdinand was still in Madrid. The emperor demanded to know whether his agent in England was a complete *imbécile*. Did he or did he not know what the English were doing?

> *I was already irritated by Spain's apparent duplicity and planned to deal with them appropriately. My concern is that I must also attend to you.*

The thought of being "attended to" by Napoleon Bonaparte was enough to send a small prickle of alarm up the man's spine. He returned to the letter.

> *Even more disturbing to me are sightings of British diplomats in Naples. Reports come to me that they have been seen near the Palace of Caserta, but no meeting has been requested with my brother Joseph. How are the British creeping about my kingdom without making themselves known?*
>
> *More importantly, why didn't you know about it and report it to me?*
>
> *Then I must ask myself, was this a feint by the British? Is this another purported wax figure wandering about in an attempt to distract me from more important war matters?*
>
> *I grow weary of your unreliable reports. I am also exasperated by this waxworker, whom you continue to assure me is an innocent in these schemes. I do not think so.*

But I offer you an opportunity to redeem yourself and solve several problems for me. So that I am no longer annoyed by these person / wax figure sightings, you are to take care of this waxworker. It doesn't matter to me what you do with her, but make sure I don't have to deal with the results of her efforts again.

The man crumpled the note and threw it in the fireplace. This had become a decidedly messy business. He hadn't bargained for this. But obey he must.

31

Nathaniel was once again lodged at Ash House, a new man. He had officially disbanded his crew, although most of them had wandered off anyway when their captain was arrested. The ship he would sell off as soon as possible. Now clean-shaven and in new clothes, with most of his interrogation injuries healed, he was ready to face life afresh.

He applied more of his cologne, a blend of rosemary and bergamot. They said Napoleon was using fragrance by the gallon. He sniffed about himself appreciatively.

If it was good enough for Bonaparte, surely it was enough for Nathaniel Ashby.

He clipped on his timepiece and made one final check in the mirror.

"You're a handsome devil, Ashby. How can she resist?" he asked himself aloud.

Ignoring his mother's questions as to where he was headed, Nathaniel left Ash House for the mews to saddle a horse and be on to his destination.

Or rather, his destiny.

For surely Marguerite said all that nonsense about never contacting her again as a feint for his mother, whose irrational hatred of her daughter-in-law was really quite incredible. No, such self-sacrifice could only mean that Marguerite was trying to secretly save him for herself without Mother knowing.

Oncc he realized that Marguerite was in London, it was a simple matter to find out where the newest waxworks location was. What a sweet irony that she was living so close to his home while he was out proving himself on the high seas.

He patted the small bundle tied around his waist. It held his journal of thoughts and plans, which he'd thankfully been able to save when the navy had shown such poor taste in yanking him from his ship. He preferred not to think about his subsequent questioning, which was also of dubious propriety.

But that was all behind him. Marguerite's devotion would be trebled when she read his profound ruminations. Any doubts she might have had about his worthiness as compared to Nicholas would be swept away like the tide.

Ah, this must be the wax exhibition. What looked like live human beings stood in the large windows, with pedestrians stopping to stare in awe. He slid heavily off his horse and tied it to a post, brushed some road dust from his clothing, and entered the exhibition to claim his true love.

He paid his admission to the thin, pale young man at the entrance, asking where he might find the proprietress. The ticket seller pointed toward the rear of the building. Nathaniel passed through the various tableaux of the exhibition, which included figures from ancient societies—Greece, Rome, and Egypt, as well as what he had to admit was a spectacular rendition of the Battle of Trafalgar. A bleeding, dying Nelson lay in the middle of the tableau, surrounded by other wax naval officers. Clever.

Was waxworking profitable? If so, he must encourage her to stay in this business.

And then there she was, chatting enthusiastically with a customer over a figure dressed in some foreign military uniform. He waited politely for her to conclude, then waved to her.

Her expression was one of pure shock, he noted with satisfaction.

She didn't realize I'd come for her so soon.

"Nathaniel, what are you doing here?"

"Good afternoon, dear Marguerite. Weren't you expecting me?"

"No, not at all."

Ah, how lovely she was, tossing her burnished hair about like that.

"Come now, Marguerite, there's no need to pretend with me. This is Nathaniel, your former brother-in-law, who holds you in the highest regard. We both know that your performance at the Fleet was for my mother's benefit and that you really wanted to know more about my enterprises."

Her quirked eyebrow was just charming.

"Nathaniel, did you think I wasn't serious that day? I meant it. I don't want to see you or your mother ever again. Ever."

"But, Marguerite, I'm getting rid of my ship, so there won't be any more naval adventures. Just as you asked. That other part you said was just silly. How could you possibly not desire contact with your brother-in-law?"

"I don't desire it. Listen to me—my two conditions held equal weight. Cease your foolish piracy and forget you were ever related to me. You and your mother are greedy leeches who prey on hapless victims, whether for money, position, or power. You are thoroughly detestable. My connection with you is finished and I will never entertain your presence ever again. Ever. Again."

"You can't be sincere."

"But I am, and I'll prove it to you. Come with me."

He followed her without question, his eyes on her swaying hips as she led him to the front of the exhibition hall.

"Mr. James," Marguerite said to the mousy little man at the ticket counter. "This gentleman is leaving. He is not welcome back to the exhibition, ever. Understood?"

The man nodded. "Yes, madam."

Marguerite held open the door for him. "Good day to you, Mr. Ashby. I expect never to see you again."

The door banged shut behind him.

He mounted his horse in disbelief. Did she really mean it? That she wasn't interested in him? She hadn't given him a chance, though. He hadn't even had an opportunity to show her his journal. That wasn't fair of her. The horse snuffled beneath him, as though in agreement.

He considered turning back. Surely he was mistaken in her attitude. She had been under tremendous strain as of late, what with being at Trafalgar, then being pressed into service with His Majesty's government. Maybe she'd come around with time.

If only her eyes hadn't been devoid of any warmth. He shuddered a little at the thought. No, there hadn't been any passion, or even kindness, in those eyes at all. When it came down to it, the visit had been altogether unsatisfactory. And he was wearing a very dapper new top hat.

No, the more Nathaniel put actual thought into it, the more he realized that Marguerite must have actually meant what she said at the prison.

So what did that mean for him?

It meant that it truly had been all for nothing. He had no glory, no title, and Marguerite had callously thrown him aside. Had he not ever been in charge of his destiny? Had he always been at the mercy of other people? All of his effort, smashed against the shoals like a ship with no captain.

How depressing.

And what now? An existence alone with Mother, who would never let him forget this. She'd always led him to believe that Nicholas was the great disappointment of her life, but lately it seemed as though she was just as dissatisfied with Nathaniel.

Oh, the carping that will go on for months and months until I am driven to the bottle.

Actually, if he wanted more interesting diversions, he'd heard about a quiet place in London where one could relax the nerves by smoking opium. He'd never tried it before. Might be interesting.

Perhaps Polly would like to sneak away with him. Mother would go completely unhinged if she found out he was cavorting publicly with a house servant. It would be even worse than a relationship with Marguerite.

The thought heartened him greatly. Perhaps he could still enjoy life after all.

* * *

Marguerite's life returned to near normal over the next two weeks. Madame Tussaud sent over a half dozen figures from the Dublin collection, and also wanted to swap the Nelson tableaux with her. Tussaud had created a scene of Nelson with Hardy in the admiral's cabin on *Victory*, poring over maps and plans together. She now wanted to see Marguerite's interpretation of the admiral's death. Marguerite and Mr. James labored quickly to dismantle the death tableau to ship it to Dublin, filling the space with other figures until Marie's replacement tableau arrived.

She had nearly washed away all thoughts of Darden, Nathaniel, Trafalgar, and the Ferdinand intrigue from her mind. Even Brax had become a rare visitor. She smiled. Probably busy crowing about his promotion to his friends.

She relished the time alone at the waxworks, with no interference by any of the men who had created such turmoil in her life. Pitt. Darden. Fox. Grey. She'd been buffeted in the wind by all of them.

Talking to awed customers, sculpting, and rearranging tableaux brought her comfort and peace. So much peace that she began missing Madame Tussaud and Joseph with a strange intensity. As though it might be worth a sea voyage to go back and rejoin them.

Foolish girl. You do Marie a far better service by remaining in London.

Nevertheless, she decided to write a letter to Marie when she returned to her rooms that evening. Letter writing bridged the distance between them.

Perhaps a letter to Claudette was in order, as well. She hadn't communicated with her aunt in weeks. Had the dogs destroyed the King James Monstrosity yet? Was Little Bitty painting family portraits by now?

But there would be no letters written this night.

She had hardly removed her bonnet and unpinned her hair before her landlady was rapping anxiously on her door.

"Mrs. Ashby, there's a gentleman here to see you. Says it's extremely urgent that he speak with you."

It was probably something to do with the shipment to Dublin.

Agents always got nervous when they inspected crates and found wax corpses in them.

"I'll bc right down, Mrs. Grove."

She repinned her hair and went to greet her guest in the parlor.

"Why, Sir Brax! I assumed with your promotion conferred upon you that you had completely forgotten your old friends. Have you come to show me your new insignia?"

"This is no time for joking, Marguerite. I'm here on serious business."

This was only the second time she had seen him without a ready smile or witty remark, the first being when he kissed her. She'd best be on her guard.

"Why? What's wrong? You can tell Lords Fox and Howick that I'm not interested in any further wax—"

"It's not that. You're in terrible danger."

"Me? From what? Or whom?"

"Hastings. Fox has had him watched ever since the Ferdinand plan was thwarted. An enemy courier was trailed after he was seen leaving Hastings's quarters in London. The courier was intercepted before boarding a ship back to France. He had a coded message to Napoleon on him. It translated to say that Hastings understood and accepted his assignment to get rid of the waxworker. Marguerite, he plans to kill you. Tonight."

"You're joking. Darden might be a turncoat, but he would never do me harm."

"You're wrong. He intends to do you great harm. Listen to me. Fox has instructed me to hide you until they can find Darden and arrest him."

"What do you mean, find him? Isn't he in his quarters?"

"No, he must have left after the man watching him went after the courier. Marguerite, there's no time for long explanations. I've got to remove you to a secure place."

"For how long?"

"I don't know. A few days, maybe?" He held his hands up in a gesture of appeal. "Please, I've got to do my duty by you. I beg you to come with me."

Oh, a curse on these pothering men about their duty, duty, duty.

Honestly. Weren't they all just serving their own means in the end? Perhaps it was time she considered her own destiny instead of flailing about inside theirs.

I need to make my own protection.

She sighed. "Very well. But I need time to put my things together. Come back in an hour."

"An hour? Ridiculous. I'll wait here. You should be able to be ready in fifteen minutes."

"An hour. And Sir Brax, you can make yourself useful in the meantime by purchasing some food. I've had no supper, and I'm famished."

With a grunt of disapproval, Brax did as she asked, warning her on his way out that he would be back in precisely an hour.

Marguerite really only needed a few minutes of privacy. She stepped lightly into the dining room, which was darkening in the setting sun. On top of the sideboard were the objects of her quest. A pair of slant-fronted knife boxes stood polished and proud at attention. She tried to slide a finger under the lid of one. It was locked. She went to the second box. It was also locked, but the mechanism jiggled insecurely.

Marguerite opened the drawers of the sideboard, looking for a thin, long-handled implement. Ah, a serving fork. That would do. She wiggled the narrow end of the handle inside the lock until it broke free.

She pulled out the sharpest, most ill-humored looking knife she could find, then quickly replaced the lid and put the fork away. She dashed up the stairs, knife in one hand and skirt in the other, to begin packing for her flight out of London.

She waited silently in the parlor, a lone traveling bag at her side, the knife in her lap should Darden show up unexpectedly before Brax. Fortunately, Mrs. Grove had gone out somewhere, so she didn't have to explain why she was sitting in a room alone with a stolen knife clenched in her fist, her only company a steadily burning lamp.

Could she use it? She wasn't sure. She was a noxious blend of fear and anger, and either one might propel her to use it to protect herself. But could she really be incited to use it against someone she once loved? She ran a finger along the blade and shivered. Please, just let Brax hurry up and return so she could escape with him.

The knock on the front door startled her so badly she dropped the knife on the parlor carpet. She picked it up with trembling hands and answered the door with the knife behind her back.

Most unfortunately, Darden had indeed arrived before Brax.

She knew he was a traitor, and now a potential murderer, and her last encounter with him had been thoroughly disagreeable, yet still she was uncontrollably drawn to him.

He wore the same woolen cape, but this time over civilian clothing. He filled it out just as well as his uniform. But what matter? He would look impressive wearing sackcloth.

"Yes?" Marguerite croaked. She cursed herself for sounding so nervous. "How may I help you?" she asked, forcing her voice to sound confident, even a little belligerent.

"I have important news for you. Your life is in danger."

"Indeed?" She held the door open without inviting him in.

What do I do? Keep him engaged in conversation until Brax returns?

Darden looked furtively down both sides of the street. "Are you going to invite me in?"

"Perhaps. What exactly is your news?"

"Who is here in the house with you?"

"No one. I mean, Mrs. Grove is out, but returning at any moment. I expect her any time. Why?"

"You're not safe here alone. Let me come in."

"Why, Captain Hastings? You can tell me your news from where you stand. Or do you not really have anything to tell me?" She gripped the handle of the knife more tightly behind her back.

Will I have to use this? Can I?

Darden sighed. "Marguerite, you are the most exasperating woman a man ever had to deal with. But deal with you, I will."

With a sudden blow of his fist to the door it banged inward, startling Marguerite backward. He stepped across the threshold and slammed it shut behind him.

"You simply can never obey anything I say, can you?"

Why does his voice sound so menacing to me?

She gripped the knife handle even tighter in her right hand. Her hand was going numb. She took several steps backward into the parlor.

"Listen to me, Marguerite. I don't know what Selwyn has been telling you all this time, but you are in great danger from him. He intends to do you great harm, probably tonight."

"How very interesting. He says the same of you. Only Brax isn't under suspicion of treason by Mr. Fox, is he?"

"I suppose not. But you don't know as much as either of them would have you believe. Stop staring at me like that. Sit down so I can talk to you civilly."

"I prefer to stand to hear whatever you have to say."

"Don't be daft." Darden reached for her left wrist. She instinctively shrank from him and raised the knife from behind her back.

They both froze, each staring at the blade poised in midair, glinting in the parlor's lamplight. It shook in Marguerite's unsteady hand.

"Good Lord, woman, were you planning to use this on me? Is your mind unraveling?"

"No, I'm just interested in my own self-preservation."

"As am I." Still holding on to her left wrist, he grabbed her right with his other hand and yanked it downward. Her hand was too numb from clenching the knife to resist him, and the knife fell with a dull thud to the carpet once again. Darden lightly kicked it to one side.

"That was very foolish, Marguerite." His voice was deadly calm.

She was fearful of him, but even more afraid of showing it. She tossed her head to one side.

"No more foolish than you, cavorting about with Napoleon and selling Britain's secrets."

He loosened his grip on her. "I can't talk about that now. Right now, what's important is that you must come with me."

"I won't. You can't force me."

"You think so? My dear Marguerite, you have no understanding of how much I can do."

And she was instantly transported back to *Victory* as Darden swept her up in his arms once again and carried her through the front door. He effortlessly lifted her onto a waiting horse, and sprang onto it behind her before she even had the wherewithal to protest, much less scream into the sparsely populated street that she was being kidnapped.

Darden pulled his cloak forward so that it protected her against the night air. She clutched at it with both hands. He wrapped one arm around her and grabbed the reins with his other hand, clicking commands to the horse with his tongue.

She was alone with this traitor and had no weapon, yet somehow she felt powerless in a dreamy, hypnotic way. Was she as unhinged as he said she was, to not struggle? Surely she could slip down into the street? Or at the very least she could cry for help. Instead, she leaned back into him to feel his strained breaths.

Darden instinctively leaned forward so that his face was against hers. It was coarse with a few days' growth. The aroma of cloves, so distinctively his, settled around her.

How extraordinarily difficult it was to simultaneously hate and love the same person.

Darden urged his horse quickly, but not frantically, through the streets of London. He said nothing to her as their bodies swayed together to the beat of the horse's rhythmic clip-clopping.

A shout in the distance behind them jerked Darden's head away from hers as he turned to find the source of the voice. He swore under his breath and spurred the horse to move faster.

"Almost there."

Marguerite finally found her voice. "Where, exactly, is 'there'?"

"It's probably better if you don't know.

Marguerite tried another approach. "Brax is coming for me, isn't he? To keep you from harming me?"

Although she couldn't quite be sure *what* his actual plan was. Why hadn't he killed her the minute he had her alone at Mrs. Grove's? Why the furtive dash through London to some unknown location?

"Selwyn is an indiscreet, foolhardy half-wit without the brains God gave a mule," he replied.

Which was no answer at all.

"Hold on tightly," he said as they approached St. James's Park.

But she didn't have to. Darden moved his arm even farther around her, clutching her so tightly she was having difficulty breathing. He skillfully guided the horse through the dark paths in the park, occasionally glancing behind him. Brax's shouts—Marguerite was sure now he was coming to her aid—were getting distant.

They were heading toward the Admiralty buildings.

Was he planning to kill her in front of Fox and Grey?

But Darden headed past Admiralty House and then beyond Banqueting House. Where was he going?

Darden hardly slowed as they approached the Palace of Westminster. He seemed to be looking for a specific entrance. He found it, and shouted to whoever was behind it to let him in. The gate creaked as it was opened by unseen hands.

Once inside, Darden sprang down nimbly from the horse and pulled Marguerite down with him. She fell into his arms in a tumble of skirts, but he allowed her no time for complaint. He set her onto her feet, grabbed her hand, and took off at a half run through the interior courtyard. Marguerite could hardly keep herself upright, much less prevent herself from stumbling.

But Darden, intent on his destination, didn't notice.

She could hear a commotion behind them at the gate.

"Brax! I'm here!" Marguerite turned and shouted, but Darden pulled her along even faster. They were now inside Westminster, long abandoned by monarchs and now used by Parliament. He led her up and down vast staircases and through long hallways, his rapid and determined stride combining with the clicking of her heels into a cacophonous echo in the palace. Marguerite's breathlessness became disorientation as they moved farther into the building.

"Stop," she pleaded, pulling back on his hand with both of hers. "Honestly, Darden, if you must do away with me, make it quick and public. Don't bury me in some secret palace room."

He paused only long enough to look at her incredulously. "Don't be ridiculous. Come on."

And so the frantic pace resumed.

He stopped before a double set of doors, painted cream with the Hanover coat of arms emblazoned on it. Darden knocked in a series of short raps, and yet another door was opened by unseen hands. Was Marguerite to be entombed in here?

Darden pulled her in. The large paneled room, dominated by an enormous oval table surrounded by men in chairs, was brightly lit by chandeliers from above and dripping candlesticks set on the table and on other shelves and stands around the room. The tapers illuminated piles of rolled-up drawings, correspondence, and other papers. The room looked like it may have once served as a court of some kind, with partitioned-off tiered seating to either side of the room and an old, unused judge's seat at the far end.

All activity stopped at their entrance. Had they interrupted some kind of state meeting?

"Hastings!" exclaimed a familiar, authoritative voice. "Why in the world did you bring her here? Have you gone raving mad?"

"Not at all, my lord. The lady needed protection, and I decided the Queen's Chamber inside Westminster was the most secure location from her enemies in London."

"I see." It was Mr. Fox, now standing and appraising Marguerite and Darden with frank disapproval.

But the foreign secretary had no time to chastise anyone or seek a full explanation, for Brax Selwyn entered, casually waving a pistol. "And what have we here? Marguerite, my sweet, you know I would never let you be trapped by the ever-lackluster Darden Hastings. But I admit to being a bit confused about the gentlemen he has surrounded himself with."

Brax eyed the room lazily. "Sirs, was there a meeting you neglected to inform me about?"

Darden took a step toward Brax. "The only neglect has been committed by you, to your own duty and honor, Selwyn."

Brax lowered the pistol. "Not true, Hastings. I've always been acutely aware of my duty to my own honor. And I fear that my honor has been impugned this very day. For example, your kidnapping of my lady love is in itself enough to call you out for. Although you seem to lack a pistol."

"I don't need one to handle the likes of you, you beetle-headed churl."

"Really, Hastings, you've no manners at all. No wonder Mrs. Ashby prefers my more refined company to yours."

Darden didn't reply, clamping his lips tight and glaring at the other man.

"After all," Brax continued, "when the British government suspected there was a spy in their midst—*you*—it was someone with skill and cunning—*me*—whom they chose to help expose you. Although you somehow seem to have walked directly into your enemy's camp."

Darden found his voice again. "You're as thick as you are vainglorious. You—"

Charles Grey stood up from his seat across the table from Fox. His chair scraped noisily on the herringboned wood floor, silencing Darden in midsentence.

Grey spoke to Brax as though addressing an errant schoolboy.

"Lieutenant Selwyn, your behavior is disgraceful and I advise you to keep silent before you reveal things you shouldn't."

"Sir, I'm afraid I'm a bit confused. Don't you find it at all disconcerting that your spy Darden has just dashed in here with the waxworker, who has served us so bravely? How does this make *me* disgraceful? Especially since I always try to be exceedingly graceful."

"*Perdóneme,*" interrupted a man near the front of the table. "Could someone please tell me who all of these intruders are?"

In the commotion, Marguerite hadn't noticed him. He was dressed in a strange military uniform and possessed a florid complexion over a wide, flat face.

"Apologies, Your Excellency," said Fox. "Captain Hastings and Lieutenant Selwyn, along with Mrs. Ashby here, were instrumental in helping us with the wax figure of Ferdinand, which was unfortunately lost. They're here because"—he turned to the trio near the door—"Why, exactly, is it that you're here?"

"I'm here to protect Mrs. Ashby from Captain Hastings. I believe he brought her here by mistake while en route to dispose of the precious lady. He's yours to arrest, my lord, and I will take Mrs.

Ashby away for continued protection." Brax reached for Marguerite with one arm while the other still held a pistol, but Darden stepped in front of her and blocked him.

"You won't touch her, ever again," he growled.

"And I won't let you harm her, Hastings. You may have once been my friend, but I'll shoot you, and you know it."

"I'll break your neck first." And with the rapid movement he'd used not an hour ago on Marguerite's wrist, Darden shook Brax's wrist and forced him to release the gun. It clattered to the floor.

Fox calmly walked over and picked it up, inspecting it in his open palm as though it were a fine piece of jewelry.

"Interesting," he said as he walked just as calmly back to the table and laid the weapon on a stack of papers. "And now, gentlemen, since there are no longer any armaments available to you, perhaps you would be so kind as to let us resume our meeting. Lieutenant Selwyn, perhaps you would care to come by Admiralty House in the morning so Lord Grey and I can address your, er, future, with you."

"My lord, what is there to discuss? I've done everything you wished in order to secure the promotion you promised, in fact guaranteed, would be mine for completion of the wax scheme. Yet here I find you seemingly taking sides with the captain."

"It wasn't a promise, actually, more of an . . . incentive . . . to have you do as we wished."

"And I did as you wished. I made sure that wax figure was made and loaded aboard the ship and I spied on Hastings for you. At great peril to myself. Presumably I have met all the requirements necessary for my captaincy. Which reminds me, I do find it rather distasteful that Hastings was promoted ahead of me." He wrinkled his nose as though the very idea smelled putrid.

Fox remained impassive. "Lieutenant, traitors are not promoted in His Majesty's kingdom. And communicating secret government activities, even if they are fictitious, does constitute treason."

"What do you mean by 'fictitious,' my lord?" For the first time since she had known him, Marguerite heard uncertainty in Brax's voice.

She cut in, her hands held out helplessly toward Darden. "I

don't understand this. I thought you—Mr. Fox told me that you were the one—"

Fox patted the top of a chair. "My dear, I can explain. Please, sit down here next to me. Lord Godoy probably deserves a proper explanation of what happened, as well."

Marguerite sat in the chair Fox proffered. Darden remained standing, his eyes fixed on Brax.

The flat-faced man nodded. "*Sí*, an explanation of tonight's events would be helpful. I assume most ministry meetings are not interrupted by pistol-carrying madmen?"

Fox coughed. "No, of course not, my lord. May I present to you Mrs. Marguerite Ashby, a waxworker of some repute and the protégé of Madame Tussaud?"

The man's eyes lit up in recognition. "Ah, I have heard of Madame Tussaud. She escaped French *revolucionarios*."

"Mrs. Ashby, you have the distinction of meeting Manuel de Godoy, the Duke of Alcudia and the prime minister of Spain. He is more commonly recognized as the Prince of Peace, since he was instrumental in negotiating the Treaty of Amiens among other European agreements. And indeed, we hope to have peace with him again."

Marguerite stood and curtsied as deeply as she could before resuming her seat. Godoy smiled his pleasure at her mark of respect. She looked backward at Brax, whose face was inscrutable.

What could he possibly be thinking at this moment?

"And also here are Lord Spencer, Lord Erskine, and Mr. Windham. Lord Grey you know. And of course you are well acquainted with Captain Hastings." Marguerite nodded politely at each man in turn, with barely a glance back at Darden.

"Lieutenant Selwyn you perhaps thought you knew, but there is much about him that has been hidden from view."

The foreign secretary then gave details of an incredible story.

In the previous year, Pitt had joined the country into a coalition with Austria, Russia, Sweden, and some German states, in an effort to repulse Napoleon's grand desire to dominate Europe. Since then, Napoleon's territorial cravings had resulted in his establishing the Kingdom of Italy and placing his stepson, Eugène de

Beauharnais, in charge as viceroy of that country. Bonaparte had also annexed the Kingdom of Naples and appointed his brother Joseph viceroy.

"As you can see, there will be a Bonaparte on every European throne if he is not stopped," Fox said.

"But we have an advantage of which Napoleon is not aware: there is a serious rift inside the Spanish monarchy, between King Charles IV and his son, Ferdinand. We suspected this was coming, since Napoleon always plays false with his supposed allies. He sold the Americans the Louisiana territory after promising to hold it for Spain, and now the Spaniards have been further demoralized by their crushing defeat at Trafalgar. In due course, Boney will undoubtedly invade them and pluck the country off for himself. And then there will be another Bonaparte on another throne on the Continent.

"We were approached through correspondence by the Duke of Alcudia about his desire to leave their French alliance and join us. Or, perhaps, to enter a state of neutrality. Obviously, these negotiations had to be conducted in the utmost secrecy, since they may involve an overthrow of Spain's king."

"Of course." Marguerite was barely following what Fox was saying. How could Darden and Brax have anything to do with this?

"It was our concern that a turncoat is getting information to France about our activities."

Marguerite sat pole straight in her chair. The story unfolding before her was too confusing to completely understand.

Who was friend in this room, and who was foe?

Fox said that Darden had been performing tasks of a confidential nature for Pitt for years, having been brought to the prime minister's attention by Nelson. Before his untimely death, Pitt was considering Darden for a posting inside the government because of his good work and unflagging loyalty. When the new government came into power, Darden was deemed too valuable to dismiss with the rest of Pitt's adherents.

Especially since he'd brought to Grey his suspicions that Brax Selwyn was secretly negotiating with one of Napoleon's operatives in England, promising valuable information in exchange for a pension, or perhaps even a generalship in the emperor's army.

"I don't understand," Marguerite interrupted. "Why would Brax tell Darden he was doing this?"

Brax answered for himself. "This is a ridiculous lie. It's Hastings who has been committing these treasonous acts, not I."

But everyone in the room ignored him as Darden finally made eye contact with Marguerite. "I told you," he said quietly. "The man was totally indiscreet. It required very little flattery to swell his ego to the point that he was dropping me liberal clues about his activities."

Fox continued the story over Brax's protests. Both Darden and Brax were recommended for the position of captain following Trafalgar. Grey concluded that since Brax was known for his great desire for promotion, that it could be used to draw him out. Grey wanted to make Brax's promotion dependent upon a "special" assignment, one involving great intrigue against France.

Fox turned a raised eyebrow to Marguerite. "He seemed especially interested in the assignment knowing you would be involved."

Marguerite could feel her face flushing but said nothing. She didn't dare look Darden's way.

"And what man would not be enamored of an assignment involving this woman?" Brax asked. "She is the sun and moon combined into one ethereal spirit. It hardly makes me a traitor."

Fox ignored him. "So we developed a false scheme whereby we were seeking a wax figure of Ferdinand made to be seen in Valencia, to convince Napoleon that Ferdinand was still in the country while we were planning to bring the duke here to cement a treaty that would assure Spanish neutrality with England and our ally, Portugal."

"False, my lord? How so? I did actually make the Ferdinand figure. I stowed it aboard the ship myself."

"Of course you did. With Selwyn's help. To make the deception as complete as possible, we wanted him to see for himself that the Ferdinand figure was on its way to its destination. We even had

Hastings follow you to ensure everything went as planned. Then that idiot brother-in-law of yours nearly ruined everything."

"Why, sir? If your deception was complete by that point, what difference did it make if Nathaniel stole the figure?"

"Because we promised it to Lord Godoy. He intended to make a goodwill present of it to Ferdinand, the heir apparent. We risked great insult to our friend the prime minister by not appearing with it as promised. But we are fortunate in my lord's graciousness in understanding our little difficulty with it."

Again Godoy smiled his gratification at what Marguerite thought was obsequious flattery.

Fox went on. "We figured Napoleon would realize soon enough that his agent was feeding him false information. We hoped it would cause Selwyn to do something bold and foolish to prove himself to Napoleon. We just didn't realize it would be something to imperil you, Mrs. Ashby.

"A French courier was intercepted after leaving Selwyn's quarters recently, and we learned that Bonaparte wanted his English agent to get rid of the waxworker as a test of loyalty. Captain Hastings went into a complete dither over it. Lord Grey and I didn't think Selwyn meant to do you any real harm, given his obvious affection for you. We thought he might kidnap you long enough for Napoleon to think he had disposed of you. Ahem—we may have been wrong on that score."

Marguerite turned to Darden. "So you were always trying to protect me?"

"Always."

"And so all of this . . . conspiracy . . . was never intended to bring me harm."

"Never."

"I see."

She sat down again while the men in the room waxed eloquent about their shrewd and clever planning. Amid the laughter and self-congratulation, two people remained silent—Marguerite and Darden.

Having finally heard enough, Marguerite stood and pushed her chair back. Its loud scrape against the floor quieted the rest of the room.

"Gentlemen, I would like to add my own conclusions to this most extraordinary story I've just heard." She gazed into each man's eyes, save Darden's, as directly as she could.

"I am astonished, simply flabbergasted, that you were so willing to ill-use me in your political games. Had Captain Hastings here not seen fit to come to my rescue—which I thought I needed *from* him, not *by* him—I might well have become another casualty in the ongoing English-French hostilities.

"How dare you commandeer the life of an innocent British subject without her consent, then sit here basking in your own self-reflected light over it? You're no better than Napoleon and his army conscriptions. I am finished with you, sirs. Never call upon me or my exhibition again."

Surprisingly, Fox rushed to conciliation.

"Mrs. Ashby, please, you must understand that what we did was for the good of the country. You were never in any real danger."

"Perhaps. Perhaps not. But you are not a gentleman, Mr. Fox. Nor are you, Lord Grey. And you!" She turned toward Darden. "You are beneath contempt."

"My lovely Marguerite, finally you've reached the correct conclusion about Hastings." Brax's carefree smile had returned.

"Do be quiet, Brax!" Marguerite's voice was harsher than she had intended. The beginnings of a headache were darting around inside her left temple. She pressed two fingers against the pain, to no avail.

Grey blundered in where Fox had left off. "Mrs. Ashby, if you desire further compensation for your troubles, be assured that we have funds at our disposal to—"

Marguerite looked at him incredulously. "First you admit that you gambled with my life, and now you accuse me of blackmailing you? Truly, sir, my brain is afire with your inconsideration and heartlessness."

The room went silent again. She shut her eyes, willing away the pain and trying to think.

What do I want from this situation, really? Mostly to be left alone. Forever. But what of Brax?

He's a traitor. And doubly so, because he convinced me that Darden was the disloyal one.

Brax deserves death. Doesn't he?

She really wasn't sure.

She opened her eyes again.

"Lord Grey, you offer me recompense for my troubles. This is what I desire: Do not punish Lieutenant Selwyn with a traitor's death. Be more lenient with him."

Grey and Fox both shook their heads gravely, but it was Fox who spoke. "My apologies, Mrs. Ashby, but we offered you that concession once before, for your brother-in-law. We won't do it again. Besides, Selwyn's crimes were far more intentional than Nathaniel Ashby's."

"Couldn't you deport him? To America or one of the Caribbean colonies?"

"Madam, no. Selwyn is no fool like your brother-in-law. He's dangerous and would find a way back to stir up trouble once again."

"So what are you saying will happen to him?"

Fox shrugged. "What happens to any traitor. A hanging."

Marguerite shuddered. Brax, hanged? She could hardly imagine that good-humored, carefree spirit hurtling down the length of a rope.

Brax all of a sudden seemed to understand his own dire situation. "Pardon me. Are you suggesting that after all I've done for the Crown, that you plan to . . . to dispose of me like an unwanted fish carcass into the ocean? Might there be some kind of agreement we can come to? Lord Grey, I've been a faithful officer to His Majesty's navy all these many years. That must surely count for something."

Grey was unperturbed. "Actually, Selwyn, your years of service to the navy are quite obliterated by the distress and irritation you caused by throwing your lot in with Napoleon."

"But you can certainly see why I was forced to it? After all, I was languishing without a promotion, with no guarantee of ever receiving one. I had to have an alternate plan. Truly, had I earned a promotion sooner, none of this would have happened, so, ultimately, *you* are responsible for all of this unpleasantness."

"I'm sure that will be an interesting defense at your court-martial."

Once again, the room went quiet. Except that Brax's breathing was heavy and audible. Yet he maintained a mask of cool composure.

"So if I am not mistaken, then, you are telling me that all of the plans for my future are to be discarded? That you would instead have me swing? Sirs, I find that not only distasteful, but insulting."

"Nevertheless, Selwyn, your fate is sealed," Fox said.

"Is it, now? My apologies, Mr. Fox, if I disagree with you. For you see, I always have an alternate plan. I wouldn't have gotten this far without claim to at least a little bit of brains and wit."

"What are you talking about, Selwyn?" Darden asked.

But Brax ignored his fellow officer. Instead, he turned to Marguerite and addressed her as though no one else was in the room.

"Dear sweet lady, this was not the outcome I would have predicted. No, not at all." He slowly stepped toward her.

"My plan was to ask you to become a captain's wife, as soon as I received my promotion."

"But Brax, I never lov—"

"Shh. Please, Marguerite, don't say the words that I don't want to hear. Let me have a perfect memory of you."

He was close enough to her now that she could sense his fear, which was tinged with genuine sadness.

"Brax, I'm sorry." What else could she say?

He reached out a hand and brushed her cheek, as he had done in front of Darden in the carriage. His eyes misted slightly.

"I really did love you, you know. At first I just wanted to best Hastings in a competition, but it turned into so much more than that. Do you believe me?"

"Yes, Sir Brax, I believe you." Marguerite was suddenly very fearful, of what she didn't know. Was he planning to run from the room? He wouldn't get far. She offered him a tremulous smile.

He gave her one back and bowed to her. "Thank you, my sweet.

And now, gentlemen"—he turned to the men at the table—"I'm afraid that I must leave this little meeting."

No, Brax, please don't try to run. You'll have no chance for leniency that way. If they don't kill you outright when they catch you.

In a move so lithe and quick that no one could react to prevent it, Brax whipped a small dagger from inside his boot and held it up for all to see. "This is my alternate plan, you see. It ensures my . . . freedom."

Darden made a move toward Brax. "You'll have to kill me first before you get to take Marguerite."

But Brax waved him away. "Hastings, honestly, you continue to live up to my expectations as the most thick-headed lunk to ever sail in His Majesty's navy. If there is a heaven, surely my reward will be that I won't find you in it."

And slowly, for the entire room to witness, he brought the knife up to his own throat.

"You are all responsible for this."

"No, Brax, please," Marguerite breathed.

"My love, you know I would look terrible in a hemp cravat. It wouldn't do at all. And now, let it be said by future generations that I was memorable until my last breath."

He looked straight at her as laughter bubbled up in his throat and he plunged the knife into his own neck. His eyes bulged as he gasped at his own audacious deed. Marguerite shrieked in horror as she heard the knife make impact with bone and turned away, unable to see any more.

She heard Brax collapse to the floor, making choking noises. Several of the men at the table jumped up to tend to him, but Marguerite knew there was nothing to be done. Avoiding the crowd of men now standing around Brax's body, she fled the room.

In her haste and anxiety, she didn't realize that she had no idea where she was and just scrambled down the nearest staircase.

And promptly became confused in the palace's maze of hallways.

She recognized the heavy steps behind her, but ignored them as she attempted to find her own way out. She slid out of her shoes and carried them in an attempt to step noiselessly, but those footsteps seemed to be instinctively following her.

She reached a door she thought looked familiar. Opening it, she found she was in little more than a forgotten storage room, with furniture covered in sheets standing by, waiting in silent hopefulness for new owners. There was no exit door across the room, so she whirled back to retrace her steps.

And was pulled up short by Darden filling the doorway, arms crossed as he leaned against the door jamb. His shirt was spattered with blood.

"You're angry," he said.

"Angry. Appalled. Frightened out of my wits. How observant of you, Captain Hastings. I suppose I shouldn't be surprised. It's your most highly polished trait. Except for your deeply imbedded sense of duty. I mustn't forget that. How do you expect me to feel? That man just murdered himself in front of me. After I learned that you've been playing me false."

"I believe I deserve an opportunity to explain myself more thoroughly."

"Do you? And I would say that these opportunities have presented themselves many times, Captain. Why the secrecy on *Victory*? Why didn't you tell me then that your future included secret work and a cabinet position? Did you think that as your wife I couldn't be discreet? You had a second opportunity to explain yourself when you visited the exhibition. And, of course, let us not forget the incredible opportunity you had just hours ago when you unceremoniously threw me on the back of a horse and raced me here like a satchel of letters on the mail road."

"You've thought about being my wife?"

"What? No! I mean, yes. Once, but it was long ago. I can hardly remember it. The only thing I can think of at this very odious moment is that everyone in the British government and Royal Navy has conspired to hoodwink me. You led me to believe you were a French spy, Brax convinced me that he wasn't, and Fox and Grey must have enjoyed themselves thoroughly at my expense, having me labor to exhaustion over a pointless wax figure. Not to mention that they were more than willing to allow me to be kidnapped at the least, or more likely killed."

"I never would have let that happen to you."

"Never would have let it happen! Darden, you were a primary cause of my being in danger."

He smiled. "Am I Darden again?"

She passed a hand across her eyes. Her headache was easing now that she had left the presence chamber. "I really don't know who you are. What I know is that there were multiple layers of deception played upon me, and you were at the center of it all."

He stepped forward to take her hands, but she wrenched free of him.

"Don't. You don't know how much your betrayal wounds me."

"I did not betray you, Marguerite. I admit that Fox and Grey can be a bit . . . inconsiderate in their dealings, but the only man who played you false was Selwyn. He deliberately courted you once he realized I was in love with you. He was already dealing with Napoleon when he agreed to the wax figure scheme. He was willing to cause you harm to prove himself to Boney, despite his professed affections for you. He was altogether unsavory."

"But Brax began courting me the minute he met me. When I was commissioned with the Nelson and Hardy figures. Are you saying you were in love with me that long ago?"

A trail of scarlet rose from underneath his blood-stained shirt and crept up his neck, settling prominently on his cheekbones. Darden cleared his throat.

"Well, I didn't mean . . . hmm . . . it's just that . . . honestly, Marguerite, the point here is that I have always tried to care for you and protect you to the best of my abilities. I'm not your enemy."

"Yet it is always when I'm with you that I'm in the greatest trouble! You seem eminently suitable for protecting and harming a woman at the same time. I can't decide what to make of you, Darden Hastings. You or that pack of jackals running the country. I need to get away from all of you."

"I understand. Perhaps some time with your relatives—"

"Oh, certainly! Where everyone can find me and ensnare me

into their newly concocted plans. Oh no, I'm going far away from you."

He stiffened. "How far away is that?"

She folded her arms. "I'm returning to Madame Tussaud. In Dublin. Presumably you'll have little reason to travel there in your duties. And once I'm out of sight, Fox and Grey will forget me, too."

"Marguerite, you can't. First of all, you find sailing intolerable, remember?"

"But I'm finding life here in London even more intolerable. I'd rather face the wrath of the Irish Sea than continue another day in this insufferable situation."

And with that, she swept past him and back into the corridor to try to find her way out of the palace. She thought she caught "But I do love you" floating in the air behind her, but she was too hurt and angry to care.

And this time, the footsteps did not follow her.

PART EIGHT

Dublin

32

Marie Tussaud expressed both delight and exasperation at Marguerite's return, happy to see her, but anxious over the closing of the second waxworks.

"I thought we agreed that the exhibition makes more money with two locations."

"Yes, but I explained to you what happened—"

"Yes, yes, man who claims to love you risks your life. The British government risks your life. You are most persecuted." Marie shook her head, but her eyes were kind. "You are a good girl, but foolish in this situation. You should have stayed in London with the captain."

"No, my place is here with you."

Marie did not broach the subject again, and Marguerite threw herself furiously back into her old life in an attempt to forget everything that had happened. Her long work hours were double even those of Marie, whose entire focus in life was the exhibition. Even Joseph, who was now displaying a serious talent for scenery design far beyond what might be expected in an eight-year-old boy, expressed concern over Marguerite's almost fiery passion for constructing wax figures night and day.

"Maman," he asked Marie, "what is wrong with Mrs. Ashby? Is she angry with someone?"

Marie patted her son's face. "Only herself, Nini. She just doesn't know it yet. Maybe we help her, yes?"

Marguerite was irritated when Marie decided she should travel to Portugal to seek out new, cheaper textile manufacturers for their costumes. She protested that they had always handled such operations through letters or hired agents. Why the need for Marguerite to make a personal trip?

But Marie was adamant. It was an important transaction and required her physical presence.

So Marguerite boarded a ship once again—a peaceable journey, thanks be to God—for Lisbon. After a few weeks of travel, she concluded her business in mere days, finding the city's cloth merchants congenial and eager to do business with someone of Madame Tussaud's fame. But it was nearly impossible to leave. She was invited to dine every evening with practically every merchant in the guild seeking an opportunity to host her. They pressed countless gifts on her, bowing and scraping their pleasure at obtaining custom with the renowned waxworker.

Really, couldn't this have been conducted without taking me away from my work? I've got four incomplete figures in the workroom that could have been finished by now.

With relief she was finally able to crate up her pile of gifts for Marie, secure their new contracts inside a specially constructed pocket in her dress, and begin the exhausting journey home.

Marguerite was pleasantly surprised to find both Marie and Joseph waiting when her ship docked. Although she had written to her friend with her planned arrival date, she fully expected Marie to be too busy with the exhibition to even consider greeting her upon reentering Ireland.

Once her possessions were unloaded from the ship and tied to the top of a hackney, the three embarked on the final leg of Marguerite's journey back to their lodgings.

Inside the rattling carriage, Marguerite sat across from Marie and Joseph. "Who manages the exhibition today?" she asked.

A curious look passed between mother and son.

"No one manages. I closed it for the day."

"Closed? The exhibit? Just to meet my ship? Marie, are you quite all right? In the years I've known you, when have you ever closed the exhibition for no good reason?"

"My reason is good." Marie smiled.

Marguerite shook her head. What had happened to her friend while she was away?

"Oh, I meant to tell you. I have all of our signed agreements sewn in my dress. I'll give them to you as soon as we arrive at our lodgings."

"Perhaps later. You need a bath and change of clothes. Need time to rest." Marie reached over and patted Marguerite's knee.

The exhibition was closed and Marie was suddenly interested in relaxation? Was the woman daft?

But after a long soak and a change from her dusty and sweaty traveling clothes, she had to admit that Marie was right. She hadn't rested since—well, when had she last lain back to simply close her eyes and be still?

She propped herself up on her bed with her wet, lavender water–scented hair drying around her, and a copy of the newly published novel *Leonora* in her hands. She read for just a few minutes with the afternoon sunlight streaming into her room, before her weariness overcame her and she shut her eyes for a dreamless nap.

Marguerite awoke like a contented cat, stretching and rolling over, her eyes lazily half-open to observe the world. Why couldn't life always be this peaceful? How had her life ended up a series of tumultuous acts in a stage play, each one punctuated by death? Well, it was all over, and she wouldn't berate herself over her temporary blindness where Darden Hastings was concerned. Life from now on would be right here, with the Tussaud wax exhibition.

I have no regrets about my return. Do I?

The sun was making its descent into the horizon. She touched her hair. Completely dry.

A soft rap at the door forced her out of her languid state.

It was Marie. "Marguerite, I left my sketchbook and pencils at the exhibit. I think in the workroom. Will you retrieve them for me? I have ideas for a new tableau and want to work on the design tonight."

Marguerite yawned drowsily. "Of course. Let me just get my keys." She went to retrieve the set of keys that locked both the front door of the exhibition and the workroom door.

Marie followed her into the room. "You plan to wear that?"

Marguerite looked down at her pale blue dress. It was a simple gown, part of the trousseau Claudette had purchased. "Yes. Why?"

Marie threw open her armoire and began riffling through the dresses hung on hooks. She pulled out a green cotton dress with a wide brown sash tied underneath the bodice.

"You should wear this one." She held it out to Marguerite.

"To pick up a sketchbook? Marie, you're acting more than odd today. Are you feeling well?"

Marie pressed the gown into her arms and kissed her cheek. "Yes, this dress is necessary for picking up my sketchbook."

After letting herself inside the dark exhibition hall, she lit the lamp kept on a small stand near the door. She stepped through the tableaux back toward the workroom where she hoped to find the sketchbook, if Marie's memory of its location was correct. Otherwise, she'd need to light up the entire exhibit and go through each tableau on a hunt for it.

How strange. There was a candlelit glow coming from the rear of the exhibition. Had Marie left lamps burning? She was never so careless. But even if she had, how could they have lasted so long?

Marguerite held her own taper up for a better view as she approached the lit area. How very strange. It seemed to be coming from the location of their Trafalgar tableau. Except . . . it was different.

It was no longer Nelson's death scene. The large canvas painted to look like the inside of *Victory* remained, but the figures and props had changed, and many-branched candelabra glowed brightly in various positions nearby. The scene now showed Nelson standing before a round table with four chairs around it. On the table were tiny wooden replicas of French, Spanish, and English ships in formation lines for battle. Seated in three of the chairs were Hardy, Collingwood, and Darden, all in uniform and looking down at Nelson's proposed battle plan.

Darden? Why would Marie select him for a tableau? He wasn't well-known to the public. She had to admire Marie's work. Darden was made so skillfully that it was as if she'd done it from a life mask.

Marguerite stepped into the tableau to look more closely at Darden's figure. She set her lamp down in the middle of the miniature ship grouping and bent to study the figure more closely.

It blinked.

She raised up and took two steps backward, a hand to her pounding chest. Surely she had imagined it.

The figure spoke in a deep, familiar voice. "I'm sorry, I just can't maintain this position any longer."

Marguerite tamped down a shriek. "What is this? Who are you?" She peered down again. "Darden?"

"I'm afraid so."

"I don't understand. Why are you here? In Dublin? After closing time in the wax exhibition? Pretending to be a wax figure, for heaven's sake?"

"Would you believe it was all Madame Tussaud's idea?"

"It was Marie's idea for you to pose as a statue in an empty wax salon?"

"Well, put like that, it's not quite as romantic as she promised me it would be."

How had she gone from a pleasant, idyllic nap to facing down Darden Hastings, all in the space of an hour?

"How could this possibly be romantic?"

Darden explained that he had written to Madame Tussaud, seeking her assistance in wooing Marguerite back. He knew Marguerite would refuse his letters and he had to come up with a more creative way of seeing her.

"But how could you know I would reject your letters? You've never sent me one."

"Marguerite, you made your feelings about me and the British government quite clear that day at Westminster. You repudiated the whole lot of us."

"Oh. Yes, I suppose I did do that. But how did you come to be in Dublin?"

"Lord Howick gave me leave. Madame Tussaud wrote to me with her conviction that you weren't happy in Dublin. She developed a plan for having me surprise you privately, before you could think to turn me away. And I believe she sent you off on some wild-goose errand to Portugal so she could have time to put the tableau together."

Marguerite shook her head in wonder. "Unbelievable."

"Are you angry with her? With us? I simply had to find a way to get you alone to talk to you one last time. I ask that you hear me out, and if you still hate me, well then, I will leave and I promise to never purposely cross your path ever again."

He pulled out the fourth empty chair with his booted foot and patted the seat with his scarred left hand. His hand, the tableau, and the movement of his foot brought all of her time on *Victory* flooding back over her once again. His warm embraces, his powerful protection of her, his ridiculous sense of duty. Her knees felt like they would not support her much longer.

I love him. God help me, I do.

She nodded her head and sat silently.

They were seated a mere foot away from each other. He had the scent of cloves about him again, on his breath and in his hair.

He must carry them about for chewing.

Darden leaned toward her. "I hardly know where to begin. I wasn't quite sure you'd even talk to me inside this rather preposterous setting of Madame Tussaud's."

"Marie has always had a talent for the theatrical. I never imagined she'd use it on me."

"I suppose we never really quite know people the way we think we do. And perhaps you haven't really known me. Not in the way you should." Darden took her hands in his, and she could see relief in his eyes when she didn't pull away.

"Quite simply, Marguerite, I love you. I have ever since I met you. Since that soirée at Edinburgh Castle where I behaved like a complete horse's ass. I tried to keep it from Brax, because he always had an easy, fascinating appeal for women, and I figured that if someone of his charm made up his mind to have you, I was lost. But I suppose my heart was completely exposed and he sensed it. Being also very competitive, he decided he wanted you and would have you at all costs."

"I was never his. Not for a moment."

"But how could I know that? His presence always brought a smile to your face that I couldn't seem to conjure up no matter how I tried." He stroked the back of one of her hands with his fingers.

"On *Victory*, I was beside myself, between worry for you and my shipboard obligations. Plus, I knew that I was seeking a responsible position inside Pitt's government, and I didn't know if my life could accommodate you. I didn't want to be a neglectful husband.

"Then when I realized Brax was up to something vile while still courting you, it took all of my own self-discipline to keep from thrashing him personally and leaving him in a sewer somewhere."

"Darden Hastings, I hardly think self-discipline has ever been a difficulty for you."

"It never was. Until I met you." He reached up to push a tendril of hair behind her ear, then resumed his light caressing of her hand. "So tell me, Marguerite, what you think."

"Honestly, Darden, I think you should simply stop talking."

Marguerite moved to his lap and wrapped her arms around his neck, a better position for nuzzling him and feeling his arms around her. He obliged by wrapping her tightly in those arms and lowering his head to hers for a kiss. One completely uninterrupted by the sounds of battle or the anguish of torn loyalties. It was deep and all-consuming, a release of desire that had been straining against its chains for nearly two years.

Marguerite felt robbed of breath, but if she died of asphyxiation now, she could have considered her life well spent. But things weren't finished between them yet. She broke away, but held her face close to his.

"Tell me, Captain," she said in a whisper, "aren't there things you wish to know about me before we go any further?"

"You mean, beyond the fact that you're a rash, stubborn little waxworker who will never give me a moment's peace the rest of my days?"

"Hmm, I guess there isn't much to know beyond that."

She saw that his eyes were twinkling with pleasure as she closed her own for another kiss.

They stayed locked together until some of the candles began sputtering out and their resultant smoke left an acrid smell in the air.

"I believe we have a signal to depart," Darden said as he broke away.

Marguerite was reluctant to leave the tableau and everything it meant but agreed. She stood and gestured to Nelson.

"Do you think the admiral would approve?"

"I believe he would want to be present at the ceremony himself if he were here today."

Together they blew out the remaining candles and made their way out of the exhibition together. At the entrance, Marguerite stopped and turned to Darden, taking his disfigured hand in her own and kissing it gently. "There's just one more thing that remains unsaid."

"Yes?" Darden's voice radiated desire.

"I've loved you for what feels like an eternity. I think I may have even fallen a bit in love with you at Edinburgh Castle, even though you were quite impossibly rude to me when I met you. But for certain I loved you after you escorted me to take Lord Nelson's life mask. And I was deeply, madly in love by the time I left *Victory*. I think that if I'd gone the rest of my life without you, I'd have gone deeply, madly insane."

33

Nathaniel sipped tea from his terrace, which ran the length of his palatial new residence in Bengal. Polly sat by his side with her own cup. Her eyes still hadn't lost their look of utter wonder at her greatly improved circumstances.

Circumstances had changed for Nathaniel, too. He'd managed to obtain employment with the East India Company, as a representative of their interests in Bengal. In a masterful move that combined his desire for glory with his new leisure pursuit, he was now an agent ensuring that opium collected here was transferred to one of several foreign intermediaries for smuggling into China. The Chinese had declared the opium trade illegal in their country.

Such a harmless, enjoyable pastime, declared unlawful. He shook his head. Ah well, all the more profit for him. Finally, a simple, secure way to earn vast sums of money in a country where he could be treated like a king.

He reached over and squeezed Polly's ample thigh. She simpered and leaned over to give him a generous view of her cleavage. Life would be uncomplicated and blissful from now on.

34

Charles Fox had died at the age of fifty-seven, on September 13, 1806, not eight months after the much younger William Pitt. Although he, too, was interred at Westminster Abbey, he was given a private funeral. Yet the crowds who turned out to pay their respects were just as large as those who came to see Pitt.

A postscript noted that Charles Grey, Viscount Howick, would be succeeding Fox as foreign secretary and leader of the House of Commons.

And so the political intrigues will continue uninterrupted.

Marguerite put down the newspaper and ticked the numbers off on one hand. "Nicholas, murdered. Philipsthal, also dead. Brax, a tragic and foolish death. Pitt and Fox, departed less than a year from one another. All men in close association with me, all expired before their times." She looked up at Darden. "Do you realize what this probably means for you?"

He gently pulled her up from her chair and put an arm around her, brushing the back of his scarred hand across her cheek. "Well, thus far it has meant a naval promotion, an opportunity to serve the Crown gloriously, and marriage to the most willful woman God did ever create. So it probably means"—he laid the same hand across her stomach—"that we'll be having a stubborn, mulish child who will have a natural desire for adventures on the high seas, no matter whether a boy or girl."

"That's not what I meant," Marguerite protested, laughing.

"But it's what *I* mean, Mrs. Hastings. The past is done, and has no bearing on our future. I'm sure Lord Nelson would agree."

He covered her lips with his own, to silence any further objections. But Marguerite had already forgotten her theory of unlucky fate inside the warm circle containing Darden, their quickening child, and herself.

AUTHOR'S NOTE

Marie Grosholtz Tussaud is one of the most interesting figures of the French Revolution. She likely knew more famous people than anyone else of her time. According to her own autobiography—which admittedly was a bit self-serving—she was personally acquainted with Marie Antoinette, King Louis XVI, the king's sister Madame Elisabeth, Robespierre, Napoleon, Josephine, and the painter Jacques-Louis David.

After fleeing France to try her fortunes in England, she traveled about Great Britain with her exhibition for nearly thirty years, her only help being in the form of her son Joseph (with Francis joining them in 1822).

There is a vast amount of conflicting information regarding Tussaud's life. Her autobiography of her life during the Revolution details a woman who witnessed more up-close carnage while narrowly avoiding the blade herself than anyone else of the time. Some modern biographers doubt many of her claims, finding them unsubstantiated. As a novelist, I chose to concentrate on her life in England, where the historical record is sketchier and I could more liberally fill in details.

I have also rearranged certain events in Tussaud's life to better fit the pacing of this story. For example, the terrifying sea voyage I describe that she takes in 1804 from Glasgow to Dublin, during which she lost much of her collection, was actually a trip from Liverpool to Dublin in 1820 to arrive in time for George IV's coronation visit.

There are also minute details that the astute reader will pick up on as having been changed. For example, the Duchess of York did indeed have Madame Tussaud do a model, and extended her patronage to her, but the model was of a young child (the duchess was childless), and Tussaud never went to Oatlands Park to visit the duchess.

The oldest surviving figure in Tussaud's collection is called The

Sleeping Beauty, believed to be that of Louis XV's last mistress, Madame du Barry. A breathing mechanism was first introduced into it in 1837, and would not have been present when Marguerite first arrived on Tussaud's doorstep in 1803.

Madame Tussaud was not the first waxworker of fame. Waxworks have been around in various use since the ancients. The most famous of her predecessors was a Mrs. Salmon, who modeled and exhibited in the early eighteenth century. However, it was Tussaud who took the genre to a completely new level of entertainment. Going to Madame Tussaud's exhibition was much like opening up a gossip magazine today. It provided a personal look at both the popular and infamous people of the day.

Charles Dickens appears to have been referring to Madame Tussaud's exhibition in his references to Mrs. Jarley in *The Old Curiosity Shop,* an indicator of Tussaud's vast popularity at the time.

Madame Tussaud married relatively late in life, at age thirty-four, to **François Tussaud**, an engineer eight years her junior. After bearing him two children, Joseph and Francis, she elected to travel to England with Joseph under Philipsthal's "protection" to make her fortune. It was her intent to return to France "with a well-filled purse," but François's terrible management of their financial affairs—including the sale of her waxwork salon in Paris in 1808—created a rift in their marriage that would never be healed. Marie refused to forgive her husband and instead had Francis sent to her. Although she remained married to François until he died in 1848, she never communicated with him again after he betrayed her by abandoning the Paris salon.

Marie lived to the grand old age of eighty-nine. She remained active with the exhibition until just a couple of years before her death. From her deathbed she admonished her sons never to argue over the exhibition, and they never did.

Philippe Curtius was a medical doctor with an aversion to blood and gore, a most inconvenient phobia for his profession. He began making anatomical figures as part of his practice, then discovered that people enjoyed looking at them and were even willing to pay to do so. He came under the patronage of the Prince de Conti, and did indeed invite Marie and her mother to come and live with him in Paris. Curtius had an uncanny sense of the rapidly changing powers in France, and always managed to stay on the right side of the shifting political winds during the Revolution. Marie always referred to him as her "uncle," but rumors have abounded that Curtius was actually her father. It does seem strange that Curtius would send to Salzburg from Paris for a mere housekeeper, and even more strange that he would mentor the housekeeper's daughter. Marie certainly inherited a love of wax sculpting from him, and eventually surpassed her mentor in talent.

Paul de Philipsthal was a French showman well acquainted with Marie Tussaud when she lived in Paris. In fact, Dr. Curtius intervened on his behalf with Robespierre when the showman was jailed during the revolutionary frenzy under one of the typical trumped-up charges used by those with axes to grind. Philipsthal viewed her show as a way to add notoriety to his own Phantasmagoria show, and invited her to join him in England under the most dreadful contract conditions, which were ludicrously favorable to him. Marie detested the man and complained bitterly of him in her letters. **John Philpot Curran** was a famous Irish judge who visited Madame Tussaud's Wax Exhibition in Dublin, although I placed their meeting in Glasgow. Upon hearing about her troubles with Philipsthal, he offered to represent her for free. When Philipsthal heard that Curran was conducting her affairs, he quickly came to terms and departed her life forever. It appears that Philipsthal later married, had children, and then died around 1830.

It's rather difficult to study the events leading up to the five furious hours at Trafalgar and not fall just a little bit in love with **Lord Horatio Nelson.** He was a complex man, as most heroes prove to be. He was clearly a naval genius, and inspired deep loyalty in his men not only because of his fairness and kindness, but because of his infirmities. Many sailors had amputated limbs or missing eyes, so Nelson's own gave him a connection to the average man. To have so great an admiral as Nelson continue on doggedly, despite his great injuries, further served as inspiration to them. Yet the hero was flawed. Although he was zealous, patriotic, and dutiful, he could at times be vain, insecure, and overly anxious for recognition. Even though Nelson plays a fictitious role in this story, I did try to use much of his own dialogue at Trafalgar from the time he was sequestered in the orlop after his injury until the moment he died.

Lord Nelson is still well-deservedly revered in England today for his efforts in assuring English naval supremacy for the remainder of the war with the French, and there is a glorious tribute to him at Madame Tussaud's in London.

Although both were married to other people at the time, Nelson and **Emma Hamilton** fell violently in love with each other. Emma's husband at the time, Sir William Hamilton, was the ambassador to the Kingdom of Naples and the two of them became involved in helping Nelson, who arrived after the Battle of the Nile to prevent a French invasion of Egypt. So respectful was Sir William of Nelson that he turned a blind eye to what he surely realized was a torrid affair between his wife and the naval hero. They formed an interesting threesome, practically living together at Merton Place until Sir William's death in 1803. Both Emma and Nelson were at his side when he died. Nelson's wife, Fanny, was not quite so tolerant, although she had the better of it upon Nelson's death. She had half his income, whereas nothing was settled on Emma and her daughter with Nelson, Horatia. Emma went deeply into debt and died from amoebic dysentery at the age of fifty-four in 1815.

Sir Thomas Hardy was Nelson's flag captain and one of the few people tolerant of Nelson's relationship with Emma Hamilton. Nelson trusted Hardy implicitly, and relied on the man's quiet, unemotional, and dependable reserve. Hardy personally delivered Nelson's last letter to Emma Hamilton. After Trafalgar, Captain Hardy received the equivalent of $100,000 of today's currency in prize money, and nearly $250,000 in compensation from the government. He was also created a baronet. Hardy went on to more crowning achievements, becoming first naval lord at the Admiralty and reaching the rank of vice admiral of the blue. He died in 1839, at age seventy.

Vice Admiral Cuthbert Collingwood also profited well from Trafalgar. He was made a baron, and granted a pension of £2000 a year, equivalent to approximately $200,000 in today's money.

However, he was not able to enjoy his reward. He was continuously on board ship for nearly five years as he commanded a fleet involved in a continuing blockade of French and Spanish ships sheltering in various ports. The hardship of being constantly at sea gradually wore down his spirits and his health, and he died at sea in March 1810 at the age of sixty-two, having not seen his wife and children since before Trafalgar. He did give **Lieutenant John Richards Lapenotière** the privilege of rushing back to England aboard HMS *Pickle* to deliver the news about Trafalgar as a debt of honor. Lapenotière was rewarded by the Admiralty Board with £500 and promotion to commander.

Mr. William Beatty was the ship's surgeon aboard *Victory*, and **Messrs. Smith** and **Westemburg** were his assistants. Medicine and surgery aboard sailing ships during the era of Trafalgar were much as I have described them, except worse. Knowledge of antiseptics, the spread of infection, and other medical concepts we take for granted today were in their infancy then. A sailor probably had equal chances of dying in battle, of disease, or at the hands of a surgeon.

The lashing of ten men for drunkenness did take place on *Victory*, but it was a mere two days prior to the battle, and I placed it a few days earlier. Discipline aboard naval vessels varied from ship to ship, as there were no specific standards for it and punishment was entirely up to individual captains. Officers like Nelson and Collingwood were very popular because of their fairness, kindness, and relative humanity in terms of discipline. However, it is well to remember that many seamen were obtained through press-gangs, and although some of them settled well into life at sea, many naturally had no desire to be there. So by necessity it was imperative to maintain strict discipline on ships to avoid laziness, or worse, mutiny. Some captains were able to inspire their men to loyalty; others were heavy-handed with the lash.

William Pitt, also known as **Pitt the Younger**, became England's youngest prime minister in 1783 at the age of twenty-four. He left office in 1801, but returned again in 1804 and served until his death in 1806. He was known as Pitt the Younger to distinguish him from his father, William Pitt the Elder, who was a previous prime minister. Pitt the Younger's second tenure was plagued by both unrelenting opposition to his plans for a broad coalition government as well as pressure from the machinations of Napoleon. His health nose-dived as a result. Pitt died of liver disease and left significant debt. Nevertheless, he was honored with a public funeral and buried in Westminster Abbey. Despite—and because of—the hostility he faced in office, he is known as one of Britain's greatest prime ministers.

Pitt's greatest political rival was **Charles James Fox.** Fox was the son of Henry Fox, himself a rival of Pitt the Elder. And so the rivalry continued into the next generation. Fox was known as a forceful and eloquent speaker in the House of Commons, as well as having a rather notorious private life. To his detriment, Fox was in constant conflict with King George III. From his intemperate influence on the Prince of Wales (the king made it publicly known that he held Fox principally responsible for the prince's many failings, including his propensity to vomit in public), to his decidedly antiroyal position on the American rebellion, the French Revolution, and the matter of the regency, Fox assured himself a greatly hostile relationship with his sovereign.

Charles Grey, Viscount Howick and first lord of the Admiralty, took over as foreign secretary upon Charles Fox's death and went on to serve the nation as prime minister from 1830 to 1834. Grey had a relatively happy marriage, producing sixteen children, although Grey did have a series of affairs with other women throughout his lifetime. His most notorious affair, which predated his engagement to his wife, was with Georgiana Cavendish, Duchess of Devonshire. She bore an illegitimate child with Grey, who was raised by Grey's parents. He became Earl Grey upon the death of his father in 1807, and, yes, the aromatic Earl Grey tea is named for him.

Charles-Philippe, Comte d'Artois and later **Charles X of France,** lived in Edinburgh after fleeing revolutionary France with his much-loved mistress, **Louise de Polastron,** who died of consumption in 1804. He was bereft the rest of his life, despite his ascension to the French throne in 1824.

Other historical figures in this story are Napoleon's minister of police, **Joseph Fouché**; the traitor **Colonel Despard; Sir Francis Burdett**, who did commission a figure of himself; **George Wright**, Marie's London solicitor; Edinburgh Castle's **Governor Sir Alexander Hope; Sir Henry Raeburn**, the painter; Marie's landlord in Glasgow, **Mr. Colin**; the female survivor of *Achille*, **Jeannette**; and Spain's prime minister, **Manuel de Godoy.**

It is worth mentioning the bigger historical picture after the British victory at Trafalgar. By 1807, Napoleon had turned his considerable attentions to Portugal, and, gaining permission from the Spanish, passed through Spain and invaded Portugal, driving the royal family to Brazil. Furthermore, by February 1808, Napoleon turned on the Spanish Crown, and proclaimed his brother Joseph king of Spain, much to the displeasure of the Spanish populace. This induced a general uprising among the Spanish, who turned on France, taxing Napoleon's military resources. The English quickly seized upon the situation by late 1808 to secure a foothold on the Continent, issuing the first major blow to Napoleon at Bailén, Spain, and thereby securing the strategic second front, eventually leading to Napoleon's downfall.

The French were the first to use balloons for aerial reconnaissance in 1794, during its conflict with Austria, and Napoleon even considered an aerial invasion of Great Britain this way, an invasion that was never realized. However, having Brax signal to the French from the shore near Dover and expecting to have his signals seen from Calais was probably a bit unrealistic. At the time, the maximum viewing distance from a balloon was about eighteen miles, and Dover is around twenty-two miles from Calais at the Channel's narrowest point. St. Margaret's at Cliffe, a little further up the Kentish coastline, is even farther away.

The lyrics that the geggy performers sing are a stanza from "My Bonnie Mary," written by Robert Burns, although Burns claimed this part of his song was actually an old Jacobite tune. Burns was an eighteenth-century poet and lyricist; today he is most famously remembered for the song "Auld Lang Syne."

A final note: After Marie Tussaud's death in 1850, **Joseph** and **Francis Tussaud** took over the management of the waxworks exhibition, which had settled at the Baker Street Bazaar in London.

Both were talented sculptors and skilled musicians, and Joseph was particularly adept at creating the settings in which wax figures were placed. After their own deaths, the exhibition went to Francis's eldest son, John Theodore, and it was under his charge that the exhibition was moved to larger quarters on nearby Marylebone Road. In 1925, a disastrous fire destroyed more than half of the 467 wax models in the collection. The exhibition was rebuilt nearby and opened in 1928. The Tussaud family continued to work in the exhibition until 1967, when Bernard Tussaud, Marie's great-great-grandson, died. The Madame Tussaud legacy continues today, where millions of visitors every year can rub elbows with the rich and famous, much as they did over two hundred years ago when she first arrived in England with her small wax exhibition.

ACKNOWLEDGMENTS

It's nearly impossible to write any book, let alone one based on historical fact, without a lot of help along the way. My thanks go to the following people who helped me with research and dispensed valuable historical advice: First and foremost is historical novelist and critique partner Leslie Carroll, who advised, consoled, and generally made ten months of writing a veritable pleasure; Cindy Vallar, historical novelist and Age of Sail expert, who assisted me with certain plotting details aboard *Victory*; and Joe Greeley, waterfront interpretive supervisor at Historic St. Mary's City, for his patience in answering my battery of questions about the Battle of Trafalgar. Any historical mistakes are mine alone.

I am again fortunate to have a supportive editor, Audrey LaFehr, who encourages me to write things my own way. My thanks to everyone at Kensington Publishing who has helped bring this book to the reader's hands.

Once again my mother, Georgia Carpenter, and my friend Diane Townsend served as able and enthusiastic readers of my manuscript in its draft form. Their coaching and encouragement cannot be overstated.

As always, this book would not have been possible without the loving support and encouragement of my husband, Jon, who spent many weekends without me while I was holed up with my computer, lavishing my time on Marguerite and her wax adventures.

Soli Deo gloria.

SELECTED BIBLIOGRAPHY

Adkins, Roy, and Lesley Adkins. *Jack Tar: Life in Nelson's Navy.* London: Little, Brown, 2008.

Adkins, Roy. *Nelson's Trafalgar: The Battle That Changed the World.* London: Penguin Group, 2004.

Berridge, Kate. *Madame Tussaud: A Life in Wax.* New York: Harper Collins, 2006.

Biesty, Stephen. *Man-of-War: Stephen Biesty's Cross-Sections.* London: Dorling Kindersley, 1993.

Bowen, Frank C. *From Carrack to Clipper: A Book of Sailing Ship Models.* London: Halton & Truscott Smith, Ltd., 1927.

Chapman, Pauline. *Madame Tussaud in England.* London: Quiller Press, 1992.

Goodwin, Peter. *Nelson's Victory: 101 Questions and Answers about HMS* Victory, *Nelson's Flagship at Trafalgar 1805.* London: Conway Maritime Press, 2004.

Herold, J. Christopher. *The Horizon Book of the Age of Napoleon.* New York: American Heritage Publishing Co., 1963.

Leslie, Anita, and Pauline Chapman. *Madame Tussaud: Waxworker Extraordinary.* London: Hutchinson & Co., 1978.

Mathew, David. *British Seamen.* London: William Collins, 1943.

Pilbeam, Pamela. *Madame Tussaud and the History of Waxworks.* London: Hambledon and London, 2003.

Pocock, Tom. *The Terror Before Trafalgar: Nelson, Napolean, and the Secret War.* New York: W. W. Norton & Company, 2002.

Ransom, Teresa. *Madame Tussaud: A Life and a Time.* Phoenix Mill: Sutton Publishing, 2003.

Smith, Janet Adam. *Life Among the Scots.* Britain in Pictures series. London: William Collins, 1946.

Strong, Roy. *Illustrated Guide to Madame Tussaud's.* London: Madame Tussaud's Limited, 1980.

Thorne, Tony. *Madame Tussaud: Waxwork Queen of the French Revolution.* London: Short Books, 2004.

Walmsley, Leo. *British Ports and Harbours*. London: William Collins, 1946.
Warwick, Peter. *Voices from the Battle of Trafalgar*. United Kingdom: David & Charles, 2005.
Wilson, Philip Whitwell. *William Pitt the Younger*. New York: Doubleday, Doran & Co., 1930.

INTERNET REFERENCES

"A Flogging at Sea, 1839." EyeWitness to History
http://www.eyewitnesstohistory.com.flogging.htm

"Domestic Medicine: Medicinal Preparations."
American Revolution.org
http://www.americanrevolution.org/medicine
/medapp3.html#anchor999782

HMS Victory: The National Museum
http://www.hms-victory.com

"Peninsular War." Answers.com
http://www.answers.com/topic/peninsular-war

A READING GROUP GUIDE

A ROYAL LIKENESS

Christine Trent

About This Guide

The suggested questions are included to enhance your group's reading of Christine Trent's *A Royal Likeness*

DISCUSSION QUESTIONS

1. How did Marie Tussaud's experiences during the French Revolution affect the way she conducted business while in England?
2. How was Marie Tussaud's lifestyle unusual for her times, in terms of her independence and entrepreneurial spirit?
3. How do you think waxworks exhibitions of the early nineteenth century were similar to those of today? In what ways do you think they were different?
4. Many French aristocrats fled France during the Revolution for places like Scotland and England. How would the émigrés' lives have been affected by Napoleon's threatened invasion of Great Britain?
5. How did Brax's background as the son of an impoverished aristocrat affect his decisions?
6. Were Marguerite's motivations for marrying Philipsthal sound? What would you have done if faced with her situation?
7. Is Darden's sense of duty admirable? How was his judgment sometimes clouded by this sense of duty? Was his attitude common or unusual in early-nineteenth-century England?
8. Were you surprised to learn that there were sometimes women aboard naval ships, and that they sometimes accompanied crews into war? What do you think were the overall attitudes toward women on ships?
9. During the Napoleonic Wars, alliances between countries shifted depending on the outcomes of battles, the rise of new leaders, and secret negotiations. How does this compare to the political map of today's world?

10. Today Madame Tussaud's wax museums sit in several permanent locations around the world. Why do you think the waxworks stopped its traveling format? What are the advantages and disadvantages of a waxworks being in a permanent location?

11. Lord Nelson's affair with Lady Emma Hamilton was considered scandalous during a time when many aristocrats conducted affairs. What was different about their circumstances that made society aghast over Nelson and Emma?

12. By the end of the novel, Marguerite has married a naval captain. What challenges might such a marriage have presented to a nineteenth-century woman? Would any of these challenges still apply today?

13. Consider Marguerite's attitudes, feelings, and thoughts. In what ways is Marguerite a typical woman of her time? Conversely, how does she chafe against social conventions?